"Cohen ha   nd interaction, and
prickly, de   heroine."
        --Publis

. "LJ Cohen deftly weaves together realistic teenage characters, futuristic technology, and big stakes for a real page turner."

    --Wen Spencer, Award winning SF&F novelist, author of the Ukiah Oregon and Elfhome series

"Get on board Derelict, and you'll take an edgy, nonstop flight into an audacious SF future with unremitting danger as your pilot -- and thrilling adventure your destination."

    --Lynn Viehl, NYT best selling author of the Stardoc and Darkyn series

"Intricate plotting melded seamlessly with delightful characterizations kept me turning pages as fast as I could go in an attempt to keep up with the unfolding story. A cracking yarn set in a lush future I'm hoping we'll hear more of."

    --Nathan Lowell, Creator of the Golden Age of the Solar Clipper and the Tanyth Fairport Adventures

THE BETWEEN

". . .a moving tale of heroism and compassion. . . Lydia is a young woman utterly unprepared for the world she's about to enter--but she learns fast. She's a character you'll want to meet again, from a writer you'll w   s a new voice to follow."

                                            nicles

ITHAKA RISING

Also by LJ Cohen

ITHAKA RISING
Halcyone Space, book 2

LJ Cohen

Interrobang Books
Newton, MA

Published by Interrobang Books
Newton, MA

www.interrobangbooks.com

First print edition: June, 2015

ISBN-10: 1942851901
ISBN-13: 978-1-942851-90-5

Original cover art by Chris Howard, copyright 2015
www.saltwaterwitch.com

For my father,
who taught me by his life and his example
what all these Ithakas mean.

Ithaka

As you set out for Ithaka, hope your voyage
is long, full of adventure, full of learning.
The Lestrygonians, the Cyclopes,
angry Poseidon are not yours to fear.
You will never meet such dangers on your path
if your thoughts stay clear, if your spirit and your body
are filled with true purpose. You will never

meet the Lestrygonians, the Cyclopes,
fierce Poseidon, unless you carry them with you,
unless you raise them up before you. Pray
that your road winds through endless
summer mornings, let joy escort you
to sun-drenched harbors where new sights await.
Stop at Phoenician markets. Purchase

their fine wares; mother of pearl, coral,
amber, ebony. Breathe in the heady air.
Buy sensual perfumes to remind yourself of pleasure.
Visit Egyptian cities, open your soul
to the learned and the wise. Always

let Ithaka live inside your heart.
She is your destiny, your home, the end
of wandering. But do not seek to shorten
your voyage, better to let it last long years;
only anchor at your isle when you are old,
rich with all you have gathered on the way.

Never expect Ithaka to give you riches.

She granted you your perfect voyage.
Without her you would not have traveled far;
she has nothing more to give. And if

you find in her a poor and meager land,
Ithaka has not cheated you. Instead,
she has let you become wise, so filled
with vast experience, that now, finally
you understand what all your Ithakas mean.

Original poem in Greek, by C. P. Cavafy
English arrangement by LJ Cohen

Chapter 1

BARRE TURNED UP the music, and it transformed his mind into a concert hall with perfect acoustics, transporting him more than a dozen wormhole jumps and a few centuries away from the ruined bridge of the broken ship. The resonance of the strings swelled through him, vibrating the bones of his skull and his chest. If Ro called, he would definitely not hear her. He clenched his jaw and focused on tracing the chaos beneath the console.

It was work a tech drone could have done, but that was another on the list of the dozens and dozens of things they needed but didn't have. So while Ro was doing something in engineering, Barre was wedged into this cramped space, comparing the half-melted mess with the schematic she had pushed to him.

The ancient symphony soothed him, and as his hands did the grunt work of stripping wires and creating splices, his mind composed a more modern counterpoint, weaving synthesized computer tones though the main theme. He knew Halcyone was monitoring and got the sense the ship approved.

It wasn't Halcyone's fault she couldn't fly. It was Ro's.

An alarm tore through the music. As Barre jerked up, his head clipped the bottom lip of the console. Swearing, he scrambled to his feet, and pressed his hand against the dripping cut on his forehead. He shut off the symphony.

Barre sent a trill of four questioning notes to Halcyone. The AI silenced the alarm and sent the same notes back in reverse order. An apology. The sudden quiet made his ears ring.

He played the command tone and Halcyone opened the internal comms. At least they worked. "Ro? What the hell are you doing?"

"Not now." Her clipped voice filled the bridge before she killed the channel.

The wound on his head throbbed and given the forty-odd-year-old ship's grime that now coated his hands, he knew he needed to get it cleaned off and sterilized. He queried Halcyone again. All calm. Whatever Ro was mucking around with, at least the ship wasn't going to go critical while he took care of himself. Barre glanced around at the half-dismantled nav console and his scattered tools. It was a miracle Halcyone had ever flown. Or at least a miracle they hadn't all gotten blown up in the process.

He updated the AI with his status in case Ro bothered to look for him, and strode to the airlock, his dreads swaying across his back. If he was lucky, his mother wouldn't be on duty in medical. Maybe he could convince one of the techs to let him grab some suture glue and a field bandage.

With his free hand, Barre unsealed the door, and stepped through into the station beyond. Before Ro resurrected the ship's AI, and before it tore loose from the station with its accidental crew and a hold full of smuggled weapons, he had been part of Daedalus's staff, at least by proxy. Now as a full Commonwealth citizen, he had his autonomy, but no real status on the station. His parents had not contested his emancipation request, and with a ship at his disposal, he figured he'd have been long gone by this point.

But Halcyone was a lot more damaged than Ro realized. Or at least that's what Barre assumed, since she'd been holed up in engineering for most of the past two weeks, only speaking to him in monosyllables after their last failed attempt to take off. And he'd been demoted to tech drone in the process.

With its stripped-down design and bare metal walls, Daedalus Station could have been an extension of the ship. Cold, clinical, like the infirmary. Like his mother. This late into third shift the corridors were deserted and the lighting set to minimal. At least neither of his folks would be in medical now, unless there were active emergencies.

He pressed his cleaner hand to the ident plate in the nexus, sighing in relief when it opened. By all rights, Commander Mendez could have revoked his access, which would have made things a lot more complicated than they already were. At the entrance to medical, he paused. He and Ro really needed to lay in their own stock of supplies. It wasn't like they could just requisition stuff, and neither of them had any money. Mendez had emptied Halcyone's storage bay of everything Ro's and Micah's fathers had been smuggling: the weapons, the battle rations, and all the medical equipment. It would have been nice to at least get a finder's fee, but Ro hadn't thought of that. And to be honest, at that point, they were all just glad to be alive.

The door slid open and the smell of the cleanser they used in medical flooded him with memories. Barre and his brother, Jem, had basically grown up in rooms like this. No matter where his parents had been stationed—from hospitals in the Hub to the asteroid that housed Daedalus—the familiar aseptic space had been a constant.

He slipped inside the silent infirmary as the door sealed behind him. The entire place gleamed, the stainless steel reflecting even the minimal illumination. All the beds were empty, their stabilization webbing packed away, their displays dark. The single on-duty tech slept in a berth built into the rear wall. Barre remembered napping in one just like it when he was little. After Jem was born, that's where the two of them had played. That had been a long time ago.

The door to the small cubicle his parents used for their office was open. The glow of a monitor brightened the room. The tech had probably forgotten to log out. Barre knew if his mother found it still on when she came in, she'd discipline the poor man. He stepped inside. Something moved at the edge of his vision and he jerked around, hitting his jutting elbow on the door frame.

"Shit." His hand jammed into the swelling wound. Pain made him woozy and a fresh trickle of warmth dripped into his left eye.

"Damn it, Barre!" Jem's urgent whisper filled the office. His little brother stood from where he'd been curled up in the high-backed desk chair and lurched across the room. "What the hell are you doing?"

Barre took his hand away from his head and blinked at it. "Bleeding."

Frowning, Jem steered him toward the chair and pushed him into it. "Wait here."

As Barre leaned forward to look at the live screen, Jem closed the window on whatever he'd been doing, leaving the station logo to slowly swirl across the monitor. Barre's good mixing headphones lay on the desk.

"And be quiet."

Barre raised his eyebrows, wincing when the motion opened the cut. Jem sneaking around? That so wasn't like him. Not the Durbins' perfect son.

He came back and dumped an armload of medical supplies on the desk. "You know this is going to hurt, right?"

"I thought Mom and Dad taught us never to sugarcoat the truth."

The corner of Jem's mouth twitched into a half-smile. "Well, keep still."

Barre held his breath as Jem cleansed the wound. It must not have been as deep as he feared.

"It's way too swollen to try to put sutures in. I'm going to seal it with antibiotic glue."

"Thank you," Barre said.

"Keep it covered and try to keep it clean."

A hint of their mom's exasperated tone echoed in Jem's voice. It would've been easy to make some snide comment about the infamous Dr. Leta Durbin. In the past, Jem would have even laughed, but in the long weeks since their return, he'd been more and more distant. Part of that was Barre avoiding his parents. Part was Jem avoiding him. Or at least that's how it seemed. Barre pursed his lips and stared at his brother, but his scars were invisible in the darkness.

Jem snatched the headphones from the desk. "We'd better get out of here before the tech gets a call or the day shift shows up."

"What were you doing with those?" He didn't mean it to sound like an accusation, but he saw the hurt in Jem's eyes as his brother offered them back.

"Just listening to something," he mumbled. "Sorry."

"Whatever. It's okay. If you need them, keep them."

"No. I'm good." Jem squinted as they moved from the almost dark infirmary to the subdued lighting of the hallway.

"Still getting headaches?"

He shrugged. "Some."

"Mom and Dad know?"

"They're doctors, right?"

Barre didn't miss that Jem hadn't answered the question. And he hadn't said anything about why he was in medical in the middle of the night.

"How's Halcyone?" Jem asked.

"Still broken. Ro hasn't said more than a few words to me in nearly a week. I don't think she's left the ship at all since we got towed in the last time. If you can, you should come by. Maybe she'll explain it to you."

As they walked in silence down the familiar path to their quarters, Barre sneaked glances at his brother. Jem held his head stiffly and kept his gaze on the floor. His hair was a shock of uneven stubble where they had shaved him for the surgery. The healing scar still stood out, raised and red along his skull.

"I'll see. Things are pretty crazy right now. Besides, Ro doesn't need me."

Barre couldn't blame him for not wanting to return to Halcyone. If he hadn't been there trying to hide Barre from their parents, Jem would've never gotten his head slammed into the corridor during the ship's first panicked burn. He wouldn't have needed emergency surgery to get his skull cracked open.

It had only been a matter of weeks, but their lives had changed significantly, maybe permanently. Micah's father was still hanging on under life support. Ro's father had escaped Halcyone in a life pod to cosmos-knows-where. And Jem, his brilliant, annoying little brother, was struggling with the terrible after-effects of head trauma.

Jem signaled the doors to open and slipped into their family's darkened quarters, leaving Barre staring after him from the corridor.

*

Ro stared up at the schematic, blinking as the image danced around her. It had taken her weeks of work but finally all the individual components of the jump drive functioned again. Or they should have. As soon as Ro had fed the AI an updated wormhole map, Halcyone refused to calculate a jump. It didn't make any sense. Ships didn't get vertigo.

She started the simulation again. Engineering faded away until Ro stood on a virtual bridge, the map of local space on its forward display, a blinking light for where she had programmed the virtual Halcyone's position just outside of the ring of satellites surrounding Daedalus Station.

"One jump. Just one small jump." Ro rubbed her burning eyes and tried to blink away the dryness. Without jump capability, she couldn't leave Daedalus Station and if she couldn't leave Daedalus, she wouldn't be able to track her father. With a quick gesture, she set the jump sequence running. The display swung around to show Halcyone in relation to the network of wormholes in this sector. Green lights indicated well established, energetically stable paths, yellow for secondary conduits or newly mapped routes, red for unstable, unexplored.

A large, green dot within flitter distance from Daedalus was the main reason the station even existed. Space was big, and no fleet in the cosmos could control it all. But the Commonwealth regulated all wormholes—even this one at the fringe of everything.

Ro sighed and turned back to her program. This should be simple. One short simulated jump from Daedalus Station to the nearest planetary settlement on an old, standard route.

A timer activated in the upper right-hand corner of the display. The programmed Halcyone moved toward the wormhole using its interstitial drive. Ro opened a new virtual window, watching the nav computer run its initial calculations. The distance between the ship and the event horizon of the wormhole shrank. The interstitial engines shut down. Good. The sim had gotten hung up here before.

As the numbers raced toward zero, the jump drive spun up. Power levels stayed stable. The null-field formed, creating a smooth shield around the entire ship that would allow it to slip through the wormhole without skipping off its walls and careening through the galaxy or worse.

At the zero mark, the ship trembled at the lip of the mapped singularity. "No, no no," Ro whispered. "Come on, you can do this."

Red emergency lights washed through the bridge simulation. The jump drive cut out. The display appeared to spin wildly, which meant the simulated ship was tumbling in space, having missed its approach to the wormhole again.

"Damn it!" she shouted, collapsing the failed program with a sharp swipe of her arm. She fought a wave of dizziness as engineering restored itself around her. Her micro buzzed. "Fuck. What?"

"Ro?" Nomi's gentle voice filled the room.

"Oh, crap."

"Glad you're so happy to talk to me."

"I'm sorry." Ro winced, even as she said it. There were far too many missed breakfasts and apologies lately. "I got caught up in something important."

Nomi paused briefly. It gave Ro time to curse herself for having her father's social graces.

"I'm heading to the commissary now. Should I wait for you?"

This time Ro paused. Waiting for her was all Nomi seemed to be doing lately. Ro glanced around the engineering compartment and the open conduits and consoles, none of which seemed to contain any clues to Halcyone's jump drive problems. Then she looked down at herself, covered in grime, dirt trapped under her ragged fingernails. "Can you give me fifteen?" It wouldn't be enough time to shower and change, but at least she could get herself clean enough to look like a programmer again, instead of an engine tech.

"No problem."

As she closed the connection, Ro knew that there would be a time when Nomi would stop calling and stop waiting. It was a problem. One she didn't know how to solve.

She left engineering behind, but not the puzzle of the jump drive. It was all her mind churned over lately. Without a functioning jump system, the ship was more of a liability than a prize. So far, Mendez's gratitude had extended to a parking spot and the free use of station power, air, and water. But for how long? What was Ro's testimony against her absent father really worth, anyway? The cache of smuggled weapons and supplies had been turned over to Commonwealth authorities; Ro had no idea how long it would take for them to build their case. Hell, as far as she knew, no one in the galaxy had any idea where her father had disappeared to, and with the senator dying they didn't have anyone on hand to blame.

They couldn't stay docked here forever. The clock was running. She just didn't know how quickly it would zero out.

Ro scrubbed her hands until the water in the sink ran clean. The captain's quarters sounded a lot more impressive than they were. Basically a small cell with an even smaller private head attached, the room had enough space for a single berth and a small desk, both bolted to the wall and floor. A shelf wrapped around the room just below the ceiling. Free-fall netting, torn in some places, missing in others, made the shelf almost useless for storage. Just as well she didn't have many things.

Her fifteen minutes were almost up. Tying her hair back with a spare bit of wire, Ro stepped into Halcyone's central corridor and stumbled into Barre. He caught her with his muscular arms and steadied her.

Frowning, she looked up at his face and the fresh bandage across his forehead. "What happened to you?"

"Another one of your simulations."

"Nothing fatal, I hope," she said, before turning sideways to squeeze past him.

"Where are you going?"

"Breakfast with Nomi." Ro hated to take time away from Halcyone, but she knew she'd be a lot more productive after a break. And spending time with the comms officer always lightened Ro's mood. "How's that bridge work coming?"

She pushed onward, heading to the ship's air lock and her waiting friend.

"This isn't what I signed on for," Barre said.

"What do you mean?" Ro stopped and turned back to him. His severe gaze bored into her.

"You really have no clue." Barre's cheeks darkened. "Me, Nomi, Micah, and Jem—none of us mean anything to you beyond how we can be used."

"That's not fair!"

"But it's true," Barre answered quietly.

Heat flooded her face, her mind ready for a confrontation her body was already shrinking away from. Was it true? She thought of the time she'd spent with Nomi since Halcyone had gotten stuck docking back at Daedalus. The times where Nomi had been her sounding board, her respite, her support.

"Nothing's forcing you to stay." In the time they'd been working together, Ro knew she had gotten too comfortable with Barre. The warning signs had been obvious, but she'd ignored them. She should have known better than to let herself rely on anyone. Not Barre. Not Nomi. Not anyone.

Her father had been right. And she hated him for it.

"Ro, that's not ..."

Cutting him off, she turned back to engineering. "I've got work to do."

Chapter 2

Nomi waited long past the fifteen minutes Ro had requested before giving up and getting herself breakfast. The commissary was mostly empty. The first-shifters had cleared out and only a few third-shift stragglers still lingered over coffee. She didn't know why she'd declined Mendez's offer to move onto a more diurnal schedule. No, that wasn't really true. She did know. The early morning hours were the times when Ro, exhausted from her night's work, seemed to be able to let her defenses down. But these past few weeks, she'd been as driven and as closed off as Nomi had ever seen her.

Sighing, Nomi pushed away her untouched bowl of reconstituted protein mush. Even with her favorite flavorings, it held no appeal this morning.

"Hey."

She looked up into Jem's bloodshot eyes.

"This seat taken?"

Ever since they'd traveled together on Hephaestus, Jem seemed to seek out her company. "Help yourself."

"Ro?"

Nomi shook her head. "She would be a no show."

"Sorry."

"Not your fault." It wasn't anyone's fault except for Ro's. And maybe Nomi's, too, for believing in her friend's promises. "So what's up with you, Jem?"

"Barre keeps asking me to help out on Halcyone."

"You haven't told him yet?"

Jem met her gaze instead of shying away like he usually did; as he tried to focus on her face, his nystagmus emerged. She stared as his eyes stuttered back and forth before he looked down. "It's not like there's anything he can do."

He was just a little younger than Daisuke had been when Nomi headed off for Uni. Jem even reminded her of her younger brother. Something in his smile, though she hadn't seen much of that since Jem came back from his last medical consultation. "What do your folks think?"

Jem laughed, but it had a bitterness no twelve-year-old should have known. "They talk a hopeful game. But I'm not stupid. I've been hacking into their assessments and the reports all the specialists have been sending them."

"I'm sorry." Nomi reached across the table to squeeze his hand. If he had been Daisuke, she would have hugged him. He squeezed back before slipping from her grasp.

"It's slow, but the text-to-speech mode you suggested works."

"I'm glad. Can you use it to program?"

He paused and slumped in his seat. "Not really. I mean, it works for really basic things. But so much of what Ro does ...What I do ..." Jem shook his head. "What I did. The

14

interface is visual-spatial."

"Look. I think you should talk to your brother. He may have some ideas from the music perspective."

"He's got enough going on." Jem pressed his lips together and for an instant, he looked as harsh and unyielding as his mother. "Nomi? Can you help me send a message to someone?"

"A message." Nomi frowned. "What sort of message?"

"There's this neuro guy. A researcher. Some of his papers are really promising." Jem's voice sped up and hitched higher. "I need to ask him some questions, but I don't want my parents to find out."

She tilted her head and raised her eyebrows.

"It's a long shot. He probably can't help me either. But my parents—I just don't want them to get disappointed again."

Nomi studied his face and traced the line of his scar as it traveled in a zigzag across nearly half his head. He lifted his gaze to hers once more, and this time she was the one to look away from his shifting eyes. "Sure, kiddo. Can you come up to comms during my next shift?"

A deep sigh relaxed his tense body. "Thank you, Nomi."

She sat there for a long while after he left, nursing her cold coffee. A few second-shift comms staff wandered in, nodded to her, and wandered out again, but for once, she wasn't in the mood to talk to anyone. Not even Ro.

*

Jem couldn't stop his hands from shaking as he walked

away from Nomi. It wasn't exactly a lie, what he'd told her, but it also wasn't the complete truth. Between the headaches that plagued him whenever he tried to focus on anything for more than a few minutes, and the nausea from struggling with the nystagmus, it had taken him over two weeks to compress and hide the real message inside the one he needed Nomi to send.

It was exhausting. Without Barre around to deflect them, his parents were on him constantly. He didn't even have his schoolwork to escape to. Even if he could have used a computer, they insisted he let his brain rest. But now he knew what they knew and refused to tell him: the damage from his head injury was too extensive. Even the best specialists money and influence could buy had nothing to offer them.

He headed back to his quarters, hoping he had enough of the sedatives left to get to sleep. The door opened. His parents were waiting for him, sitting at the dining room table, grim expressions on their faces. He had to force himself not to bolt. Now he knew how Barre had felt before his emancipation. It didn't help.

"Hey, what are you two doing home?" He meant it as a joke, but even he heard the sharp edge to his voice.

His father held out a nearly empty pill container. "Why didn't you tell us you haven't been sleeping?"

Jem swallowed the lump in his dry throat. "I didn't want you to worry."

"So you stole sedatives from the pharmacy?" His mother's voice cracked with barely controlled fury.

They were playing their usual good cop/bad cop roles. He

had seen this show before, too many times to count. Only it had always been played for Barre's benefit.

"Jem, sit down," his father said.

He clamped down on the back of an empty chair so hard his fingers ached.

"We're here to help you," his father continued. "These can be dangerously addictive. There are other ways of dealing with sleep problems."

They had no idea how bad it had gotten. How much the pain and the roiling of his insides made his days and nights hell. The neo-benzos were the only thing that let him function as well as he did. And that was barely tolerable. It had taken some trial and error, but he finally knew the exact dose that would let him walk around without feeling like he was jump-sick all the time, but not knock him out if he sat down. And a few milligrams more let him fall asleep without the room spinning out of control.

His mother was glaring at him. Her lips were pressed together so tightly all the color had bled out of them. Her dark eyes smoldered with a strange combination of worry and fury. Jem opened his mouth and closed it again. There was nothing he could say that would help. If it had only been his father, then maybe. He closed his eyes, feeling the press of frustrated tears.

"We have an appointment with a neurologist at the University of Avencia next month."

He took a deep breath before staring his mother down. "And this doctor is going to tell us something different from every other specialist you've dragged me to?" The room was starting to spin; he knew the nystagmus would already be in full force. His mother winced, but didn't look away. He clamped down on the chair even harder. "We've been through this. The only thing that even has a chance at helping me is a neural. And no one will consider it."

All the expression drained from his mother's face. Only the distant doctor looked out of her eyes now. "You know the risks. Your brain is not fully matured. The guidelines specify sixteen for a reason."

That was four years away. Four years of pain and motion sickness and frustration.

"I know it's hard, Jem," his father said, pocketing the bottle of pills, "but you need to trust us and be patient. We won't give up."

He wanted to throw the chair, but right now it was the only thing keeping him from falling down. "You have no idea." His voice was a harsh whisper. The toast he had eaten at breakfast with Nomi threatened to come up for a second appearance. His knuckles cracking, Jem let go of the chair and lurched toward the far wall of their apartment. He squeezed his eyes shut on the conflicting world his inner ear couldn't resolve, until he stumbled into his room and sprawled across his bed.

The trash can was nowhere nearby when his stomach heaved, spilling bile and half-digested toast in a bitter stream across the floor.

*

When the message from medical finally came, Micah

carefully carried the contents of his father's bar to the kitchen and smashed each bottle against the side of the disposal. The senator had preferred traditional single-malt scotches, imported directly from the Hub, but he had kept a stash of expensive wine as well, just in case. The amber liquid mingled with the dark burgundy. It swirled around the drain like blood.

The empty bar and the overlapping water rings on the coffee table were the last remnants of Senator Corwin Rotherwood, alcoholic, morally corrupt—if charming—public servant. The rest of his father's things were already recycled into their base fibers, plastics, and metals. Maybe they would do some good somewhere, though Micah had no illusions that the scales of his father's life would ever balance.

His own belongings, as scant as they were, had been packed for a long time now. Except for a few changes of clothes and his micro, there was nothing Micah needed and as soon as he was released from active therapy, he was headed back to the Hub and a new life at Uni under a new name.

Turning his back on the generic space he had lived in for less than a year, Micah slowly hobbled to medical. The skin on his feet was still healing, and he winced as it stretched with every step, despite the custom molded shoe inserts and the local anesthetic implants.

But he had functioning feet and had been cleared to walk several weeks earlier than Kristoff Durbin had anticipated. If it hadn't been for Barre, Micah would probably be getting fitted for prosthetics at this point.

He threaded his way through the light traffic following

morning shift change, nodding at occasional staff. His practiced, neutral expression was a legacy of his father's that he used even as he resented it. Far simpler to slide away from any kind of social interaction than to deal with awkward sympathy from people he hardly knew and would likely never see again.

The infirmary was also quiet, which suited Micah just fine. He eased himself into a chair and closed his eyes, waiting for the throbbing to fade.

"My condolences," Dr. Durbin said.

Micah glanced up at the tall, imposing man standing in front of him, his lab coat clean and crisp over the utilitarian bronze and black jumpsuits he and his wife favored. They had both done stints as active military and they both still looked like they could pass a space physical without blinking.

"I can walk one klick without any seeping at the graft sites."

The doctor narrowed his eyes, staring down at Micah's feet as if he could see through the shoes to the damaged skin beneath. "Room one. You know the drill."

Dr. Durbin followed behind as he walked to the examination room. Micah moved carefully, focusing on smoothly shifting his weight from right foot to left, ignoring the pulling and tearing at the scars. The pain was manageable. He'd dealt with a lot worse. And he didn't want to give Durbin any reason to keep him at Daedalus Station longer than was absolutely necessary.

Micah settled on the treatment table. "When can I get back to regular shoes?" These were heavy and thick. Peeling back the compression socks, he uncovered the mottled skin beneath. It wasn't pretty, but it looked a whole hell of a lot better than it had after he had blasted his own feet escaping from the hellish restraints on Halcyone. Damn Ro's father. And his own, for that matter.

Dr. Durban disinfected his hands and slipped on the thin durable gloves before examining Micah's feet. "Did he have specific funeral plans?"

"What?" Micah jerked his foot out of Durbin's hold.

"Your father. Did he specify arrangements?"

Micah sighed and closed his eyes. "A parade. With elephants."

"Excuse me?"

"How well did you know the senator?"

"The senator?"

Micah opened his eyes and met Durbin's gaze with a direct stare he knew his father had employed often. "He hadn't been my father in a long time. And I don't care what you do with the body. Now, am I ready to be discharged or not?"

"I'd prefer you remained here under treatment for a few weeks longer."

"My term starts in eight days. I am planning on being there when it does."

Durbin nodded. "I see." He pulled out a portable scanner and ran it over Micah's feet in a deliberate pattern. "No sign of infection. The grafts have integrated into your remaining tissue. No areas of necrosis." He pulled out the sensory testing wand. "Tell me sharp, dull, or nothing. Ready?"

"Dull. Dull. Nothing. Dull." A sudden zing traveled through his foot from heel to arch. He jerked away. "Ouch!"

"Your sensory nerves are healing well. But you may have some area of persistent numbness."

"Better than the pain."

"Not really. Pain is your body's alert system. Without it, you stand a higher risk of injury and potential infection. You're going to need to monitor your feet for a long time."

It hadn't worked that way for his mother. She didn't need the pain to tell her she was dying. But that was a long time ago. "So am I done here?"

"I have a colleague at the Commonwealth Medical College who is a burn specialist. I'd like you to check in with her when you get settled."

"Fine."

"You need to identify and release the body."

"Fine."

"I don't think you are."

"Are what?" Micah crumpled his socks in his fist.

"Fine."

Micah couldn't stifle the laughter that shook through him. "Seriously? You're seriously analyzing my relationship with my father?"

Dr. Durbin silently put his scanner away and peeled off his gloves, his expression the medical equivalent of his father's politician-face. "Go ahead and put your shoes back on."

It was so hard not to say something about Barre and being a father to him. Something said with feigned politeness that would be sarcastic and biting and so very clever. But it wasn't his place, and baiting Dr. Durbin wouldn't do anything to defuse the anger that still burned through him. Anger that he thought would die when his father did. "Let's get this over with."

Durbin nodded and Micah shuffled after him to the infirmary's small morgue.

As he stepped into the cold, sterile room and saw the sealed body bag, memories swept through him.

The days and weeks of sitting at his mother's bedside, helpless in the face of the pain that twisted her once bright smile into a grimace, broke something in Micah. Her long illness had broken something in his father, too, but the fault lines had been there long before. And once Nina Rotherwood had transformed from the charming, intelligent, and fiercely passionate presence by the senator's side into an inconvenient liability, those cracks had fractured through all their lives.

Micah just hadn't understood how deeply until he found the weapons the senator had smuggled with the help of Ro's dad. That's when he realized his own father had been more concerned with his illegal business than his only son's life.

Maybe he should have realized a lot sooner, but he wasn't much older than Jem when his mother died. When his father found his support network at the bottom of a bottle and left a guilt-wracked Micah to grieve on his own.

Dr. Durbin leaned over the body and unzipped the head of the body bag.

Micah couldn't look away. The expression on the rigid face was the most honest he could remember seeing in a long time. "Fine. That's him."

"Do you want some time alone?"

"I'm done here." Micah limped to the door, waiting there

as Durbin resealed the body, the sound of the zipper loud and final.

Chapter 3

Ro had no idea how long it had been since her confrontation with Barre when her micro buzzed, pulling her out of her latest battle with Halcyone's jump drive programming.

Shit. She had never called Nomi. *Damn it. Damn it. Damn it.*

Blinking through layers of virtual windows, each running a custom diagnostic, it took her a few minutes to locate the small device. By the time she snatched it from where it lay on the main nav console, the call had ended, leaving a high-priority message scrolling across the screen.

The call had been from Commander Mendez. She wasn't sure if she should be relieved or upset that it hadn't been Nomi.

Ro had known this was coming. There was only so long she could lean on the station's resources before Mendez's gratitude expired. Sighing, she pushed away her guilt before sending a reply. Mendez first. And then try to fix things with Nomi. Her father would have ignored the call and the messages—both the explicit one and the implicit one behind it. Maybe she wasn't entirely like him after all.

Shift change turned the corridors and the nexus into a traffic jam. Or at least the equivalent on Daedalus. The outpost station had few enough staff that even Ro was able to put names to all the faces she passed on her way to command. What surprised her was how many of them looked at her, smiling and nodding. It was unsettling.

Lieutenant Commander Emma Gutierrez stood at attention at Mendez's office, her uniform crisp, her sidearm gleaming in its holster, her expression neutral. Older than Mendez by at least a decade, Gutierrez had the look of a lifer and the scars that marked her as having seen hard combat, probably in the war that had downed Halcyone. Part of her left arm and hand had been reconstructed—old battle tech that Gutierrez had never bothered to replace with more natural-looking prosthetics. But there was nothing wrong with how they functioned.

"The commander asked to see me?"

Gutierrez nodded and the door opened. Ro stepped through, feeling the intensity of the lieutenant commander's gaze, like the laser sight of a gun on her back.

The last time Ro had been in this office, Mendez had given her Halcyone.

"Ms. Maldonado. Please sit down." Mendez came around the front of her desk and waved Ro toward a small table and two chairs in an alcove at the rear of her office.

She studied the commander, wondering what kind of meeting this was to be. So far, it didn't seem like any kind of hearing or disciplinary action. Then again, Ro was not technically under Mendez's command. The commander sat and Ro followed her lead. The woman had always seemed stern and distant, but Ro saw the lines of fatigue at the corner of her eyes and the deep furrows across her brow, legacy of the mess that led to an ongoing Commonwealth investigation into her father, the smuggled weapons, and the war they were meant to spark.

The door opened again and Gutierrez entered, carrying a tray with two steaming coffees. Ro frowned, but watched as the old soldier easily set down a cup next to each of them with her bio-electronic hand, not spilling a drop.

"That will be all," Mendez said. Gutierrez nodded, turned crisply, and left.

Ro waited until the commander picked up her cup before taking a sip of the coffee. It was the real deal—a smooth, dark roast, imported from the Hub at great expense. And served black, just the way she liked it.

"There's been no word on your father."

He was out there—Ro had no doubt about that. Alain Maldonado was too smart and too vindictive to be dead. She knew she needed to find him before he came for her.

"There was enough evidence just based on dereliction of duty to strip him of his rank in the engineering guild and his Commonwealth citizenship."

It was far less than he deserved after what he had done to Micah, what he had threatened to do to her and Barre. Ro focused on the welcome burn of the coffee as she swallowed.

Mendez put down her cup. "They also confiscated his assets."

Unfortunately, Ro had also expected that. She finished

the coffee and carefully placed her cup on the small table, waiting for Mendez's third and final blow. A freighter without jump capability was space junk. Sure, she could live aboard Halcyone. The water recycling worked, as did the air scrubbers. The ship had enough aduronium to fuel the interstitial engines for a thousand years, or until the base metals disintegrated back into star stuff. But being forced to drift through the sector where Daedalus Station orbited felt like slow suicide.

"As little as Halcyone draws from the station, there is a cost."

Ro kept her gaze steady, but she couldn't help the heat that rose to her cheeks. It wasn't as if she hadn't been expecting this. That's what drove her to work nearly through all three shifts during the past long weeks, irritating and alienating both Nomi and Barre in the process.

And for nothing. The ship was likely irretrievably broken. And there was a good chance her relationships were, too.

"I appreciate all you've done for me, Commander Mendez." Ro was shocked at how steady her voice was. "I understand. Thank you for your time." She pushed her chair from the table and stood to leave.

"Sit down." Mendez's command filled the room.

Ro sat, the heat spreading out from her cheeks to her whole face.

"You need resources. I need an engineer."

"Sir?"

"Until this mess with your father is straightened out and Commonwealth Command decides to fill my staffing request, I am short one chief engineer. You have the skills to do the job and a ship that won't fly."

"You're offering me a job?"

"Such as it is. My budget is stretched thin. When they claimed your father's resources, they also froze his salary. I can manage to continue your intern's stipend, along with supplies for Halcyone in return for a part-time commitment."

"But I'm not military."

"Consider yourself an outside contractor."

"Oh."

"I've taken the liberty of pushing a standard agreement to your micro. Am I correct in assuming you'd prefer to stay aboard your ship, rather than return to your previously assigned quarters?"

Ro nodded. One of the first things she had done on her return to Daedalus was to salvage anything of value from the small living space she had shared with her father. At least the Commonwealth didn't get the contents of his workroom. Though if they knew she'd taken his notes and his spare memory cube, they would come knocking. It was encrypted and locked, but Ro knew her father as well as anyone and given enough time, she was going to crack it. And then she was going to go after him.

To find her father, she needed a ship with a jump drive. To fix the ship, she needed to step into her father's old job. Mendez had assured her she was not her father. She hoped the commander was right. But now she would have even less time to work on Halcyone and to try to repair her damaged relationships.

"Welcome aboard, Acting Chief Engineer Maldonado."

Ro jerked, unable to quell the involuntary response of

looking for him over her shoulder.

Mendez studied her carefully. "You are not to blame for your father's crimes. And you will not be judged by his actions, but by your own."

The coffee soured in her stomach. "Thank you, sir."

*

The pounding in his head woke Jem hours later. He risked opening his eyes. Fortunately, he found only soothing darkness. His room smelled like the outflow of a decontamination line, and the sour taste coated his mouth as well. At least he'd been able to sleep. He sent a voice command and the air scrubbers kicked on high, dissipating the nauseating odor.

Jem shuffled to the small head in the back corner of his room. Everything was organized so he didn't have to open his eyes and risk spewing the contents of his stomach again. It took three rounds with the ultrasonic tooth cleaner before Jem had finally rinsed out the memory of sour vomit. Now he had to figure out how to make it through the station to comms without the calming effect of the meds.

It wasn't fair. He needed those drugs. This wasn't like his brother's old bittergreen habit. His hands shook and Jem slammed them on the stainless steel counter. He needed those meds to function. Why couldn't his parents understand? They were the damned doctors.

His stomach roiled and a flood of saliva filled his mouth. Jem whimpered and swallowed. His body was bathed in a cold sweat. This was worse than space sickness. At least there were meds for that; they were so common, the cabin crew gave them out like candy on commercial flights. Cheaper and less noxious than cleaning up after someone's first jump.

Well, that would be better than nothing. He groped in the back of the single cabinet above the sink, looking for the in-flight comfort bag he'd taken from their last disappointing trip to a neuro specialist his father knew. Rummaging, Jem ignored the earplugs and compressed pillow in search of the blisterpac, which he finally found at the bottom of the bag. One dose. It shouldn't be all that hard to find more. The hard part would be hiding it from his parents.

Jem let the tablet dissolve on his tongue, hoping it would at least take the edge off. He ran his hand along the wall of his room toward the door. Pausing, he listened. It was well into third shift and his parents would be long asleep, unless one of them was on call and there were emergencies. Well, if he didn't take the jump, he'd never make it out of local space.

"Okay, then," he said, grabbing his near useless micro. "Time to send a message."

His head pulsed with his heartbeat, but the nausea was manageable, even when he had to look up into the corridor. The dimmed illumination bounced off the hard, shiny surfaces, making his head ache and his vision waver. At least the station was quiet. Jem had grown to love the late-night silence and the soft lighting.

At the door to comms, Jem paused. What if Nomi had

changed her mind? Or suspected his message was more than it seemed? If she hadn't been wearing the uniform, Jem would have told her flat out what he was doing, but as a Commonwealth officer, she'd have to report him. Even if she thought he was doing what he had to do.

Jem liked Nomi too much to put her in that position.

He hit the ident plate and frowned. The old Jem would have been able to cover his tracks. Now, he had only limited concentration to code and he hadn't been willing to waste it. The message had to come first. If he was lucky, he'd get a reply before anyone thought to look at his station access logs.

The doors opened onto what looked like a near silent star-scape. White lights glittered against the dark background of a large, curved display. The interior lights were set to night vision. The red glow of Nomi's instruments didn't trigger any of his symptoms.

"Hey Jem. Practicing for an exciting career as a third-shifter?"

"I wish." The door sealed shut, cutting off even the small amount of light-leak from the corridors. Jem stepped into comms and relaxed into a soothing dark lit by the glittering ansible nodes. "Is this a good time?"

"Sure. Nights are pretty quiet around here. What do you have for me?"

"You sure you're okay with this?" He risked glancing at her face and the frown that briefly covered up her smile.

"Is there a reason I shouldn't be?"

Jem shook his head slowly. Nothing swam in his vision. Good. "No. I mean, I don't want my folks to know."

Nomi smiled at him. "As far as I know, the Commonwealth hasn't made sending mail a crime."

He relaxed his hiked-up shoulders.

"There's not a lot of traffic passing this time of night. It should route directly, without much node-hopping."

Jem nodded as he unlocked his micro and handed it over to her.

She looked at the node address of the outer message he'd crafted. "Even all the way to the Hub won't take long. It's your lucky night."

It would only be lucky if the true message got delivered. The black market didn't advertise its node address. But everyone knew The Underworld was where you could find what you needed outside of Commonwealth control. If you had enough credit or they were interested enough in you to respond.

Nomi smiled at him before turning to her softly lit console. "This will be out in a nanosec."

Jem held his breath as she pulled the message from his micro and formatted it for transmission. If Daedalus found his hidden program, Nomi could lose her job. There was a limit to what they could do to him since he was a minor, but that didn't mean the consequences would be pleasant.

The old Jem could have created the layered message in a blink. And it would have been solid. This had taken him forever, but without going to Ro for help, it was the best he could do.

"Here you go." Nomi handed back his micro. Jem let out the breath he'd been holding.

"Thank you."

"I've asked Daedalus to auto-ping you on delivery and reply. You'll get that researcher's message relayed right to your micro."

He looked away, ashamed of the lie. "Thank you," he said again.

"Hey, what are friends for?"

It was a good question. And one he'd been asking himself ever since they all got safely back to Daedalus. Ro had barely spoken to him in weeks and he couldn't bring himself to really talk to Barre. His brother would try to help, but all Barre would accomplish was an escalation of hostilities with their parents. No, it was easier just to keep things to himself.

Jem had been surprised when Nomi and Micah started coming by to see how he was doing. Neither of them owed him. If anything, it was the other way around, especially with Micah. He hadn't forgotten Micah's kindness on Halcyone, when he took care of Jem after the injury.

"Try to get some sleep, Jem. You can't heal when you're strung out like this."

"I know. It's just ..." He didn't want to get her involved in his parents' crap. "No, you're right. I'll try."

The gentle chime of an incoming message resonated through comms. "Hey, look, something for me to do." Nomi turned to her console.

Jem stood by the door watching her work for a moment before heading back out into the still too-bright corridor. There was no way to know how long it would take for his message to be received. And even if it was, that was no guarantee if or when he would get a reply. If his AI interface code mods didn't at least pique The Underworld's interest, Jem was screwed. And if by some miracle they *did* answer him, he still didn't know how he was going to pay for the neural or get off Daedalus without his parents finding out.

Chapter 4

BARRE ROLLED OVER and fell out of the narrow berth onto the floor in the cabin he had claimed on Halcyone. Swearing, he untangled his legs from the blanket and stood, rubbing his shoulder. The junior officers who lived aboard must have been a lot smaller than Barre. The closet-sized space had been quarters for two. Each of the bunk beds bolted to the wall had an integrated storage locker. The padding had broken down long ago, but Barre had been able to scavenge a mostly intact jump cushion from a decommissioned medi-bed. Other than a few changes of clothes and his micro, the room was generic. Anyone could have lived there.

He missed his instruments. Collected over more than a decade, with money Barre had struggled to earn and save, they represented who he was. And if he was going to stay aboard Halcyone—and broken or not, he didn't see that he had much choice—maybe it was time to make this look like some kind of home.

The tiny sink and toilet slid from the panel in the rear wall as he triggered the proximity detector. At least some things still worked. Barre washed and changed before heading out to the station in search of coffee. They were going to have to figure out the food situation on Halcyone eventually. He'd bought a bunch of food bars from station supply, but even if that's all he wanted to eat, Barre's limited funds would only stretch so far. Ro hadn't volunteered to pitch in.

Shift change had finished and Barre was able to swipe a cup of coffee from the empty commissary. He dumped a small heap of sweetener into the synthetic brew and gulped the first bitter sip. Micah would drink station coffee only under protest. Barre raised his cup in a silent toast to his friend before taking another drink. At least the caffeine hit it contained was indistinguishable from the expensive stuff.

Taking the covered cup with him, he walked through the station to his family's quarters. His mother would probably be relieved when he moved his stuff out for good. The few times they'd run into one another since Barre's return to Daedalus, she'd had very little to say to him. Her cold gaze and lined brow were enough to tell him she still blamed him for Jem's head injury.

That was nowhere near as bad as the blame he placed on himself. If his parents hadn't suspected he'd been using again—no, that wasn't the full truth. Barre was done with blaming others for his choices. If he hadn't been using, his parents wouldn't have threatened to send him to rehab. And Jem wouldn't have smuggled him aboard Halcyone in the first place. Even if the tainted bittergreen had been to blame for starting it all, that wouldn't have happened if Barre hadn't taken it.

He was surprised when the door still opened for him. He half figured his folks would have revoked his access by now. In the weeks since he had last been here, nothing had really changed, even though everything had changed. The living area reflected his mother's sensibilities—clean, utilitarian, and functional. The only decorations, if you could call them that, were the holos of his parents receiving their commissions. He paused to glance at the photos, hardly recognizing his stern mother in the smiling young woman, her hair in a wild afro, her eyes gleaming, as if looking off into a future she couldn't wait to meet. Her father was the more pensive, more reserved of the two. He stood to the side of his medical partner and wife, his face serious, his arms folded across his chest. What had happened to make them change?

A choking cough startled Barre. "Jem?" His brother was usually out of their quarters and working on some experiment or his coursework by now. The sound muffled. Barre leaned his forehead on his brother's door. "Jem? Are you all right?"

"Go 'way." Something thudded against the door.

"Let me in. If you're sick, I can help."

A long silence answered him. Ro could easily override the lock. If this were Halcyone, Barre could have opened it with a few musical notes, but he had no influence over Daedalus, and Ro was too busy for him or his brother these days.

"I'm worried about you," Barre whispered, his words never penetrating the closed door. "I'm sorry." Before he could move away, the door opened and he tumbled into Jem's room. The smell hit him first. It was the sour reminder of cleaning up vomit in infirmaries all across the galaxy. Then as he recovered his balance and looked up, Barre was stunned by the chaos. Permapapers lay scattered across Jem's desk. His micro balanced on the edge of the chair and clothes littered the floor. Beside his bed was a half-empty travel container of mouth-rinse.

Jem huddled under a heap of blankets, his head hanging off the bed's edge over a spare storage bin.

Barre swore under his breath and headed back to the main apartment to rummage for cleaning supplies. After setting the environmentals to deodorize the room, he gloved and cleaned up the thin vomit. It wasn't as easy to retreat into the routine of his parents' training. This wasn't some anonymous patient. He continued the work in a guilty silence.

After bagging the cleaning supplies and the dirty cloths, he stripped off the gloves. Either he was acclimating to the smell, or the disinfectant was doing its job. Probably some of both. He sighed and turned to his brother. "I thought it was getting better." He winced at how accusatory he sounded.

Jem slowly sat up, leaning against the molded headboard. "I lied."

"Damn it, Jem. Why didn't you say something?"

"There's nothing you can do. There's nothing anyone can do."

He sat at the edge of Jem's bed, really looking at his brother for the first time since they had reunited on Daedalus. His thin body seemed even thinner, his face drawn, his skin sallow, his mouth downturned. "Here." Barre handed him the mouth rinse.

"Thank you."

As Jem leaned over the bed to spit the fluid into the

storage bin, Barre visually traced the line of the jagged scar. In the weeks since his emergency surgery, Jem's wiry hair had started to grow back, but the scar meandered its way across his head like a river cutting through a savannah. It must itch like crazy. Barre had an urge to scratch his own head, but shook it instead, feeling the sway of his dreadlocks across his spine. "How bad is it?"

Jem leaned back against the wall. "You really want to know?"

"Yes."

"It's bad." Jem looked up and locked his gaze on Barre's face.

For an instant, Barre didn't know what Jem was showing him, but then Jem's eyes started stuttering back and forth in a rhythmic beat, rapidly to the right, then slowly back to the left. He couldn't look away.

Jem did, ducking his head and tilting it up to look back at Barre. His eyes quieted in their jerky dance.

"It's bad. I can't look at my micro or any fixed screen for more than a few minutes. Bright lights give me headaches. And when I try to move, the world spins around me. Hell, when I close my eyes, the world spins around me."

Barre swallowed, imagining the taste of bile in his own throat. "What do Mom and Dad say?"

His brother laughed and it was a bitter sound. "Can you believe it? They're actually lying to me."

That was the one thing they never, ever did. Not about medical stuff. They were brutally honest with their patients and their own sons. "Are you sure?"

"I'm not stupid, Barre. I see the way they look at me. I've

been around enough medical people to know when the specialists are being evasive. It hasn't gotten any better. It's probably not going to get any better."

He tilted his head to look directly in Jem's eyes. "They're not moving so much now. Are you still dizzy?"

"I'm always dizzy. But if I can keep my head in this position, I can manage. At least I can use my micro for a few minutes."

"Oh, Jem, I'm so—"

"Stop! Just stop. Don't you dare apologize." Jem lifted his head and his eyes began to flick again. The color left his face and he turned away. "Mom found out I was using sedatives and had a super-nova."

Barre heard the suppressed sob in his brother's voice.

"Short of a neural, the meds were the only thing that let me function. Even a little bit. I don't know what to do."

Even if Jem had the money, no surgeon in the Hub or beyond would implant a neural in a kid his age. "Shit, Jem, is there anything I can do?"

"I'd even risk bittergreen at this point. I don't suppose you could hook me up?"

Barre couldn't stand the twisted smile on his little brother's face. "The contaminated shit from Hadria was the last of it." Everything else had gotten flushed from Halcyone when Micah broke down his makeshift botany experiment.

"That was a joke, stupid," Jem said.

But Barre didn't think so. It would have to be pretty bad for Jem to want to use.

"Wait—you're a citizen, now. You can buy stuff without Mom and Dad finding out."

"What do you need?" He hoped whatever money he had left would be enough.

"The stuff they hand out for space sickness. It's not as good as the prescription shit, but it helps."

"How are you going to hide it?"

"How did you hide your bittergreen?"

"In my room. Can you walk? I'll show you."

Jem sighed and rolled out of bed, holding his head in the strange, awkward position that seemed to slow down the nystagmus. It hurt Barre's neck just to watch him.

At the door to Barre's room, Jem placed a light hand on his arm. "Why did you come back?"

"My instruments. I shouldn't have left them."

"Oh."

A pang of fear moved through Barre's chest. "They didn't get rid of them, did they?"

"No. It's okay. Well, Mom wanted to sell them—"

"Fuck! No!" Barre pounded on the door with his fist.

"She was going to leave the money. In trust for you. But me and Dad, we convinced her to leave your stuff be."

Barre brought his breathing under control. His music. His instruments. She had never understood. The money didn't matter if he couldn't play. He blinked away the tears gathering in his eyes; glancing back at Jem, he understood his brother's desperation. If Barre were cut off from his music, the way Jem was from his ability to code, part of him would be dead.

He keyed the door and it slid open. His room was just as he'd left it. Unnaturally clean and organized. But at least his instruments were still there. He stroked the neck of the twelve-string guitar without sounding a single note. It would be woefully out of tune. Of all his collection, this one was his most valuable. It was only a replica, but unlike the others, it was handmade from real wood and not only did it sing, it was a thing of beauty. He loosened the strings one by one, slipped it into its shock-proof case, and slung it over his shoulder.

Barre glanced at the row of drums against the wall and sighed. This was going to take a million trips.

"You could requisition a trundle."

A work cart would make things simpler, but Barre wasn't a member of Daedalus's crew. "On whose cred?"

Jem cracked a rare smile. "The Doctors Durbin, of course."

"Will you do the honors?"

"Daedalus," Jem signaled, "send a trundle to Habitation ring/05 Alpha, authorization Durbin, Leta, zero zero zero zed nine six three."

"Authorization accepted. Trundle located. On route to Habitation ring/05 Alpha."

The voice of Daedalus always sounded slightly bored to Barre. Before he could thank his brother, the door chime sounded and the boxy cart wheeled itself inside.

While Jem sat on Barre's bed, resting his head against the wall, Barre packed the drums, pausing to look at the *djembe* his grandparents had given him on his twelfth birthday. The synthetic dark wood gleamed in between the webbing of rope that secured the membrane to the drum head. The base was covered in carvings. Barre tapped lightly on it listening to the low sound boom in the small space. When Jem was younger, he used to like to pound on it when Barre played guitar or one of his horns.

"Here," he said, passing the *djembe* to Jem.

"What am I supposed to do with this?"

"Look at the waist strap."

Jem frowned and tried to focus on the brightly woven material. Barre leaned over and guided his brother's hand to the end seam.

"Feel the clasp? Press it gently and it will open. There's enough space inside the padding to hide what you need."

"Clever."

Barre shrugged. "Mom searched the drum base, figuring if I was smuggling shit, that's where I would put it. But all anyone would have to do is play the thing and hear the change in its tone."

"I don't know, Barre. Maybe you would." Jem squeezed the seam closed again. "In case you haven't noticed, most people don't have your ear."

Barre felt his face get warm. He wasn't used to being noticed for what he loved, what he was good at. "Yeah, well, you're not so ordinary yourself."

A long silence filled Barre's room. Jem hugged the drum, closed his eyes, and turned away. "What am I going to do if I can't code?"

"It's not going to come to that. We're going to figure something out. I swear it."

Jem sighed and didn't say anything else as Barre finished packing up the practice guitar and the odd collection of flutes and recorders, along with the clarinet and compact keyboard. It was going to be a challenge to fit this all in his room on Halcyone.

"I'll message you when I have the space-sickness stuff. We can meet up in the commissary or something." He really didn't want to risk coming back here with anything his mother could use against him. "Hey, you're not going to get in trouble for this, are you?" Barre said, patting the boxy cart.

"I'm the golden child, remember?"

"Jem, I'm—"

"No. This isn't your fault. None of it."

But that's not what it felt like. Even if the shit that had gone down on the ship had had nothing to do with him, once they'd gotten back here, Barre had left Jem alone with their parents. "Look, if you need me, you know where I am. It's not like we're going anywhere soon. And maybe you can talk to Ro. Nobody else can, these days."

Jem sighed again. "I'll try. Now get out of here before Mom or Dad comes home."

He keyed the trundle to his micro and turned to leave, the cart following closely behind. "Hey, kiddo? Don't give up, okay?"

Barre paused by the apartment door, but never got an answer.

Chapter 5

AFTER A RESTLESS sleep, Ro grabbed a quick shower and rummaged through the pile of clothes on the floor of her quarters for the least dirty set. She wrinkled her nose. Now that she was official again, everything needed to be sent through the cleanser on Daedalus.

At least Halcyone wouldn't get kicked out of her docking space. But Ro would be so much busier now. She'd already cut down her sleep to four hours with the liberal use of caffeine and stimulant pills. There was a limit to how long her body would tolerate the abuse.

She worked her hair into a tight braid. A memory of Nomi unbraiding it made her hands tremble, and she dropped the wire she was using to tie it off. "Damn it." Ro knew she owed Nomi an apology. And not just Nomi.

Her hair rebraided, Ro stepped into Halcyone's main corridor and nearly tripped over a trundle loaded with musical instruments. Barre emerged from his quarters across the hallway and stopped short, staring between the cart and her.

"I have nowhere else to go," he said, his dark eyes staring directly at her. "And despite your belief to the contrary, you do need me here. Unless you can play one of these for Halcyone."

"Look. I'm not—" Ro was going to say she wasn't good at this. At this friendship thing. Or the communications thing, but Barre cut her off.

"I'll do what I can to get the ship working. I know I'm not my brother." A frown narrowed his eyes for a moment. "But I owe at least that much to you."

He didn't understand, she could tell. It was so much the other way around. She just couldn't find a way to say it. Barre pulled several stringed instruments from the cart. Her micro beeped with a list of tasks Mendez had prioritized for her. Ro waved her hand over it to silence the alert. "Can I help you?"

Barre shrugged. "Knock yourself out."

They emptied the cart into the tight confines of his room without speaking. It felt comfortable to just be doing something. It was what she was best at. The words were so much harder. "I can take the trundle back." Ro sighed, thinking of all time she would have to spend away from Halcyone. "Mendez put me back on staff. I have to head to the depot anyway."

"That's new."

"As of yesterday. But we get to keep Halcyone here as long as we need to and have access to the resources to fix her." If they could fix her. Ro squashed that particular fear and looked up at Barre. She hoped he got her use of 'we' and heard the apology in it. "It means I have to spend time at the station. Do you think ... are you willing to keep working on her? Can you get Jem to help?"

He was scowling at her, his expression just like his mother's. She hoped he didn't think she just insulted his abilities. But Jem was better at troubleshooting. Even Barre knew that.

"You haven't even asked about him once since we got back here. Now you want to use him?"

It was hard not to look away. Yes, she was going to use him. The same way she used and drove herself. If Jem was anything like her, that's what he'd want, too. Something in Barre's eyes made her bite back her sharp reply. She took a deep breath and replayed what he'd said. She hadn't asked about him ... Shit. "What's wrong?"

"He has a head injury, that's what's wrong." Barre's face darkened.

"But the surgery—that was supposed to fix it, right?"

"He's broken. Like Halcyone. And I don't think anyone can fix him."

"Oh, crap. I'm sorry."

"Sorry that he can't help anymore? Or sorry that he got dragged into your mess?"

Heat rose up through her chest and burned across her face. Ro turned, nearly tripping on an upended drum at her feet. She wanted to kick it, to leave it in pieces strewn across the floor. Instead, she compacted the anger into a tiny black hole and added it to all the rest. Someday, it would eat its way through her, leaving emptiness behind.

"Shit. I'm sorry," Barre said. "That was out of line."

She slammed her hand down on the trundle, paired it to her micro, and turned to go.

"Ro?"

Why wouldn't he leave her be? "What?"

"It wasn't your fault. What happened to Jem."

The pain in his voice was as unsettling as her own anger.

"He wouldn't even have been there, except for me screwing up."

Ro closed her eyes, wishing for the clean problems of code and machine. "I'm sorry," she repeated, not sure what else to say.

"I know. Me too."

Her micro buzzed again. "I've got to go." She turned around. He was leaning against the doorway, his head bowed, dreads falling forward to cover his face. His large hands circled the neck of some kind of flute, his grip so tight Ro was sure the instrument would snap. In the silence, she could only hear the pulse pounding in her ears.

With shaking hands, she stepped forward and reached for the flute. Barre jerked his head up and for an instant, his knuckles tightened even further, turning gray against the shiny silver metal, before his hands loosened and his shoulders slumped.

Ro set it down on the bare steel desk and left, the empty trundle following her out of the ship and into the station.

*

Jem carried the *djembe* into his room. There was a time

when the thing had been taller than he was. It was still pretty big for him and heavier than it looked when Barre played it. He ran his hands over the taut material stretched over the top, remembering the sound. Barre could make the thing really sing. All Jem could do was pound on it.

The secret pocket in the waist strap was cleverly constructed. Short of taking the entire thing apart, or running it through a scanner, the compartment was impossible to accidentally find. Now he'd be all set, as long as Barre could make good on his promise.

He set the drum next to his desk, climbed back into bed, and pulled out his micro. If he canted his head down and to the side, he could manage to focus on the screen for almost twenty minutes. Of course, there would be a price afterward. That's what the bucket was for.

Unlocking the search history, Jem glanced at his specialized feed. Culled from research journals, university symposia, medical news, and a smattering of fringe sites, anything that related to neurals and implant technology got pushed out to him. He scanned the headlines, but there wasn't anything new or noteworthy. Just the same answers. Twelve was too young. His head trauma made him a risky candidate. Of course the newest article about the Common-wealth turning implantees into mindless soldiers amused him. Somehow, he couldn't see Barre as the perfect and orderly recruit. He pushed that one to the text-to-speech engine and listened to the paranoid rant for a few minutes. The artificial voice couldn't really do it justice.

Even if there were a shred of reality to it, he'd still take the risk for the chance at a neural and being able to go back to his life.

Jem could feel it when the nystagmus kicked up again. And he had hardly even tried to focus. The screen blurred and danced in front of him. He set the micro down and shut his eyes. Too late. The room began to spin. Groaning, he leaned over the edge of the bed only to dry heave into the bucket. More of the space-sickness tablets would have been nice about now.

He took deep, slow breaths trying to get his revved-up nervous system to settle down. His micro buzzed. Opening his eyes would be a big mistake. Accessing voice commands, he waited for the read out.

The neutral-gendered, slightly flat voice filled the room.

"To Jeremy Durbin. From Dr. Land, IBNI. Regarding clinical research protocol, neural implant study."

His heart pounded. The saliva that had been flooding his mouth dried away. They got his message and they answered him. The Underworld answered him.

"Message follows.

"Thank you for your interest. We are not enrolling subjects at this time. If you wish to be removed from our mailing list, please do nothing and we will eliminate your information from our database. If you wish to receive continued updates as our research needs change, please reply to the appropriate department. Our directory is attached.

"You may unsubscribe at any time in the future. If this message has reached you in error, please accept our apologies.

"This communication and all such communications from

the Integrative BioNeural Institute complies with Common-
wealth privacy and disclosure directive seven three eight
eight two slash gamma.

"Message ends."

Silence filled the room. That was it? Jem risked opening
his eyes to look at his micro. The message text scrolled
across the screen. Not enrolling subjects. Shit. Did that mean
they had rejected him? Please do nothing? He threw a pillow
across the room. Nothing is what he'd been doing. And it
didn't help.

He scanned the message again. What was he missing?
There was no Dr. Land or neural implant study. The IBNI
was a shell corporation he had discovered in his research
into the black market. So why send a message asking for a
reply? There had to be something buried in the message or in
the attachment. Something they thought he could decode.
And if he couldn't decode it, and didn't reply, his request
would go no further.

His stomach heaved again and he leaned back against the
headboard waiting for the world to settle. He'd have to do
this in small bites. The irony wasn't lost on him: if he had a
neural, he could examine the file and any code it contained
without risking nausea and the blinding headache that would
come with it. But if he had a neural, he wouldn't need to be
proving himself to The Underworld.

Fixing his head position at the null point, he felt the
world stabilize back to his new, slightly queasy baseline. It
wasn't perfect and it wasn't pretty, but it was the best he had.

*

Micah was pacing his empty quarters when the door chimed. "Daedalus, identify."

The AI announced, "Durbin, Bernard."

His shoulders dropped. "Come in," he called.

Barre stood at the threshold, shifting his weight back and forth. "Hey. Heard about your dad."

"Yeah." Micah shrugged and waved him in.

"You okay?"

He didn't know how to answer that. "My feet are better," he said, working to keep his gait smooth as he walked over to the sofa. There was still a limit to how long he could stand without the fluid building up at the graft sites. It would have been a lot worse but for Barre's quick thinking and medical knowledge back on Halcyone. Micah let his body sink into the cushioning and propped his feet up on the coffee table, covering the water rings.

Barre sat at the other end and drummed his hands on his knees. "When do you leave?"

"There's a jump shuttle tomorrow. I figured I'd get there early and settle in."

"Yeah."

"I have to set up a whole new lab."

Barre grinned widely. "You're crazy, you know that? It's one thing to be messing with bittergreen in a place like Daedalus, but in the Hub? If the cartels don't kill you, the Commonwealth will."

"What can I say, I like a challenge." And even though he

and Barre had dismantled his lab and flushed all his plants out the airlock, he wouldn't be starting from scratch. He had his data and he knew at least a dozen ways that didn't work. With the resources he could tap at Uni, he should be able to solve the seed sterility problem. And then he'd have to worry about the cartels. Well, they would have to worry about him. "Besides," Micah said, "there's something to be said about hiding in plain sight."

"There's hiding, and there's broadcasting your story on all ansible frequencies. Have you listened to the news bands lately? It's all Rotherwood, all the time."

"Yeah. Too bad he's not running for anything this term."

Barre winced. "Ouch."

"Don't worry. I'm not a Rotherwood anymore. I had my name officially changed to my mom's family name. Micah Rotherwood's breadcrumb trail ends at Daedalus Station." Michael Chase would start a botany degree in his place. It was fitting to use her name; having him study at Uni was what his mother had wanted more than anything. And he would use her name and his position to break the monopoly on bittergreen and punish the cartels in her memory.

"Keep in touch, okay? If we ever get Halcyone working again, the Hub's only a few jump-days away," Barre said.

Micah leaned over and held out his hand. Barre shook it, folding Micah's in both of his larger ones. "Thank you. For everything. For Jem." The big musician pulled away.

"Right back at you," Micah said, his voice rough. It wasn't easy making friends, given who his father was. First because the senator insisted Micah only have the right friends— friends whose families had influence and money. Then later, because of the price on his father's head. Micah couldn't risk letting anyone get too close. "If I had to almost get killed by a deranged AI and tortured by my father's co-conspirator, I'm glad it was with you."

"Next time, can we skip the part where you nearly burn off your own feet rescuing us?"

He shrugged. The memories were still strong enough to make him queasy, the smell of burnt flesh even clearer than the pain. Ro's father was on the very short list of people he owed some significant payback. "How is Ro, anyway? Haven't seen her since you guys limped back here."

Barre twisted his lips into a wry smile. "Ro is Ro. If I were Nomi, I'd have tossed her out of the air lock by now."

"And Jem?" Micah felt bad. He'd meant to stop by to tell him he was leaving. Of the two of them, Micah's injuries were more visible, but less disabling.

Barre shook his head.

"Still throwing up?"

"You knew? You knew and you didn't say anything?"

"Whoa." Micah held up his hands. "He's your brother. I figured he'd have told you."

Barre turned away. "His vision and his balance are pretty messed up. I don't think he's going to get better."

"Oh, man, that burns. Nothing your folks can do?"

"He thinks a neural will help."

They were still pretty rare. And still risky enough that Micah hadn't wanted to be a beta tester. He had to admit, Barre's had come in pretty handy communicating with Halcyone.

"Hell, I'd give him mine if I could." Barre gave him a half

smile. "Sorry, man, you've got enough to blast through. Be safe. Message me when you get settled."

Micah struggled to his feet, wincing as the skin grafts stretched with the weight. He stepped closer to Barre and stuck out his hand again. Instead of shaking it, Barre embraced him. Micah stiffened briefly before pounding Barre's back.

"If there's anything you need, just ask," Micah said.

Barre stepped away. "Just don't get yourself killed, okay?"

"Deal."

After Barre left, Micah drifted through his empty quarters, but there was nothing left to do except wait. His micro pinged, the sound echoing strangely in the metallic space. He glanced down, wondering if Ro was finally going to talk to him. His father's smiling face filled the small screen. Micah blinked, the room wavering around him.

"What the hell will it take for you to leave me alone?"

Micah unlocked the micro, his hands shaking. All he wanted to do was delete the message unread, but his father had known he wouldn't do that. For his mother's sake, he would suffer through whatever rambling justification his father had prepared for him in the eventual case of his death. It was pure Senator Rotherwood. All theater and full of manufactured drama.

He fell into the sofa and played the message. It would be the only way he'd be able to put this whole business behind him.

"Hello Micah."

"Well, hello, Father. How's hell treating you?"

"If you're seeing this, it means I've died. I'm sorry, son."

Sorry that he was dead, most likely. Micah snorted. The only time his father called him 'son' was for interviews or when he needed something. The man was space dust. What could he possibly need from Micah now?

"I've done some unwise things in my life." He paused to look into the recorder, all Rotherwood sincerity. Micah wanted to throw up. *"But the past is in the past. I hope that you can find it in your heart to forgive me. It's what your mother would have wanted."*

Micah slammed the heel of his hand on the screen and his father paused just as he'd taken a breath. He looked like a gaping fish. "Way to go with the guilt play, Dad. Damn you're good." There was nothing to do but get it over with. It didn't matter. In another day, Micah Rotherwood would effectively disappear, and his connection to his father would fade along with the memory of their shared name. He triggered the playback once more.

"I hope you know I loved you. Even if I wasn't very good at showing it."

"That's not fair. Damn it, that's not fair!" he shouted at his father's image. The man paused as if somewhere beyond the grave he was listening. Micah clenched his teeth as his father leaned forward out of the screen, returning with a full glass of scotch, ice cubes tinkling.

"I can't change the past. But I can help your future."

What had he done? What the hell had he done? Micah's hands shook and he pressed them on his legs.

"Attached to this message is the access code to a private investment account. It's in your name. Use the money as you see fit. And don't blame yourself. You were just a kid."

"Son of a bitch!" Micah nearly flew from the sofa, his father's words echoing in his mind. *Don't blame yourself. Don't blame yourself.* His micro clattered to the ground, his father's telegenic face frozen in a well-practiced expression of humble sincerity. "It was your fucking fault. You left me to deal with Mom's pain. You used us. The poor, brave senator, soldiering on while his noble wife was dying. You used us!" Tears blurred his vision. Micah stumbled around the room wishing he hadn't dumped all of his father's scotch. The burn would have been more than welcome.

Chapter 6

Ro ran down the list of priority issues, marveling that Daedalus was actually still in one piece. There was more broken here than she could get to in a month of work shifts. The station was old, its AI was old, and it orbited the dead end of one of the least-traveled jump paths in the sector. No wonder the Commonwealth wasn't in any hurry to replace their AWOL engineer. Ro sighed. No wonder they had given her father a contract to begin with.

She was better with programming than with pure hardtech, but so many of the work orders were for basic repairs. Boring but essential. An intermittent cutting out of the ansible grid display was marked a priority. Ro glanced at the time. Nomi would still be asleep. Part of her wanted to get it over with now, so she wouldn't have to deal with how thin her own excuses were going to sound, but the job could take down the ansible relay for some time. Better to do that on third shift. And third shift meant apologizing to Nomi.

Between now and then, Ro needed to do inventory. She

made her way to the narrow passage between the inner and outer command rings where spare equipment was stored. She wasn't sure her father ever used the place much, but it would be a good idea to separate station work from her own work on Halcyone.

Her credentials opened the access door—not much more than a narrow panel in the corridor that linked sick bay with hydroponics—and she slipped inside. The service corridors were the remnants of the original scaffolding used to lay out the station. Everywhere else, the metal bracing had been skinned with stainless steel walls. The sounds of the station fell away and Ro could believe she was trapped inside the skeleton of some mechanical beast, with the whoosh of the air moving through the scrubbers its breathing.

Remnants of broken machinery, decommissioned bots and drones, tangles of wiring and random piles of spare parts lay in unlabeled boxes along the structural lattice of service corridor 7. Some of the more specialized work drones were stored here, as well. They would come in handy if she had to get into Halcyone's wiring or superstructure. She hoped Mendez had meant what she said about Ro accessing station resources.

Now that she had the full station schematic on her micro, Ro realized that these corridors snaked their way all through the station, and that it was possible to get from any point on Daedalus to any other point without ever entering the station proper. That was how her father had been able to disappear so effectively during their time here. She'd have to remember that. Ro smiled to herself. No, she didn't need to hide anymore. She had a position here and she had

Halcyone. And even if the ship couldn't jump, it was hers.

She collected what she needed and organized it on the utility cart. At least she could knock down the list by a few jobs, then get back to Halcyone for a bit before she had to face Nomi again.

There was a quick repair she could finish in the command ring hydroponics bay, so Ro used the service corridor network to pop out behind the main water manifold. She pulled out the sensor and double-checked the pressure readings before adjusting the flow through the reducers. It was something the hydroponics tech should have been able to do, but it landed on her work schedule. She didn't really mind. There was something satisfying about a problem that she could solve as opposed to the puzzle of Halcyone and the jump drive.

Leaving the tools in the crawlspace, Ro squeezed through the access hatch into a larger and wilder version of the botany lab Micah had set up on Halcyone. It had the same modulated sunlight, the same artificial rain and controlled humidity, the same enriched soils. The main difference was no bittergreen grew here.

And instead of a practical lab environment, hydroponics doubled as a tiny park at the heart of each of the station's two interlocking rings, providing fresh oxygen, source material for the synthproteins that made up a good portion of their diet, and rare open space. It made a welcome change after hunkering down in the service corridors, and being there reminded Ro a little of the openness of comms during third shift with Nomi.

"Ro?"

She jerked around and nearly bumped into the tall, slender comms officer. Nomi was off duty, dressed in a bright green kimono layered over slim black leggings. "What are you doing here?" Ro asked, hearing the ghost of her father's accusations in her voice.

Nomi's smile vanished. Crap. Ro had screwed up already.

"I walk here nearly every day," she said. "It reminds me of home."

Ro heard the unspoken rebuke. If she'd paid attention, she would have known that. "I'm sorry—"

Nomi shook her head sharply, her black hair swinging around her head. "I know. It doesn't change anything."

Heat flooded Ro's face and she turned away. Anything she could say felt like a ragged excuse, so she stayed silent. But that seemed wrong, too. "I have to check the ambient humidity. Do you want to walk with me?" It sounded lame and stupid, but it was the only thing she could think of that might keep Nomi from leaving.

It would have been easy for someone else to miss the slight narrowing in Nomi's brown eyes, but Ro had a lifetime of experience gathering clues from the smallest changes in her father's expression. It had been a matter of survival then, and it felt like a matter of survival now. She waited as Nomi stared, aware of time moving away, of the work orders scrolling through her micro, of the broken ship that she had to fix.

"Fine," Nomi said.

Ro exhaled. She would count even that short reply as a little victory. They walked side by side in silence. Every few meters, as Ro stopped to measure the humidity in the air,

Nomi bent over to examine a plant or a flower. They all seemed the same to Ro; just greenery, useful and beneficial. Micah's interest was something she understood, but Nomi saw something beyond the utilitarian.

They had circled around to where they had started. Ro slipped the monitor into her pocket. "Are you on shift tonight?"

Nomi frowned, lines creasing her forehead. "Don't. Just don't. It's better when you don't make promises."

The pulse pounded in her ears and Ro froze, anger trying to push its way out of her in hurtful words. She swallowed them as she had done so many times in the past, but this wasn't her father. She wasn't her father, either. "I have a repair to do in comms. It needs to be done third shift." That was the logical, safe thing to say.

Ro paused. Silence fell between them. Nomi nodded and turned to leave. Something inside Ro cracked, fault lines spidering across her as if she were a viewport struck by an asteroid. Nomi paused, but didn't turn around.

"It's a boring job," Ro said, her voice breaking. "Is it okay ... I'd really like the company. If you don't mind."

"You know where I'll be."

"I know," Ro said softly, as Nomi walked away. She ducked back into the service corridor and packed up her tools, replaying the terse conversation over and over, wondering how she could have said things differently. Her micro buzzed. A message from Jem scrolled across her screen.

<u>I need your help. There's no one else I can ask. Please.</u>

"Damn it, Jem," Ro said. Her voice echoed in the

enclosed space. "Fine." She messaged back. <u>Meet me on Halcyone.</u>

*

Jem hadn't set foot on Halcyone since Hephaestus's medic had taken him off the ship in a stretcher. He wasn't sure what he expected, but the sense of falling back in time wasn't it. The ship was silent and it could have been the first time he'd sneaked aboard, looking for Ro, and finding the ruin of the bridge instead.

If he had known then how it was going to turn out, he might not have tried to follow her that day. But then Barre would have been on his way to mandatory rehab and getting the music wiped from him along with his craving for bittergreen, courtesy of their parents. Jem sighed and retraced his footsteps, this time walking close to the shining walls of the corridor. With his eyes squinted, and his head held motionless, he slid his hand along the grab rails. There was no reverse in a wormhole.

The bridge was silent, the soft illumination soothing his double vision. He set his micro down on the blast-burned console, waiting for Ro to show up. "Halcyone, locate Durbin, Bernard." The AI didn't answer. "Blast it, Barre," he muttered. "Fine. It's your ship. I get it." He triggered his micro. "Daedalus, locate Durbin, Bernard."

"Command nexus."

Good. He didn't want his brother to see him here, asking for help. It was bad enough Barre knew how bad it had become. Jem hoped he was getting the motion-sickness meds.

He glanced up at the cracked viewscreen, dark now that Halcyone was grounded, and looked away. It reminded him too much of his damaged brain.

The door slid open. Jem kept his head still and waited until Ro came to him.

"You doing okay?" she asked.

Her concern surprised him. "No."

Ro's eyes widened slightly. He guessed he'd surprised her, too.

"I have to decrypt something and I can't focus on the display long enough to do it."

"What do you want me to do?"

Jem exhaled in a rush. He didn't realize how worried he'd been that she'd refuse to help. "Be my eyes. Do what I tell you." He wasn't sure she could do that without asking questions Jem wasn't going to answer, but there was no one else he could go to.

"Show me." She pulled out her micro and slid it toward his.

Their micros were still paired from their time on Halcyone together. It was the slower way, but Jem used voice commands to navigate to the message from The Underworld and pushed it and the attached file over to Ro's machine. "I spent an hour fighting with it and all it got me was a brutal headache. I'm sure it's a program, but I can't find the executable anywhere." It was like a solid sphere, and everything he hit it with slid away.

"Do you mind if I ...?" Ro gestured at Jem's micro.

"Go for it."

She moved her arms in a blur that he couldn't have tracked even if he hadn't had double vision most of the time. A cone of light formed over both micros. The small, slippery message file hovered in the air in that space, spinning slowly.

"Can you stop that?" Jem asked. He closed his eyes on the irritating motion.

"Sure. Sure. Sorry."

The sphere halted, hanging there like a perfect circle of shining mercury.

"It looks like a basic database. Are you sure there's a program inside?"

"Just because I can't focus doesn't mean I suddenly turned stupid."

"I know ... I didn't ..." Ro turned back to the holographic display but not before Jem saw the red flush on her cheeks.

He hated himself for the surge of satisfaction that followed.

"What is this, anyway?" Ro asked.

"It's personal." He wasn't sure how he was going to get her to help him crack it without her finding out what he was up to, but when you were out of air, you took a hose from the closest spacesuit.

She glanced at him with eyes narrowed, but then shrugged. "I guess I deserved that."

They all had secrets, Ro more than most. "I already ran through the standard decryption algorithms." It had been a waste of time and Jem knew it, even as he used up precious moments of concentration. But there was value in being systematic. Even when things didn't work, they often yielded useful information. "You have things in your toolbox that I don't." Jem hated admitting that, but it was the truth. She was better and this was too important to let his ego get in the way.

"Who's Dr. Land? Someone your folks drag you to?" Ro rummaged through her customized hacking kit.

"Not exactly."

She fidgeted and the display wavered. "Look, I'm sorry I didn't come to see you. I got caught up fixing Halcyone. Besides, I didn't know." Her arms relaxed down to her sides. The hologram collapsed into a blinking dot hovering at eye level. "I thought … It doesn't matter. I'm sorry. If this is something that can help you, I'll do what I can."

Jem turned away, his face hot. They trusted him—Nomi, Ro, and Barre—and he couldn't tell them what he was doing.

"What makes you think there's a program hidden inside?"

"I can't tell you that. But there is and I need to crack it."

Ro held his gaze for several seconds before nodding. Her arms created a blur of light as she opened the display, the file hovering above Jem's micro, tiny colorful boxes representing her customized programs twinkling over hers. Jem closed his eyes before the display triggered a fresh headache and a new round of nausea.

He listened to her hum tunelessly as she worked and could imagine her tossing box after box at the message. If the stakes weren't so high, he would have enjoyed seeing her struggle.

"You're right. It's not any of the standard encryptions or even some of the experimental ones. Hell, my toolkit doesn't even recognize the thing as having any. Even the checksums are valid."

"It has to be there, Ro. It just has to."

"I don't know, Jem. It just looks like a plain directory file attached to an ordinary, routine ansible message."

Jem looked at the floor, where he had spent so much of his time on Halcyone, and felt tears burning his eyes. "That doesn't make any sense." Why would The Underworld reply to him unless their message had something buried in it? The answer was there, circling him in an erratic orbit he couldn't match. He shook with the need to hit something. A wave of dizziness nearly took him to the ground and he slammed his arm into the wall for support. The pain cleared away his frustration. "Wait."

For an instant, Jem felt the fog of his head injury lift as he made the connection. An ansible message. Forty years ago, the rebels had found a way to hide programs in ansible messages. It's what had downed Halcyone along with a host of other AIs during the war. "What if it's not in the file attachment at all? What if it's something in the ansible message itself?" The file could just be a red herring. Anyone intercepting the transmission would be wasting their time trying to access it.

"Like a virus? Daedalus would have scanned for that."

"A really old virus. Like the one that killed Halcyone."

"Modern AIs aren't susceptible to that anymore." Ro frowned at Jem, then her eyes went wide. "Shit!" She collapsed the holographic interface and separated their micros.

"No, it's okay. It's not like the AI killer."

"How the hell do you know that?"

There was so much Jem wanted to tell her: Because there would be no point in sending a malicious virus rendered obsolete decades ago. Because it was a puzzle and a test, not a threat. It had to be. He forced his wandering eyes to focus on her. "I just do. You've got to believe me. I swear, I wouldn't do anything to put Halcyone at risk."

She pursed her lips, but didn't look away.

"Do you still have the sandbox with the AI source code?"

"Are you sure about this?"

Jem nodded, hoping he was right about Halcyone not being in any danger.

Ro paused, searching his face. He could feel his eyes starting to stutter back and forth.

"Okay. Give me a nano to set it up."

Out of the corner of his eye, Jem watched the holographic display shimmer and bleed a rainbow of colors as Ro ran Dauber and May's original AI source code in a protected space. "It's not a full implementation. It can't be. Not enough resources in the sandbox."

"I know. It'll be okay. It'll work." It had to work. It had to. It was the only thing Jem had to hold on to; everything else in his world just kept spinning. He forced himself to watch as Ro pulled the ansible message into the virtual AI.

Nothing happened. The display hung at Ro's eye level, softly pulsing in its ready-for-input mode. Jem held his breath, not even caring as his eyes began to drift back and forth more quickly.

The numbers at the base of the display kept changing as seconds bled into minutes and still nothing happened. "Shit." His voice cracked. "Shit. Shit. Shit." He had been so sure.

"Jem?"

He slid down the wall until he collapsed on the floor, dropping his head in his hands. "Forget it. Just go. Please. Leave me alone." The bridge spun around him and he swallowed the saliva that pooled in his mouth, desperate to not vomit here, where Ro would see.

He felt her hand, warm and light, rest on his shoulder. "Where would I go? This is my ship."

"I think I'm going to be sick."

"We'll make your brother clean it up."

They sat in silence for a few minutes and the nausea passed. Jem risked opening his eyes. Ro was sitting beside him, her knees drawn up, her head leaning against the bulkhead wall.

"I'm sorry."

"I know it's in there. It has to be." Jem hated the pleading sound of his own voice.

"Then I'll keep looking."

An insistent beeping blared through the bridge. Jem jerked his head up, triggering another surge of dizziness. He staggered to his feet, staring open-mouthed at Ro's virtual machine. The text of the ansible message scrolled across the virtual space, and as he watched, the letters wavered, rotating and blinking, each at a different rate.

"What the hell?" Ro said. "That's enough to make me hurl."

"Welcome to my world," Jem said, softly. He couldn't look away, no matter how his stomach churned. The screen brightened, washing out the warping letters, forcing him to close his eyes. Afterimages danced behind his lids. The room darkened. Jem opened his eyes as the display redrew itself. The words were gone, replaced by tiny black puzzle pieces suspended on a white background.

"Whoa," Ro said.

As they watched, the black shapes fell in a rhythmic rain, and as they hit the bottom of the display, they melded together, forming a small box, with tiny white script letters on its side spelling out 'Read Me.'

Chapter 7

Ro stared at the bridge door long after Jem had staggered out clutching his micro to his chest. Whatever that message contained, it was important to him. As important as Halcyone was to her. Ro could still feel the ghost pressure of Jem's arms where he'd hugged her. She smiled. At least she had done something right for someone for a change.

Her micro still projected its holographic display, a blank shimmering canvas hovering in front of the ship's damaged viewscreen. Even if her father's assets hadn't been confiscated, there wouldn't have been enough credit to replace it. Besides, what use was an intact viewer if the ship never jumped? Ro sighed and played the recorded command fanfare Barre had given her. Halcyone trilled in return.

"Halcyone, run diagnostics. Propulsion: jump drive. Verbal and visual display."

A gentle beeping filled the bridge. Barre would probably know what note it was. Ro just wished it would stop. It was the insistent blare of an alarm she could neither silence nor fix.

Halcyone's calm voice gave Ro the same bad news she'd been getting for weeks. "Jump drive off-line. Wormhole mapping functions off-line."

"I know. But why?"

Halcyone didn't answer. Ro studied the detailed output scrolling through the display. As far as she could tell, all the individual components of the drive tested fine. They just wouldn't work together. And nothing would synchronize with the wormhole maps. It was as if the computer didn't even recognize them. Which made no sense. Halcyone's core mapping functions worked—the AI could plot interstitial courses just fine. What was different about the jump drive?

There had to be something she was missing. Ro stuck her arm in the middle of the display and crumpled up the virtual report in her fist. Throwing it away wasn't as satisfying as destroying permapaper, but it did leave her with a blank screen again—which was its own problem. Ro sighed and paced the bridge. What was she missing?

The alarm she set on her micro buzzed. Ro glanced up, blinking at the time in the center of the display. It was an hour from the end of second shift. An hour before she had to face Nomi again. An hour to clean herself up and figure out how she was going to make amends to her friend. If she had been more like her father, she would just fix the problem in comms and be done with it.

She wasn't her father. Mendez had told her that. So had Nomi. Ro had to believe it. Besides, Alain Maldonado was long gone. Ro didn't need to stare at his closed workshop door anymore, wondering when and if he was going to emerge and in what mood.

"Oh," she whispered, an image of his desk clear in her mind with the permapaper schematics of Halcyone spread across it. She had taken images with her micro and stitched them together in a 3-d rendering. "Oh." A smile spread across her face. Raising her arms, she thought of Barre. Ro was no musician, but this was her symphony. And she was the conductor.

A second window opened beside the first. She called up her model in one and displayed the actual jump drive schematics from Halcyone's internal sensors in the other. Her hands became part of the light patterns of the display as she rotated and reoriented the ship's original plans to center on engineering. Then she peeled back layers and zoomed in on the jump system, orienting both displays to the same magnification and perspective.

Standing back, she looked at her two windows. It wasn't perfect. Her construct had been created with images, not original data, but she thought she could compensate. Ro crossed her arms, considering what she had in her toolbox for the actual analysis.

Her micro buzzed again. Forty-five minutes of her hour were gone. She glanced down at her rumpled jumpsuit. So much for cleaning up. Fifteen minutes. There was no way Ro could finish a compare and contrast routine in fifteen minutes. Hell, it could take all shift or longer.

Her promise to Nomi warred with her need to fix the jump drive. Even without analyzing the schematics, she knew this was where she'd find the answer. She opened a third window and rummaged through her inventory of tiny hacks, each a complete and robust program that could be combined with any of the others to create custom tools. But most of what she'd created was meant for raw code, not analysis of images.

She glanced up at the time stamp. Nomi's shift would start in five minutes. Ro swore and swept her hand through the virtual stack of subroutines, scattering them across the display before storing all the windows back to her micro. There had to be some way to figure this out. For now, at least, the problem in comms was something she could fix.

Her clothes were a mess, but Ro didn't want to risk taking the time to change. Besides, there was the very real chance that once she closeted herself back in her quarters, she'd find some reason to push off the job in comms for another day. She glanced down at herself one more time before organizing her work trundle and leaving Halcyone's bridge for the station proper and Nomi.

This was who she was, rumpled, stained jumpsuit and all.

Ro walked through the mostly silent station. Dim lights brightened as she triggered their sensors, and returned to low power once she'd passed. This was third shift on a sparsely populated station, far from the midst of anything important. It suited her mood. A functioning jump drive would have suited it better.

At the entrance to comms, Ro hesitated. The old trundle's sensors were slow to react and the little drone bumped into her. Like just about everything else on this station, it mostly worked. Comms was waiting. Ro sighed. Nomi was waiting.

It was probably just a switch or a relay that needed to be swapped out. Not fatal. Not complicated. Just annoying and time-consuming. If her father had been doing his job, he would have checked the system's integrity as part of his routine and this wouldn't have happened.

The door opened and Ro stumbled away from comms, her heart racing.

"Were you going to wait there all shift?" Nomi asked, her face shadowed, her soft voice floating in the darkness of an artificial night sky.

Ro's cheeks got hot. She stepped over the threshold, hoping the trundle would follow without any additional prompting. "Hey Nomi."

The doors whooshed shut behind her. Nomi didn't say anything and Ro blinked, still unable to see past the dim red lighting that shone down from the underside of the consoles. "There's a problem with the display?"

There was just the slightest pause before Nomi spoke, the hint of a sigh never fully voiced. "I don't usually see it on third shift. It seems to be an issue with screen redraw during heavy ansible use."

Ro bent down to rummage through the compartments on the trundle. She needed to simulate full load conditions and then see what happened. No use taking the system apart to replace components if it was a programming hiccup.

"Or as heavy as this place ever sees."

There was a bitterness to Nomi's voice that Ro had never heard before. She took a few steps closer to Nomi's terminal and fidgeted with the tester in her hand. Nomi's face was still shadowed. "What's wrong?"

"The screen cuts out and then we need to reboot the whole system to get the ansibles to talk to the main—"

"Not with comms." Ro stood sweating in the perfectly climate controlled room, her fingers curled around her tools in a death grip.

"It doesn't have anything to do with your ship or the station, so why would you care?"

That wasn't fair. She was here, wasn't she? A familiar pressure squeezed her throat closed. Heat spread through Ro's chest. She'd walked away from her own work to be with Nomi. That had to count for something. A lifetime of swallowing anger and resentment kept her silent, now. She took a step away, glancing at the door and then back to where Nomi sat, her slender form a dark blot beside her console.

The artificial stars shimmered against the display. Every few seconds, a node would brighten as it identified itself to the network before fading back to standby. No real traffic was being passed in the silence. She and Nomi were like two of those ansible nodes, pinging one another in the darkness and getting no response.

Walking away would be the safest choice. But she knew where that jump landed her. She could just fix the display and leave. That might strand her in an even worse place. "Because ... Because you're my friend," Ro whispered, not sure Nomi would even hear her. Not sure she wanted her to.

Seconds passed and Nomi didn't move. She didn't answer.

Ro looked down at the tester and the other tools in her hands. She fixed things. "I'm going to need access to your console," she finally said, if only to break the tension in the room.

Nomi stood and stepped away from her station. Ro took a shaky breath, moving closer. Under the red glow of the night-vision lights, Nomi's eyes looked haunted, her face sallow. They were close enough to touch. Close enough that Ro caught the light floral scent of Nomi's soap. It reminded her of one of the hanging plants in hydroponics, and she had the urge to ask what the flower's name was.

"My grandfather ..." Nomi's voice broke. Ro held her breath. "My grandfather died. More than a week ago."

Ro didn't know what to say. There was no way for her to even find out if she had a grandfather. Or any grandparent. The only relative Ro knew of for sure was her father, and it would be better for all concerned if he was dead. She set down her tools on Nomi's workstation before twisting her fingers together in the strained silence.

"The message got lost. Routed to the wrong node address. Funny, right?" Nomi's laugh was a high-pitched, strangled sound. "I missed the memorial service. I didn't get a chance to say goodbye."

"I'm sorry."

"It doesn't matter. Even if I'd gotten my parents' message sooner, there's no jump path in the Commonwealth that could've gotten me there in time."

"Is there anything I can do?" The unfamiliar words came tumbling out. Ro shook as she said them, but they couldn't be unsaid.

Nomi turned away. Her voice was small and hoarse with unshed tears. "Stay here. I don't ... I don't want to be by myself, tonight."

Ro had been awake nearly a full cycle. Her eyes burned

and her spine ached. But she'd pushed off sleep before. It was just one more shift. She could rest later, once Nomi was all right. "I'll stay."

"Thank you." Nomi reached out and gently squeezed Ro's fingers. Ro rubbed her calloused thumb across the soft skin of Nomi's hand.

"Do you need to send a reply?" Ro asked. "I have to take comms off line for a little while."

"No, I'm good."

Ro slipped her hand free and turned to Nomi's console, still feeling the warmth and comfort of that light touch. She paired her micro with the main system, keying in the override that would send out a signal to reroute all ansible traffic before shutting down Daedalus's comms.

The red lights pulsed. "Warning: comms off-line."

"Yeah, I got that," Ro said, and forced the system into debug mode.

"Is there something I can do?" The near-darkness seemed to swallow Nomi's small voice.

Ro's first instinct was to shake her head. Trying to explain to someone else what she needed would take more time than running the diagnostic on her own. But the problem in comms was not the only reason Ro was there. She stilled her hands and the heads-up display paused, floating between them. "Actually, yes." With a flick of her fingers, Ro opened another window linked to the first that mimicked the standard comms terminal interface. She pushed over the test file. "When I tell you, run that. It'll simulate maximum node traffic. All good?"

"Five by five," Nomi said, a brief smile lighting her somber face.

It was an archaic expression from the days of analog radio and had absolutely no relevance to ansible transmissions, but it made Ro happy to hear Nomi say it.

Ro paired the tester to the program. It would assess both the software that ran comms as well as the signal integrity of the transmitter. "Okay, let her run."

The file simulated an eight-hour shift of heavy ansible traffic within an eight-minute span. Test messages were received so quickly, the display was nearly one continuous flare of brightness that washed out the red night-vision lighting. Despite that, the minutes seemed to crawl by. Ro watched her micro analyzing the data, not trying to read or interpret any of the thousands of lines written across the virtual screen, but letting the patterns flow through her. So far, nothing looked particularly wrong.

"What was he like?" Ro asked.

"My grandfather?"

Ro nodded.

"Sofu was a quiet man. With a big laugh. He always had treats hidden in his coat pockets. Nothing like the candy we could buy in the colony. I have no idea where he got them." Tears glittered in Nomi's eyes. "Little sweet cakes in the shape of a fish, hard candies with little flower designs inside them. We pretended to like them, but as soon as Sofu would turn around, we'd spit them out."

"Did he ever figure it out?" If she had done something like that, her father would have hit her. But then again, she couldn't imagine her father ever giving her much of anything, especially not candy.

"Maybe. Probably. At one point, he stopped bringing

any." Her lower lip trembled. "The last time I saw him was at my graduation. He gave me a whole box full of them."

As her micro beeped twice at the end of the simulation, Ro took the opportunity to look away from Nomi and the uncomfortable range of emotions in her expression. "Well, it's nothing internal to comms programming or the transmitter. But I figured as much."

"I wish you could have met him."

"It's probably just a bad component." Ro kept her gaze focused on her micro. "I have to access the service tunnels to get at it."

Nomi stepped closer and lightly squeezed Ro's hand. "Thank you."

"For what?" She hadn't repaired the problem in comms, and there wasn't anything she could do for Nomi.

"You're here."

Ro took a shaky breath, not wanting to move or break the contact between them. Nomi slipped her hand away and walked back to her console.

"Go fix it. I'll be okay." She stared up into the stilled display.

"You sure?"

Nomi nodded.

Turning back to the trundle, Ro filled the pockets of her coverall with the tools she figured she'd need. They had mass and heft and she knew just how and where to apply them to take care of the problem in comms. She glanced back at Nomi. Things were better. At least a little bit. Maybe she wasn't so useless with people after all.

Chapter 8

IT HAD BEEN almost too simple to get Jem the space-sickness meds he needed. Daedalus had an automated system for purchases and Barre didn't have to explain or justify his request. All he did was choose what he wanted from central supply's inventory and push the order to the AI. A trundle delivered the small package to Halcyone. The perks of citizenship. And his parents never needed to be involved.

Barre tucked the meds in a pocket and only wished he could do more for his brother. He hesitated at the entrance to the commissary. It was late enough that his parents should have eaten and gone, but if they had somehow lingered, this could be a very unpleasant interaction.

The first time Barre had come for dinner here after his emancipation, his mother had stared past him and led Jem to a table across the room. That was the last time he'd tried to meet Jem for meals, choosing to eat on Halcyone or slipping into the commissary either before or after shift change in medical.

Tonight, Jem sat alone at a cleared table staring down at his micro.

"Hey." Barre said.

Jem jerked his head up and then looked away again, wincing against the brightness. "Don't worry. They were already here and gone," he said.

Barre hated that Jem kept trying to protect him. "You have dinner yet?" he asked.

"Kind of."

"Can I get you anything else?" Jem had always been small for his age, but he seemed so much thinner and more fragile since the injury. When Jem shook his head, Barre pulled over an empty chair, turned it around, and straddled it. "Well, I have a present for you."

They were alone in the far corner of the commissary. Barre's back was to the room. Even the ubiquitous presence of Daedalus's oculars wasn't trained on them. Leaning forward, he handed Jem a small tube of space-sickness pills in their familiar sealed packets. Jem curled his shaking fingers around it. Barre nearly choked on the irony: he was smuggling his little brother drugs.

It wasn't bittergreen, and the anti-nausea pills weren't illegal. But still.

"Will that help?"

"A little." Jem's voice sounded so small and so lost.

"Micah's leaving on the morning transport."

"I know."

"He asked about you."

Jem didn't answer; he simply stared down at the pills in his hand.

Maybe getting him connected again with the work he loved would help. Even a little. Anything to change the defeated look in Jem's eyes and the slump of his shoulders. "Look. Do you think with the meds on board, you'd be able to help us with something on Halcyone? Ro's driving me crazy. She can't—"

"No."

Jem looked away, but not before Barre saw the hunger and resignation in his gaze. It was how Barre had felt when he was Jem's age, after he understood their mother would never understand his passion for his music, could never give him what he needed.

"I'm sorry. I can't. I just can't," Jem said.

Barre closed his hand around a polymer cup. Fractures spread across its surface before it splintered. "I'd give mine to you if I could," he said, quietly, though his voice shook with anger. "I'd rip the damned thing right out of my head."

"I know." Jem smiled, but it looked more like a grimace. "I'm sorry," he repeated. "Ro will get it. She's good. She's the best. And she has you."

He set the broken cup on the table. "Once we have jump capability, I can take you anywhere. There's got to be someone who can help you."

Jem pressed his fist to his mouth and stifled back a sob. "Mom and Dad have already done everything they could."

"Damn it, there has to be another way."

"Go help Ro."

"It'd be easier with you," Barre said.

"I know. I know. She can be a pain in the ass. And she'll try to push you away. But you know what? You guys make a good team. Even if she won't admit it."

Barre leaned forward and squeezed Jem's shoulder. It should be him on Halcyone, working on the AI with Ro. "Are you sure there isn't something else I can do?"

Jem shook the tube of pills in his hand. "These will be a big help. Really."

"I'll check in with you tomorrow, okay?"

"Okay."

Barre stared down at the table for a long minute. When Jem wouldn't meet his gaze, he flipped the chair back around before heading out of the quiet commissary. There had to be something he could do for Jem. His parents had to be wrong.

*

Jem sat at the empty table long after Barre had left. The message Ro had decoded spun through his mind. He scowled down at his silent micro daring it to change. At least for the sake of his limited reading attention, the reply from The Underworld was mercifully brief. He had already memorized it.

It consisted of three sets of numbers: jump coordinates, a date, and an amount.

And it was utterly impossible. There wasn't anything

anyone could do, not without a large amount of money he didn't have and a jump-capable ship with a captain who wouldn't ask a lot of questions.

He stared at the meds Barre had gotten him. Jem wanted to rip open the package and down a few of them. Maybe it wouldn't feel as hopeless if he could really examine the numbers without wanting to hurl.

Refusing Barre had been hard, but even with the more powerful sedatives his parents had confiscated, he only had a small window of functioning. He couldn't waste whatever time the over-the-counter alternatives would grant him, even for Ro. He had to find a way to make the numbers work. He needed transportation and money. And he needed it now.

If only. If only Halcyone could jump, Barre could get him to the rendezvous point and Jem would escape into The Underworld. Get his implant. But he'd have to tell his brother what he was doing. Besides, that didn't solve the money problem. Jem sighed. It didn't matter. Halcyone couldn't jump. Not now. Maybe not ever, judging by Ro's frustration.

Jem was on his own. He'd begged, but his parents wouldn't even consider letting him get a neural. It was too risky. Unapproved. Not prudent. But prudent wasn't going to fix him. And if Jem couldn't be fixed, there was nothing for him. Why couldn't they understand?

Jem ripped open two of the pill packets and let the contents dissolve on his tongue. As the bitterness faded, his nausea receded. The dizziness didn't go away completely and neither did the involuntary movement of his eyes, but Jem could at least turn his head a little without feeling like he was spinning in space. It would have to do.

The numbers were waiting on his micro. Of the three, the biggest hurdle was probably getting off Daedalus without his parents finding out. It would be simple if he were a full citizen like Barre, but his parents would never grant Jem's emancipation.

It was ridiculous that he couldn't travel on his own. At twelve, Jem had logged more jumps and more flight hours than most people twice his age. He and Barre were even accredited flitter pilots. Which didn't help him here. Even if he could steal one of the station's few flitters, it would take him weeks limping through interstitial space just to get to somewhere that would have jump-capable ships. And without travel documents, he was just as out of fuel.

Jem pushed his micro away and rested his head on the table, cushioned by his folded arms.

If only he were a citizen.

If only his brain didn't feel like protein mush.

Plenty of minors traveled. Hell, over the years, he'd taken trips with and without Barre when his parents had been too busy to accompany them. His competence hadn't changed just because he struggled with headaches and dizziness now. But his parents wouldn't let him go alone these days. In the past month, one of them had accompanied him as he'd left Daedalus almost a dozen times to consult with one specialist or another.

Forging citizenship papers was near impossible. Probably on par with the fake diplomatic seals the senator and Ro's dad had created or bought to smuggle their weapons. It would almost be funny if they had obtained them through

The Underworld. Almost.

Jem had neither the resources nor the time for something as elaborate as that. But if he had what scanned as a valid authorization, it wouldn't matter that he was a minor.

He sat up, blinking away his double vision. He still had all of the travel authorizations from his recent trips stored in his micro. How hard could it be to reverse engineer the tiny embedded programs that made up a basic exit pass? Especially if he had so many examples to pull apart. And nearly all of their prior trips had passed through Gal-3.

For the first time in a long time, excitement pulsed through him. It would be worth whatever price his head trauma exacted. Even if it meant using up all the meds Barre had gotten him in one night. Jem swallowed two more of the mild sedatives before pulling his micro back to the center of the table.

Fixing his head into the position that caused him the least amount of vertigo, he pulled up each of his travel authorizations, stacking them one on top of another. There were a number of assumptions he could make: They would each have identity information, origin, destination, and travel time embedded in the code. He wasn't starting from zero. He knew who he was, and had all the details from all of his trips.

Jem might not have as sophisticated a tool set as Ro did, but analyzing programs was something he did well. Even she admitted that. He worked deep into the shift, stopping only to take more anti-nausea pills and small sips of water. Hours slipped away.

He had no idea what time it was when he'd finally crafted something that might pass the cursory exit scan from

Daedalus. The commissary was eerily silent. Jem's eyes felt gritty and his neck ached from the stress of holding it in such an awkward position. Leaving the table littered with half-filled cups, he stumbled into the corridor, heading back toward the residence ring.

*

Micah was too restless to sleep, and he didn't want to stay in his quarters alone anymore. Even with everything that belonged to his father removed and his own things packed away, the space held too many unpleasant memories. Besides, there would be plenty of time to sleep on board the ship in the morning. Instead, he spent a good portion of third shift walking the quiet corridors of Daedalus.

He wandered as far as the umbilical that led to Halcyone before turning back to the station proper and the residence ring. Ro wouldn't thank him for interrupting her work. It would probably take her several days to realize he was gone. There was something comforting in her single-minded focus. It reminded him of his own.

A muffled cough startled him. Micah glanced up. Jem was leaning against a bulkhead, clutching the grab rail. "Hey, you okay?"

"I've been better," Jem said.

"Here, let me help you." Micah slipped his arm beneath Jem's shoulders and led him into his quarters.

"I think I'm going to be sick," Jem said.

Micah sat him down on the sofa. "Nothing that hasn't

happened here before."

Jem rested his head in his hands. "I feel like crap."

"Close your eyes and concentrate on taking slow, deep breaths." Micah rummaged through a box in the galley for a towel. He ran it under cold water and wrung it out before handing it to Jem.

Jem wiped his face. "Thank you."

Micah swapped the towel for a cup of water, wishing he could do more to help. "Sip it slowly."

"Barre told me you were leaving tomorrow."

Micah glanced around the empty quarters. "Even if I wasn't headed to Uni, I couldn't stay. It's like he's still here, you know?"

"Hey, I'm happy for you. Really." Jem looked up. At least his face wasn't pasty gray anymore. "I'm sorry I was such a jerk. Before Halcyone." Jem had all but attacked him, back when he was sure Micah was the source of the tainted bitter-green that had made Barre sick.

"Yeah, well, I probably deserved it." Micah shrugged. "There's more of my father in me than I like to admit."

"I'm sorry. About your dad." Jem leaned forward to place the empty glass on the table where so many of the senator's had sat.

"Don't be," Micah said.

Jem looked down at the bare floor.

"You feeling sick again?"

"No. Just thinking," Jem said.

"I'll be in the Hub in a few days. And classes don't start until next week. I'll poke around. See if there's some new research that might help you."

"Good luck with that. My folks have already tried."

"I'm sorry."

"Hey, this is not your fault. And you have your own shit to deal with. Just don't get yourself killed by the cartels."

"Thanks. I'll do my best."

Jem stood and gave Micah a fierce hug. Just as when Barre had embraced him, Micah nearly pulled away. The last person who'd hugged him had been his mother, just before she died. His father wasn't much for physical shows of affection, except during photo ops—and even then he'd only place his hand on Micah's shoulders.

Micah circled his arms around Jem's thin frame. "Barre is lucky," he said, patting Jem's back before letting him go. "Are you sure there isn't anything I can do?"

Jem barked out a short laugh. "Not unless you have a ship and a lot of money hiding in the couch cushions."

"Well, about that ..." Micah paced from one side of the small room to the other and picked up his micro. "How much do you need?"

"I don't ... I didn't ..." Jem stared at Micah until his eyes began to jerk back and forth.

"It's blood money and I don't want it." The only money Micah would use was what his mother had left in trust for him. It wasn't as much as in his father's secret account, but it didn't make him physically ill to think about. "Maybe my father's crimes can do some good."

"I don't know what to say."

"Look. He hurt a lot of people. This is my way of balancing the scales." Micah looked down at his micro. "I've sent you a message with the access key to a bank account.

Use it or not. Give it away or not. I don't care. I'm done with him in my life."

Jem's face flushed. "There's a doc doing some experimental work. It's expensive and it's risky."

"What do your folks think?"

Jem looked away. "I can't stand to see them crushed again. There's a good chance this clinic can't even help me. But I have to try. I could get the consult and be back here in a day. Then even if it doesn't work out, I'll know I've done everything I could do. Barre would take me, but Halcyone won't jump."

Micah thought back to those last months with his mother. If there had been a chance, any chance at all, he would have tethered all his hopes to it. It was fitting that his father's money would pay for this. If the dear senator and Alain Maldonado hadn't been using the old freighter for gunrunning, hadn't been manipulating Ro into repairing it, Jem wouldn't have been aboard when Halcyone went nuclear. "Where do you need to go?"

"The medical complex on Galileo 3."

"Hmm." Micah accessed his micro again and smiled. "Well, my friend, you're in luck. That happens to be one of our jumps on the way from this back-end-of-nowhere station to the Hub."

"What time does the jump shuttle leave?" Jem's voice cracked.

It was good to see him so excited about something. Micah only hoped he wouldn't be disappointed. He smiled as he triggered his micro. "Zero six hundred hours. There. Micah Rotherwood just bought a ticket on that shuttle. First class. I hope you're packed."

"Won't it look odd that you have two cabins?"

"Ah, but that is no longer my name. And this will be the last official act of Senator Rotherwood's son."

"You did this for me?"

"What are friends for?"

"I owe you. Big time."

Micah laughed. "I'll put it on your bill. Now get going. Our transport leaves bright and early."

Chapter 9

I⏆ was hard to return to his quarters. Jem wasn't worried about waking his parents. They had pretty much resigned themselves to Jem's impaired sleep schedule. No, the hardest part was leaving his things behind.

This must have been how Barre had felt when Jem hid him aboard Halcyone. Jem didn't have a collection of instruments to abandon, but through all their family's moves, he'd kept a collection of antique books along with archived perma-paper editions of some of the big research breakthroughs in the world of coding. He even had a reproduction of Dauber and May's first joint publication; the work was widely regarded as the beginning of the AI revolution, and probably would have earned them the Nobel Prize if they hadn't both been killed in the war.

All Jem took was a few changes of clothes and his micro. If the implant worked, he'd be able to access everything he needed using the neural. If not, then nothing he had left behind would matter. He did feel bad for keeping his plans from Barre. No matter what his brother thought, Jem's head injury wasn't Barre's fault. Jem hoped the note he left in the hidden pouch of the *djembe's* strap would help Barre understand. And if he made it back to the station with his brain in one piece, he could destroy the apology before anyone read it.

It would have been a lot harder getting aboard the jump ship if Daedalus had been a major port. But there was nothing important to protect or inspect here. Just a few routine staff rotations and some supply deliveries, mainly. It was good timing. There were actually several ships in and around Daedalus, all leaving about the same time. Even if his parents discovered Jem gone, it would take them some time to check them all.

Jem's biggest worry was his hacked travel authorization.

It had taken him the rest of the shift to check and recheck his work. He'd been right—he burned through almost all the sedatives Barre had gotten and, despite that, spent too many hours with his head over a bucket. He felt as if he'd been shoved through a wormhole in a flitter.

He waited until the final boarding call. The fewer people who remembered seeing him, the better. A bored steward signaled for his micro and scanned the authorization. Jem's heart raced as the seconds seemed to crawl by. He was afraid to look at the uniformed man, but afraid to look away, too. What would happen if the checksums came back invalid? Micah had purchased his ticket. Would they haul him off the ship, too? Micah, Barre, Nomi, and Ro had all helped him and he'd lied to all of them.

How was he going to face them?

His hands trembled. The sweat chilled on his arms. This was taking too long. Something was wrong.

The authentication signal seemed as loud as a vacuum alarm. Jem stumbled backwards and nearly fell as the steward handed him back his micro.

"Cabin 09. Port side."

Jem stood there, with his mouth open.

"Sir?"

"Thank you," he said automatically, his fingers closing around his micro. He followed the narrow corridor around to his cabin. It wasn't fancy, but it was private, a two-meter-high tube just wide enough for him to turn around in, with a programmable viewscreen on the far wall. Currently, it displayed space over the large asteroid that housed Daedalus.

Now all he had to do was wait.

Jem slid into the narrow bunk and found a sealed package on the pillow. It ripped open easily. Out tumbled an eye-shade, a travel-sized cleanser kit, and motion-sickness pills. "It figures," he said, staring down at the packet of pills in his hand. It would almost be funny if he wasn't struggling with the ever-present vertigo.

He popped the pills from their packaging and let them dissolve on his tongue. They must have been stronger than the ones Barre had been able to get; the slight fogginess that meant they were working had already settled over him. He pulled out his micro to message Micah. How's your quarters?

My bags have more space inside them.

Yeah, well, you had your chance for the super deluxe accommodations and you gave them to me. Jem snorted as he glanced around the room. The ship was old and tired. Not as old as Halcyone, but not a whole lot newer. He threw his arm over his eyes. Halcyone. If things had gone differently, he'd be there now, helping Barre and Ro get her working again.

His micro beeped softly with the notice of an unread message from Micah.

If I don't see you before we reach Gal-3, good luck, kid.

Thanks. You too.

Bright chimes sounded through the cabin. The ship's AI went through the pre-board announcements and safety check. Jem powered down his micro before tightening the jump netting. Once they were clear of Daedalus, he'd be free.

Or if the implant didn't work, he'd be dead.

Either way, the nightmare would be over.

The thrum of engines vibrated through him. Seconds passed and he felt the pressure change as the interstitial drive came on line. The burn was a gentle one, nothing like Halcyone's wild flights. The bunk's padding was a hell of a lot better than the rotting stuff they had salvaged from the crew quarters on the derelict transport.

Jem wondered if his folks had figured out he was gone yet. A flutter of fear moved through him. He held his breath as the burn went on. Surely they were out of hailing range now? And as soon as they made a jump, Daedalus would have to node-hop to get any messages aboard.

Besides, this wasn't the only ship to leave. The station would have to track them all to make sure. Jem's heart settled into a slower rhythm. Then the warning tones for their first jump came and his universe shrank to the dimensions of the shining metal tube.

He shut his eyes tight, hoping the meds would ease the symptoms. Passengers were encouraged to fixate on a still point in the distance during a jump. The display screens helped by projecting a simple vista with parallel lines, like a forest, or monorail tracks. Something that gave a geometric reference helped the strange wobbly feeling that jumpers experienced from being slightly out of temporal phase. But Jem knew that trying to stare straight ahead would only make things worse for him.

It was like he was jumping all the time, his body at war with the signals from his brain and his eyes and ears. The times he had jumped since his injury were miserable. He braced himself. The ship spiraled into the wormhole. Colors swam across his eyelids. A star-scape sparkled through his mind. His vertigo surged and he lost all sense of his own boundaries. Jem knew that it was impossible for his body to actually turn inside out, but that's what it felt like. Nothing held. There was no up or down, no stable gravity. His thoughts fractured into a thousand glass shards.

The memory of his latest consult replayed like a vid with a sync glitch between visual and audio tracks. After his parents had left the room, Jem asked the question that had been burning in him for weeks. The doctor's mouth moved and then her answer hung in the air, the sound cycling in frequency from low to high, from slow to fast. *"I'm afraid you're far too young. And even if you weren't, the damage may be too great for your brain to integrate the implant. I'm sorry."*

Sorry.

Soooooorrrrrrrrrryyyyyy.

Sor.

Ry.

The word melted. The colors behind Jem's eyes flared brighter and brighter, melding to a white that seared his vision.

Pain blossomed in the space the colors left behind.

After what seemed like an eternity, his body coalesced back onto the cushioned berth. The all-clear sounded.

One jump down. Two to go.

*

An alarm blasted. Ro struggled to free herself from the wreckage littering Halcyone's bridge, but she couldn't move her arms or her legs. For a wild moment, she thought the ship had made an emergency burn, except there was no crushing weight on her chest. She thrashed, and suddenly Ro was airborne. It was as if gravity had abruptly stopped working. Then she hit the ground, the impact forcing the air out of her.

"Ow," she moaned, when she finally caught her breath. The alarm resolved into a bright fanfare of trumpets and drums. She was trapped, not in the former ruin of ship's bridge, but in her own bedding. "Halcyone! Turn down the damned volume!" Ro shouted, as she wriggled her arms free. How the hell had she gotten herself so wound up?

The music blared on. She could hardly hear her own voice against Halcyone's broadcast. "Damn it. Barre!" What in the cosmos was he doing? "Fine." She triggered the command fanfare that he had programmed for her. The playback was lost in the cacophony, but that shouldn't matter to Halcyone. Several seconds passed, but the AI didn't respond. "Son of a bitch."

Ro tossed the tangled blankets back on her bed, splashed water on her face, and threw on some clean clothes. Coffee would have to wait until she found Barre. And strangled him.

Snatching her micro, she stormed across the hall and pounded on his door. It was just as loud in the corridor as in her quarters; there was no way he would hear her. But just because he had found a way to communicate directly with Halcyone through his neural and his music, it didn't mean Ro was completely shut out. The locks, along with a host of other basic functions, could be accessed without the AI's conscious permission and control. She brought up the program that interfaced with the autonomics on the ship. Overriding locks was simple stuff.

The door slid open. "What the hell do you think you're doing?" she shouted. Cutting through the noise was like trying to move a planet with a flitter. Barre didn't even notice. He stood beside the bunk bed. His eyes were squeezed shut and sweat beaded his upper lip.

The auditory chaos beat against Ro's ears with physical force. His face an ashen gray, Barre wrapped his arm around the metal rail of the bed frame. She wanted to shake him, but was afraid if she interrupted whatever he was doing, the assault would only get worse.

A sharp pain pierced her head. Ro clasped her hands over her ears and curled up on the floor, trembling as Halcyone's barrage of sound intensified. The musical instruments secured in Barre's room vibrated in response, but their voices were overwhelmed by the ship's. Barre swayed. His knees buckled but he held on to the bed. There was nothing Ro could do. She wasn't even sure she could leave the ship. If Halcyone believed it was under attack, the AI would take control of the main airlocks from the autonomics.

It was up to Barre.

As painful as the sound was for her, it had to be much, much worse for him—he was directly linked to Halcyone through his neural. *Damn it, Barre, what the hell are you doing?*

Maybe she could help. The waves of pressure made it hard for her to think. Taking her hands from her ears would be painful, but she could try to overload the autonomics and give Halcyone other things to deal with. Ro tried to prepare herself for the full brunt of the sound.

There were frequencies in it that her ears couldn't hear, but her body felt. Even her bones resonated in response. Struggling to focus, Ro opened the link to the ship's subconscious functions. It wasn't elegant and it wasn't sophisticated, but it was the best she could do under the circumstances. Her hack rapidly changed the state of every basic function on the ship. Lights blinked on and off. Temperature settings cycled. Fan speeds on the air handlers varied randomly. Noncritical doors opened and closed. Sensors all over the ship pinged their statuses simultaneously.

Ro's head pounded. Her eyes couldn't focus on the micro's screen. She let it slip from her fingers and curled up again, her hands covering her ears in a futile attempt to block out the terrible noise.

She shuddered, jerking upright at a touch on her spine. Her hands relaxed. The pain in her head focused to a cold stab behind her left eye.

"What the fuck did you do?" she shouted. Her voice filled the room.

Barre winced and backed away.

She could hear herself.

The sudden silence was nearly as painful as the noise had been. Her ears rang with it—a single note that was practically beyond the audible. As the pressure and confusion eased, she realized the lights were still strobing. The door to Barre's quarters whooshed open and closed in a rhythmic syncopation. Ro scrabbled for her micro and shut down her hack.

"Are you trying to kill us?" Her voice seemed harsh and too big for the room.

Barre wiped the sweat from his forehead and collapsed onto the lower bunk. He sat in the strange silence cradling his head in his hands.

"You okay?" Ro whispered. Even that seemed overly loud.

"No," he said.

She picked her way through the piles of instruments to the sink and poured him a cup of water. "Here."

"I'd kill for some bittergreen."

"That didn't work out so well the last time."

He lifted his head and smiled at her before downing the water. The color returned to his face. "This wasn't supposed to happen."

"Y'think?"

"I was poking around in engineering, looking for any logs we might have missed and I found this huge file."

"And?"

"All I did was try to read it. Halcyone kind of freaked out."

"What the hell kind of file turns into a sonic cannon?"

"I have no idea," Barre said. "But I think I'm going to need some backup to find out."

"You think?" Ro said again, this time smirking. She reached her hand out to him.

He grabbed it and stood. "Yeah. I do."

"Then let's get to work." She retreated from the cluttered room.

"Not without coffee," Barre said. "My head is still rattling."

"Come on. I brought some of the insti-synth stuff from the commissary. Perks of station employment."

"Some perk."

"You have a better offer?" Ro asked, looking back from the doorway.

"Fine."

They walked down the now silent corridors to the small galley. It was no bigger than her quarters and consisted of hot and cold water dispensers and an induction coil to heat up redi-meals. There were no chairs, only a few small tables built at counter height and bolted into the floor.

"And I thought the commissary on Daedalus was primitive," Barre said.

Ro shrugged. Nothing she wasn't used to. "Well, haute

cuisine wasn't in our current budget." It came out a lot harsher than she intended. Barre turned away. Shit. "Sorry. Open mouth, insert mag-boot. It's one of my hidden talents."

"Hey, this is great. Coffee would be amazing. Really. You should have seen some of the placements my folks dragged us to. Hardship doesn't even begin to cover it."

She filled the two cups she'd filched from the station with hot water and sprinkled a pack of the coffee substitute into each. At least it smelled like coffee. "Here. Breakfast, too." Ro tossed Barre one of the least objectionable of the food bars. "Let's get to work."

As they headed to engineering, Ro sipped the hot drink. It was bitter, but she hadn't thought to get any sweetener or creamer. She hoped Barre liked black coffee. "How's Halcyone?"

"Quiet. I think she's sulking. Or something."

"It can sulk all it likes, as long as we don't get blasted again."

They stepped into engineering. Barre set his cup down on the nav console along with his untouched food bar.

"Not hungry?"

"My brain feels scrambled. If this is even a micron of what Jem is going through ... No wonder he's so miserable."

Ro nodded, hoping the message she decoded had good news for Jem. The kid deserved a break. "So where did you find that file?" She paused with her hand hovering over her micro. "And is it safe to trigger Halcyone?"

"In the nav subsection. And, um, probably?"

"How about you do the honors, then?"

Barre's lips twitched into a half-smile. "Why, thank you."

He braced himself against the nav console before closing his eyes.

Ro held her breath. Blessed silence continued to fill the room.

A virtual window opened above Barre's micro. Ro exhaled slowly. Barre opened his eyes and smiled fully. "See. No problem."

Ro snorted before studying the file list. "May I?" she asked, wiggling her fingers in the air.

"All yours."

She expanded Barre's window to show the file properties. Then she sorted by last accessed. And stood back. "Holy mother of the cosmos. That's huge." How had she missed something that took up so much space? "It's definitely not a log file. But it shouldn't be an executable, either."

"Yeah. Tell that to my aching head."

"Maybe I can trace it to its core process. See what accesses it."

"Can you wall it off?"

"Maybe." Ro wasn't any more eager than Barre to trigger another sonic attack, but she had to figure out what the hell it was. Having a primed weapon in the virtual hands of a damaged AI wouldn't let Ro sleep easily. And it was an anomaly in engineering. If it had any connection to the problem with the jump drive, she would have to risk poking it with a stick. "I'm going to need to pair our micros."

Barre nodded. There was no hesitation in it. Ro nodded back. There was a time she wouldn't have asked for permission and they both knew it.

Ro interlaced her fingers and cracked her knuckles.

"Okay. Let's get started."

The last time she stood poised beside her virtual screens, she had been staring across two essentially identical projections of engineering schematics. She pulled them up again, arranging them all around her until she was standing in the center of a circle formed by the heads-up displays.

"What are you doing?" Barre stepped into the middle of the data readouts, color rippling across him as they redrew.

"I have a hunch. Let's see if I'm right." Nothing revealed itself as she examined the file's properties. It looked like random data. A mega-waste-ton of data. But it was a file type Ro had never seen before. "What the hell reads you?" she muttered. "I'm going to have to dig a little deeper. Let me know if anything changes."

"Um, Ro, I think you'll hear it when I do."

That was what she was afraid of. But if she could sift through some of the raw data, something there might give her a clue. Or at least a starting point. Her main concern was avoiding triggering Halcyone's panic response. Frowning, she rummaged through her tool set. "Wait. I'm an idiot."

Barre snorted. "I didn't say that."

"Just shut up, you." Ro set up a virtual protected machine and copied the suspect file over. Going back to her hacks, she chose one that would lock any program into safe mode and require her express permission to run. A fail-safe for a fail-safe. Given the AI's unpredictable nature, it didn't make Ro feel any more confident. "Tell me if Halcyone starts to get agitated." The last time he had run interference for her with the AI, they had been lost in interstitial space with a ship making random, wild burns.

"Aye, aye, Captain."

"Shut up, Barre."

"Aye, aye—"

Ro whipped her head around before he could finish, but her glare was ruined by one look at him as he stood at attention, his hand raised in a mock salute. She pulled her hands away from the displays she was manipulating and swatted him across one shoulder. His lips twitched and they both broke up laughing. Then he stepped outside her circle and back to the single virtual screen above his micro.

"Here we go." She deployed her hack, and started examining the file parameters. "Barre?"

"All quiet."

"Okay. Next step." Double checking to make sure she was working in the sandbox, Ro associated the file with a basic text renderer. If it didn't blow up in her face, she should be able to read something. Nearly every programmer left some sort of signature or hint. At the very least, she was hoping for even the briefest of comments.

A string of gibberish wrote itself across the window. Line after line after line. Random strings of letters, numbers, and symbols. As soon as the text hit the end of the display's right hand border, it would scroll down and start again. She watched, unblinking, until her vision swam and still the file continued to spit out nonsense. Ro sighed.

"Hey, at least Halcyone didn't blast us again," Barre said.

"Well, there's that ..." But that didn't get them any closer to fixing the jump drive or figuring out what the hell was lurking in the AI's scrambled brain. At this rate, it would take hours to scroll through the entire blasted file. She threw another of her hacks at it; this one searched for readable text fragments. Even automated, it would take a few minutes to examine the entire hulking mass. Ro stepped back from the running code and shook out her arms.

"I don't know about you, but I need more coffee. Do you want to get it, or would you rather babysit—"

"Oh, shit," Barre said, looking past her with narrowed eyes.

Wincing in anticipation, Ro glanced at the transparent windows hanging at her eye level. Only one was active, but it wasn't connected to Halcyone. So what was the matter?

She turned back to Barre.

"I have to go."

"Go? Where? Is it Halcyone?"

Shaking his head, Barre moved toward the door.

"Then what's wrong?"

He didn't answer.

She caught up with him in the corridor. The harsh light reflected off the bulkhead walls, washing out his dark face, turning his eyes into deep shadows. "What the hell, Barre?"

"It's Jem."

Her stomach clenched.

"He's disappeared."

Chapter 10

Barre brushed past Ro, seeing only the memory of his brother's pain-wracked expression. How could he be missing? "Daedalus, locate Durbin, Jeremy."

"Out of area. Unavailable."

"The hell? What does that mean?"

"Please restate your query."

"Locate. Durbin. Jeremy." He nearly spit the words out.

Daedalus's implacable voice repeated the prior status. "Out of area. Unavailable."

His parents' message had been terse and accusatory. Hell, if Barre could have, he'd have taken Jem off-station just for the principle of it. Ignoring the passing staff, he stormed through Daedalus. Where the hell was Jem? Barre halted mid-stride. Could he be using Ro's ghost protocol? If Jem was hiding on the station, he probably had a good reason. And if he was hurt or in trouble, Barre needed to get to him before their parents did.

He triggered his micro and sent Ro a message.

<u>how would I know if jem was ghosting?</u>

<u>hang on a micron</u>

Barre leaned against the corridor wall beside his family's quarters. Each beat of his heart seemed to take an age. *Damn it, Jem. What are you doing?* Barre refused to think of any other reason that Daedalus wouldn't be able to locate his brother.

<u>not that I can tell</u>

<u>are you sure?</u>

<u>yes</u>

He paused, trying to get his breathing and his racing heart under control. The door slid open. Barre glanced around the living room area, hoping it had been a computer glitch and Jem would be sitting there. But it was both of his parents who were waiting, instead. His mother stood rigidly, her gaze fixed on the doorway while his father paced a tight line back and forth across the room.

"If you care about your brother at all, you'll tell us where he is," his mother said.

Barre hesitated at the threshold, feeling like a child again under her cold gaze.

His father paused and placed a warning hand on her shoulder. "Come in, Barre. Please," he said.

"I'm not the one who drove him away." Barre blocked the door from closing. His head ached. The after effects of Halcyone's auditory storm were intensified by the anger and fear that shocked through him, but his voice remained dead calm. He guessed he was his mother's son, after all.

A flash of pure rage burned in her eyes for an instant before she regained control. "Get in and close the door. This is a family matter."

So Barre was family again. He balled his hands into tight fists and fought the urge to run. If it hadn't been for Jem, he would have. "Fine." As he moved into the room, his father steered his mother to the sofa. They both sat rigidly, side by side. Barre dropped into the chair opposite, glad of the low table between them.

His mother drew breath to speak. Barre cut her off. "I don't know where he is. I didn't even know he was gone until you messaged me. Believe me or not, but I'm as worried about Jem as you are."

"I know," his father said. "We know."

"Did he say anything to you?" his mother asked. Her eyes were bright with unshed tears.

Barre looked away from the naked pain in her expression and leaned forward, supporting his arms on his thighs. His dreads fell to cover his face. What could he tell them? That Jem was furious about the meds? That Barre had supplied him with what he could? He had hated the look of defeat in his brother's eyes. Their parents had failed him. They knew it and Jem knew it. "Do you have any idea how bad things were?"

"Of course we know," his mother snapped. "We're doctors. We treat head injuries all the time."

"Leta." The warning was clear in his father's voice. He cleared his throat. "All the specialists said that he was young. That his brain had a good chance of healing. That it would take time."

"He wasn't getting better." Barre looked up. His mother wouldn't meet his gaze. "The nausea, the dizziness. It was getting worse. He thought ... he thought he was running out of time."

His mother's head jerked up.

"Look. I don't have a working ship and I don't have a stash of credit. I was trying to help him, but I didn't send him off-station." His parents shared a look Barre couldn't interpret, but it sent a wave of cold through him. He frowned. There hadn't been a station-wide alert that he could tell. "You haven't told Mendez. Why not?"

"This is a family matter," his mother repeated quietly.

Barre bolted out of his chair. "What if he's hurt? What if he can't respond? What if he's—"

She stared him down and Barre clamped his mouth shut. "If your brother was somewhere on-station, the AI would be able to locate him. Even if he was injured. Even if he was non responsive."

Even if he was dead. Barre let out the breath he had been holding. If Ro was sure he wasn't ghosting, then he wasn't hiding somewhere on station. Given Jem's condition, Barre didn't think he could have written any kind of location override on his own. So that left escape. "Daedalus, message Commander Mendez."

His mother leapt to her feet and confronted him from across the coffee table. "Daedalus, override."

The AI answered in its perpetually bored voice. "State override authority."

Barre smiled tightly. "You can't do that anymore, Mother. I earned my citizenship. Remember?"

"Medical override, Durbin —"

"Leta, no." His father stood. "Barre's right."

Barre couldn't remember a time when the two of them had openly disagreed like this. He waited for the stalemate to break. His father had a half-meter in height over his mother, but that didn't mean she would back down. She would never take Barre's side in anything—she would insist that vacuum was breathable if he tried to hand her an air hose.

For a long moment, she tried to stare Barre's father into submission, but for once, he held his ground. She closed her eyes and turned away. His father nodded at him.

"Daedalus, message Commander Mendez," Barre said in a soft voice. "Mark message urgent."

"Recording."

What the hell should he say? Barre glanced at his father for support, but he was staring down at his feet. "Commander, my brother, Jem ... Jeremy Durbin, is no longer on the station. As he is a minor and in fragile health, I ... we are concerned for his safety. We believe he has taken a transport and request assistance in searching for him. Durbin, Bernard, out."

His mother turned to him with a look that inspired fear in her medical staff. "Satisfied?"

"No. Not until my brother is safe." Barre nodded to his father and strode out of their quarters.

The sound of heavy footfalls echoed close behind. Barre kept walking. If he got to the north nexus, there would be too many people around for his father to trap him into a conversation Barre didn't want to have right now.

"Bernard, please," his father said.

He flinched. It was the same appeasing tone of voice the

man had used on Barre's mother. "Fine." They were at the end of their residence corridor. It was public enough that whatever his father had to tell him would have to remain civil. "Say what you need to say and get it over with. I have work to do."

"You sound just like your mother."

Barre turned to confront him and the expression in his father's face made him hold back the snippy reply that came all too easily: *And whose fault do you think that is?* Instead, he swallowed the anger and kept silent.

"For what it's worth, you did the right thing." He brushed his hand over the short dark stubble of his closely cropped hair. It glistened with silver that Barre didn't remember being there. But then again, when was the last time he had really examined his own father?

He always had thought of him as a tall man, but now they stood eye to eye. It was all Barre could do not to slump and look away. "Thank you." The words felt awkward and formal in his mouth.

His father glanced up and down the empty corridor. "She loves you. You and your brother, both."

He knew that, even if she couldn't show it. But that wasn't enough. It was like she only loved the version of Barre she wanted him to be. Maybe it was the same for Jem.

"She's afraid."

He looked up into his father's space-pale face, frowning. The fierce Doctor Leta Durbin, afraid? Not hardly. Barre had seen her take on a desperately strung-out junkie with her bare hands and her cold stare. The man had been waving around a live laser scalpel and she hadn't even broken a sweat. Barre and Jem had been playing in the back of the medical clinic where they had been stationed. His mother never once glanced back at them.

No. The only thing his mother was afraid of was one of her children failing to live up to her exacting standards and marring the perfect construct of her life.

"It's not my place to tell her story, Barre, but I swear, she loves you. Everything she's done, every choice she's made, comes from that love."

"I wish I could believe that," Barre said, remembering the fury in his mother's face when she'd first caught him using bittergreen.

His father reached a hand out as if to touch Barre's shoulder, but let it fall back down to his side. His blue eyes were bleary and red with fatigue. "Please. Find Jem. She won't survive losing both of you."

Barre turned away from the sadness and fear in his gaze. "I won't let anything happen to him." It was a promise and a warning.

*

Ro paced out the narrow corridor that ran down the center of engineering. It was exactly thirteen steps from end to end and barely wide enough for two people to pass. Two small people. Like her and Jem. She worried the end of her braid as she walked. It couldn't have been a coincidence. The message she helped him decode had to be related to him leaving.

Maybe Barre would have some more pieces of the puzzle.

At the end of the engineering bay, Ro turned back to her running programs. From where she stood, the heads-up displays were a wash of light and shifting color. A loud alert tone made her flinch even though she knew it was just the text salvage routine completing its run. She made it back to her micro in ten long strides.

The little hack opened a fourth window with its results. Ro studied the isolated words that had been gleaned from the massive file of gibberish and frowned. There wasn't a lot to go on. She scrolled past the two- and three-letter words looking for something more substantial. If it was a disguised program, some developer comments would be nice. There was nothing more irritating than undocumented code.

The door slid open and Barre stomped inside. "I don't know how he managed it, but he's gone off-station. We have an ansible alert out for him."

Ro knew all about what a minor needed to book passage. Maybe he had the money, but Jem certainly wouldn't have travel clearance or documentation.

"Did you help him?" Barre asked.

"No." Ro backed away from his glowering face. "Those kinds of permissions are risky to forge." Hell, if she had had the skills, she would have used them years ago to escape her father.

Barre pushed past her and walked the length of engineering. Ro counted eight of his long strides. "Where do you think he went?" she asked. He glanced at her and frowned. "I know you're worried, but think. The how doesn't really matter at this point. If he's gone, we need to figure out where he is."

"I don't know," Barre said. His eyes were red, but Ro couldn't imagine him crying. "He was getting worse. And he was getting hopeless."

Ro nodded. "Does the name Dr. Land mean anything to you?"

"Why?" He stared at her from the opposite end of the room. The suspicion was back in his gaze.

"Yesterday, he came to me, asked me to help him open something in a message he'd gotten."

Barre crossed the bay and towered over her. "What message?"

She struggled not to step away. "I don't know, exactly."

"What do you mean you don't know?" Barre's hands began to shake.

"I was trying to help!" The old Ro would never have respected his privacy. The old Ro would have made a duplicate. She would have gleaned all the information she could from it and kept it hidden from Jem. Her face flushed as she held her ground. "I just know the header had a Dr. Land's name in it. From some medical institute."

Barre looked away, his eyes unfocusing briefly. When he looked back at her, he was frowning.

"What?"

"That's not one of the specialists my folks took him to."

"So now what?"

"I wish I knew." Barre pushed his dreads back from his face. "All Mendez can do is push an alert with Jem's info to all the ships that left Daedalus last shift. At least it's not like there were a lot of them. If he stowed away somewhere, they should be able to find him."

"And then what?" Ro asked. Jem had looked pretty desperate. As desperate as Ro had ever been during the years of her father's abuse.

"I need to get to him before anyone else does."

Ro nodded. Anyone else meant his parents. "He didn't tell you anything?"

Barre winced and turned away. "No."

"We have the evidence of an ansible message and a name. It's a start."

"It would be easier to find a stable wormhole in an uncharted galaxy."

"It's been done," Ro said, shrugging.

"And even if we find where he's gone, how are we going to get him back?" He glanced around the engineering bay.

"I don't know, Barre." Ro stared up at her bright displays and sighed. "But I'll keep trying."

"Give me something to do." Barre pounded his fist against the surface of a nearby console so hard Ro thought he was going to dent the composite.

"Here." She shifted the results window closer to him. "Sift through these and see if there's anything that makes sense. I'll keep trying to figure out what accesses the damned file."

*

Barre kept glancing over at his micro, even though it would ping his neural if Mendez or his parents messaged him. "I should have known."

"Hmm?" Ro stood in front of her virtual windows, manipulating lines of code with careful fingers.

"Jem. I should have known he was going to run away." It must have been even worse than Barre had feared. Jem was convinced the only thing that would help him was a neural. Barre could only imagine how that conversation had gone with their parents.

He sighed and pulled his attention back to the list of words Ro had him searching. So far, there was nothing relevant, nothing that hinted at the file's purpose or creator. Jem would have figured out a way to assign point values to each word and sort them in order of importance. Barre scrolled through them manually, letting the letters go by in a blur.

"Ro? If you were underage and needed a neural, where would you go?"

She stopped what she was doing and turned to him, frowning. "The Underworld."

"Right. The holy grail of every small-system-smuggler and wannabe hacker." There were rumors about The Underworld. Some people thought it was a place, others believed it was an organization. If everyone who claimed to be connected to it really was, it would be bigger than the Commonwealth itself.

"No. Really."

Every time an ansible relay hiccupped or a Commonwealth ship crashed, someone blamed The Underworld. "It's not like implants are an off-the-shelf item. You need a modern medical facility and cutting-edge neurocyberneticists. Not to mention the imaging equipment. There are only a finite number of places that have all those things." Barre remembered the implantation procedure vividly. It was something you had to be awake for, but restrained, with brain activity closely monitored. The memory of the way the nanoemitters made his brain crawl and the whine of the injector as it drove them through the catheter still had the power to give him nightmares.

"You said it yourself. No accredited doc is going to put a neural in Jem."

"Then where is he going?" Searching for a Dr. Land got Barre nowhere, even when he filtered by specialty.

"The Underworld is real," Ro said quietly. "It's not easy to make contact, but if I were Jem, that's what I would have done."

"You're serious."

"Yes."

"Well, where the hell is it?"

"That's the thing. No one knows. Every cybertrail fades away. You don't go to The Underworld; they come to you."

"That's crazy. How could Jem get hold of them?"

Ro shrugged. "I'd say he was pretty motivated."

Barre turned back to the endless display of irrelevant words. "If that's where Jem is headed, then we need to get there first."

"And how do you propose we do that without any clue where to find them or a functioning jump drive?"

"I have no idea," Barre said. He crashed his palm into the flat surface of a nearby console. "But I can't just do nothing."

"You're not doing nothing. You're waiting on information, and you're fixing the ship. Both things that need to happen before we can rescue Jem."

"We?" Barre looked at Ro from across the aisle. Her cheeks were flushed and her green eyes stared a challenge back at him.

"What? He's a pain in the ass, but he's also my friend." She looked away. "And so are you."

"Okay." There was nothing else he could risk saying without breaking down.

"You're welcome," Ro said, flashing him a small smile.

After another futile glimpse at his micro, Barre returned to the boring task Ro had passed on to him. He started scrolling entire screens at a time, hoping that something useful would jump out. Most of the intact words were conjunctions, articles, and short verbs—lots of *the/as/and/am/is/was/were*. Whatever the text had been, too much of it was garbled to make sense of what remained.

A strange word flashed by. Barre blinked and stopped the display, rolling it back to center on what had caught his eye. *Ithaka.*

Ithaka.

He had seen that word somewhere before.

"Ro? Does 'Ithaka' mean anything to you?"

"Not really. Look it up," she said, focusing back on her screens.

Barre sighed. Without context, he'd be swamped with irrelevant data. He restarted the display, this time scrolling more slowly. Another word leaped out at him. *Cyclopes.* "Hmm. Ro?"

"What?"

"Who started the naming conventions for AIs?"

"What do you mean?"

"Haven't you noticed? Daedalus. Halcyone. Hephaestus. Those are all names from ancient Greek mythology."

She shrugged. "They're just names."

"I don't think so. This is an old file. At least forty years old, right? Halcyone was already named then, so the practice had to have started before that." Now he remembered where he had seen Ithaka before. It was a place. From Homer's *Odyssey*. "There's a poem I learned once called 'Ithaka.' 'As you set out for Ithaka, hope your voyage is long.' That's the first line. Or at least a reasonable translation from the old Greek."

Ro turned to him and put her hands on her hips. "Why would a hidden file have a reference to some dusty poem in it?"

"I don't know. But it's kind of a strange thing to put into a program or a file unless it had some significance." Barre looked at the glowing words, hovering at his eye level. "Is there a search function here?"

"Yeah. Top right. Tap and pull down."

Barre found the search command and paused, staring at the blinking cursor and thinking of the poem. He queried the edudatabase. The text appeared on his micro and he mirrored it to another virtual window. With all the shifting displays, engineering looked more like a VR lab. Scanning through the readout, he picked out the words that wouldn't likely be part of anything else and searched for them in the corrupted file. Poseidon. Lestrygonians. Phoenician. Mother-of-pearl. Ebony. Egyptian. They weren't all there, but enough of them were. "Why would someone put the entire text of a centuries old poem in a computer file?"

"Hell if I know. Ping me when you figure it out."

Chapter 11

Every time Barre called her name and interrupted her train of thought, Ro had to fight not to snap at him. He wasn't doing it to drive her crazy. Besides, she'd invited him to help. But it was the same physical sensation she used to have when her father would startle her in the midst of her work. The same wave of cold settled in the pit of her stomach, the same prickling of the skin on the back of her neck.

She sighed and turned to him. Barre wasn't even remotely like her father in any way. And after a lifetime of living in perpetual mistrust of every other human she encountered, Ro realized she trusted the tall musician.

If he thought all the Greek mythology references were relevant, then they were probably relevant. That was something he was going to have to sort out. Her job was tracing the file. And following her hunch that it was somehow related to the problem with Halcyone's jump drive.

She activated the windows that rendered her two views of engineering and linked the redraw so the actual schematic was the master and her father's reconstruction the slave. Testing the limits of the images, she zoomed in on the isotope chamber. There was a flicker as the screen recentered and refocused. After a several-second pause, the reconstruction repeated the process. But where the real structure remained crisp, Ro had reached the limit of data her micro could extrapolate from the stitched-together images. The display blurred out at this magnification. It would have to do.

Now that their surprise sonic boom was walled off from Halcyone's hair-trigger artificial mind, Ro could poke at the copy of the program and see what shook out. Colors washed across her vision. She could see Barre outside the circle of her displays, but he wavered as if he were virtual and only her work real.

So. A file written at least forty years ago. And maybe earlier than that. A lot had changed in forty years. Some things hadn't. "Follow the ion trail," she whispered, digging in to the file parameters. This time, she wasn't worried about triggering Halcyone's protective response or blowing up the program.

Ro quickly put together several of her small utilities into something that would test the file against known file types. Or at least the ones that were common several decades ago. The program icon transformed into a moon, rapidly cycling through its phases, her version of the hourglass that was still a default image for waiting, though no one had used one in centuries. Maybe it belonged in the same universe where Halcyone and Daedalus came from. She'd have to ask Barre.

The moon phases slowed until her icon settled on a full moon with a happy face drawn in the center. She tapped it and held her breath as the massive file winked out. Oh, well, Ro hadn't thought it was going to be that easy. The display brightened until it washed out the entire engineering bay.

"What did you just do, Ro?"

"Nothing that should have caused that." The light seared her vision and she shut her eyes. The afterimages followed. It was better than the blast of noise that Barre had triggered, but this shouldn't have happened either. Unless ... Ro squinted at the display. The light level fell to merely uncomfortable. Unless she'd activated some kind of self-destruct.

"What kind of file would obliterate itself?" she asked.

"This ship was in the middle of an active war. Invasion plans? Schematic of some weapons system?"

"Stored in the engineering subsystems of a tired old freighter?" That didn't make a whole lot of sense, but the file had to be important if it was set to detonate.

"Don't ask me. I'm just a musician, remember?"

"Okay. Let me make another copy and try again. Any luck figuring out what Ithaka is?"

"Not what. Where."

Ro and Barre both turned to the open door in engineering. Nomi stood yawning on the threshold, bleary-eyed.

"It's a place," Nomi said. She walked in and the door slid shut behind her.

"Well, yeah, in the Homeric sagas, it was an island back on Earth. The home of Odysseus," Barre said. "We already know that."

"Sure." Nomi nodded. "But I'm talking about the more contemporary Ithaka."

Ro shrugged. At least Barre didn't seem to be any more

knowledgeable than her.

"It's the ultimate prize of ansible operators and jump navigators." Nomi looked back and forth between the two of them, shaking her head. "You've never heard of Ithaka? The lost colony?"

"Nope." Ro answered for her and Barre.

Nomi stepped inside the circle of Ro's displays.

"You look terrible," Ro said and immediately felt the burn on her cheeks. "I mean ..."

"I know what you mean." Nomi smiled and gave Ro a quick hug. The heat burned a path into her chest. "Mendez sent out a comms-wide alert about Jem. I had just fallen asleep."

"Sorry," Barre said.

After squeezing Ro's hand, Nomi turned to Barre. "No. I'm sorry. I should have said something."

"About what?" he asked.

Nomi sighed and dipped her head. The razor sharp lines of her black hair fell forward to cover her face. "He came to visit me in comms the other night. Asked me to send an ansible message. Said it was to a researcher that might be able to help him."

"Let me guess. A Dr. Land." Barre said.

"That was the name."

Do you remember the node address?" Barre leaned forward. His hands were knotted together. "Or anything that could help me figure out where he went?"

"All traffic that originates on Daedalus gets logged. I can't access the content without a Commonwealth order, but the headers are all a matter of record. When I get back to comms, I'll push the log entry to you both."

"Thank you," Barre said.

Ro looked across her displays at the text of the poem Barre had put up. Ithaka. He was right. If it was in the file, it had to be important. It had to be connected somehow.

"Halcyone: define Ithaka," Ro said.

There was a pause before the AI's flat voice filled the engine room. "Ithaka. As you set out for Ithaka, hope your voyage is long, full of adventure, full of learning. The Lestrygonians, the Cyclopes, angry Poseidon are not yours to fear."

"What the hell?" Barre asked.

"You will never meet such dangers on your path if your thoughts stay clear, if your spirit and your body are filled with true purpose. You will never meet the Lestrygonians, the Cyclopes, fierce Poseidon, unless you carry them with you, unless you raise them up before you. Pray that—"

"Halcyone: end definition," Ro ordered.

The AI stopped its recitation mid-sentence.

She frowned at the words of the poem on Barre's display. "Well, does anyone else think that was weird?"

"Someone had to program her with that," Barre said.

"Y'think?"

"But why?" Nomi asked.

Ro stepped as close as she could to the virtual window where the suspect file was rendered. Colors rippled through engineering as she blinked at Nomi. "How do you lose a colony?"

"Actually, a small planet," Nomi said. "It was one of the original mining colonies during the diaspora. At the some point during the war, a group of rebels claimed it, changed its name to Ithaka, and tried to break away from the Commonwealth. It didn't end well."

A chill settled between Ro's shoulder blades.

"Seriously? You can't simply lose a whole planet," Barre said.

"Well, it just disappeared. No ansible signal. No stable wormhole coordinates. There's a whole network of old-timers who keep looking for it, though." Nomi shrugged. "Official word is it was destroyed in the war."

"It's out there, somewhere. I'm sure of it." Thoughts jumped around Ro's mind like ansible packets. "You're at war. Say you're on the losing side. Say you retreat to some backwater colony and need to make yourself invisible. To lick your wounds. To survive." She looked through the hazy display to Nomi. "What would you do?"

Nomi's eyes widened. "Make sure I was somewhere that's not on any ansible grid or jump map."

"Because if it's not on the map, it doesn't exist," Ro said. She shifted her gaze from the corrupted file to the engineering schematics. "What if it used to be on the map? What if the planet is still there, but the map is wrong?"

"What do you mean?" Barre asked.

"Look. I've been over this a thousand times. Every piece of the system. Halcyone's jump drive should work. All the individual components check out during the sims, but the AI just refuses to calculate coordinates. There are fail-safes for fail-safes and a ship won't jump if it can't make the quantum calculations balance out. What if it's not the drive that's the problem, but the map?"

"So you need a forty-year-old map for a forty-year-old drive?" Barre asked.

"Maybe."

Nomi studied the two side by side schematics. "I think it's more complicated than that. There are plenty of old ships around navigating wormhole space just fine with current maps. The system is designed to be reverse compatible. New wormholes are discovered all the time and updates are passed through the ansible system to every ship with a Commonwealth beacon."

"Not this one," Ro said. Halcyone didn't have a beacon, or at least not one she could find. She figured that was because the ship was so old, but now she wasn't so sure. "I know this is all connected somehow. The drive, the poem, and the planet." She glanced over at Barre. "And Jem." It made sense in her mind, only she knew there were pieces missing.

"Jem? What about Jem?" Nomi asked.

"We think he's looking for a black-market neural."

"Shit, Barre. If I had known, I never would have—"

"I know. It's not your fault."

For the hundredth time, Ro stared at the windows displaying two versions of the jump drive and found nothing. She raised her hand, about to scatter them both back to their respective photons.

"Ro?" Nomi stood close beside her, close enough to touch. Frowning, she leaned just centimeters from the display and used two slender, precise fingers to zoom in on one small component of the actual drive schematics. "What's this?"

Shadows and light blinked across engineering as the second window zoomed and recentered to match. Ro glanced between the displays. The tiny black box Nomi pointed to didn't exist on the original plans for the ship. She'd been studying the two windows for days. How could she have missed that? It looked like an ordinary linkage, one of dozens that moved data from one part of the drive system to another. "I don't ... How did you ..." Ro stuttered to a stop, trying to catch up with her racing mind. A ship with no beacon. A forty-plus-year-old drive with altered schematics. A drive that wouldn't work with a current jump map. Greek mythology. A planet that didn't exist. The Underworld. A poem that made no sense in a protected file nothing could read.

"Ro?" Barre touched her shoulder and she flinched.

Then it was as if neither Barre nor Nomi were in engineering with her. There was only Ro and her displays and an idea she could barely articulate, even to herself.

With quick gestures, she collapsed all the open windows including the copy of the strange program before opening the original. She removed the protections that kept it from running in real time. Then she triggered the drive system to open in debug mode. "Halcyone: execute Ithaka."

"What are you doing?" Barre shouted.

It was too late. A soft ringing filled engineering. If she'd just triggered Halcyone to blast them again, holding her ears wouldn't do a damn thing. "Following the ion trail." It made sense. She just wasn't sure she could explain it. Now all they could do was wait.

*

By the time the ship arrived at Galileo 3, Jem had started to regret his decision. Three jumps, and his reaction to them had only intensified. But there was no going back. He only hoped wherever he was headed after this, it would be through interstitial space instead.

Once he lost himself in the spaceport, Jem knew he'd be pretty much untrackable as long as he didn't use his micro to make any purchases or try to use the ansible network. And after The Underworld made contact, Jem would disappear from Commonwealth view as effectively as they had. But he had to get off the transport first. He joined the short queue to disembark. No one gave him a second glance. Why should they? Anyone leaving a ship had to have the clearances to have been on it in the first place. The only way he might run into problems was if he tried to board an outbound ship. Jem wasn't sure his creative travel authorizations would stand up to repeated scans.

There would be a visual record of his passing in the passive eye of the station's AI, but the same laws that granted the Commonwealth license to collect that data also protected it from third parties. But the Commonwealth didn't care about Jeremy Durbin, one runaway minor. No matter how much influence his parents thought they had, no tribunal would query the AI database for anything less than a threatened political coup or a high profile murder. He was as invisible as anyone could be. Jem wanted to thank Micah again, but now that he was in the station and off peer-to-peer messaging, he couldn't risk broadcasting his whereabouts. Unlike visual records, ansible messages could be traced.

Galileo 3 was built on the same basic footprint as Daedalus, only to a much large scale, and with multiple levels. And unlike the small station built into the asteroid, Gal-3 was integrated into a major spaceport, large enough that it even boasted an Earth-standard rotational day. After bypassing the line for baggage claim, Jem staggered his way down into the main terminal on the topmost level. With so many people coming and going, it would be simple to hide in plain sight.

Food dispensaries filled what would have been the outer ring on Daedalus. Instead of a transit corridor with rooms carved out of the interior, there was an open space. View ports lined the exterior wall. Seats and small tables were bolted to the floor with mag-locks. Travelers crowded the narrow path between seating area and each kiosk and queued up in front of the more popular ones. The sheer number of people made Jem uneasy. He hadn't seen that much of a crowd in one place since the riots on Tresthame where his parents had been stationed, managing a blood-fever outbreak when Jem had been seven.

He shuddered and turned away from the throngs of people, looking for an empty table.

The noise and the commotion were easier to process from the relative peace of a quiet corner. Jem took out his micro and pulled up the brief message from The Underworld. He had gotten off Daedalus and was here, right on schedule. Thanks to Micah, he had the credit. Now he just had to wait. Closing his eyes, Jem leaned against the bulkhead. The metal was cool on his head.

He traced the path of his scar, the outline rough against his finger. The doc on Hephaestus had done his best. It just wasn't good enough. Voices came and went. Jem heard snippets of arguments, the brief whining of a child, the alert tones of an impending departure, but he let the sounds flow over him.

There was no way he could find The Underworld. But if they were as good as they were supposed to be, they would find him. As long as there was a 'they.' Jem pursed his lips. There had to be a 'they.' They had answered him and he was here. He had done it all just as they asked.

"You shouldn't keep a live connection open in a place like this," a rough male voice interrupted Jem's anxious thoughts.

"How else would you have found me?" Jem asked, opening his eyes. He didn't know what he had expected, but it wasn't this thin, pinched-faced, scruffy man.

The man placed his index finger on his nose and gave Jem a mini-salute. "I didn't know you were lost."

Jem smiled wryly and swept his hand through his short brush of hair. "Pretty much since this."

His companion tapped his own head. "I'll show you mine if you show me yours."

When Jem looked closer, he saw what looked like the ropy tissue of an old burn scar nearly hidden in a patchy hairline. It was thin, precisely carved across the man's head, and had the characteristic look of a high-energy weapon burn. Jem took a more careful look.

"Some of my scars are more visible than others."

Jem nodded. "I'm Jem Durbin."

"We know who you are," the man said. When he smiled, scar tissue pulled the right corner of his lip into a grimace. "Call me Charon."

"Sharon?"

The man laughed. It was a startlingly big sound coming from his scrawny frame. Jem looked around, but no one paid any attention to them.

"What's so funny? Jem asked.

"Charon. The ferryman?"

"Sorry. Nope." Frowning, Jem reached for his micro. Charon's hand clamped around his with the unbreakable grip of a work drone.

"They told me you were smart. Were they wrong?"

"You're hurting me," Jem whispered. He looked up into the man's cold gray eyes. Charon's gaze didn't falter, even when Jem felt his eyes start their mad dance. Taking a deep breath, Jem relaxed his hiked-up shoulders and stopped tugging against Charon's hold.

He had chosen this. Jem knew he could probably make enough noise and commotion to cut through the disinterested cacophony of the travelers around him, but what good would that do? Charon would vanish, along with any hope of a neural.

Going back wasn't an option.

"Fine." Jem looked away. Charon let go.

"Clever, maybe. Which is not the same as smart. Your brother would know who I am."

Jem jerked his head up, wincing as his stomach heaved in response.

"You didn't think we'd let you this close without digging, did you?"

"No." He wished Barre were here, but that ship had crossed the event horizon. "So now what?"

"Now we see just how committed you are." Charon handed him a slender wrist cuff. "Put it on."

"What does it do?"

"Does it matter?" Charon grinned again, the right side of his face as stiff as a leather mask.

He examined the smooth metallic surface, but there was nothing to betray its purpose.

"Put it on, or I walk away." It wasn't a threat. Charon spoke casually, his eyes half closed, his body relaxed against the chair back.

Jem took a shaky breath. He passed the cuff from hand to hand. It was as cold and as unyielding as Charon himself.

He put it on.

Nothing happened.

"So what's that supposed to prove? That I can follow commands?"

"Partly," Charon said. He slid his left sleeve up past his forearm, revealing the cuff's twin and another series of scars. They reminded Jem of the twisted snake on his parents' medical service IDs. Charon followed Jem's gaze. "They go all the way up. Makes for a hell of an icebreaker. Especially with the ladies."

"I'm sorry." Jem's stomach churned and for once, it had nothing to do with the head injury.

"You didn't shoot me. Hell, you weren't even born when I got wounded." Charon ran the fingers of his right hand across the metal cuff. "Did you know that if the burn is deep enough, you don't actually feel any pain?"

Jem nodded. The burn sims had been awful. He and Barre had to work through them multiple times until their parents deemed their skills proficient.

"I wasn't so lucky. Deep enough to scar, shallow enough to sear. Those Commonwealth engineers really knew how to make a weapon."

Micah had been lucky. Treatments were better now. Thanks to the war. Jem bit back the urge to apologize again and watched Charon's fingers dance over his cuff. It wasn't just a nervous habit. There was a deliberate pattern to the man's movements.

"Don't move," he said, before tapping one final time on the metal bracelet.

Jem's cuff snapped closed, fusing into a solid ring around his wrist just loose enough that he could rotate it and not squeeze his wrist bones. "What the hell?"

"A precaution."

"Against what?" Jem resisted the urge to tug at it.

"In case you were followed. And so you won't get lost. Among other things."

Jem glared across the table. "What other things?"

Charon pulled his sleeve down over his cuff. "I wouldn't use my micro, if I were you. Not until Ithaka. Not until she has a chance to make up her own mind about you."

Ithaka. He stared at Charon until his eyes started to drift back and forth. Charon sat, expressionless. Jem broke eye contact first. Ithaka. So it wasn't a spacer's tale. It was where The Underworld was. Of course. Where else did you hide a black market but on a planet that didn't exist? Jem itched to check his micro, but he didn't want to risk frying it. The cuff probably had some kind of EM scrambler. It was a pretty sweet bit of engineering, but Jem would rather admire its schematics than have it clamped onto him. "So you'll take me? You'll take me to Ithaka? I can get my neural there?"

Charon glowered down at him. "We honor our agreements. Which is more than I can say for your Commonwealth."

"Is it far? Are we going to have to take many jumps?"

"Why do you care? People far more clever than you have tried to find Ithaka. She hid us pretty well."

That was the second time Charon had said 'she' in that reverent tone. "Wait, Ithaka is a person?"

He laughed, a gravelly sound. "No. Let's get moving."

"Wait. I don't understand."

Charon yanked Jem's arm and pulled him out of his seat. "There isn't much to understand. You contacted us. And here we are. A simple transaction. Apparently we each have something the other wants."

What could they possibly want from him, other than the money Micah had given him access to? Jem looked down at the table. His micro, now a useless brick of shiny black, and his small travel bag were all he'd taken with him. He snatched them with his free hand and nodded. Charon let go.

Jem followed him out of the food dispensary and on a serpentine path to one of the minor docking bays in the transport area. Only a few of the berths were occupied. One of the ships looked just like Halcyone. The pang of regret surprised him. He hoped Barre and Ro could fix her.

They stopped beside a small hauler that looked like its better days had seen better days. He groaned. Jumping in a small ship was a lot rougher than in the larger vessels.

Jem swallowed the flood of saliva that pooled in his mouth as they walked up the gangplank and into the ship. There was no one waiting. A ship this small only needed one crew member. It could be fitted with either three tiny jump cubicles or a small storage bay. This one needed some of Ro's attention. Bulkhead panels were missing from most of the corridor, exposing conduit and wire like the schematic of the human circulatory system.

He hoped Charon was a better pilot than conversationalist.

They stopped beside a small cubby built into the corridor.

"Strap in." Charon took Jem's bag.

It was just a tube, angling down into darkness. Barre wouldn't have fit in it. At least not comfortably. Jem hesitated, his hand on the grab rail above the opening. "Look. If we're going to jump, I need to take more medication." It was hard to know just how much information Charon had.

"I'm not here to babysit you. Strap in or leave."

Jem bit his lip. Where would he go? He swung himself up and slid into the bunk. The jump foam smelled like fear and sweat. He engaged the clamps. "The head injury. Makes the jumps really bad." Jem's voice echoed flatly in the confined space.

Charon's voice softened. "Yeah. It can get pretty ugly. Don't worry. These bracelets aren't just fashion accessories.

We'll get you to Ithaka in one piece. Nighty night."

Something cold pricked the inside of his wrist, and his body was suddenly heavy and warm. Charon's laughter was the last thing he heard before darkness took him.

Chapter 12

BARRE SPREAD OUT his feet and leaned into the closest console. Given their past experience with Halcyone, another panicked blast wouldn't surprise him. Nothing would. He hesitated, the musical command sequence that would attempt to wrest control of the ship in the front of his thoughts. In the weeks since their grounding on Daedalus, he had gotten better at communicating with the AI. At least he thought he had. The last time Barre had directly linked his neural to her inputs, he'd been nearly deafened.

"Brace yourself," he called to Nomi. She looked as confused as Barre felt. What the hell was Ro thinking? She leaned over the main jump controller as if waiting for something to happen. The program she executed pulsed through the engineering bay. Strange tones accompanied the light that spilled from her display. It wasn't anything like the musical programs Barre had created with the AI. He triggered his neural to capture it. The sounds rose in pitch, moving rapidly through what was audible to the human ear until they vanished, leaving a kind of pressure behind.

Nomi's face paled. She slid to the floor, her hands over her ears, but that wouldn't block the not-noise. Nothing could.

His head throbbed to the music's invisible pulse, reminding him of the intense pain of his implant procedure. How could Ro stand it? Barre feared he was going to be sick. At least he could close his eyes and shut out the strobing light, not that it helped much. Gritting his teeth against the backlash, Barre risked sending the musical fanfare that would pair his neural to Halcyone.

Silence.

Barre's heart pounded in a syncopated, rapid rhythm. His mouth dried.

Silence.

The terrible sound wave receded. The intense brightness against his eyelids slowed and faded to a steady glow. Barre opened his eyes.

"What the hell, Ro?"

She rubbed her forehead, staring blankly at the navigation console.

"Jump drive on-line. Wormhole mapping functions on-line." Halcyone's voice filled the engineering bay with its eerie programmed calm.

"What?" Ro said.

Halcyone took Ro's startled shout as a request. "Jump drive on-line. Wormhole mapping functions on-line." After a pause, the ship added, "Navigation ready."

"Oh." Ro turned to Barre, a huge grin on her face. "Would you look at that."

Barre reached his hand out to Nomi and helped her to her feet. "You okay?"

Her narrow brown eyes thinned to slits as she glared over at Ro. "You could have ... That was ..."

"Gotten us killed? Stupid?" Barre filled in the blanks. Nomi's cheeks were flushed, her breathing ragged. The three of them stood within arms' reach, Nomi nearly vibrating with anger, Ro staring at the nav display, her mouth open. Barre took a breath to yell at Ro. A laugh emerged instead.

Nomi whirled toward him. "It's not funny. Do you know how much damage this ship could have done?"

"Yes." Ro's quiet voice answered for him. "I'm sorry. I took a calculated risk."

"It wasn't your decision to make," Nomi said.

"I'm sorry. I had no right to put you in harm's way."

"It's not me that's the problem! What about everyone on Daedalus? Do you know how lucky you were that you didn't get anyone killed the last time you mucked with Halcyone?"

Two red blotches colored Ro's cheeks. She took a step closer to Nomi. "Look. I didn't mean—"

Barre put himself between them, interrupting Ro. "Shut up. Just shut up." He turned to Nomi. "She's an idiot. I think we've already established that. Let's get you out of here before Ro creates an artificial wormhole from two micros and a cup of coffee, okay?"

Nomi glared at Ro before nodding. "Fine. But we're not done."

Ro opened her mouth.

"Don't," Barre warned, before turning his back to her and walking with Nomi out of engineering, through the quiet corridors of Halcyone, to the unsuspecting station. "I don't know how her brain works, but I know she cares about you."

Nomi stopped at the station air lock and slammed her hand against the wall.

Barre winced in sympathy. "If it's any consolation, I wouldn't have let Halcyone blast off again."

"That's not the point." Nomi cradled her hand against her stomach.

"So what is the point?"

"She could have gotten us killed. She could have gotten herself killed."

"Possibly." Barre smiled tightly. He couldn't believe he was apologizing for Ro. "It's who she is. You follow protocols, map a trajectory from one ansible node to another. Ro jumps first and calculates the course after."

"How does it not drive you mad?"

He put his hand on her shoulder. "Oh, trust me, it does. But I think if she can't find Jem, no one can."

Nomi took several deep breaths. "Fine," she said again. "I won't kill her until after she finds him."

Barre sighed. His brother could be half a galaxy away by now. No messages had come through from Mendez. But that didn't make sense. Jem had to have been on one of the ships that left Daedalus. He wasn't here. He had to be somewhere.

"We'll find him," Nomi said.

"Thank you."

"He reminds me of my little brother. Sometime you want to strangle them first, before you dump them out the air lock."

"Yeah."

Nomi gave him a quick hug. "I'll do what I can. See if I can track whoever answered Jem's message." She stifled a yawn. "I'm going to score some coffee. Go back to engineering, Barre. Keep Ro from blowing us all up, okay? I'll ping you if I find anything."

He opened the airlock. "I'll do the same."

"Thanks." Nomi stepped inside.

"She's lucky to have you," he said.

"Funny, I was thinking the same thing." She smiled up at Barre. "Ro certainly has good friends for someone so infuriating."

"Let's make sure she learns to appreciate us."

"You're on," Nomi said, as she triggered the airlock to cycle.

Barre watched her until she turned out of sight at the end of the temporary corridor. Ro was lucky. He hoped she'd continue to be lucky. Jem's life might depend on it.

*

A half-remembered melody drifted through Jem's mind. It was something Barre had written years ago. Years before the drugs and the arguments with their parents that had spilled over and poisoned the brothers' relationship. It was a song Barre had written just for him—a lullaby that had filled the emptiness and chased away the fear Jem had felt when strapped into the small jump chamber on their parents' ship.

The sound faded as Jem woke to darkness.

"Barre?" His own voice sounded small and thin. The stale

smell of the jump chamber brought him back to the present. This was Charon's ship. Jem tugged on the restraints, but they didn't retract. "Hey! Get me out of here!"

Jem squirmed. The old compression foam bottomed out, and his spine pressed against the hard frame of the acceleration couch. He rotated his arm and groped for any kind of release mechanism. The cuff Charon had given him clanked against the metal straps.

Charon had drugged him. Jem didn't know whether to be furious or grateful. His head didn't ache and he didn't desperately need to vomit, so maybe the gratitude just edged out the anger. At least for now.

"Hello?" Whatever Charon had given him had knocked him out hard, but now that he was conscious, his body was making its needs known. He had to pee. And he was hungry. "Look. I'm awake. If the ship is going to make any more jumps, you're going to have to sterilize this bay."

The ship had to have an AI to calculate the jumps. And AIs were programmed with emergency overrides. Medical overrides. Jem smiled in the darkness. His parents made sure he knew the codes as well as the consequences of using them inappropriately. Releasing jump restraints mid-jump had messy and often lethal outcomes.

Ignoring the pressure in his bladder, Jem focused on the ship. There was no sound other than the humming of the air handlers. Since he didn't feel as if his body were being pulled inside out in the human equivalent of a Möbius strip, Jem knew they weren't mid-jump. But they weren't under normal propulsion either. Even the quietest of interstitial drives made a ship vibrate. And a ship this old would definitely have a shimmy.

So they either had landed, were docked, or were adrift.

In any case, Jem wanted out. He channeled his best Dr. Leta Durbin. It was a brook-no-nonsense attitude coupled with an absolute certainty of being obeyed that made his mother brutally efficient in a crisis. "Emergency medical override Alpha Alpha Alpha. Disengage jump restraints." This might not count as a crisis in her world, but Jem wasn't above using any advantage he could.

The restraints clicked open. Jem blinked his tearing eyes as light flooded the compartment. Wriggling out a little at a time, he was able to reach the grab bar, slide free the rest of the way, and land on his feet in the corridor.

"You're more resourceful than you look."

Jem jumped at the sound of Charon's voice right behind him. The man leaned against the only intact bulkhead panel, spinning the metal cuff on his wrist.

Whatever Charon had injected him with was nearly out of Jem's system and the nausea had returned. It wasn't so bad yet that he had to hold onto the wall, but it would get there. He needed to find the head before that. "I get that a lot." Jem shrugged. "You should block all the primary over-rides. Everyone forgets the medical ones."

"And where would that have left you?" The woman whose voice filled the narrow corridor wasn't much taller than Jem. She limped closer, favoring her left leg. As far as he knew, she hadn't been aboard on Gal-3. So unless they'd stopped to take on a passenger while Jem was in dream-land, they had landed. Or docked. And she came from wherever they had parked.

"Not too far from where I am now. Only still horizontal. Is there a head on this boat?"

Charon snapped to rigid attention as she stopped beside him. "Major Doc, sir!" he shouted, saluting.

"At ease, ferryman. I'll take it from here."

"You sure, Doc?" Charon asked, ignoring Jem.

"Aren't I always?"

Jem studied her short white hair and the deep parallel lines that carved a path across her forehead. She wore a stained engineer's coverall. Its pockets were filled with delicate tools, but her hands were clean. Her blue-eyed gaze took him in and seemed to judge him by standards Jem couldn't hope to match. She reminded him of a future version of Ro.

The old soldier squeezed Jem's wrist just above the cuff. Jem winced, but gritted his teeth to avoid crying out. "Welcome to The Underworld," Charon said. "Don't do anything stupid or I'll ferry you out into interstitial space myself." He nodded to the old woman. "I'll be monitoring."

"Of course you will," she answered, smiling, before turning to Jem. "You need to use the head; then I think some food is in order, and after that, answers."

"Yes." The pressure in his bladder was becoming painful.

"Well, follow me." She would have stumbled if not for the intact grab rail along the remaining sealed bulkhead.

Jem glanced down at her feet. The heel and sole of her left shoe were a good two centimeters thicker than the right and still it wasn't enough to erase the limp.

"Souvenir. A gift from the Commonwealth." She glanced

at where Charon had disappeared. "One of many."

So many questions filled his mind. The most pressing one was if he had made the right choice. No one knew where he was. Hell, he didn't know where he was. He swallowed bitter saliva and lurched after her.

Chapter 13

IT WOULD BE simpler if Nomi could just walk away from the frustrating engineer. But even now, when Ro had nearly done something so intensely idiotic, something that could have put them all in danger, Nomi wanted to be near her. Of course, she also wanted to throttle her.

It was a good thing Barre had separated them.

Nomi walked through Daedalus's outer ring to the commissary. Just shy of shift change, most of the tables were occupied. Stifling a yawn, Nomi drifted over to the coffee dispenser. Any other day, she'd be asleep now, but she had made a promise to Barre. Knowing there'd be a price to pay later, she added an extra caffeine shot to her cup.

In the months since she'd been posted here, Nomi had started to make friends among the staff—especially the comms crew, and especially after her role in tracking down the missing Halcyone. Several of the second-shifters waved her over to their crowded table.

"Hey, Nomi! To what do we owe the honor?" Cam Lowell shifted his chair over to make a space for her.

He was the senior comms officer, a veteran of the final years of the war. Nomi couldn't figure out why he wasn't sitting on some pension somewhere on a Hub world instead of fielding the occasional ansible message here at the edge of nowhere.

"Haven't you found someplace better than Daedalus yet?" she asked.

"And leave all this?" He swept his arm out, nearly knocking a meal tray out of Emma Gutierrez's hands. The grip of her prosthesis was all that saved the lieutenant commander's lunch. Lowell jumped up and apologized.

"At ease, Lieutenant," Gutierrez said and strode toward a table in the back corner of the commissary. The three staff members sitting there nodded to the station's second in command before vacating their spot. Gutierrez sat with her back to the wall, watching the room.

"Someone needs to tell her the war ended," Nomi muttered.

"Has it?" Lowell said so quietly Nomi wasn't certain she'd heard him right.

When she looked more closely at him, he was laughing at something one of the other comms staff had said. Then the ten-minute warning to shift change sounded and the people around her started gathering their trash and their trays.

Lowell's hand rested lightly on Nomi's shoulder. "You should spend more time with the two crew. I think you would fit right in. Besides, aren't you getting bored up in comms on your own?"

When she'd first come to Daedalus, Nomi had dreaded the silence and the isolation of third shift, but now she'd grown to crave the quiet nights. She shrugged. "I don't set the duty schedule. But how about you save some work for me?"

He laughed, but Nomi noticed he'd kept his gaze locked on Gutierrez. That was interesting. Leaning back in her chair, Gutierrez seemed to be monitoring the entire commissary.

"Later, Lieutenant," Nomi said. Lowell jerked his head toward her. It took him a moment to remember to smile.

Whatever was between Lowell and the lieutenant commander wasn't Nomi's business. She yawned again and frowned at her empty coffee cup. Any more of the stimulant and she'd be utterly unable to sleep. There was little worse than experiencing a wide-awake tired. Maybe she could get some research done here and still have time for at least a little rest before her shift.

Nomi placed her micro on the table and opened a small window. She wasn't nearly as skilled as Ro with the kinesthetic commands, but it was faster than typing and more private than voice input. The holo projection was clear and sharp, perfectly focused at her eye level. It would blur out at any distance and any other viewing angle. Not that anyone was paying attention. The commissary had emptied, leaving Nomi alone at her table and Gutierrez across the room, working at her own micro.

She hesitated before accessing the comms logs. It wasn't against regs, not exactly, but it wasn't standard practice, either. Frowning, Nomi searched for Ithaka first. What if Ro was right? If Ithaka hadn't been pulverized during the war, then someone had found a way to make a planet disappear from all the jump maps in the Commonwealth. That was a hack to end all hacks. And worth a fortune to the person who uncovered it.

The first result was about prize money some reclusive communications engineer had offered for discovering the coordinates to Ithaka. The credits had gone unclaimed, left to gather interest for nearly forty years, and the payout was truly astounding. That amount of money would settle all her debts to the Commonwealth, fund Daisuke's full Uni course, buy her parents a top of the line ship, and there would still be enough left over to travel for the next ten years. And maybe even fund all of Halcyone's repairs.

Nomi's cheeks warmed. It was one thing to spend an imaginary prize for finding an invisible planet. But she and Ro were still figuring out their relationship. Besides, there was the stunt Ro had pulled on Halcyone.

Ithaka. It all seemed to circle back to Ithaka.

But that wasn't going to help her track Jem.

Nomi pulled up a second window and signed into comms. She had logged Jem's outgoing message, just as all ansible traffic was logged. The messages themselves were private, but the headers and the routing were not. As far as she could tell, this was just an ordinary text-only, thin-band transmission, sent to one of the medical research centers in the Hub.

But Jem hadn't been trying to contact a researcher. He was sending a message to The Underworld. To Ithaka, if Ro was right. Ro's brain might make what seemed like dangerous leaps of logic, but this one made sense. If you could hide a whole planet, you could easily use it to hide the seat of the black market. No wonder the Commonwealth hadn't been able to obliterate it.

What the hell was Jem thinking?

She copied the metadata and pushed it to Ro and Barre. With the three of them poking at it, maybe something useful would shake out.

"Think you have a lead, Nakamura?"

Nomi jerked, jostling her micro. Gutierrez stood just outside the glow of the two wavering holo displays. How had she moved so silently? Heat rose to her face. "Sir?" It wasn't unheard of for staff to work remotely, but this wasn't Nomi's shift and this technically wasn't official station business—though Mendez's earlier alert justified it in her mind. Would Gutierrez see it that way? Nomi couldn't afford to have anything critical show up on her official file. Not if she ever wanted to get off Daedalus and find work closer to the Hub. Closer to home.

And she wouldn't throw Jem under the afterburners. He was just a kid. A desperate kid.

"Nothing, sir. I was just checking to see if Jem had contacted Daedalus." Nomi closed the connection to comms, casually, a diligent part of the crew just doing her job. She glanced up at the formidable lieutenant commander. The woman's prosthetics were a visible reminder of the war so many had paid for in blood and more.

"And dreaming of the prize money should you locate more than one lost boy in the process?"

Nomi traced the line of Gutierrez's gaze. The woman was staring at the search results for Ithaka, a tight smile on her lips.

"Um, no, sir," Nomi answered, unable to look away from

the scarred veteran. Had Nomi just betrayed the connection they suspected between Jem and Ithaka? "It was something one of the crew mentioned. Sir. Just a curiosity." It was amazing she didn't stammer on the lie.

"I've taken note of your interest and dedication," Gutierrez said, before turning to leave the commissary. "Oh, and Nakamura? Trust me. There are some things too dangerous to find."

Nomi collapsed the display with shaking hands and slumped in her seat. What the hell? Was that just a threat? "Holy mother of the cosmos," she whispered. *Ro, what have you dragged me into this time?*

*

"One of these days she's going to walk away and not come back," Barre said, from where he casually leaned against the doorway in engineering.

He was probably right. But trapped between her promise to Barre and her obligation to Jem, Ro wasn't sure what else to do. She shrugged, but any awkward reply she could have made was interrupted by both of their micros pinging simultaneously.

A message from Nomi. The tiny icon of her smiling face made Ro feel absurdly happy. And this was just a forward of Jem's message parameters. No note. No signature. Still, they were communicating. It was more than Ro probably deserved, especially after this morning.

She paired her micro to the main nav station and started

setting up yet another jump simulation. No matter what Halcyone reported, Ro wasn't going to risk getting her insides jumbled without testing the system. There were limits to even her stupidity. A virtual bridge unfolded around her. A star chart with a blinking icon labeled 'Daedalus' lay in the dead center of the viewer. Ro smiled. It was probably the only time the station was the center of anyone's universe. "I'll figure it out after we find Jem."

"If you're right and he's somehow made contact with Ithaka, then what?"

"We go and get him."

"Do you really think we can just pop into interstitial space in orbit around the home base of the separatists, who, by the way have been effectively hidden for forty years, and ask them for help? We're Commonwealth citizens. In a Commonwealth ship. Hell, as far as they're concerned, you work for the 'enemy.'"

"Barre—" Ro tried to interrupt, but his deep voice drowned hers out.

"If we're lucky, they'll only try to capture us. Halcyone is an ancient freighter. Her shields are meant for space dust. She has no weapons. Most likely, they'll shoot first and analyze the wreckage later." He barreled through her sim, scattering light across the room. "And I thought Micah was crazy."

"Barre!"

He ignored her and paced the tight confines of engineering. "I can't believe Jem did this. What was he thinking?"

Ro stopped him with a touch on his arm. "That he could get his life back. Is that really so hard to understand?"

Barre's shoulders slumped. "No."

"One thing at a time. We have the message headers. Maybe it'll help us figure out where Jem went. It'll give us a place to start." Ro set up the sim to take a small jump, just out of local space. The wormhole she chose was an old, very stable one. "Theoretically, we have a functioning drive. We have a map. Sort of ..."

"Sort of?"

"We can't use current maps—Ithaka won't be on them. But even with Halcyone's original maps, it's not like we can just search for the place. Remember? Nomi said that wasn't the planet's original name. There were a lot of colonies and it was a long time ago. Many of them were destroyed or abandoned in the war, or resettled under new names right after. Besides, not only are our maps inaccurate, there's been some damage to the files."

"Which means?"

"We could jump into an unstable wormhole. Or one that's shifted position. Or tumble into one that wasn't there when these maps were created."

"What about all the fail-safes?"

Ro frowned at the virtual star chart. "They rely on the maps. Garbage in, garbage out."

"Can you merge the new map with the old?"

"Not without significantly more time and processing power than I have access to. The problem is, they aren't just visual schematics. What you see here is actually a computation, a construction from a mathematical representation of fluid space. Get one data point wrong, and the whole thing slides sideways."

"Then what are we going to do?"

Ro drew her breath in sharply. To alter the jump maps to hide one small point in space? And with the resources available forty years ago? Maybe Dauber and May could have done it, but even then... "It's impossible."

"It can't be impossible. Jem found them. We can find Jem."

"No. Not that." It had to be possible to make contact with The Underworld. That's what Jem had done. Despite the Commonwealth's best efforts, the black market existed and thrived. Her own father was probably working with people at least loosely connected to it. But was The Underworld formally linked with Ithaka? If so, how? Ro had no way to prove it, but it all made sense.

"Then what?" Barre gripped her upper arms. "He's my brother. Don't shut me out."

She frowned up at him. Is that what he thought? Is that what Nomi thought when the ideas exploded in Ro's mind? "The maps. Whoever hacked the maps to hide Ithaka was either a genius or the luckiest idiot in the cosmos."

"And what about us?"

"What do you mean?"

"We're going to trust a decades-old jump map to find a planet that definitely doesn't want to be found, using a ship that intermittently loses its shit. So which are we? Geniuses or lucky idiots?"

Ro remembered the horrified expression on Nomi's face when she told Halcyone to run the damaged program. "Both."

"Fine. What do you want me to do?"

Pausing, her arms raised to set the jump sim in motion, Ro smiled. "Brace yourself?"

"Seriously?"

"Well, yeah, but I think it's going to work this time."

Barre tilted his head and raised his eyebrows.

"No, really. While I'm doing this, can you set up some quick shutdown routines? They need to be passed through the autonomics and they each need a verbal trigger. I want to be able to isolate Halcyone's subsystems if I need to. Can you do it?" She wouldn't have had to ask Jem. He would have been able to create the programs without a lot of guidance. And they would work. But that was before his head trauma. Barre had his own ways of communicating with the touchy AI. Ro didn't understand them, but that didn't mean they weren't effective.

"What do you need?"

"Interstitial drive, jump drive, life support, comms." That should be enough. That way, she wouldn't have to take Halcyone completely off line if something went critical.

"I'm on it." He took what would probably be the junior nav officer's console.

"And Barre?"

"Hmmm?"

"Brace yourself."

Ro wedged herself in a space between two consoles and gave the signal to start the sim.

Tiny circles glowed across the map, greens, yellows, and reds indicating wormhole status, at least as it had been in this sector four decades ago. Not that much had changed way out here in that time, which made this initial jump a fairly innocuous one. Once they were satisfied the sim was solid, they could risk a real jump. Ro wasn't sure what they would do if they had to travel to more dynamic regions of mapped space.

She gnawed on the cuticle at the side of her thumb as she watched the avatar of the ship slip closer and closer to the target wormhole's gravitational field. This was the go/no go point. If they had been jumping in truth, Ro would have mere seconds to abort before the ship and field started interacting with one another. In a few more heart-beats, the jump would be inevitable.

Unless the drive errored out again.

The timer slowly counted down toward zero.

The jump drive whined. A stable null field cocooned the virtual ship. Ro held her breath, but the ship met the event horizon in perfect alignment. In a real jump, time and reality would twist and melt until they re-emerged in interstitial space. The sim simply blinked once and then the star chart redrew itself to reflect the virtual ship's new position.

"Good job," Ro whispered, patting the engineering console. She wiped the sweat from her forehead and turned to Barre. "Now all we have to do is find Jem."

Chapter 14

BARRE PULLED SO hard against the grab strap he'd been holding that it broke free of its wall anchor. He threw it at her. "Ro, this damned ship is falling apart. And where are we going to look for Jem? It's a big universe." Guilt, fear, and anger filled his mind in a symphony of dissonance. He disconnected his neural from Halcyone before it spilled over into the AI.

Ro laid her hand on his arm. "I don't know. But I'm not giving up on him."

"What if we're too late?" Implanting a neural was supposed to be safe, but people still died. And that was in the best research hospitals with the best doctors and equipment. Who knew where Jem was going to end up?

"We have the ansible headers. It's a start." She squeezed his arm. Ro wouldn't quit until she found him or lost Halcyone in uncharted space trying. The warmth of her touch and her fierce intensity comforted him more than her words.

Maybe Ro could work her magic on the message data Nomi had sent, but Barre didn't have those skills. "I know," he said. "I just need a break."

"I'll be here."

Barre strode off Halcyone and through the corridors of Daedalus and was halfway to the residence ring before he realized where he was headed. His family's quarters. He stopped, leaning against the cool metal wall of an empty hallway. "Daedalus, locate Durbin, Leta and Durbin, Kristoff."

"Durbin, Leta, command. Durbin, Kristoff, command. Status: emergency only."

He exhaled and relaxed his shoulders. At least he wouldn't end up in another confrontation with his parents while he was feeling this frustrated and helpless. And it would give him the chance to search Jem's room for any clues. At the door, Barre hesitated. Why were his parents in command? Other than some station medical crisis, the only reason both of them would be there would be to talk to Mendez. About Jem. Barre wondered if there was any news. Would they even tell him?

The doors opened for him and he slipped inside. If his parents were meeting with the commander, Barre certainly didn't envy her. He hesitated again at the door to Jem's room. Maybe if he'd tried harder, done more for his brother, Jem wouldn't have felt he had to run away. "Damn it, Jem," he whispered. There was nothing he could have done. The both knew it.

His brother's room was as neat and organized as Barre's had always been barely contained chaos. There was no trace of the acrid scent of vomit that had greeted him the last time he'd been here. Jem had barely been able to keep his head up, much less clean his room. His parents must have done it after Jem left, which meant they had already searched it, top to bottom.

Barre wasn't even sure what he was looking for. Jem's micro was gone, but it didn't look like his brother had taken much of anything else. The intricate model ships the two of them used to build when they were little filled a clear display cabinet. Permapapers were stored in a neat pile on his desk. The bed looked like it was ready for a military inspection.

Nothing seemed out of place, except for Barre's *djembe*, hanging by its colorful strap from a hook on the wall. He took it down and sat at the edge of the bed, wrinkling the smooth surface of the tightly tucked blanket. A soft sound whispered through the room as Barre slid his palm over the drum's head.

He ran his fingers across the strap and triggered the hidden clasp. The lining gapped. A small piece of folded permapaper fell out. As Barre leaned over to pick it up, the sound of his parents arguing burst into their quarters. He palmed the note, slipped it into a pocket, and sealed the compartment.

"Jem?" His mother's voice cracked.

"No. It's me," Barre said. "I was ..." His mother glared at him from the doorway. What excuse could he give for being here? "I miss Jem." And it was true. What they went through on Halcyone had burned away all of Barre's anger and jealousy and he remembered how close the two of them had once been. He looked up into his father's tired face. "Any word?"

"No," his father said.

His mother turned and retreated into her bedroom.

Barre tapped a traditional rhythm across the drum. The sound echoed his sadness.

"I need to check on your mother."

As his father left, Barre let the drum speak for him. His parents' voices rose and fell, muffled by the sound baffling in the walls. The words might have been indistinct, but the emotion in them carried. Barre hit the top of the drum one last time and waited until the sound died out before hanging the *djembe* back on the wall and leaving.

Outside his family's quarters, Barre pulled out Jem's note. His brother's usual measured handwriting was rushed and sloppy.

<u>Barre—this isn't your fault. This was my choice and I'll take full responsibility for it. Don't let Mom and Dad twist you around. When I get back, I'm going to need your advice on how to face them, okay? I don't know where I'm headed, only that my rendezvous point is on Gal-3. Don't be mad at Micah. I lied to him, too.</u>

"Oh, Jem," Barre said. He wondered what Micah's part in this was. At least they had some place to start looking. He wiped the message, wincing as his brother's words vanished. For the smallest instant, Barre considered telling his parents what he knew, but Jem wouldn't thank him for that. And he owed his brother—not only for what he had been willing to risk on Barre's behalf, but for all the ways he'd supported him against their parents.

*

Jem followed the limping woman as she escorted him out into what looked like a clone of a standard Commonwealth installation. The stations must come prefab in a kit. There were the familiar metal bulkheads, the overly bright industrial lighting, the ancient ident plates.

She triggered the ident plate at a set of closed doors, waving a cuff that was the twin of Jem's. That was different than the hand- or voice-prints Daedalus used. Interesting.

"After you," she said, ushering him inside a generic living apartment. "Head's through there."

Jem struggled to walk normally across the small room, but it had been too long since he'd taken anything for the dizziness and the glare of the overhead lighting seared his vision. Stumbling, he made it to the head in time to spit sour saliva into the sink. He sat to empty his bladder, afraid of pissing all over the small compartment if he tried to stand. This had to work. The neural had to be the answer.

Leaning his head against the wall, he remained seated until the worst of the nausea passed. He cleaned up as best he could and fished through his bag for the container of mouth rinse. A packet of space sickness pills crinkled in his hand. He tore open the package and swallowed them dry, shaking at the sink until he thought he could risk walking out of the head.

The woman was sitting on a colorless modular chair. A tray of food had been delivered while Jem had been in the bathroom. The smell of synthetic protein and coffee made him both hungry and queasy.

"Where am I?"

She leaned forward and handed him a cup of hot coffee. "Ithaka."

He sipped the coffee, grimacing at the bitter aftertaste. "I contacted The Underworld."

"So you did."

She waited, smiling thinly, waiting for Jem to make the connection. He thought of everything he had learned about the black market since he'd been researching ways to obtain a neural.

"The Underworld isn't a physical place."

"Good," she said. "Continue."

"It's a loosely connected network of everything from almost legal to seriously illegal goods and services."

"More loosely and less connected, which is a problem, but yes."

The Underworld couldn't exist without some kind of home base. At the very least, someone had to maintain and update the software that kept them out of Commonwealth hands and that allowed currency to move between the virtual and the physical worlds undetected. It was hard to believe that such a place could exist without serious safeguards. Only a place that didn't officially exist could manage it.

And according to legends, Ithaka had vanished well before The Underworld emerged.

"Oh," Jem said, as he started to put it together. "You created the black market. You protect it."

She smiled. "Not exactly."

"No. Wait. It's the other way around. The Underworld

protects Ithaka." He thought of all the money traded through The Underworld. "It funds this place."

She nodded. "Among other things. I knew you could work your way to it."

He studied his ... what was she? His captor? Guide? Judge? She had talked about scars, but her face and arms were unmarked. Either she was referring to Charon, or to the kind of scars that were invisible. Jem had seen his parents treat enough of those kinds of scars in remote postings and conflict zones all over the known galaxy. Judging by her age, it was a good bet she had been in the war. But as a combatant or a civilian?

Charon had called her 'Major,' which leaned toward military. And definitely not under the Commonwealth banner. 'Major Doc' made Jem think of his parents. Could she have been a medic on the rebel side? Charon had mentioned her in pretty reverent tones. She had to be someone important. Maybe even the person he had come here for. Jem's heart beat faster. "Will you help me? I can pay you."

"We have The Underworld. We don't need your money." Her bright blue eyes seemed amused.

Jem slumped in his chair. "Then why did you drag me out here?" Was he in danger? But that didn't make any sense. Charon could have killed him as easily as he had drugged him before the jumps. And if they didn't need Micah's money, he certainly wasn't a ransom candidate. The available credit in the late senator's accounts was far more than anything his parents could raise.

"You know everything about me. You have to know why I'm here. What I don't understand is why we're even talking.

I need a neural. If you're not willing to give me one, I'll find someone who can." Could he even leave? He was effectively trapped here, at least for now. That should have bothered Jem more than it did.

"Was that your program?" she asked.

"What?" Jem relaxed his hold on the chair arms.

"The program you sent, wrapped in the ansible message you broadcast. Was it yours?" She leaned forward and locked her gaze on his, not even flinching when his nystagmus started up again.

"What is this, a test?" Jem thought back to when he had created those code mods. It was the last big program he had written before his head injury.

"Was it your work?" Her voice was low, intense.

"Yes. That was mine." He kept staring at her, willing her to break eye contact first. Even if he paid for it by throwing up again, it would be worth it.

She held her gaze steady, her expression curious, as if he were some interesting kind of specimen to study.

"What is your problem? Can you help me or not?"

"Well, that remains to be seen. On both counts." Her lips curved into a slight smile which widened until she was out and out laughing. Jem leapt up from his chair, trying to ignore the sensation of the room spinning around him.

"Sit down, young man. I can't help you, not directly, but I didn't say *we* wouldn't help you."

He collapsed back down and closed his eyes.

"The problems I work with tend to be a lot less emotional and generally don't try to get up and walk away. You were an exception I made. And not everyone here agreed with my decision."

"I don't understand. Why me?"

"Your code mods. They were more than very good. They were elegant. Something I should have thought of in the original."

Jem stared at her, narrowing his eyes.

She laughed again, but this time there was no mockery in it and for an instant, she seemed decades younger. "You have no idea who I am. That's actually kind of refreshing."

"Look, I feel like crap and I'm really confused. Would it seriously be all that hard to just tell me what's going on?" Jem knew he sounded as rude and entitled as he had assumed Micah to be long before he'd gotten to know the senator's son, but it had been a long day. Maybe days. He hadn't checked his micro since Charon slapped the cuff on him, so Jem had no idea how long he'd been traveling.

She reached a surprisingly delicate hand toward him. "Jeremy Durbin, I am Adiana May. It's a pleasure to meet you."

Jem shook her hand on automatic pilot. Adiana May. May. Dauber and May. As in the SIREN code that made true AIs possible. He dropped her hand as if it burned. "You're ... you're Dr. May. I thought you were dead."

She nodded. "I get that a lot. And call me Ada."

Chapter 15

Nomi didn't think she could sleep now, even if she wanted to. She got up and shifted over to the table Gutierrez had just vacated. The back corner of the empty commissary between shifts was as private a place as any on the station. It wasn't unusual for staff to use the common room to catch up on mail, arrange a tabletop game, or watch vids. Other than hydroponics, it was one of the larger freely available spaces on Daedalus. They were lucky to be housed on an asteroid rather than isolated in orbit somewhere, but there was still little opportunity for getting outside, and there was a limit to the amount of hours it was healthy to spend in tiny, sealed rooms.

What was Gutierrez up to? Was she interested in Jem or in Ithaka? Nomi called up the message headers again and stared at the data, hoping it would tell her something different this time. There had to be something she was missing.

Her micro beeped with a private text from Barre.

If it helps, he was on a ship to Gal-3. Probably the same

one as Micah.

Hoping Ro was as good as she claimed to be, and this chat program was secure, Nomi answered. <u>Thank you. I can check if any incomings got logged to him from there</u> At least she only needed to search a few shifts' worth of reports. For the first time, Nomi was glad this was such a low volume posting.

<u>We know he got a reply. Ro saw it.</u>

If Jem got a message back, Nomi would find it. There were ways to alter the headers and metadata, but even the most sophisticated methods usually left clues. Knowing where to look was half the battle. <u>We'll find him</u>

<u>And then what?</u>

Even through the flat, impersonal text-based program, Nomi could sense Barre's hurt and fear. If Jem was able to find someone to give him a neural, there was a good chance it would make things worse. And if that someone was connected with The Underworld and Ithaka? As far as the Commonwealth was concerned, one small boy would be considered a justifiable sacrifice if it meant being able to crush the black market once and for all. Nomi glanced down at her uniform. She was the Commonwealth, as much as Gutierrez or Mendez.

What would she do if she heard from him? Fulfilling her obligations could mean betraying his trust and his life. Concealing what she knew could lead to charges of treason. For now, all she knew for sure was that Jem was missing. Everything else was pure conjecture. Silence was the safest path.

And if Ro and Barre found him first, then what was he

coming home to? She answered Barre, hating this terrible mix of helplessness and dread. I'll ping you once I have anything

Barre's messages and her replies faded out. She opened a remote session to comms again and queried Daedalus about the past three shifts. It had been less than two days since Jem had visited her in comms during her shift. He had seemed so quiet that night, so subdued, and Nomi had attributed that to his ongoing symptoms. He'd been lying to her, but she couldn't find it in herself to feel betrayed. She probably would have done much the same in his position.

The logs scrolled across her display and she scanned them with a well-practiced eye. Most of the incoming traffic was routine sector maintenance or official announcements. She ignored anything with a Commonwealth header. There were several priority communiques for Commander Mendez, significantly more than she expected for a station this small and this remote. The rest of the messages were personal mail for station staff. Her own name popped up several times: messages from her folks, condolences from school friends about her grandfather, the latest vid from Daisuke. Nomi could have searched for Jem, but queries of the database were logged. It was enough that her session would show up.

She was getting as paranoid as Ro.

Nomi got to the end of the file and didn't find anything for Jem. "Huh, let's try that again." This time, she scanned the logs from most recent to least, looking for anything tagged with Durbin. Several listserv subscriptions a day were delivered to both of the doctors, but nothing else. No personal mail at all. Not even to Barre or Jem. Maybe that wasn't so strange, considering they were all here on Daedalus. Nomi was surprised they weren't in regular contact with any friends or colleagues, though.

And especially strange, there was nothing for Jem. Which wasn't possible. Ro had helped him decode the reply he'd gotten. It had to have come through the ansible system. It had to have been logged. It took a command override to alter an official ansible record.

Frowning, Nomi checked the outgoing side. It could have been a database error. The incoming message might have been filed with the outgoing. More sophisticated systems did have threaded logs. She scrolled rapidly, looking for her shift from the night before last.

All traces of the message she had sent on Jem's behalf were gone. The only proof she had existed in the copy of the metadata Nomi had forwarded to Ro and Barre earlier. Before her strange not-quite-confrontation with Gutierrez.

This was no error.

A shiver moved through her and she shut down her session with comms. Gutierrez had command override privileges. How much did she know? How much did she suspect?

How much trouble was Nomi in?

She needed to talk to Ro. In person. On Halcyone. Her heart pounding, Nomi walked out of the commissary, seeing only the lieutenant commander's enigmatic expression.

There was the usual sparse foot traffic between the commissary and the temporary air lock where Halcyone was docked. Nomi flinched each time she passed one of Daedalus's oculars. It didn't matter that the Commonwealth limited real-time visual tracking to the passive variety.

Anything recorded and saved could be hacked. Hanging around Ro had taught her that.

As Nomi walked through the short section of umbilical tubing, Halcyone's outer door unlatched with a loud clunk. "Welcome Nakamura, Konomi," the AI said as the hatch swung open. Ro must have programmed that. "Thank you, Halcyone."

She knew Ro would tease her for being polite to a computer, but it was something she'd picked up from her grandparents when she was a little girl. Her grandfather had programmed his house AI to use formal Japanese honorifics when it spoke to them. Nomi preferred her grandfather's house and the AI who called him *Ojiisan* to the boring AI with its default voice and prompts at home. She smiled, lost in the past. It took her a minute to remember the name her grandfather had given the computer. *Tetsujin.* Japanese for Iron Man.

Ro was in engineering, exactly where she'd been when Nomi had stormed out earlier.

"Hey," Nomi said.

"Hey, yourself." Ro stood with her hands upraised, several blinking windows floating at her eye level. With a series of quick gestures, she shut them down, one by one, until there was nothing between the two of them except the length of a walkway.

"I'm sorry." Ro's light skin blushed a dusky pink. "I keep saying that to you."

"Yes. You do." It would be easy for Nomi to rekindle her earlier anger, but that wasn't going to get them anywhere. And it wouldn't help Jem. Barre was right. This recklessness was part of Ro. Part of what excited Nomi about her. There was nothing reckless about Nomi, except maybe for wanting to be near Rosalen Maldonado.

"I'm trying."

Nomi broke into a wide grin. "Yes. You certainly are."

Ro opened her mouth and closed it. "I jumped right into that one." She shook her head and her long hair slipped free of its tie-back. Nomi wanted to catch its golden length in her hands.

"I suspect it's a talent," Nomi said.

"I'm not sorry you came back, but why are you here?" Ro winced. "I mean, you're on shift in a few hours and you've been up practically since last night."

"How secure are we?"

Ro narrowed her eyes briefly before pulling up a fresh window and creating an oily rainbow of color with her hand gestures. "As secure as I can make us without someone getting curious."

That would have to do. "Jem's messages are gone."

"What do you mean?"

"There's no record of the message I sent for him and nothing inbound either. Someone altered the logs—and I think it was Gutierrez." Nomi described her uncomfortable conversation with the lieutenant commander and Lowell's odd reaction to her.

"I can't take Halcyone and search for Jem without filing a flight plan and getting Mendez's approval. There's no way Gutierrez won't know about it."

"I know," Nomi said. "And I don't know what she wants. But I think it's bigger than Jem, and it's definitely something to do with Ithaka."

She shrugged. "We have to find Ithaka if we want to save Jem."

"You're not the only one looking. And if you find it, then what?"

"That's up to the Commonwealth, I guess." Ro paused and cocked her head. "But look on the bright side. Maybe we can claim the prize money."

A wave of warmth crept up to Nomi's face. *We.* She liked the sound of that.

Ro took a step closer and pushed a strand of hair out of Nomi's eye. "Go rest. If Barre and I figure anything out, we'll find you in comms later."

Nomi leaned into Ro's touch and the skittish engineer didn't stiffen or move away. It was a start.

*

After Nomi left, Ro rubbed her finger and thumb together, still feeling the smooth texture of her friend's black hair. It was a minor miracle, but Nomi seemed willing to look at her as a work in progress. Ro wasn't going to waste that chance to prove her right. The habitual tension in her shoulders eased. For a moment all the problems around her didn't feel so impossible. Halcyone would fly. They would find Jem. Ro would come back to Daedalus and Nomi would be here.

Nomi would be here.

But Gutierrez was a puzzle. Less second-in-command and

more Mendez's silent shadow, the scarred vet had primary responsibility over training and management of the small military staff on Daedalus, leaving Mendez to run the station. Ro had never had much contact with her. It had been Mendez who supervised her father and now passed along her orders.

Did they really believe they could dismantle the black market if they found Ithaka? It would probably take all the resources of the Commonwealth and then some. Especially if people like her father and his smuggler associates were connected with it.

Ro hated the thought of Jem being beholden to them. The Commonwealth could have Ithaka, as long as they could get Jem free first. And maybe Ro could get a line on her father. That would be an extra bonus.

She headed toward command, wondering what she'd have to trade for permission to leave Daedalus. Gutierrez was sitting in the small anteroom to Mendez's office.

"I need to see the commander," Ro said.

"She's in a meeting, Chief Engineer Maldonado. You're welcome to wait."

Ro suppressed a shudder as an image of her father filled her mind. The chief engineer's position was hers now, for good or for ill, and he was long gone. He had no more power over her. The past had no more power over her. She thought of Nomi again and took a deep breath.

She chose a seat near the door and fidgeted with her micro. Indistinct voices rose and fell, masked by the constant hiss of the air handlers, but Ro could pick out Mendez's higher-pitched tone against a man's deeper voice. Their conversation paused and the door opened.

"Thank you, Commander," Mendez said.

Ro stood as Mendez escorted her visitor out. The tall, silver-haired man paused before glancing at Ro. She recognized the piercing blue eyes and the burn scar that meandered across the right side of his face.

"Commander Targill." Ro inclined her head.

"I hope you are enjoying your ship, Ms. Maldonado."

"Halcyone has been a challenge, sir," she said, suppressing a smile. He had tried to claim the former derelict ship as salvage, but Ro had had possession of it at the time and legally, a slightly stronger claim. Which wouldn't have made a bit of difference, except Mendez had fought for her. If for no other reason, Ro wanted to believe the commander hadn't altered the logs.

"Are you waiting for me, Chief Engineer?"

Targill's eyebrows rose. "Congratulations."

"Thank you." She turned to Mendez. "Yes."

Mendez smoothed her uniform top and brushed her hand over her nearly shaved head. "Emma? I think I'll need you for this."

Gutierrez pushed past them both to stand at parade rest just inside the door. Light glinted off her crude prosthetic claw. Mendez settled into a chair with a sigh. "So you have repaired your ship's jump drive."

Ro paused just as she was about to sit. "Sir?"

"Ever since Halcyone nearly tore half my station apart, I've had Daedalus monitoring her drive signatures. It has changed. And I suspect you are here to file a flight plan."

She wanted to see the expression on Gutierrez's face, but

the lieutenant commander was behind her. Mendez just looked weary. "Yes, sir." Was Nomi was right? Had Gutierrez ordered the erasure of Jem's messages? And if so, why? "We think we may have a lead on Jeremy Durbin's location and would like to pursue it."

"His parents have been in to see me. They are quite concerned."

Ro nearly snorted. That would explain Mendez's exhaustion. "Commander, we believe it would be premature to share our information with the Durbins. There is a high likelihood that it's a dead end." Besides, Ro owed them nothing. Gal-3 would be in their flight plan, but if Gutierrez had been the one who eliminated Jem's messages, the headers would likely have already given her that information. It would be a race to track him from there.

Mendez glanced at the readout integrated into her desk and frowned. "We don't have the resources to mount a search out of sector."

Daedalus's 'fleet' consisted of several short-range flitters and evac pods. Which is why Mendez had called on Hephaestus when Halcyone had woken up and blasted off. Probably more for the ship than its accidental crew.

What was Targill doing here now? Ro had a hard time believing they would provide a Commonwealth ship to bring home one runaway minor, no matter how outraged his parents were. And if Targill was here to track Jem to Ithaka, his orders wouldn't include rescuing him. Jem would be collateral damage to a massive Commonwealth victory. "We do. Sir. Both of Halcyone's drive systems are functioning within normal parameters."

Mendez nodded. "You are cleared to leave Daedalus."

That was too easy.

"Lieutenant Commander Gutierrez will be your liaison with the station. I will need you to be in regular communication with her."

Ro remained silent, staring past Mendez. Was there any way she could avoid the LC?

"Chief Engineer?" Mendez leaned forward, studying her. "Do I need to remind you that even without a military commission, you are still part of the Commonwealth chain of command simply by virtue of your position here?"

"Understood, sir."

"Emma, coordinate ansible frequencies before Halcyone files her flight plan."

"Yes, sir," Gutierrez said, her voice flat, emotionless as any AI.

"Am I dismissed?" Ro asked.

Mendez nodded before shifting her attention back to her desk. Ro took her cue to leave. As she passed Gutierrez, the stern veteran relaxed her stance and followed Ro out of the commander's office.

"Shall I speak with Nakamura?"

An all-too-familiar fear filled Ro, making it hard to swallow, trapping her breath in her chest. She wanted to warn Nomi away from the lieutenant commander, in the same way she had been desperate to keep her clear of her father's influence. But while Alain Maldonado had been a threat, she had no proof concerning Gutierrez. Only Nomi's suspicions and her own unease. "I will let her know you'll be in contact," Ro said, keeping her voice level.

Gutierrez nodded, dismissing her.

Ro backed out of command, not breaking eye contact until she reached the corridor. Outside command, she closed her eyes and leaned against the bulkhead, dripping with sweat.

*

Jem continued to blink, staring open-mouthed at the small silver-haired woman sitting across from him. She seemed like someone's grandmother—intense blue eyes in a sharply lined, narrow face that looked like it was more comfortable frowning than anything else. All the official photos of her were from the war. In Jem's mind she was permanently in her twenties, but as he studied her, he recognized the high cheekbones and the widow's peak in her hairline. Her hair had once been darker, but her eyes were the same vivid color they had been.

He wanted to touch her, to make sure she was real. And then ask her a million questions. "I don't understand. You died in the war. Rebels shot your ship down."

"Not exactly," she said. "Chaz was killed. But not by the rebels." Her lips writhed as if she had tasted something caustic. "The Commonwealth killed him. He paid the price of his doubt. I kept my mouth shut and continued to write code. At least until I could manage to get away."

"No, that's not possible." Dauber and May were Jem's heroes. There had to be some mistake. This bitter old woman couldn't be Dr. May.

"That's what we wanted to believe. It's why we kept working for the Commonwealth, even after Chaz found out what they wanted us to do. He spoke up and then he was gone. His beautiful mind, destroyed for the sake of expediency. I'm told we did make perfect symbols for the war effort."

Jem jumped up from his chair and stared down at her, blinking furiously. None of this made any sense. What had the Commonwealth ordered them to do? How did she end up here? "But you work for the black market. The drug syndicates. Gunrunners. How could you do that?"

"I was once like you. Smart. Driven. Passionate. The Commonwealth found me and used me, the way it used any number of its resources. You are being mined as systematically and as methodically as aduronium."

"I'm no use to anyone, now." Jem clutched the chair arm and closed his eyes as the room began to spin.

"Sit down before you fall," May snapped.

Jem sat.

"You blame me, yet here you are, willing to pay the same black market."

"That's different," Jem said, swallowing thickly, trying not to vomit.

"Is it?" Her voice softened. "We are all hypocrites for our desires, Jeremy. Even me."

"It's Jem."

"My apologies. I should have remembered from your record."

His eyes snapped open. "My record?"

"We don't let just anyone make the trip to Ithaka. You, my friend, are a special case."

"Meaning?" So they did want something from him. He wondered what their price would be and if he could pay it. If he would.

"My people passed along your hack to me. Within hours, we had compiled a dossier on you, Jem Durbin."

"Then you know why I need a neural."

"Yes. I know."

Was that sympathy in her voice? Regret? "What will it take?" He had known contacting The Underworld was a dangerous decision. That changed nothing. Neither did finding out about Ithaka and Ada May. Fine, Jem was a hypocrite. But at least he'd be a hypocrite with a functioning brain.

"We have access to technology the Commonwealth has not yet adopted. The doctors tell me it's possible to insert a neural, even in someone as young as you, but there is still some risk."

"It can't be worse than living like this."

"You're young. You have no idea what you can live with."

There was that bitterness again. The question burned in his mind. What had she learned to live with? But Jem couldn't ask it. He had no right. "If you don't want my money, what do you want?"

"Your future. Your potential." She stared right into his wandering eyes. Hers were the blue of Earth's seas from space. "Your loyalty."

"And if I say no?"

May sighed. Her shoulders slumped and she seemed to fall in to herself, suddenly aging decades. "Then Charon takes you back to Galileo 3 and you do what you wish from there."

"No threats? No ultimatums?"

"You know nothing the Commonwealth doesn't already know. Even if they compelled you, you couldn't show them the way here. Besides, we do not threaten. You have a choice. No one will judge you for it. Least of all me."

"What happened to you?" Jem didn't realize he had spoken aloud until she looked away, blinking tears.

"I met Chaz when we were both not much older than you. You remind me of him." She stood, grimacing as she put weight on her left leg. "These are your quarters for as long as you choose to stay with us. You are free to use your micro to access the intranet. Lethe will respond to all basic household functions, but you will not be able to broadcast or receive beyond this compound. I've pushed a local map to you. The layout should be familiar from your time on Daedalus."

Jem curled his hands around his micro.

"And don't bother trying to hack around Lethe. I programmed her."

May limped toward the door and left without looking back.

This was what he'd been working towards since he returned to Daedalus. Since all the specialists had given him the same answers. Since his brain was getting worse, not better. And he got himself here. So why was he so uneasy? Jem's head ached as much from the after effects of the jumps as from his confusion. He had to get some real rest, or none of this would make sense.

Curling up in the uncomfortable chair, Jem found a position that didn't set the room spinning and fell into an exhausted sleep.

Chapter 16

Too jittery to actually sleep, and leery of missing her shift if she used a sedative, Nomi let her body simply rest for a few hours. When the alarm beeped, she stifled a yawn and slid from beneath the warm pile of covers. She frowned at her wrinkled uniform. There wouldn't be anyone to write her up for it on third shift. Ro was turning into a bad influence on her.

After splashing some cold water on her face and brushing out the tangles in her hair from the pillow, Nomi headed to comms. She was early. The 'two crew,' as Cam Lowell called his two second-shifters, was logging off. Her friend, Simon Marchand, was working. He looked up from his station and smiled a greeting. They had bonded after the search for Halcyone, and Nomi would have liked to ask him if Lowell and Gutierrez had a history she should know about. That would have to wait until Nomi was off shift; then they could catch up.

Nomi sat down in one of the empty comms stations,

waiting for the official turnover. Lowell shut down his console and walked over to her.

"Ready for another exciting night in comms?" His light brown eyes glittered as he smiled.

Nomi smiled back. "It's not so bad."

"We used to rotate the shift. Before you got here."

"Was that your bright idea? Stick the newb with the crap shift?"

His hands tightened briefly on the back of her chair. "Actually no. The lieutenant commander made the duty changes."

Something to thank Gutierrez for. And something else between Lowell and the LC, though Nomi couldn't imagine why he'd object to being freed from the drudgery of third shift in comms. "Any word about Jem?"

Lowell glanced back at the display of the ansible network. "No. Poor kid."

"Well, maybe we'll hear something tonight," Nomi said.

"Maybe."

She shifted to the center console as the other comms officer, Yizhi Chen, closed out her station. "Anything I should know about?" Nomi asked.

"Just the usual," Yizhi said. "I keep telling Cam that he could easily replace us with a pair of drones, but he's not buying it."

"Regulations. Which means job security for you two," Lowell said. "So quit complaining."

"You free later, Simon?" Nomi asked.

His blue eyes glinted with his usual amusement. "You asking me on a date?"

LJ Cohen

She snorted. "I only love you for your coffee." He had family on New Louisiana and they sent him real coffee and fresh spices every few months.

"Well, it's always good to know where I stand." He stretched his spine and twisted his neck until his joints cracked. The sound always made Nomi wince. "Going to scrounge up some supplies and cook up a gumbo later. Come on by."

"Will do." She had some time to figure out how to pump Simon for information without making him suspicious.

After they left, Nomi slipped on her headset and dialed down the lights. It wasn't stimulating work, but it did pay back her obligations to the Commonwealth. She wondered why the rest of the staff were stuck here.

"If you want, I'll put in an official request to get you off nights."

Lowell's unexpected voice in the room's stillness made Nomi twitch. She swiveled around in her workstation's chair and squinted at his shadow by the door. "No, really, I'm good. The first few weeks were tough, but it's easier now." Having some friends on the station helped. Having Barre and Ro in her life helped even more.

"Well, if you change your mind, let me know."

It was almost as if Lowell was trying to get her to swap shifts with him. How strange. Nomi waited until he left, continuing to watch the door long after it had closed behind him.

*

"You told her Halcyone was ready to fly?" The bridge was still a mess, but that wasn't what Barre was concerned about. "Weren't you the one who said we could jump into oblivion or something?"

Ro pointed to the display she'd set up in front of Halcyone's damaged viewscreen. "See? Gal-3 is just a few jumps away and nothing has changed in that sector since they built the station. It's on a stable Lagrange point. There isn't anything else in the entire system. If there's one safe place to jump to, that's it."

"What about the map problem?"

Ro sighed and looked away. "I told you. They're a little damaged." Her voice dropped into a mumble.

Barre's head began to throb. "Define 'little.'"

"It's hard to tell. There's definitely data missing. But the data that's intact looks good."

This was crazy. They were going to go after Jem and would probably get themselves blown up in the process. "But you don't know for sure."

"Look. I get this is a risk. But I made a promise. To you. To myself. You don't have to come. Stay on Daedalus. That way if Jem contacts you—"

"No." Barre's anger drained away, replaced by a reckless hope. "You jump, I jump."

The humming of the fans was loud in the silence. "Are you sure?"

"Yes. I trust you," Barre said, answering the question she

hadn't asked.

She looked down at her micro. "Oh."

"Besides. You need my help."

"Well, if you put it that way." She smiled up at him.

A warmth spread out from Barre's chest. They made a good team. Who would have guessed? "I still need to finish programming those shutdowns."

"I need to raid Daedalus for some supplies." Ro shrugged. "Mendez wants us to go after Jem, right? That's official station business."

"Do you need help?"

"Take care of those routines. I got this."

It was third shift. "Ah," he said. "Give Nomi a hug for me."

Ro blushed so fiercely even her ears turned red.

Barre laughed as she stuck out her tongue. So Ro was human after all. After she left and the door sealed shut, the silence of the bridge pressed down on him. He linked up with Halcyone and sifted through the fragments of musical commands he had built with her repertoire of sounds. But his worry for Jem created a counterpoint that interrupted his concentration. Again and again Barre created odd little melodies that Halcyone would respond to, only to hear his fear threaded through the song.

An hour had passed. Barre shut down his connection with the AI and paced the bridge, avoiding the place where his brother had lain, his brain quietly bleeding.

The bridge held a lot of uncomfortable memories. He headed to his quarters. Maybe he needed to do this the old-fashioned way. Barre tuned the twelve-string guitar and strummed it softly, listening to the overtones fade. Reluctantly, he put it away. The beautiful instrument didn't have enough range for what he needed. He pulled the small keyboard from the top bunk and sat down on his bed with it across his lap. The bunk forced him to hunch over, but there was always something soothing about playing music with his hands instead of through his neural.

He'd been programming the keyboard with Halcyone's tones. The scale was unlike anything he'd studied. It wasn't the seven-tone scale of old Earth's western musical canon, nor was it the twelve fundamental notes of ancient Chinese music. Halcyone had a near infinite range of sound, with sliding pitches and changing resonances. Barre had only begun to master its complexity.

After linking his neural to the keyboard, he played in a sandbox so nothing he did would trigger the AI. She was listening. Barre would say she was curious, but Ro would mock him for humanizing what to her was merely a program. A complex one, to be sure, but code that Ro saw as essentially understandable and controllable.

Music was a kind of code, but it wasn't as delineated as Ro believed. There wasn't a one-to-one correspondence between her programs and his music. The melodies carried emotion and nuance. The same song, played in a different way, could have a totally different meaning. Which was why Barre kept wiping what he'd constructed and starting over.

His fear for Jem kept creeping into the song fragments. Barre growled and slammed his hands onto the keyboard, creating a loop of reverberating dissonance.

One bright note sounded in his head, higher pitched than what was coming from his keyboard. Barre lifted his hands from it. The terrible noise died away leaving only that one note, pinging through him.

It was Halcyone's query tone.

Barre sucked in his breath. Over the course of the past several weeks, ever since Barre made the connection between the damaged AI and his music, he had been communicating to her. But this was the first time the AI had reached out to him first.

He played a brief fanfare in a major key. She silenced the repeating tone and played his fanfare back to him.

"All right. So I can't keep Jem out of it. He's the reason we're trying this in the first place." He'd never tell Ro, but he was sure that's what Halcyone was trying to tell him. "Thank you." Barre shook out his hands and returned them to the keyboard. It only took him a few minutes to record and set the triggers for all the shutdown routines Ro asked for.

The door chime sounded. Barre opened it to find Ro with a trundle nearly buried beneath a pile of jump snugs. "I'll take that hand, now," she said.

Barre set the keyboard aside. "How's Nomi?"

"Fine." This time the blush didn't do more than color her cheeks. "Do you know how to use these?"

"Yeah." His parents had made sure of it as part of their emergency medical training. The jump snugs were effective, if a little primitive. They were usually deployed in disaster situations. Once a body was wrapped inside and the bag triggered, it created a dense webbing that was better and more reliable than a force field. They were cheap, too, which was a good thing because without any external visual stabilization, you were almost guaranteed to vomit in one. Most people called them 'air-sickness bags.'

Ro helped him latch his into his bunk. The old cushions should give them a little extra insurance, too.

"How many of those snugs did you snag?"

"Not enough.

"First class all the way with you," Barre said.

"Nothing but," Ro answered, smirking. She handed him a pile of anti-nausea tablets. "Stock up."

He sealed them in his jumpsuit pocket, thinking of the ones he had gotten for Jem. Wherever his little brother was, Barre hoped he had enough. He picked up a second snug. "For Jem." Ro nodded as he cleared the top bunk and stowed his instruments, filling every bit of storage in the room. Without a word, Ro reached up and helped him secure the snug.

"Ready to roll?"

"I have the programs you wanted. I'll pass the triggers through to your micro."

"Good. We'll do one easy burn to get us aligned with our first jump target. Then it's three jumps to Gal-3."

And that was the closest major nexus in this entire sector. At least three jumps from anywhere. That was Daedalus. He wondered how far Jem had had to travel to get to Ithaka. And how they were going to find him. "And you think Halcyone's ready?"

"I've run the sim a dozen times—the entire trip from Daedalus to Gal-3, including the interstitial burns. No errors."

"Then let's fire up the rockets."

Ro smiled. No one had used rockets and propellant fuel in generations of space flight, but they still used the expression. "Give me a few minutes to jettison the umbilical."

The last time Halcyone had flown, she'd torn clear of Daedalus, trailing the temporary corridor material with her and, in the process, knocking out the station's ansible capabilities. It had been a miracle she hadn't done more damage.

"Can you sleep underway?"

"Whatever it takes to get to Jem." It wouldn't be pleasant if they had to pull a lot of g's, but the faster they found his brother, the better.

"Then we might as well stay in the snugs for the burns. I'll program Halcyone to run the entire flight sequence and patch it to my micro. If there's a problem, you'll know about it."

Yes. He would. At least until the ship broke apart or depressurized or got lost in jump-space. "See you on the other side."

Ro paused at his door, but didn't say anything. They both knew it was too late to back out.

*

Jem opened his eyes to an unfamiliar room. It took him several minutes to remember where he was. The sleep had cleared his head, but didn't do much for his anxiety. After washing up, he walked to the door and triggered it. When it opened, he sagged against the wall of the compartment. So he wasn't a prisoner. At least not one confined to quarters. He gestured at his micro.

"Lethe, activate voice commands and voice feedback."

"Voice command and feedback mode on." The AI's voice sounded a lot like a digitized version of Dr. May's.

"Guide me to medical."

"Turn right. Proceed to the north nexus."

He risked glancing down at the schematic. It could have been the twin to Daedalus Station with its double ring and spoke design. If the sick bay was in the same location, Jem needed to access the command ring. He'd find out what May's assurances meant soon enough. The door to his assigned quarters closed behind him. Jem turned right, walking close to the curved wall so he could steady himself if he needed to. It was quiet and the lights were dimmed.

"Lethe, what is the local time?"

"Zero six hundred hours and twenty seven seconds."

He hadn't thought he'd slept that long. It would be nearly the end of third shift back on Daedalus. Nomi would probably be sitting in the midst of her sparkling ansible network display. He wondered what Ro and Barre were doing. Probably trying to follow his trail. They would at least get to Galileo 3. Beyond that? Even if Jem could hack into the ansible network—assuming Ithaka had one—he had no idea where in the cosmos he was.

What chance did they have of finding him?

He was on his own here, which is what he had wanted. So why was he so conflicted? He stopped in the empty corridor. If they went by the standard Hub-centric clock, medical would be ready for shift change soon.

Voices echoed off the metal walls. Jem froze as several people walked toward him. They were joking and laughing, and if it weren't for their clothes, Jem would have believed he had woken up back on Daedalus. They were all wearing neutral-colored coveralls that were identical to May's. There were no insignia, no ranks or identifications of any kind. No one had any sidearms, either. But they all had the same wrist cuffs.

Jem fiddled with his cuff. Even Charon didn't have any weapons. He hadn't needed any, judging by how easily the ferryman controlled Jem through the metal band.

They fell silent as they passed Jem, looking at him with mild curiosity. He kept walking. Between the residence ring and medical, he passed dozens of people. A few nodded to him, but most ignored him. No greetings. No questions. Probably everyone here knew who he was. It made him uneasy. Jem was used to being ignored, but not like this.

In the north nexus, he tapped his wrist against the ident plate.

The door opened onto the command ring—or what would have been the command ring on Daedalus. But instead of discrete walled-off compartments, most of the area was an open space, divided by clear terraforming bubbles like Micah had used for his plant breeding. Jem groped for the rail in the corridor as he was hit by a wave of vertigo. Too much brightness. Too much motion. Too much open space. Groaning, he closed his eyes.

Charon's hoarse voice whispered into his ear. "I told the doc we should've left you on Gal-3, but this is her show."

"What is this place?"

"Welcome to the heart of Ithaka. Where the best and the brightest, or at least the most frustrated and the rebellious, come to play."

"I don't understand." Jem opened his eyes, blinking against the harsh lighting.

"Do you know why the Commonwealth hates us?"

Jem didn't risk answering. Ithaka was the home of the rebellion. They were the ones who'd started the war. Who wanted to destabilize the government.

"You think we're the enemy. It's what they taught you in school. It's what everyone's been conditioned to believe. But that's not why they want to find this place and turn it back into elemental particles."

"Then why?"

Charon smiled and half of his face puckered, his lips twisting into a jagged line. "The doc says you're smart enough to figure it out. I think she's wrong about you, but we'll see."

Jem had to resist the urge to try to tug off the cuff. "Why are you helping me?"

"Because she asked me to." Charon stared at Jem until he closed his eyes again, discomfited by the man's extensive scars. "Because she saved me when she could have left me behind. Because she never blamed me for following my orders."

Something May had said bumped up against Charon's words. "Wait. You were a Commonwealth soldier."

Charon didn't answer. "Come on. Medical's this way."

Jem hesitated. Following orders. What had this man

done? Charon never turned back and Jem had to race to catch up with him. The visual chaos made his balance even worse. He wanted to stop until the vertigo eased, but Charon didn't slow his pace.

Medical was at twelve o'clock on the outer command ring, just as it was on Daedalus. In contrast to the open space in most of the ring on Ithaka, it was in an enclosure. Charon triggered the door and waited outside until Jem entered. The door closed a centimeter from his back with Charon on the other side. Jem's heart beat double time. Would the door open for him again? Was he trapped here?

The sounds of the medical bay—the beeping of monitoring equipment, the low hushed conversations of the staff, even a cry of pain—created a familiar music. It was strangely comforting. He could do this. Jem looked up into the sharp gaze of a tall man. Dressed in the same bland coveralls as everyone else here, he might have been the chief medical officer or a janitor.

"I've been expecting you."

"Then you have the advantage over me."

"Damiano Land." He put his hand out. Jem clasped it automatically.

"Dr. Land. You weren't just a bot."

When he smiled, his eyes nearly disappeared. "No. I am very much a real person. A neurocyberneticist, to be precise. You've come a long way to see me, I think."

It was hard not to smile back. Dr. Land had an intense enthusiasm that came through even in such a generic exchange. The doctor leaned forward slightly, with his head tilted as if not wanting to miss the next thing Jem said. "Can you help me?" Jem's voice caught. He blinked back tears he hadn't shed despite disappointment after disappointment.

Dr. Land handed him a gauze square from one of the deep pockets in his coverall and steered him into a small office. "Let's talk in private, shall we?"

Jem sat across from Land's desk. The tall man sat and leaned his elbows on its pitted surface, interlacing his long fingers. "Lethe, lights at fifteen percent, please."

"Certainly, Doctor."

It was disconcerting to hear Dr. May's voice in the AI. "Thank you," Jem said.

"We were able to scrape some of your records, but I'll still need to do some scans. Our equipment is somewhat specialized."

"You're not going to tell me I'm too young? That I need to be patient? That I'll learn to adapt?" The bitterness that spilled out of Jem had been trapped inside for weeks.

"Would that change your mind?"

"No." Jem crumpled the wet gauze in his fist.

"Then such platitudes are a waste of of time for both of us. You're here. At least let's see what's possible first."

Jem closed his eyes and exhaled heavily. "You're not what I expected."

"For a black market doc?"

"I didn't ... I mean ..." His face burned with heat.

"No. I'm sorry. That was out of line."

He looked up again, studying Land's face. "You don't think Dr. May should have let me come either."

"It doesn't matter what I thought. You're here now. That makes you my patient. You of all people should understand what that means."

His parents had treated anyone who needed help. No matter their beliefs. They treated prisoners with the same care as heads of state. They weren't perfect people by any stretch of the imagination, but they were good doctors and Jem respected that, even when he wished they could be better parents. "So what's the plan?"

"We do a brain scan. Then an arteriogram. Though the route of entry is less problematic than the implant itself. If all your tests look good, then we can talk about the risks and potential benefits."

"Doc, if you were the patient, would you do it?"

Land paused and watched Jem for several seconds, his face unreadable. "If you were in my position, would you?"

Jem had no answer.

"Let's get you prepped for the brain scan. I'm going to give you a light sedative. Do you have any allergies?"

"No."

"When did you eat last?"

He hadn't touched any of the food Dr. May had brought and barely sipped the coffee she'd handed him. "I don't know. Before I landed at Gal-3. However long ago that was."

Dr. Land nodded. "Good."

So the good doc wasn't going to let slip anything about how far Jem had traveled, either. He'd have to figure it out some other way. Dr. May had to realize she had issued him a challenge, not a warning, when she told him about Lethe. Jem smiled. Ro would be proud of him.

Chapter 17

Ro worked her way from the airlock to engineering and finally the bridge, stowing loose gear and checking systems as she headed back to her quarters. Everything was as shipshape as she could make it. She opened a direct voice channel between her micro and Barre's. "You set?"

"Aye, aye, Captain."

"Aye, aye, yourself. Get secured. There won't be a lot of time between the initial burn and our first jump. Our deepest burn will be close to three g's. And before you ask me to recalculate, it's the best compromise between speed, safety, and the risk of overshooting a jump."

There was a brief moment of silence before Barre answered. "I know."

"We'll get there."

"Roger, that," Barre said.

After securing her jump snug, Ro swallowed a handful of space-sickness tablets. She hated the way jumps made her feel as if her stomach had turned inside out. If that was half of what Jem experienced just trying to get through a normal day, she understood why he had run away. But a black market neural? That was a risk no one should have to take. There had to be a better option for him.

"Okay, baby, time for you to shine." Ro paired her micro with Halcyone and initiated the holographic interface. Jem's work. Brilliant and elegant. It would be a tragedy if he couldn't continue to code. Despite her own sense of urgency, Ro carefully examined the nav program she had written. It linked the jumps to a series of precise burns, each designed to get Halcyone close enough to each wormhole to minimize transit time and the effects on the ship and her and Barre.

What she had told Barre was true. This was the safest course she could plot. All the wormholes were fairly short and extremely stable. Nothing had altered local space where they were traveling. But it didn't mean there wasn't risk. Every jump was a risk. Any engineer would tell you they hated jumping, because they knew in intricate detail all the things that could go catastrophically wrong.

"Halcyone, check jump equations Alpha, Beta, and Gamma."

"All equations valid."

It should have eased Ro's worry. But no amount of sims could save a ship from a bad jump. She wriggled into the snug, her micro secured in a mesh pocket within reach. "Halcyone, file final flight plan and obtain launch approval." There. That would appease Mendez.

"Launch is a go."

"Halcyone, load launch sequence 'Jem,' sixty-second delay."

"Program loaded and ready."

Ro triggered the snug, wincing as the bag tightened around her. "Execute."

The minute seemed to last an hour. Finally, when Ro thought the program had terminated, her weight doubled, pushing her into the jump snug's impersonal embrace. At least it was a hell of a lot more gentle than Halcyone's first wild burn. The burn that had cracked Ro's ankle and given Jem the head injury that ultimately led to this trip.

Just when Ro had decided that the acceleration had gone on too long and something was wrong, it stopped. Her breathing eased. "Halcyone, countdown time to first jump." She hoped Barre was secure. And that he'd taken the space-sickness tablets.

The AI's calm voice counted down to zero and Ro remembered why she hated jump travel. Rumor had it that there were some people who weren't affected by the twisting of time and reality in a wormhole, but Ro figured that had to be a lie. Without an external horizon to track, her brain was bombarded by mixed signals, her eyes at war with her inner ear, her kinesthetics, and her viscera. Even with the meds, she felt her stomach twist.

There was a reason most spacers didn't eat for at least an hour before jump time.

"Jump Alpha complete. Commencing second burn in five, four, three, two, one, go."

Then Ro was flattened again as Halcyone sped through interstitial space to their next jump. Even knowing exactly what was happening as it happened, Ro was miserable. She could only imagine how much worse it was for Barre. There wasn't a lot of time to feel sorry for him before they jumped again and she lost all sense of time as well as the contents of her stomach, as meager as they were.

*

The scans were routine, if the setting was not. There was something perversely comforting about being a patient for the moment. For being taken care of. For as far back as Jem could remember, his parents had pushed him and Barre to be self-sufficient. That included things like dealing with cuts, bruises, sprains, and burns. Pretty much anything that didn't require surgical-level care was left up to them. It made Jem very skilled at triage, which was not something most people twice his age could say.

Dr. May was waiting for him in medical. "It will be at least an hour or so before Damiano and his team come up with a consensus. While you're waiting, I want to show you something."

Jem wanted to object, but he'd spent enough time waiting in medical bays lately. And besides, this was Adiana May, coinventor of the SIREN code. And she wanted to show him something. The sedative Dr. Land had given him had damped down the vertigo and nausea a lot better than the space-sickness tablets had. Maybe now he'd be able to keep some food down. Maybe even play with his micro a little.

"Fine. Can I eat on the way?"

May nodded. "I can do better than that. Lethe, have

lunch for two delivered to my lab, please."

"Certainly, Dr. May."

"Don't you ever get tired of talking to yourself?"

"It wasn't my idea. My colleagues thought it would be amusing." She laughed and for a moment the bitterness eased. Jem laughed with her.

"What happened to you?" As soon as he asked the question, he regretted it. Her expression closed down, all hints of her smile disappeared. They walked the rest of the way around the command ring and its busy manufacturing and development pods until they stopped at a security door.

May waved her cuff, but motioned for him to wait.

"Lethe, security override, computer lab. Set access parameters for Durbin, Jeremy: approved with escort."

"Durbin, Jeremy, approved with escort. Please tap security cuff for confirmation."

Jem stood, waiting.

"That means you," May said.

"Oh." Jem pulled up his sleeve and touched the cuff to the ident plate.

"Durbin, Jeremy, access confirmed."

"Thank you." Ro always teased him about being polite to the AI, but it seemed weird not to acknowledge something talking to you.

"Just to make this explicit, so there's no risk of you misunderstanding. If you attempt to access this area without an approved escort, you'll be rendered unconscious and security will be called."

Jem fiddled with the cuff and nodded.

"Well, let's see what you're made of," May said, her tone

brighter. She stepped into her lab. Jem followed, stopping short just inside the room. It was larger than Halcyone's bridge, but smaller than the cargo bays. One wall was a huge viewscreen. The largest holoprojector Jem had ever seen was built into a workstation to its right. In the center of the lab was a sitting area with a sofa and several soft chairs around a low table. A tray with small sandwiches and stay-hot mugs of coffee had been placed there, but whoever brought it had gone. Jem and Dr. May were alone in the lab.

He didn't know where to look first. This was Adiana May's computer lab. The look on Ro's face when he told her would be priceless. His smile faded. There was a good chance Jem would never be able to share this with her, regardless of May's promises. This was Ithaka. They didn't trust him. Jem had to remember that.

"Have something to eat, first. Then I'll show you around."

Jem nibbled on a few sandwiches. They were just enough to quiet his stomach, though fairly tasteless. The chair he sat on was worn, the material thin and shiny in spots. He glanced up at the wall-sized screen and then back at the chipped table.

"Our resources go into what's important. Uniforms and furniture are not."

Or food, judging by the generic protein spread. "It looks pretty hi-tech out there."

"Have you figured out why yet?"

"You do the R and D. Then sell what you invent throughout the Commonwealth via contacts in the black market."

May clapped her hands. "Bravo."

"But you're working against them." Jem frowned. "Right?"

"It's a different kind of arms race. Why do you think they created the system of Hub universities and their scholarship programs? They know if they don't snag the most talented students, Ithaka will." She leaned forward. "I know for a fact that several were already interested in you."

"Until this." Jem gestured at his scarred head. So far the nystagmus was manageable. But the effects of the sedative wouldn't last forever.

"Tell me."

"Tell you what?"

"How you were injured."

"I thought you had a dossier on me."

"Our methods are not perfect. And we have only had a few days to put it together. I'm curious. Some of your records have been redacted."

"Redacted?" Why would the Commonwealth go to the trouble of blanking out some of his data?

"All references to your accident have been removed. To be honest, your code got me curious. The coverup in your records sealed the deal."

"You don't know about Halcyone."

"Halcyone?" May leaned forward again, her eyes bright.

"A ship. A wreck from the war. Daedalus was built around it." Jem thought back to his first glimpse of her ruined bridge. How all he saw was the gleaming ship she had once been. "The code mods I wrote. We grafted them onto the SIREN source code. To repair the AI."

"Go on."

"It worked. Sort of." Jem ran his fingers along the scar. "No. It did work. The only problem was Halcyone was as damaged as I am. She blasted off from Daedalus in full fight-or-flight mode. Totally melted down."

"And?"

"We got jumbled around. My head slammed into a bulkhead. The rest you probably know."

May was staring past him, frowning. "Who named her Halcyone?"

"That's what she called herself."

"What kind of ship was she?"

"A freighter. One of the bumblebees."

"Halcyone." May turned back to Jem. "That was one of mine. The AI was one of the original ship controllers. First gen. She's still running?"

"No. I mean yes." He scratched his head where his growing hair made the scars itch. "She was dormant for decades. Since the war. Then we woke her up."

"We?"

She didn't know about Ro. Should he tell her? Halcyone was Ro's ship now. "Me. My brother. Our friends." Let her think Jem had been the force behind Halcyone's resurrection. Safer for Ro that way.

"Where is the ship now?"

Jem shrugged. "Docked on Daedalus. The jump drive is damaged. Really, it's a wonder the ship can fly at all."

"You are an interesting young man. I was right to bring you here." May set her coffee cup down and stood. "Come on. I think you'll like this."

He followed her to the corner of the room that held the holoprojector.

"Your idea was pretty elegant."

She didn't add 'for a kid.'

"And all you had was a micro to do the actual grafting?"

"It was the only way. Halcyone was too badly damaged for us to directly access her code, and there was no way to link her with the station's AI." Jem picked at a seam in his pants. "Well, there might have been a way, but it wasn't officially sanctioned." He glanced up at May and she raised an eyebrow. "And at that point, only her autonomics were functioning anyway. So that's what we did."

"Let me show you my sandbox," May said. A grin transformed her face and for the moment, the cynical woman faded away. The light in her eyes reminded Jem of Ro, lost in her work. In another life, another universe, Adiana May might have been Ro's teacher and mentor. But that was before the war with the Commonwealth had changed everything.

Dr. May triggered the holoprojector. For an instant the room went dark. Then pieces of code assembled around them, each a colored block floating in space. Each block was inscribed with a symbol. One tumbled closer to him and Jem touched it with a finger. The block spun end over end. He cupped it in his palm; it had mass. Or at least it tingled against the skin of his hand. Reaching out, he tapped the corner nearest him when it flashed with a blue light. The box opened and flattened into a two-dimensional square. Lines of code wrote themselves on the virtual sheet of paper.

"Wow," he whispered. "How did you do that?" Ro should be here, not him. She would intuitively grasp the system May had devised and figure out how to use it to create astonishing code. Jem was good, but he wasn't as good as she was.

"Want to see what your code mods look like?"

"Hell yeah."

May swept her work away. The bright blocks jumbled together before disappearing. "Here you go." New blocks appeared in the space between them and assembled into what looked like a crystalline shape. "The yellow represents definitions and variables. The blue, commands. Red shows the real-time interactions as the program runs. The more symmetrical the shape, the cleaner the program. And yours is quite lovely."

"You made that from my code?"

"Your program is unchanged. This is just another way to visualize it. You can work in code view or in holographic view. Like this." She waved her hand and again Jem thought of Ro. The colors melted away and his program wrote itself, line by line, in the air in front of him. The moving text triggered a wave of dizziness.

Jem groaned. "I'm sorry. I can't ..." He reached out for the wall, but misjudged the direction in the visual chaos and tripped over the low table. The floor met him, hard. Pain spiked through his head. His lunch tasted and smelled a lot worse on the way out. Not the way he'd wanted to impress Dr. May, but he figured she'd never forget him, now.

"Lethe, lights daylight normal."

The holoprojector powered down with a low whine. The room brightened. Jem wished it hadn't. Dr. May handed him a damp cloth.

"So it's as bad as your records say."

"This was a goddamned test?"

She sat down as Jem used the chair to pull himself up off the floor. His vision had quieted, as had his stomach. The nausea was always better for at least a little while after he vomited. He threw the cloth on the spreading mess before folding his arms and glaring at her.

"Less a test and more a corroboration."

"You're making it really hard to like you."

"That's not my job. My job is to keep Ithaka and its people safe. And to fully vet any potential candidates."

The AI interrupted. "Incoming message from Land, Damiano."

"Patch him through, please."

"We have Jem's test results."

He jerked fully upright. He didn't have to like Adiana May. He didn't have to like Ithaka or The Underworld or any deal they needed him to make. He just needed a neural. And May's little stunt here only proved to him how badly.

"We'll be there shortly." She turned to him. "Ready?"

*

Nomi turned over the logs to her first-shift replacement and headed out of comms, yawning. It had been another quiet night. Struggling to stay awake, she spent much of her shift walking a circuit of the room. As she'd feared, there was no message from Jem. Now, having been up for more than a full day, all she wanted was to fall into bed.

She headed to the residence ring on automatic pilot, answering morning greetings with a grunt. The mystery of the missing logs pulled at her. As did Lowell's strange behavior. There was no logical reason why a senior officer would want a third-shift stint. Unless he was doing something that couldn't bear scrutiny. Could Lowell have been the one to erase the log entries? Nomi didn't think he had the clearance. Lowell and Gutierrez. Now she was seeing conspiracies everywhere.

What had Ro done to her?

With a sigh, Nomi walked past her quarters and headed to Simon's room. He was already cooking; the scent of Cajun spices had wafted into the corridor. She announced herself and the door opened. Her eyes watered at the aromatic assault.

"Come on in!" Simon called. "Hope you like it hot!"

Nomi smiled. "How's the rice?"

"Dirty."

"Need any help?"

"You've managed to show up just in time to watch me clean up." He handed her a cup of fresh coffee.

"Oh, man, that's good." It was worth the caffeine jolt that would keep her tossing in bed hours into her off shift.

"See? Can Ro do this for you?"

Nomi took another sip, hiding her face behind the cup.

Laughing, Simon started loading bowls and utensils into

the cleanser unit. "So how's things on the graveyard shift?"

"Why do they call it that?"

"Because it's quiet and peaceful?"

She yawned into her now empty cup. "More likely because you get bored to death."

"Well, they can't keep you on it forever. You know, they used to rotate us through there until recently."

"I know. Lowell told me. He almost seems disappointed I'm still assigned." Nomi stood next to Simon at the counter and handed him her cup. He reached for the carafe, but she shook her head. "Either he's an insomniac or he's worried about my mental health."

"Don't think you're so special. I think he misses the overtime bonus."

"Seriously?"

"Yup. He used to offer to take mine as an extra shift whenever I got rotated to third. It wasn't out of the goodness of his heart."

Gutierrez assigned Nomi to this shift. The LC probably figured the most junior member of the staff wouldn't complain too loudly. And it got Lowell away from comms at night. Nomi ran her hands through her hair as if tugging at her head would pull her thoughts together.

"Look, I'm sure you could put in a request through Mendez. The rotation wasn't so bad. None of us minded all that much. And the crew thinks it's unfair to stick it to you. Seriously. It was just one extra shift every couple of cycles."

"Actually, I don't mind it." Ro was a night person, and she often found an excuse to come up to comms during Nomi's break time.

"Better watch out or command will think you're searching for Ithaka on work time."

Nomi's hands grasped the edge of the counter. "What?"

"Don't tell me they've stopped tantalizing the comms students with stories of the famous lost colony!" He smiled before refilling his cup. "There's a huge prize offered by some anonymous donor. It'd be enough to buy your own small planet, or close to it. Get Lowell drunk enough and he'll tell you all about how he'd spend the credits."

Her heart rate returned to its normal speed and she relaxed her hands. This was almost too close to what she had told Gutierrez in the commissary. "Yeah, that's still a thing. There's always some wager going on between the nav and the comms classes. No one's been able to claim the money yet."

If Lowell had erased the logs, then he also suspected a connection between Jem, The Underworld, and Ithaka. It didn't make sense. How would he have figured that out? Her thoughts returned to Gutierrez and the way she'd looked at Nomi's search results in the commissary. And what was the bad blood between the comms officer and the LC? She wanted to ask Simon, but felt that she'd already said too much.

"Well, if you're not searching for phantoms, what are you doing up there in the quiet?"

"It gives me time to think."

Simon burst out laughing. "I figured Daedalus would have cured you of that by now. You've been here, what, twelve, fourteen weeks? Do your work. Don't expect much in the way of interesting and your time here will be over soon enough." He checked his micro. "I have seven months, one week, and four days before I can have real gumbo in a real restaurant, instead of what I can pull together here."

"Well, it smells like the real deal. And a lot better than what's in the commissary. When's dinner?"

"You sure you're ready to feel the burn?"

His gumbo would have nothing on her grandfather's wasabi.

Chapter 18

DR. MAY WALKED him back to medical, letting Jem set the pace. Sweat beaded across his forehead and his stomach cramped. Would they recommend a neural? Would they refuse him one? There were no guarantees. He had no idea what kind of pull May had. If she really wanted him here, could she overrule the docs if they said no?

Did she really want Jem to work for Ithaka? Would it make him a traitor? At this point, he wasn't sure he really cared.

He thought of Barre and stopped short, his hand slick on the railing. If it meant never being able to see his brother again, then yes, Jem did care.

"Everything all right?" May asked.

Jem didn't risk shaking his head. "Just outstanding," he said, his voice thick with sarcasm. "Everything's auroras and quasars."

She answered him with a sigh and stayed silent until they stood by the door in medical. "This is where I leave you. I trust you will make the decision that is best for you."

"Where are you going?" The question sounded a lot more desperate than Jem intended it to be. It wasn't that he liked Dr. May. He didn't even really trust her. But she was familiar in a way Dr. Land was not.

"When you're done here, have someone escort you back to my lab."

"Fine." Jem waited beside the door to medical until May's uneven footfalls faded away. He dried his damp palms on his pants. This is what he wanted. If they couldn't help him, no one could. And if he walked away now, he would never know. With trembling hands, he signaled for entry.

The door opened. Just as before, Dr. Land was waiting for him. Jem tried to read his face, but the doctor's expression was full-on professional neutral. Cold gathered in the pit of Jem's stomach. In his experience, that usually meant bad news.

"The team is in the conference room. We can review your scans together."

Jem followed him, feeling as if he was heading toward his own memorial service.

The room was mostly one large table surrounded by eight chairs. Four of them were filled. Three men and one woman sat waiting, dressed in what Jem thought of as Ithaka's generic uniform. One of the men looked at him with open curiosity. The rest didn't glance up from their micros. Land took the seat at the head of the table. He gestured for Jem to sit opposite him.

"Jem Durbin, our team. Mariana Chote, our head researcher." The woman nodded and smiled. "Wen Yingjie is the neurointerventionalist who will do the actual deployment." A compact man with long, slender fingers looked up at Jem briefly before returning to his micro. "Terrance Brown is our neuropsychologist, and Martin Johnson is our ethicist."

Land waved with one hand and the lights dimmed. A three-dimensional representation of a brain hovered over the center of the table, rotating slowly. "This is the holo-imagery of your resting brain."

Jem knew enough neurology to identify the different functional areas, but he couldn't tell where the damage was.

The doctor gestured again. It was as if someone had poured a prism of color through the model. Streaks of red, blue, yellow, and green traveled across the map of Jem's mind.

"This was when we had you complete several cognitive and physical tasks. It's a simplification and vastly slowed down, but it helps tell the story. Blue is sensory data. Yellow is motor activity. Green is healthy synapse response. Red shows abnormal signal."

There was a lot of red. And it wasn't only in one area. Jem rubbed the scar where it traveled across his head.

"There is damage from two basic processes." Land manipulated the model. The colors stopped pulsing, and instead of the whole brain, the display showed a series of slices. "You sustained a minor bleed. That's why they had to do the emergency surgery. There are other ways of dealing with hemorrhages, but by the time you received help, the damage was already done."

Clearly Dr. Land had been trained in the same brutal truth school as Jem's parents. Jem took a deep breath and tried to focus on the words as if Land were talking about someone else.

"But the more significant problem is also more subtle." He put the slices back together into the whole. "Your original trauma caused diffuse axonal injury. When you got bounced around, your head decelerated at a faster rate than your brain. Your brain continued to move around in your skull, and the shearing forces caused damage to axons throughout its structure."

"Tell me something I don't already know." Jem could have given this exact lecture on head injury, now that he was living it from the inside.

Dr. Chote stood up. "Dr. Land asked me to give you some background."

Jem nodded, still unsure of where this was leading. A clean, surgical 'no' would be preferable to this drawn-out process.

"The technology that led to the current neural implant came out of the war. The first prototype was a trans-cranial receiver that allowed soldiers with prosthetics to control their artificial limbs using their own sensorimotor systems." She tapped her micro and Jem's brain disappeared, replaced by the image of an upper-extremity amputee wearing what looked like a clumsy headset. "Once the nanoemitters were perfected, we were able to boost the relevant neural signals and use smaller and smaller control modules. Now we can deploy the emitters to the brain through the vascular system and slip the transmitter under the skin."

Jem looked down at his hand, opening and closing his fingers.

"Neurals work because axonal activation creates electrical activity. The nanoemitters read that activity, amplify it, and broadcast it to the transmitter." The injured soldier was replaced by a schematic of a brain. A silver web originating from multiple sources spread across both hemispheres. "That is a near-field quasi neural net. It allows the transmitter to integrate signals from all over the brain. Part of the integration process is to learn how to control the input and create a cohesive output."

Barre had done it. Jem knew he could, too.

"We generally don't do this in the immature patient. There is some concern about long-term effects of near-field stimulation on the developing brain. And with the subject's ..." Land cleared his throat and Chote nodded an apology before rewording her statement. "With your head injury, it becomes an open question whether you can manage the training."

The woman sat. "Thank you, Mariana," Land said. "Yingjie?"

He looked up from his micro and nodded. "We are also concerned about the distribution of the nanites for maximum effectiveness of the net given your brain injury. However, there is nothing abnormal about the vascular anatomy. Deployment would be routine."

"Martin?"

Dr. Johnson cleared his throat and stood, studying Jem. The lines on his face made frowning his natural expression.

"An ethicist? Seriously?"

"We are not a group of mad scientists, young man." Jem immediately took a dislike to him and his patronizing tone of voice. "Because you are underage, we must approach your request with greater scrutiny. It is up to you to convince us you are making this decision with full understanding of the potential risks, benefits, and consequences."

Jem risked staring back at the man, hoping his nystagmus would make him uncomfortable. "I know the risks and consequences of doing nothing. If I can't get a neural here and now, I'm four years away from any hope of one out there. Four years of being unable to function. And even if I'm a candidate then, then what? What I know, what I can do, will be outdated, useless. I'll be useless." His eyes started to shift back and forth and he leaned forward, his palms flat on the table, daring the man to look away. "It's not even that I can't program. I can't read. I can't use a computer. I can't even walk a straight line without throwing up most days. What do you expect me to do? So there are risks. I know the statistics. But I also know this statistic and it's more accurate than any studies you can cite: I am one hundred percent sure that this is the only future for me."

Johnson blinked and looked away. Jem slumped back in his seat, sweating, the saliva pooling in his mouth.

"I would say Mr. Durbin understands the risks, benefits, and consequences of this procedure," Dr. Land said. "Do you concur?"

A moment's silence fell in the room. Jem kept his eyes closed.

"Then we are agreed. There are no absolute contraindications, Jem."

He opened his eyes and looked up at Dr. Land, his heart beating wildly.

"However, we believe it is important to temper your expectations. Aside from the typical complications of accessing the brain, even in a minimally invasive way, you present a special set of issues. There's a good chance the neural won't create a functioning near-field net, given the widespread damage. If that's the case, there are several possible points of failure. You may not be able to establish a full link between your thoughts and the field, between the field and the control module, or between the module and any connected devices."

"I'm willing to take that chance."

"It could cause new damage. Make things worse," Dr. Chote said.

Jem swallowed against the lump in his throat. "I know. No matter what my parents say, I know and they know the odds of my brain healing much more are slim. This is a chance to get my life back."

"Lethe, please record consent of Durbin, Jeremy to undergo neural implantation."

"Recording."

"Jeremy, do you understand the risks as they have been outlined to you, including but not limited to risks related to sedation, to deployment of nanoemitters, and to insertion of hardware?"

"Yes."

"And do you further understand that this procedure is not an approved treatment for traumatic brain injury and may make your symptoms and functioning worse?"

"Yes."

"And do you understand that even if the procedure itself

is successful, there still may be complications in the training and orientation for this device?"

Jem sighed. "Yes."

"Lethe, end recording."

"Recording complete."

Jem pressed his hands on the table top to stop them from trembling. "How soon can we do this?"

"The catheters and deployment system can be printed in a few hours," Dr. Wen said.

"Terrance?"

The neuropsychologist looked up from his micro. "I have several sets of assessments from his records. This young man has a very well-studied cognitive process."

His parents had paid for the best and most thorough of specialists. Jem dreaded running through the tests again.

"They are consistent. I can use them as his baseline."

"Martin?"

The ethicist sighed, and Jem held his breath.

"I can offer no formal objections. His consent has been obtained without coercion and with full understanding."

Jem exhaled heavily. His shoulders dropped.

"However, I would like to state for the record that I am concerned at the precedent this sets."

"Noted," Dr. Land said. "Any further questions?"

As the rest of the team left the conference room, Jem realized Land was talking to him. "No. I'm good."

"Nervous?"

"Yeah."

"I'd be worried if you weren't. I think you have unfinished business with Ada."

Jem nodded.

"When you're done speaking with her, we'll prep you for the procedure. Nothing to eat or drink until then."

That shouldn't be all that hard. Even taking into account the vertigo and nausea, his stomach was in knots.

"One of the techs will take you to the computer lab. See you in a few hours."

"Doc?" Jem put his hand on Land's sleeve. "Thank you."

"Don't thank me yet," he said.

Jem shivered as he followed the tall doctor out of the conference room.

*

Dr. May was standing next to the sitting area, waiting for him. She'd cleaned up the floor where Jem had vomited. The tray of food had vanished. The only thing left was the faint combined odor of protein spread and industrial cleanser. "So you've made your decision."

Of course Land had briefed her.

"And have you considered the cost?"

Her voice echoed in his mind: *Your future, your potential, your loyalty.* Without a neural, Jem had no future. And if the Commonwealth and all its resources couldn't help him, did he really have another choice? Besides, he was just a kid. He didn't know any government secrets. It wasn't like his parents had any particular political connections. "I'm not going to hurt anyone for you."

"Is that what you think, Jem?"

Jem pressed his spine against the door. "I don't know what to think. You're the enemy, right?"

"We're not your enemy. We want to help you. Help you find your potential in a place where you have the freedom to pursue your ideas."

"I'm sure it's all sunshine and happiness here on the utopia of Ithaka."

May glared at him. "You haven't earned the right to that degree of cynicism."

"I know when I'm being sold something."

She limped around to the front of the chair and sat. "Everyone's always selling something. We happen to be a bit more transparent about it than the Commonwealth. We think you're worth our investment."

"So I'll be supporting the same black market that nearly started a war with smuggled weapons and just about got me and my friends killed in the process."

"I have no idea what you're talking about."

"Oh, I forgot. That information was redacted. So how could you know?"

"Jem, come and sit down." May sighed. "Believe me or not, but there's a lot about the arrangement with The Underworld I don't control. And more than a little I regret."

There was nothing to be gained from standing and Jem was starting to feel a little wobbly. He took a seat opposite her.

"Think about it for a moment. We gain nothing and risk everything from open warfare. The Commonwealth has a fleet. We have a few ships, no standing army, no caches of hidden weapons. We fight in other ways. Quieter ways. If

anyone is looking for out-and-out war, it's the Commonwealth, not us."

"I don't understand."

"There's been relative peace for forty years. There are
those even within the Commonwealth who believe that
priorities are skewed and more resources should be devoted
to commerce and technology instead of the military. What
does a military organization do when it feels its relevance
threatened?"

"Don't tell me you believe the radiation from traveling
through wormholes turns people into zombies, too."

"It's only a conspiracy theory if it's not true."

Jem dropped his head into his hands. "I don't know what
to believe anymore."

"Believe this. You may need us, but we also need you."

Her uneven footsteps rang in the room. She placed her
hand on his shoulder. Jem looked up into her tired face.

"I've been looking for someone who could take my work
into the future. Maybe you're that person. Maybe you're not.
But if you never get the chance to try, I'll never know."

A shiver moved through him, part anticipation, part
terror. Ro was much better at this than he was. She was the
one Dr. May wanted. He looked away again. But Ro wasn't
here, and she wasn't the one who needed a neural. "Fine. But
if I find out you're lying to me, I'll walk away. I'll find a way
to lead the Commonwealth right to your doorstep."

"I wish Chaz could have met you. You're so much like he
was. Before."

The ache in her voice made Jem want to give her a hug.
But she wasn't Barre or Ro. He didn't really know who she

was or if she had anything in common with the young, brilliant programmer Jem had idolized for years.

"So are you going to draw up an agreement? Have the AI witness it?"

She shook her head. "I think we both know where we stand."

Chapter 19

It could have been worse. Maybe. Halcyone could have cut off life support, or they could have crash-landed on Galileo 3. In either case, Barre figured he'd have been put out of his misery by now. His room was sour with sweat and his head felt like someone was playing a full drum-set inside it.

"We made it." Ro's voice coming through his micro sounded as shaky as he felt.

"Meet you in the bridge?"

"Sounds good."

Barre wriggled out of the jump snug. It would be less than pleasant to have to wrap himself back in its sweaty embrace, but it beat using only the worn-out acceleration foam. Jump sickness wasn't pretty, and even though it could be treated now, it left its mark on survivors.

Rolling off the bunk, Barre hit the ground hard and grunted. Well, he was certainly awake. He took a minute to check how his instruments had fared in transit and to wipe the sweat from his face with a wet towel before heading to meet Ro.

Her voice wasn't the only thing that matched how he felt. She looked wilted.

"If we're going to be doing that more, we're going to have to figure out a more permanent solution than the jump snugs," Bare said.

"Everyone's a critic."

"I should demand my money back." He dropped into the comms station chair and looked up at the cracked screen. Galileo 3 spun like a slow top orbited by dozens of small satellites, ansible nodes, and ships coming and going. "So what's the plan?"

"Well, Jem didn't answer my message."

Barre sighed. "Did you think it would be that simple?"

"No. We have clearance to dock. Maybe someone will remember seeing him."

Either Ro was being extremely naive or she was staying optimistic for his sake. Most of Gal-3 was a transient way station. In the handful of hours since Jem arrived here, thousands of people had moved through it. "We knew it was a long shot."

"Fine. Let's dock and show his picture around. Maybe we'll get lucky."

Ro mumbled something to Halcyone about a docking bay. Barre figured she could take care of it. Finding a picture of Jem would be a more difficult challenge. His parents didn't take family holos; the only image he could find was of their official intake when they had gotten to Daedalus. It was from less than a year ago, but Jem looked so much younger in it. He was missing the scar that carved its path across his head. And the defeated look in his eyes. In the official image, Jem looked excited, eager for whatever the universe would present to him. Barre didn't think he'd ever been like that, even when he was as young as his little brother.

"Jem, you idiot," he muttered.

"Barre?"

"Hmm?"

"What are you doing with Halcyone?"

He looked up. "What do you mean?"

"I was trying to send an ansible message to Daedalus, but Halcyone's not responding to my commands. Not the verbal. Not the holo interface. And we're moving."

"I'm not doing anything. I'm not even jacked in." Barre had ignored the low rumble beneath his feet, figuring Ro was giving the ship docking instructions. He glanced up. The station seemed smaller, more distant. "Where are we going?"

"Halcyone, review course and speed."

The ship ignored Ro's request. Barre triggered the command fanfare. "Sorry, I thought I'd fixed that. Halcyone, review course and speed."

The AI still didn't respond. Barre looked up again. Gal-3 had dwindled until it measured only a few centimeters in length on the viewscreen.

"Brace yourself. I'm going to try to isolate navigation and kill the process," Ro said.

Barre spread out his legs and stabilized his thighs against the wide lip at the edge of the seat. He clung to the armrests.

"In three, two, one." Ro triggered one of the fail-safes he'd programmed. The ship shuddered but didn't stop. The engines continued to thrum softly as Halcyone moved further away from Gal-3 in interstitial space. "I'm going to try that again."

Her voice was calm but Barre could see her growing tension in the tightness across her shoulders and the way Ro opened and closed her hands in a pressured rhythm.

"Fuck."

"Ro, what's happening?"

"Fuckfuckfuck."

"Ro!"

"We're headed for a wormhole."

"What?"

"We're going to jump. We're going to fucking jump." She stared at him, her eyes wide and glassy. "Go. Go. Go."

Barre launched himself out of the nav chair and the two of them reached the bridge door side by side. They raced through Halcyone's corridor. Ro slammed to a stop at her door. "Hurry," she urged him before slipping inside. Barre triggered his door release and jammed his legs into the damp jump snug. His heart slammed against his ribs with every beat. His breath burned in his throat. How much time did they have? He slid his arms into the snug and closed his eyes as it tightened down around him.

Silence.

He reached out to Halcyone, linking his neural to the AI and listened.

Silence.

Even when Halcyone was busy, she 'hummed' to herself. It was a strange outcome of the musical language he had taught her. But now, there was nothing. The ship seemed to hiccup beneath him. She was getting ready to jump.

He risked playing a few notes of what he thought of as his

basic hello. The sounds faded away in his mind. And then space folded him inside out as Halcyone took them through a wormhole, to a destination only the ship knew.

Barre lost track of the number of jumps Halcyone made. It was much worse than the trip from Daedalus Station to Galileo 3, if only because there hadn't been time to take any more of the space-sickness tablets. His stomach felt bruised. The room reeked of sweat and vomit. He had a lot more sympathy for what Jem had been going through.

He lay in the jump snug listening to the ship. They hadn't moved for at least twenty minutes; Barre couldn't stand being trapped in his room for another instant. "Ro?" He called out, hoping Halcyone's intercom system was still functional. "Ro? Are you all right?"

"I'm never jumping again." She groaned and Barre could well imagine what the inside of her quarters smelled like.

"Do you think we're done?"

"We'd better be. I'm getting out of here."

Barre disentangled himself from the snug, rolled it up, and shoved it in the recycler. Risking jump sickness had to be better than subjecting himself to that bag again. He pulled out the small sink. Contorting his body, he put his head under the faucet and let the water cool him down. He squeezed the water from his dreads before wetting a towel and sponging his face and hands clean. It was better than nothing.

"Deja vu," Barre said, meeting Ro in the bridge. Again, she looked like he felt. Her long hair was plastered against her head. She was wearing a clean shirt. "Where are we?"

"Haven't a clue."

"Gee, we've never been here before."

Ro laughed and it broke the tension and fear between them. Then she frowned again. "Can you get in?"

"I'll try." He didn't want to tell her about the unnatural silence he found earlier. And maybe now that they were wherever the AI had decided to take them, she would respond to him. Taking a deep breath, Barre triggered his neural, reaching out to the ship the way he had that first time, before they had even learned Halcyone's name. He played the equivalent of a basic scale, using all the myriad sounds the computer could create. The sound faded into silence. Barre waited. No response.

"Try again," Ro whispered. "Please."

Barre closed his eyes, focusing on his fear for Jem, for himself, and for Ro. He let the emotion crest over him in a wave. The wave turned into sound, the sound into music. *I need you to hear me. I need you to help us.* He played his fear in a loop, pausing between repetitions. It was like ancient sonar, sending out pulses of sound and listening for the echo.

A single warning tone nearly deafened him. It rang in his head and through the bridge. Ro winced.

Halcyone? Barre called to her, replaying the same tone, only softer, like a question.

"Proximity alert." Halcyone's flat voice filled the bridge.

"What the hell? Now it responds?" Ro asked. "Are we back in business? Barre?"

"I don't know. Maybe? Try a command."

"Halcyone, screen on, one-to-one magnification."

The cracked screen flared to life. Barre exhaled, his

breath whistling through his pursed lips. They were in orbit over a planet that wasn't a lot more colorful than Daedalus. "Where the hell are we?"

"Halcyone, identify location."

"Unable to determine."

"Seriously?" Ro turned to her micro.

"Proximity alert," Halcyone repeated.

"No shit," Ro said. "It's a planet."

"Um, Ro?" Barre stared at the screen as two small objects approached.

"What?"

"I don't think that's what she's talking about." As they got closer, they resolved into two flitters. "We have company."

"Fine. Halcyone, open comms."

"Comms open."

Ro flashed a smile at Barre. "Well, that's better, at least. Let's see if we can ask for directions. Small crafts approaching, this is the freighter Halcyone. Our navigation is malfunctioning. Request—"

Her message was interrupted by a loud clank. The ship rocked as first one, then another tow line was fired at them.

"What the hell?" Ro stared at Barre as if this were somehow his fault.

"Do not attempt to disengage clamps or we will be forced to fire."

Barre wedged himself between the console and the chair bolted in front of it. *Stay calm. Stay calm.* The melody he played sounded a soft counterpoint to his racing heart. The last time Halcyone felt threatened, she'd made an emergency burn. If she flipped out now, with two flitters attached, it would tear her apart.

Ro's knuckles whitened as she held on to the command chair back, but her steady voice broadcast over the open channel. "We are a Commonwealth ship, registration Epsilon Delta Niner Seven Nine—"

Again, she was cut off. "Set your engines for towing."

The ship bucked as the flitters pulled with their powerful engines. Halcyone pulled back.

"Shit. Halcyone! Stop!" Barre shouted. The vibration beneath his feet increased until it was an audible growl.

"Halcyone, power propulsion down and engage landing gear!" Ro ordered.

Barre sent a plea through his neural. The ship continued to rumble for a few seconds longer before her engines faded away to a soft whine. "Are we under arrest?"

"This has to be some mistake," Ro said. "We have a legal flight plan."

"But we're nowhere on that flight plan."

The flitters towed Halcyone in a smooth trajectory toward a small spaceport, planetside. The ship trembled as it entered the atmosphere, but the freighter was designed for planetary landings and their escorts seemed to know what they were doing. At the precise moment, they disengaged and Halcyone glided down, her landing gear snatched expertly by the docking mechanisms waiting for them.

"Now what?" Barre asked.

"I have no idea."

At least Halcyone was alive again. When he queried her through his neural, she responded, but she had no memory of her recent flight. The navigation system was a little frazzled. It kept trying to reconcile their current position with the coordinates of Galileo 3 and crashing. It was as if the AI had some kind of seizure.

Ro tugged on his arm. "Let's go meet our hosts."

"They don't seem like hosts." They seemed more like smugglers or cranky military types.

"No, they don't. But I'm not going to cower in here while we try to figure out who they are."

They headed to the air lock in time to watch Halcyone disengage the clamps. That was interesting. Why was she opening up without their approval? The door opened and two jump-suited guards, one man and one woman, stepped through. The man was slight. Old scars traversed his face and head, and disappeared beneath his shirt collar. The woman stood a full head taller than him—nearly eye to eye with Barre. Neither seemed to be wearing weapons, but they both were definitely former military. Barre had seen his parents treat enough wounded vets to know the look.

"Why have you taken my ship?" Ro demanded.

"You'll have to talk to her about it," the man said. He wasn't referring to his fellow guard. The way he said 'her' seemed significant. As if he referred to whoever it was in all capital letters. Barre and Ro shared a puzzled look.

"We are Commonwealth citizens outbound from Daedalus Station on official business," Ro said.

"This is not the Commonwealth," the woman said.

Barre stopped short. Not the Commonwealth. He caught Ro's wide-eyed gaze. If this wasn't Commonwealth space, it had to be The Underworld. How in the cosmos had Halcyone jumped here?

"You need to follow us," the woman said, in a way that brooked no disagreement. Her eyes were a nondescript brown, as was her short, spiky hair, but the sharp gaze she trained on the two of them was the look of someone who was used to being in command. And listened to. Tribal-style tattoos spiraled their way around her left arm. When Barre took a closer look, he could see thin silver threads of old scars hidden by the ink.

She turned back to the door. The man circled behind them. The two of them were really going to herd him and Ro out of Halcyone.

"Where are we?" Ro asked.

"Nowhere," the woman replied.

Barre's breath was trapped in his throat. There was only one place he knew of that didn't exist. And that was Ithaka. Was Jem here? Did he dare ask? Was his little brother also a prisoner?

The man pushed Ro in the center of her spine. "Come on. She wants to talk to you."

"Wait. What are you planning to do to our ship?" Barre asked.

"Your ship?" He smiled. "That's up to her."

Barre shut his mouth and walked, following the woman's lead.

*

A series of familiar beeps sounded above Jem.

"Telemetry is live."

LJ Cohen

He didn't know which of the lab techs was speaking. If this worked, he could thank them all later. If it didn't work, it wouldn't matter.

"Vitals are stable."

Jem figured his rapid heartbeat was something they expected. The procedure room was cold. All medical bays were cold. Maybe it was something left over from some old belief about healing and disease; more likely it was just another way to make a patient feel helpless.

It definitely worked. Jem lay quietly on the padded table and let the team putter around him. Gentle hands engaged restraints at his forehead, chest, wrists, and ankles. At least his vertigo had eased, courtesy of the powerful sedatives running through his IV.

"Jem, are you comfortable?" Dr. Land's voice startled him from his drifting thoughts.

"Let's just get this done."

"We need you awake and responsive for the procedure. Some patients experience more pain than others. We'll do our best to manage your symptoms."

"Fine."

"We're going to numb your leg where the catheter will be inserted."

"Fine." This was going to get tedious if Land insisted on narrating every freaking nanosecond. Something even colder than the room swiped across the inside of his thigh and he flinched.

"Hold still, please." It was the precise, clipped tones of Dr. Wen. "You will feel pressure."

Jem kept his eyes tightly shut. His bare backside pressed

237

against the medifoam lining the table. The heated surgical drapes barely cut the chill. Beeping monitors, hushed voices, and the smell of antiseptic brought back an old memory of the small cubby his parents had created for him in the medical bay of one of the many remote 'hardship' postings they had taken when he was small. In a strange way, it was comforting.

He thought of Barre and the silly songs he would compose for him when Jem was scared or upset and their parents were otherwise occupied. There were a lot of songs.

Something sharp and hot pierced his leg. Jem gasped. His body struggled against the restraints.

"Easy, Jem. This is the hard part." Dr. Land's voice cut through the pain. "I'm putting some more pain meds through your line, but you need to stay awake. Can you do that?"

Something got between him and the pain in his leg. It didn't make it go away, exactly, he just stopped caring so much about it. "Yeah. I can do that." His tongue stuck in his mouth. His voice sounded faint and dreamy. The words were like an ansible message drifting through space. Jem was drifting. Was this how it felt when Barre drank bittergreen tea? He could see the appeal.

Something heavy leaned on his leg and he wanted to complain, but he couldn't figure out what to say. It was as if someone was sitting on him, but that didn't make sense and he didn't want to get the doctors angry by complaining.

"Guide wire deployed. Placement scans are good."

Jem understood each of the words, but they refused to make sense as a total whole. He repeated the word 'guide' to himself over and over again until the sounds became a kind of percussion. He wished Barre were here to sing to him.

"Ready the catheter."

The pressure on his leg made Jem irritable. "Find somewhere else to sit," he said.

"Jem? Don't fall asleep."

"I'm not 'sleep. My leg." It made perfect sense in his mind, but he knew something was missing.

"Ready the first dose of the emitters." That was Dr. Wen.

"Jem," Dr. Land said. "We're getting ready to place the first of three sets of nanoemitters. But first we need to do a few tests. I need you to open your eyes."

"Can't," he mumbled. Well, he could. He just didn't want to. It was so comfortable to drift and not feel as if the world was tumbling around and around.

"Jem, this is the part where you have to work with us." Dr. Land's voice was a point of cold in the warm cocoon Jem was floating in. "We can't do this without your help."

He opened his eyes to a terrible darkness. "I can't see! I can't see!" Jem tried to move, but his body was paralyzed. All he could do was hear the acceleration of his heartbeat through the telemetry monitors.

"Take a deep breath, Jem. You're all right. There's nothing to see yet." Dr. Land stayed so calm. As calm as his mother always was, no matter what was going on. Except for Barre and the bittergreen.

Thoughts of his brother chased away the panic. The memory of Barre's music filled his mind.

"Your head is in a kind of VR display. We're going to

project some images. We need you to track their movement so we can map your visual cortex. Do you understand?"

"Not stupid," he murmured.

"Get the magnet online."

"All set."

"Are you ready, Jem?"

There was blackness. Darker than space. Darker than the place he had fallen into after his head injury. Then brightness seared across his vision. He couldn't pull away, couldn't get away from the light even when he shut his eyes.

"Jem, open your eyes."

He tried again. This time, the light was bearable. It moved across his field of vision from left to right and he followed it. The light winked out. This time the darkness was soothing. A splotch of purple stained the middle of the display. Color dripped down and vanished further down than he could see.

"You're doing great."

He snorted. How hard was it to look at lights? A few more color trails followed. Then darkness again.

"Okay, now we're going to quickly show some images of arrows. Just tell me if they're pointed up, down, right, or left. Ready?"

"Right."

Flash.

"Right."

Flash.

"Up."

Flash.

"Down."

Flash.

"Right."

This was boring. Jem let his attention drift, trying to capture one of Barre's old songs.

"Jem."

"What!" he snapped.

"Okay. You did great. We're going to inject the first dose of emitters now. You're going to feel a buzzing in your head. Most people describe it as a tickle. There are no pain endings in the brain itself, so giving you more pain meds won't help. It will pass. Are you ready?"

"What do you think?"

"Injecting now."

A racing heat moved through his neck and into the middle of his head. It wasn't painful. It was weird, like someone had painted his brain with light.

Then a swarm of burrowing insects crawled through his head. "Get them out of me!" He fought against the head restraints, but he couldn't move. A thousand tiny pincers bit their way into his brain. Fragmented images lit up in his mind.

He was on Halcyone's ruined bridge, wide-eyed as red emergency lights flashed their warning and klaxons drowned out the sound of his own thoughts. "It wasn't my fault." Jem voice played in his memory. *My fault. My fault. My fault.* Something tore the memory into shreds.

A light flared in Jem's field of vision and he was staring out the observation lounge viewport as their ship left Hadrian space and the planet dwindled in the distance. Behind him, Barre and his mother were arguing again. "I'm old enough," his brother had pleaded. "Look. They only accept a handful of musicians a year. And they want me." He tried to show her his micro. She tossed it aside. The pain in Barre's eyes burned through Jem's mind as a white hot ball of flame. It seared away the memory, leaving Jem panting, a faint warmth at the back of his head.

"Okay. Okay. I'm okay." He choked back a sob, afraid that if they knew what was happening, they would stop the procedure.

"One down, two to go. We're going to move to sensorimotor mapping. This time we need you to tell us sharp or dull and where you feel the stimulus."

He struggled to calm his breathing and let his body be somewhere else, let the pinpricks happen to someone else. While he gave the doctors their information, his thoughts drifted far from the procedure room. Did Ro and Barre get Halcyone's drive working? Were his parents mounting a search? He wondered if Micah had gotten to Uni yet. Good old Micah.

"You're doing great, Jem. Here comes the second dose."

This time Jem knew what to expect, but it didn't make the sensations any easier to bear. His breath echoed harshly in the procedure room. His heart lurched against his ribs. All over his body, his skin crawled and burned. Muscles he didn't even know he had twitched. Jem gritted his teeth as his brain seemed to writhe within his skull.

Across the room they had shared when Jem was small, Barre leaned over his guitar, his dreads only long enough to cover his eyes. He plucked at the strings; a layer of sound resonated through the air. The chords thrummed louder and louder, each one building into a higher crescendo than the last, until Jem's skull shook with the vibration. His head pounded in time with his heartbeat. His ears rang.

And then silence. Another memory jumped forward.

He stood in their family quarters shaking Barre's unconscious body. His brother was dead weight, nearly impossible to turn over, and Jem's arms quivered with the strain. Pain arced through his shoulders, leaving his arms trembling against the restraints.

A laser scalpel gleamed in the harsh light of a medical bay. His mother walked closer to the crazed patient holding it as Barre threw his arms around Jem in the small compartment they shared. The weight of his brother's strong body kept him pinned to the berth. He couldn't move. He couldn't breathe.

And then his mind and body were his own again. The cold of the table pressed into his spine.

"One more. And then the hard part is over."

"You said that before."

"The final emitters target visual spatial perception. It will be a particular area of weakness, given your head injury. The mapping and the placement may trigger your vertigo. I'm going to give you something for nausea ahead of time."

Great. Just great. He wasn't miserable enough. "Bring it on."

"Keep your eyes open again. You'll feel as if you are falling, but it's just an illusion."

If he threw up, it would be their problem. Jem stared straight ahead at the X in the center of his visual field. Then it was as if he was spinning, his body flailing in open space.

His stomach rebelled. Dry heaves shook through him and bitter saliva pooled in his mouth. Tears blurred his vision. Not this. Not again.

"Inject. Now."

The vertigo intensified. Jem wanted to curl up into a tight ball and rock until it was over. He knew his body was restrained, that any sensation of motion was artificially induced, but it didn't help. He relived every jump he'd ever taken, one after another in such quick succession it was like one continuous involution.

He wanted to scream. To beg them to stop. But he couldn't draw a breath. His lungs were pressed flat as if he were accelerating at impossible g forces. His brain crawled with insects again. The itch was intolerable.

"Neural net starting to form. Looking good."

"Let's give this boy a break."

The visual display shut off. Jem welcomed the darkness. Then a thin stream of warmth meandered through his arm, and he followed it into a blessed oblivion.

Chapter 20

ALL THE WAY through what looked like a clone of the residence ring on Daedalus Station, Ro struggled not to lash out at the guards. Halcyone was her ship. Hers. She had brought it to life, nearly getting her friends killed in the process, and she would be damned if she was going to let someone else take it.

Barre was walking silently beside her, his face set in a scowl. It wasn't hard to work out where they were: there weren't many places in the cosmos that were both 'nowhere' and outside the Commonwealth's influence. If not Ithaka proper, then they were certainly somewhere controlled by The Underworld. She knew Barre was thinking about Jem. There was a better than good chance that even if he wasn't here, someone on this settlement knew where he was. Had Jem convinced them to do the implant? Could they stop him? Even if they could, she wasn't sure it was the right thing to do.

If she were in Jem's place, she'd have done the same thing.

Ro never gave too much thought to the Commonwealth or

politics. Her father had been as dismissive and paranoid about their system of military government as he had been about everything else except his own self-interest. Mostly she just tried to stay beneath anyone's notice. But she was a Commonwealth citizen now. And this was The Underworld. What did that mean for her and for Barre? Neither of their escorts was obviously armed. Were she and Barre prisoners?

They hadn't passed anyone else in the corridor. Either there were only a handful of people here, or the common areas had been cleared for them. She glanced at Barre. He shrugged.

The woman waved her tattooed arm at the door sensor. A gleam of metal around her wrist caught Ro's eye. The door opened.

"This is where we leave you," the man said. He and the woman took up guard positions on either side of the door.

A woman's quiet voice came from somewhere inside. "I'm sure you have questions. At least I do. So you may as well come in."

Barre nodded. He looked relaxed, but his shoulders were rigid. Ro gave his hand a quick squeeze. They walked in. The door shut behind them, leaving them in shadow. The only illumination in the room came from a task light in the sitting area. It took all of Ro's self-control not to step back and check if the door would open again for her.

The woman sat back in a chair too large for her small frame. The light didn't reveal her face. "First, who are you? Second, how did you find your way here? Third, what are you doing with one of my ships?"

Ro lifted her chin. "One of your ships?" She stepped

further into the room. "Halcyone was salvage. A wreck. I resurrected the AI. The ship is registered in my name."

The woman laughed. "I like your confidence, young lady. Please, both of you, sit."

As Ro moved toward the sitting area, the woman leaned forward. The light reflected the silver of her hair. Her face was deeply lined. Her eyes shone a bright blue.

"Neither of us have any idea where 'here' is," Ro said. Or at least they didn't have any jump coordinates, which amounted to the same thing. "And you have no right to keep us against our will." Ro would have rushed the woman if Barre hadn't put his hand on her shoulder.

"Sit." The woman's voice was an unmistakable command. They sat. Three chairs formed a small triangle. The single light created harsh shadows between them. "And you are?"

She still hadn't given them her name. Ro narrowed her eyes and stared a challenge back at her.

Barre sighed, answering for both of them. "This is Ro Maldonado. I'm Barre Durbin. We are both full citizens of the Commonwealth. If we are under arrest, then name the charges and allow us to exercise our rights."

Her gaze flicked to his face and then away again, but not before Ro saw her eyes widen in surprise. "You have no rights here, young man."

"Who are you and what do you want with us?" Ro asked quickly as Barre nearly sprang out of his chair. "I'm not a fan of being abducted."

"Let me ask you a question first. Did you really bring Halcyone back from the dead?"

It was a strange way to word it, as if the AI were alive,

instead of merely a sentient machine. "Yes."

She raised an eyebrow. "All on your own?"

"I did the major reprogramming. But I had help with the holo and voice interfaces." Ro glanced at Barre and then back to their host. "Among other things."

"So are you as good a programmer as I suspect you are?" Ro frowned.

"She's better," Barre said quietly.

The woman nodded. "I'm Ada May. And I think I know a friend of yours."

Ro sat stunned, blinking at the old woman perched on the edge of a too-large chair.

Barre bolted out of his seat. "Where is he? What have you done to my brother?"

"Holy mother of the cosmos," Ro whispered.

May looked up at Barre's looming presence. "Are you threatening me, young man?" There was no fear in her eyes even though he probably out-massed the frail woman by more than 2 to 1.

He collapsed back down, releasing the tension in his fists.

"I didn't think so," May said.

"You're supposed to be dead," Ro said.

"Where's Jem? Is he okay?" Barre's husky voice cut into Ro's. She felt a twinge of guilt.

"I suspect so. He's quite a remarkable and resourceful young man. Are you a coding savant as well?"

Barre's cheeks darkened. "No. I'm just the musician."

Ro squeezed his knee. She wanted to tell May just how talented Barre was. About the way he figured out how to get through to Halcyone when no one else could. Not Jem. Not her. But her father's suspicious nature was as ingrained in Ro as her ability to see code as a three-dimensional thing. May brought them here for a reason. Until Ro figured out that reason, she wasn't going to tell the woman anything she didn't need to know. No matter who she was.

Ada May. No shit. Ro tried to seem young and awed. It wasn't hard, despite the habitual mistrust. "Dr. May, why are we here?"

Barre shot her a quizzical look.

"Yes, that May," the woman said. "As in Dauber and May."

"Oh," Barre said. "My brother practically worships you."

"Yes, he was quite earnest."

"I need to talk to him."

May stood. She couldn't have been more than one-and-a-half meters tall, but her physical presence meant nothing compared with her giant influence. "I will arrange that as soon as it's possible. For now, you are guests of Ithaka. Please remain in these quarters. If there's anything you need, signal the area AI. She responds to Lethe." As she turned and walked towards the door, Ro took in the modified shoe and the pronounced limp. Something May had been born with, or a war injury?

"Excuse me, what?" Barre asked. "So we're prisoners here."

"Not exactly." May sighed. "But we do need to figure out what to do with you."

"Seriously? I don't like being threatened either. Have you got my brother locked up somewhere in here too?"

She turned back from the door. "Not exactly," she

repeated.

The door opened to let May leave and then shut again, silently. In her brief glimpse of the corridor, Ro saw their escorts were still there.

Barre strode to the door. It didn't respond. He hit it once with his fist. Ro winced on his behalf. "How do we get out of here?" he asked.

"I don't know, but I'm not going to wait around, either."

Barre clenched his fist again. Ro covered it with her hand.

"That's not going to help." She sat back down again, tucked her legs beneath her, and pulled out her micro. "Unless he purged it for some reason, Jem's micro still has the peer-to-peer messaging program I installed. It should just tunnel through the AI's autonomics like on Daedalus."

"Okay. Fine." He shook out his fist as he paced the bland room.

Ro activated the little program. The screen blanked and a blinking cursor replaced her usual icons. "What do you want to say?"

"What do I want to say? How about 'you fucking idiot, what have you gotten yourself tangled up in?'"

"Yeah, no." She started typing. <u>Jem. We're here. Me and Barre. Fellow guests of Dr. M. Worried about you.</u> The words glowed on the black background and hung there. She hit the manual SEND button. Still nothing. "Huh."

"What?"

"It's not working."

"Maybe his micro is busted. Maybe they took it from him. Maybe—"

"This is something at my end," Ro said, her voice calm,

even though the ramifications of what she was saying terrified her. "Something's blocking the outgoing message. Which shouldn't be possible." Frowning, Ro turned back to her micro. That particular program was something she had adapted from code traded through virtual hacker spaces. Which most likely had a direct connection to The Underworld. She bit her lip. Which meant it couldn't be trusted. Here, especially. How many of her hacks had been put together with, or at least were based on, bits of scavenged utilities and programs that could be traced back here? "We're screwed. Spaced without air. If that really was Ada May, then she knows more about programming and hacks than anyone alive."

"So that's it? Ro Maldonado caves?"

"That's not it, Barre! Look, we don't even know if we're in any danger ..."

Barre stared at her and Ro wanted to hide under her chair. "I get it," he said, his voice cold enough to make her shiver. "This is the first time in your life you've been slapped down by someone smarter than you. It sucks. It makes you want to crawl into a hole. But you know what? You don't have that option. We don't have that option. So put on your real spacer p-suit and step outside the air lock."

He was right. But it didn't make it any easier to take. Ro looked away, her face burning.

*

Ro could give up, but Barre wasn't going to. Maybe he

was just fooling himself. Certainly he wasn't as smart as Ro or Ada May or even his baby brother, but none of that mattered. Jem needed him. Whether Jem knew it or not, he was in over his head.

Barre stopped pacing and leaned against the empty counter in the tiny kitchen area. He triggered his micro and sent a trill of sound to Halcyone. The notes trailed off into silence. There was no reply. He sent wave after wave of music, the notes getting darker and more insistent until his head rang with the cacophony.

Tears burning in his eyes, Barre hung his head, an image of Jem curled on his bed in a miserable bundle clear in his mind. Seeing Jem's eyes start their odd shifting dance was almost more than he could take, even in memory.

Instead, Barre let his worry and his fear create a melody, a tune that meant 'Jem' to him, filled with his brother's irritating energy and relentless curiosity. That was the Jem who drove him crazy, the Jem he wanted to think about. The Jem he used to sing silly songs to when they were little. How had his parents forced a wedge between them?

His anger made the music falter. No, it wasn't his parents' fault. Cosmos knows they weren't perfect, but whatever had frayed the bond between him and Jem had been caused by Barre's own insecurity. He knew that now. And he wasn't going to let it happen again. Barre followed the music, let it fill him and resonate in his skull. There was annoyance in the song, but also love.

Barre? Barre, I'm scared. Everything's dark and I don't know where I am.

Barre jerked upright and slammed his shoulder against a

cabinet. The song stopped. He looked around the room. "Jem?"

Ro jumped out of her chair and went to him. "What's going on?"

The voice was in his head. His brother's voice was in his head. He squeezed his eyes shut as he turned away from Ro, focusing on the faint whisper. *I'm here, Jem. I'm right here.*

I knew you'd come.

This isn't possible. You're in my head. How are you in my head? Barre knew he was repeating the same damn thing over and over again.

I don't know. I was scared. I started thinking about the songs you used to sing me. You always used music to communicate. Long before Halcyone. That's when I heard it. The music. I knew it was you.

This didn't make any sense. Barre could communicate with the ship, but that was just an extension of his neural making a basic link. Telepathy was the stuff in old sci-fi books. *Are you hurt? Did you hit your head again?*

Barre. I let them do it. The neural. It was hard and it hurt like hell, but they did it.

Shit! They were too late.

Only, I think something's gone wrong. I can't see anything. I can't feel my body. I'm just drifting.

We're here. Ro and me. On Ithaka. We're going to find you. And then we're going to go home. Barre had no idea how they were going to get out of here, but there was no way he'd abandon Jem. *Just breathe. We're going to find you.*

Barre? I'm sorry.

The voice drifted away. "Jem!" Barre shouted, the sound

reverberating in his head and through the room.

"What the hell? Where did you just go?" Ro stood in front of him, her hands grasping his arms. He hadn't even felt it.

"He's here. They did the implant."

"Wait. How do you know?"

"He was talking to me."

"That's not—"

"Possible? I know. No one's ever been able to make direct neural-to-neural communication happen."

"What were you doing?"

"It doesn't matter! We have to get the hell out of this room. We have to find Jem. Something's wrong. Something's seriously wrong!"

Ro dug her fingernails into his arm. That he did feel.

"We can't help him unless you can reach him again. We can't reach him again unless you can figure out how you did it in the first place. So focus."

Barre gently disengaged her hands and rubbed the indentations on his arms. "I don't know!"

"Please. Just think."

He started pacing again. "I was trying to trigger Halcyone. Nothing happened. And I was so worried about Jem. The music followed."

"What do you mean, 'the music followed?'"

"It's how I think, all right? You see the world in code. I deal with it in sound. Everyone has their own particular melody stored in my head. And it changes over time as the person changes." He felt her staring at him and his face got hot. "Yes, even you. There's music for you."

"Oh."

"So I was focusing on Jem's, thinking about how the head injury has changed him. And then he was in my mind. Talking to me."

"That's just ... I don't know. A little spooky?"

"Maybe. It's not all that different from communicating with Halcyone. Except that's just with music, not words." Barre stopped talking and looked past Ro. "I think ..." He shook his head, but the idea wouldn't leave. "I think Halcyone did something. Like an ancient switchboard. I called in and Jem called in. For whatever reason, she's having a hard time talking to me, so she connected us."

Ro stood and stared at him for a long minute. Just stared. She didn't blink; she didn't breathe. Just stared. "You're serious."

"We have to get Jem out of here." His parents would know what to do. He choked back a laugh. When was the last time he had turned to his parents for anything? But this. This was bigger than him. They would blame him and he didn't care.

"How. We can't even get out of this room. And you said Halcyone isn't responding to you." Ro frowned. That was her thinking face.

"What?"

"Something or someone is blocking the higher AI functions. What about the autonomics? That's how I've tunneled in to Halcyone before."

"But you said your micro was blocked."

"Yeah, but your neural isn't. Here." She handed him her micro. "These are the specs of the autonomic control module. All you have to do is translate this code into your notes. Music. Whatever. It should get us in."

"How does that help us?"

"If we can establish our own conduit, then I'll have a chance to figure out what's blocking Halcyone and retake control."

He narrowed his eyes, scanning Ro's program. There were a lot of lines of code. "I don't know, Ro. This is loads more complicated than the little routines I've created before."

"And?"

Barre's hands dwarfed her micro. "This may take a little time."

"I don't think we have any other commitments."

Chapter 21

THE ALERT TONE on her micro brought Nomi instantly from deep inside a dream to full wakefulness. She bolted upright, still blinking away the sense of being in her grandparents' house. Ro was there too, and she was arguing with their AI about something. The details fell away, leaving Nomi bemused, a single image of her grandfather bowing to Ro, persisting from the dream. A pang of regret had her blinking back tears. He would have liked her, prickly nature and all.

Nomi's micro was still buzzing. "I'm awake. Shut up, already." The noise stopped. "Retrieve message."

Schedule change alert: Konomi Nakamura. Effective as of 2300 hours. Log in for new assignment.

Canting her head, she stared at the message. That was interesting. She checked the duty roster for the first time in weeks. Gutierrez had pulled her from third shift, reassigning her to days. It looked like third shift was back to being covered by rotation.

"Huh."

And Nomi had an unexpected day off.

She eyed the pillow, slowly filling in from where her head had left its indent. It would be so easy to curl back under the covers and sleep. Cosmos knows she was tired. Since she was already up, maybe she could check on Ro. It might not be her shift in comms, but Mendez had assigned her to be the liaison between Ro and Gutierrez.

A hot shower wasn't a full cycle of sleep, but it helped. Nomi considered her off-duty clothes, but went for the uniform instead. There would be fewer questions that way. She stopped at the commissary to nab a coffee and a food bar to go. A bunch of the crew from other comms shifts were at their usual table, probably all talking and complaining about the schedule changes. Nomi slipped out before they noticed her.

She hesitated at the entrance to comms. Unless Gutierrez had changed everything, this was Lowell's shift. But maybe Simon would be there, too. She'd love to get his take on things.

The door opened at her request. Lowell was in the supervisor's chair. Simon and Yizhi Chen, his usual crew, were both also working. That was interesting. So it wasn't a global reassignment. Just her.

Lowell spun around in his chair. "Nomi. You're not on my watch."

"No. I know. I'm supposed to be coordinating communications for the search."

"Don't trust us to do our jobs?" Lowell kept his voice light, but there was an intensity about his stare that made Nomi uncomfortable.

"The schedule change alert woke me anyway, so I thought

I'd check. Any messages come in?"

"Nothing," Simon answered. "It's been a quiet shift. Want me to ping Halcyone for you?"

"I have nothing better to do. If you don't mind?" Nomi looked at Lowell and waited for his confirmation. It would be odd if he did have objections. Outside of a red alert situation, life in comms was pretty relaxed; during the day shifts, staff often wandered in to send their messages directly, rather than have them pile up in the queue.

"Take a station. Knock yourself out," Lowell said, after a long silence.

Simon raised an eyebrow at her. At least she wasn't imagining things. Lowell was acting strange.

Nomi took the outermost station in the horseshoe around the supervisor's chair. Lowell would have to actively turn to watch her. Of course, he could access her screen from his, but that wasn't the same. It only took a moment for the headset to conform around her ears and the chair to mold to her contours. She double-checked the logs, not caring if Lowell assumed she didn't trust him.

No word from Halcyone. Which didn't really surprise her. Ro would communicate the bare minimum that regulations dictated. Still, calculating the jump route between here and Gal-3, Nomi figured they certainly should have gotten there long before now and checked in.

Since she made the effort to look the part, Nomi needed to do this officially. She created a status request and routed it through the ansible net to Gal-3. It shouldn't take long to get a reply.

Several minutes passed. Nomi rechecked the message

path. There was no signal drop, and besides, the network was self-healing. If one node malfunctioned, traffic would be automatically rerouted. People credited the AIs and their wormhole mapping skills with the ability to truly conquer space, but it was the ansible that made communication during travel and across distances possible. It was the ansible that allowed the Commonwealth to expand.

Ro, why aren't you answering?

Nomi tried to convince herself that there were plenty of reasons. Maybe they had found Jem. Maybe they had transited elsewhere on his trail and neglected to file a revised flight plan. Maybe they were ignoring Mendez. That last one she could believe, given Ro's issues with authority. But would she risk her now-official position on the station? Nomi didn't think she was that contrary.

Well, maybe she wouldn't answer official station traffic, but what about a personal message? Nomi pulled out her micro and opened the private communication program Ro had put there. Somehow she'd hacked into the locator beacon pulse system and figured out how to use it as an out-of-band network. It was ridiculously inefficient and didn't have the error correction that full duplex ansible channels had, which made communication frustrating and prone to delay. However, it was also a lot less traceable than ansible traffic. Especially if Ro did any sort of path randomization. Though the more randomization, the longer delivery took.

<u>Any word?</u> Nomi paused her typing, wanting to add something about protocol and responsibility, but wasn't sure how to say it. Then she continued. <u>Gutierrez will get suspicious without an official update.</u> That should get her

point across without triggering Ro's personal repulsors.

While she waited for Ro's response, Nomi flagged the official outgoing message for resend. That was standard procedure and she didn't want to give the LC any reason to mistrust her. Her micro buzzed and Nomi smiled. Ro may have been incredibly smart, but she was predictable. Nomi hoped she had some word on Jem.

The incoming message wasn't from Ro.

Nomi read and reread the summons. <u>Nakamura, report to Command.</u> Her head jerked up. She stared at Lowell wondering if he had made a complaint, but he was engaged with the display and didn't spare her a glance. If not him, than who or what would have triggered the order? What could Mendez know about Jem or Ro and Barre that wouldn't have come through comms?

She logged off her terminal and removed her headset with trembling hands. "You were right. A lot of nothing."

"Like I said." Lowell didn't bother to turn around when he spoke.

"Catch you later, Nomi." Marchand turned to give her a smile.

"Sure thing, Simon."

"I'll save you some left over gumbo."

"Appreciate the chair, Lowell." It hadn't been technically necessary to ask for his permission, and he certainly wasn't owed any thanks, but ticking off a shift supervisor wasn't smart.

"Didn't cost me anything."

All the way to command, Nomi fought to keep her worry at bay. Images of Barre, Jem, and Ro, always Ro, filled her mind. What if something happened to Halcyone? Ro was certain the jump drive would work, but no sim could predict the dangerous quantum forces of a wormhole. In the early days of jump travel, ships went missing, never to be heard from again. They were the lucky ones. Her grandfather had been one of the original drive engineers and he did everything he could to avoid jumping. That was one of the reasons her family had all moved back to Altara after her grandmother died. When he'd come to Nomi's graduation, it had been his first jump in over a decade.

What if Ro had been wrong and Halcyone was even more broken then they thought? The fail-safes were supposed to prevent a ship from jumping if the coordinates couldn't be verified. But this was a forty-year-old ship with damaged maps.

Nomi heard her name being called. When she looked up, she was surrounded by a group of laughing comms personnel just outside the commissary.

"What's the matter, Nakamura? Sleepwalking?" Jenna Carlisle was also on Daedalus to pay back her debt to the Commonwealth. She was in her last rotation.

She untangled her thoughts from her grandfather's stories of jump disasters and the first maimed survivors of jump sickness and forced herself to smile. "Must be. Just wait until you have to cover your first late night in comms."

"Yeah. How'd you manage to get off nights? Not too shabby for the newbie."

Nomi shrugged. "Ask command. Sorry, duty calls." She deliberately glanced down at her micro, not wanting to get drawn into a lengthy conversation with the talkative group.

It was rude, and it was all Nomi could do not to run down the corridor to command.

She entered Mendez's anteroom. The commander's office was open—and empty.

"Nakamura."

Or not empty. Her head jerked up. Gutierrez stepped from the shadows in the corner of the room. "Sir? Mendez wanted to see me?"

"The commander is in a meeting. I called you." Light glinted off Gutierrez's artificial arm.

"Oh." Nomi wondered why the LC had never upgraded her prosthesis. The technology had made huge jumps forward since the war and Gutierrez could have gotten an arm that was virtually indistinguishable from her intact limb.

The woman lifted it, bringing the metal arm fully into the light. The wrist ended in a crude claw. "Does it make you uncomfortable?" Gutierrez paused. "Good. It's a reminder—for me, for others—of the sacrifices we made so citizens like you can serve their obligations to the Commonwealth in safe places like this."

"Yes, sir." Did Gutierrez want to scare her? Warn her? Nomi waited, standing at parade rest. It was the safest response.

"I suspect you want to know why I altered the logs."

Nomi rocked back on her heels and nearly stumbled. "Sir?" She knew she sounded like an ansible message set on repeat.

"We don't have a lot of time. And as much as I regret it, I am forced to trust you. Mendez is speaking with Targill on a secure connection right now. He's out there searching. If you care about your friends and their survival, I need to know everything you do about Ithaka."

This time Nomi did fall out of her rigid stance, struggling to make sense of what the LC was telling her. Okay, Gutierrez had been the one to alter the log. Nomi had figured that out, for the most part. What confused her was why. And why was Gutierrez admitting it?

"They were going to look for Jem on Gal-3," Nomi said, trying to pull her thoughts together.

"We both know that was simply a meeting point. If you know where they were headed after that, you'd better tell me."

Nomi shifted her gaze from the LC's shining arm to her scowling face. "How do I know I can trust you?"

"You don't. But if Targill finds them before I do, I suspect it will not end well for your friends."

"Why?" Nomi was aware of moments passing. Gutierrez kept glancing to her micro.

"Do you really need to ask?" The stern woman almost smiled.

"No." The Commonwealth wanted Ithaka. They hadn't been able to locate it for more than forty years, despite the searching by the best and the brightest of its citizens. And Jem had blundered into it.

As if reading her thoughts, Gutierrez continued. "Are you aware the boy tried to catch their attention with evidence of his programming ability?"

"I sent that message. It was just plain text."

"Not quite 'just.'"

But the content of ansible messages was supposed to be private. How had Gutierrez gotten the overrides? And if the LC knew what Jem sent and who he sent it to, then the Commonwealth knew. Didn't it? Her brows knotted together. "Wait. You don't want Targill to find them?"

"I owe a debt that tests my loyalties more than you could ever understand. Whatever decision you're planning to make, make it quickly."

The desperate tone of Gutierrez's voice sent cold rippling down Nomi's spine. Would Ro trust this woman? And if not, would that be the right choice? The sound of voices from the corridor made her freeze.

"Time's up," Gutierrez said.

"But I don't know where they are," she whispered.

"That's unfortunate."

Then the door opened and Mendez stepped inside. Gutierrez snapped to attention. "Oh, good, you're here. In my office, please. Emma, would you please bring in some coffee? Status report, Nakamura."

Nomi sent Gutierrez a helpless look, but the woman's face reflected no emotion.

Chapter 22

Barre sat down with Ro's micro, his face creased in concentration. She paced the little apartment—or rather their comfortable jail. It was hard not to stop and ask him how he was doing every twenty-three nanoseconds. Harder still because he looked like he was daydreaming. At least when she was programming and using the kinesthetic input, she was physically doing something.

"You're making me nervous," Barre said. "Can you just sit down?"

"Sorry." Ro stopped and sat, but as the minutes passed, her hands began to fidget, drumming against the arms of the chair.

"This isn't helping."

She folded her arms against her chest.

"Okay." Barre leaned forward to hand her back her micro. "It's not perfect, but it's the best I can do under the circumstances."

"Can you trigger it so I can hear?"

"Yeah. Sure. If you want. Ready?"

Ro stood again and pulled up six virtual windows in a circle around her. It was the maximum one micro could reasonably maintain without a significant performance hit. She hoped it would be enough. Each display contained a different kind of hack, each designed to troubleshoot and scan a different system on Halcyone. If Barre could make the connection, maybe, just maybe Ro could get the AI to respond.

And even that was only a baby step.

"Ready."

Barre nodded. A strange hissing emerged from the inadequate speaker of his micro, a soft static that started and stopped in a syncopated rhythm. It sent shivers down Ro's spine. She almost regretted having asked him to make it audible. "Anything?" she whispered.

"Not yet."

Nothing stirred in any of her virtual windows either, though Ro suspected Barre would hear from Halcyone before she did.

The sounds changed, became more melodic, though it wasn't music in the way Ro thought of music. It meandered up and down a discordant scale, playing sounds that were often painful and sometimes merely uncomfortable. And the song—such as it was—never resolved. "Anything?"

He glared her way. The auditory program played on.

It wasn't working. It wasn't going to work. What had May done to Halcyone and how was Ro going to get her ship back? She glanced at Barre and her face blazed with heat. It was Jem they needed to worry about. Jem who was in danger.

Something flashed in the corner of her eye. Ro turned as Barre shouted.

"I'm in!"

Ro half expected to feel a rumbling at her feet as Halcyone blasted off, without them, to parts unknown. But she doubted they would notice this far away from the dock, and besides, Barre was monitoring. Now all they had to do was reestablish contact with the AI proper. Right. Only.

The heads-up displays were a riot of color in motion as each of her hacks made its connection with a different part of the autonomic pathways that formed the supporting code for the SIREN program. The Self-learning Interactive Recursive Enhanced Network schema that Dauber and May had developed couldn't function without it. And for now, that was a vulnerability Ro could exploit.

The music died away as the program Barre had translated finished running. Ro watched her windows. Every single one of the six was stable, querying the system, and running its diagnostics. "You're a genius," she said.

"No, that would be the other Durbin brother," Barre said. "The one I'm going to find and carry out of here if I have to."

"I'll be right there with you. But first, it's time for me to get to work."

"Anything I can do?"

"Keep an ear out. I'm going to be poking around Halcyone's subsystems. Depending on what May has done to the ship, it may get messy."

"Aye, aye, Cap. I'm on it."

It felt natural to be working with him like this. When had that happened? Nomi would be proud of her. Ro felt her cheeks warm again as she thought of her friend. No. More than friend. Much more.

"Okay. I'm getting solid readings from all the autonomics." So far, nothing she had touched triggered any of Halcyone's old fight-or-flight responses. It was better than she'd hoped. "I want to try and force Halcyone to reboot."

"Are you sure that's a good idea?"

"I'm not sure we have any other good options." This would be just like her original repair attempt. The one where she had run Jem's code mods in real time without telling him. And set off the ship's alarms in the process. They couldn't risk that here.

Barre exhaled heavily. "Then do it."

Her hands trembled as she prepared to start the reboot. But this time she had Barre, the AI whisperer, and Ro was no longer a stranger and potential threat to Halcyone. It would have to be enough.

She pushed five of the displays to one side, letting them stack one behind the other. The final window, she enlarged, and ran the SIREN code that contained both her enhancements and Jem's in update mode. Now they waited.

Instead of watching her programming windows, Ro watched Barre. He sat, listening, his head slightly canted to one side, dreads sliding behind his shoulders. His dark eyes focused on a spot just past her. It was as if she'd jumped back in time to when she realized he first had a neural—when she'd run into him in Daedalus's nexus, just a few days before her former life blasted off along with Halcyone.

And to think she had mocked him because he used it for 'just' playing music.

"How's Halcyone doing?" Ro asked.

"Quiet. But I can tell she's listening."

She. AI's were always 'it' to Ro. It seemed silly to personalize them to such an extent, but she had to admit Halcyone and Barre had a different kind of relationship. "Let me know if anything changes."

The minutes crawled by in a tense silence. Ro was tempted to poke at individual subsystems just to make sure Halcyone was alive and responsive. But that would have been a waste of resources. She had to trust in Barre and in her own troubleshooting. The time for second guessing had been over a long time ago.

Every few seconds, she glanced up at her running program, comforted by the continuous scrolling of code. Then a trumpet blast echoed through the room. The screen went dark. Barre winced and clapped his hands to his ears. Shit. What was wrong? Ro lifted shaking hands to her virtual screens, but didn't know what to do.

The sound died away.

"Barre?" Ro whispered. "What's going on?"

"Sorry. Forgot to turn off the speakers." He moved his hands away and shook his head as if to clear it.

"Barre, are we okay?"

"Oh." He smiled. "Yeah. She's back."

"Okay." She relaxed her shoulders and rolled her neck. "Okay. Then we're in business."

"Halcyone, record following transmission to Daedalus Station, attention Commander Mendez."

"Unable to comply."

Frowning, Ro teased out one of the stacked windows.

"Halcyone, run diagnostic, ansible receiver and transmitter. Verbal and visual output, auxiliary display."

After a brief pause, Halcyone's welcome voice filled the room. "Status as follows. Ansible receiver, functional. Ansible transmitter, functional. Schematic displayed."

"That doesn't make sense," Barre said.

Ro studied the simplified diagram of the ansible system and swore. "Yes it does. There's nothing wrong with the ansible itself. We're being blocked. Same reason I couldn't get a message to Jem."

"So now what?"

"I don't know. I'm thinking." She pressed the heels of her hands against her eyes. "We have a functioning ship we can't access. We don't know where Jem is being held. We have no idea where in the cosmos we are."

"And?"

"And what?" Ro let her hands fall to her sides. "I'm not seeing a whole lot of good news here, Barre."

He bolted from the chair, but she kept talking.

"Look, I'm not giving up, but maybe we need more information. We're just going to have to wait for May."

"Waiting is not an option. Not for Jem. You didn't hear how terrified he was. I've been trying to get Halcyone to connect us again, but it's not working. Maybe it was a fluke. All I know is I'm not going to sit here, helpless, while he could be dying."

Ro turned away from the raw pain in his eyes. "I'm sorry. I don't know what else to do."

Barre walked around so he was in front of her and took hold of her shoulders. His hands were warm and gentle.

"You're a hacker. A damned good one. And you just got around Ithaka's safeguards to free our ship. Is that the best you've got?"

"I'm sorr—" She interrupted herself. No. Wait. Barre was right. She had taken advantage of the AI's inherent vulnerability to hack into her own ship. Could she do the same with Lethe? All they needed to do was to find some way in. Even hacking as basic a function as room lighting or temperature, and her programs would run.

She didn't have enough firepower to break into their AI. But with Halcyone's help, maybe she would.

"Okay. I have an idea."

Barre squeezed her shoulders and let go.

"There's a decent chance it won't work, but it's worth trying."

"I'm listening."

She sketched out her idea while he nodded. "You're better at communicating with Halcyone than I am."

He raised a single eyebrow at her admission.

"Yeah, see? I'm the new and improved Ro."

Barre snorted.

"I need the ship to make as many basic requests of Lethe as it can simultaneously. If we can overload the underlying autonomic functions, I may be able to slip in and establish my own conduit."

"I can set it the way I did the shutdown routines, to deploy on your mark."

"Perfect." Barre was brilliant. As talented and original a thinker as Jem was. When this was all over, she needed to figure out a way to get him to believe it.

It didn't take him more than a minute before he nodded. "All set."

"All right, music man. Let's see what you got."

They coordinated silently, with an ease Ro had never really believed possible. A few seconds later, she had her own programs up and ready to run in their protected windows. She smirked to herself. *Will wonders never cease.*

"On my mark," Ro said. "Three, two, one, now!"

He set his program for audible again. She listened to the strange music that translated lines of code and commands into a different symbolic language. One Halcyone seemed to gravitate to.

The last warble faded away to silence. All Ro could hear was the artificial breath of the station and their own ragged inhales and exhales as she and Barre waited for her chance to hack into Lethe.

A handful of seconds passed. Nothing. She glanced at Barre. He shook his head. Nothing. If Ro could feel their chances fading by the minute, it had to be much, much worse for him.

Still, Ro waited, her arms upraised, ready to trigger her little programs into Lethe's subsystems as soon as Halcyone gave her an opportunity. The old Ro might have demanded to review Barre's program. The old Ro would never have trusted him to help her in the first place. The old Ro was an idiot.

"Nothing," Barre said into the intolerable quiet. The despair was clear in his voice.

The room lights flickered so subtly, Ro wasn't sure she even saw it. Then she heard Barre's indrawn breath. "Go! Go!

Go!" he shouted.

Without any hesitation, Ro deployed her attack. The second thoughts and fears came after. There was no time for a test run. She was in unexplored space, in more ways than one. If Lethe had the same core vulnerability as Halcyone. If her hack penetrated Ithaka's security. If she could establish some measure of control over the station AI. If.

The room plunged into darkness, illuminated only by her displays.

Ro smiled fiercely.

When.

Time to get to work.

Minutes flew by as she struggled to create her own links to Lethe. Ones that would let her free Halcyone from its restrictions without triggering a station-wide alert. Barre kept an open audio link with the ship; the sound was the soft rumbling of what he called Halcyone's thinking music.

The door opened. Ro jumped. Light flooded the room and her heart pounded as Ada May limped into the little apartment. Her shoulders were rigid and the lines of her face deepened by her scowl. "What the hell do you think you're doing?"

"Finding my brother."

"Freeing my ship."

Ro's and Barre's voices tangled together.

"Lethe, security protocol Alpha. Authorization May, Adiana. Confirm."

"Security protocol Alpha, confirmed. Authorization confirmed."

Ro's windows collapsed. The music coming from

Halcyone climbed in pitch and volume until it abruptly cut out. Barre staggered back, clutching his head.

"Lethe, review surveillance. Compress and play back, analyzing for relevance and risk." She studied her micro, nodding at whatever the AI showed her. "I suspect you are more than 'just' a musician, young man. And you?" She turned to Ro. "You and I need to talk."

"What's wrong with my brother?" Barre stood so quickly, his micro tumbled off his lap onto the floor.

May didn't flinch as he loomed over her. "The doctors are examining him."

"I need to see him."

"Yes, I think you do," May agreed, and stood still, watching the two of them.

"And you're not going to let us unless we agree to your terms." Ro knew she was right even before May's slight nod.

"What do you want?" Barre asked.

Desperation made his voice crack. He sounded too much like Jem.

She tapped on her micro's screen. "You may have just stumbled upon a secure form of communication between two people with neurals. One that would be extremely difficult to hack. And your friend here has managed to break into my computer system. What do you think I want?"

"But I don't know—"

Ro interrupted Barre before he discounted what could be their biggest bargaining chip.

"And if we share this with you, you'll let us see Jem?"

"Of course."

Barre started toward the door. Ro held him back with a

light touch.

"I think you were going to let us do that anyway, right, Dr. May?" There had been real worry in her eyes when she mentioned Jem. "I suggest something in addition." As long as May was talking and interested, it meant they weren't in more trouble. Maybe it was time to push their luck. "My commander knows we went out looking for Jem. They had our flight plan to Galileo 3. We're obligated to check in and report every shift. I suggest you unlock us and let me send an update, before they scour every wormhole for several sectors around Gal-3."

"You're that important?"

"No, but I think you are. The CO on Daedalus is no fool. She'll organize a search for us. And if they find us, they find you."

May canted her head. "I don't think so. We haven't hidden ourselves for more than four decades only to be discovered by accident."

"And what's to stop me from figuring out where Ithaka is once we leave?"

"Ro, Jem needs me." The panic was clear in Barre's voice.

"Are you so sure it will be so easy to leave?" May said.

"I don't think you're in the business of murdering guests, uninvited or otherwise. Am I wrong?" If they were, the hack Ro'd just attempted would have gotten them put in shackles. Or worse. She thought of the lack of weapons on their escorts, and the general shabbiness of what she'd seen of Ithaka in contrast with the incredible infrastructure of the R&D space. Whatever their power, it wasn't in force of arms. "The last time you faced off with the Commonwealth, it didn't go very well for you."

"No. It didn't." May winced. Ro's gaze flicked down to the woman's damaged foot. "And you think you can accomplish what the Commonwealth has failed at for so long?"

Ro ignored Barre, who was nearly vibrating with anxiety beside her. "We have an advantage they lack. I know how you were able to hide. You altered the ansible maps and figured out a way to push your new maps through to every ship carrying a Commonwealth beacon."

May nodded. "And all the freestanding AIs as well, though there weren't as many of them in those days."

"Halcyone doesn't have a beacon," Ro said. "Which means she wasn't a Commonwealth ship. I repaired the jump drive and located her maps. Ithaka will be on those maps."

"But you're here, and so is Halcyone."

Ro thought fast. Even if May suspected the lie, the woman couldn't take the chance. "I copied all my data before we left. It won't be all that hard for a motivated engineer to figure out what I did. And all your protection will be lost. I can safeguard it from here, but you need to unlock my micro."

"And I will see Jem. Now." Barre's face was set in the same stark angles and planes she had seen in his mother's face.

May closed her eyes briefly before nodding. "Just so we understand one another, Ro Maldonado. I will instruct Lethe to remove the lock on your communications. I will allow you to reply, but all messages need to be sent through us."

There went any privacy. Ro started to object, but May cut her off.

"Do you really think we'd let ourselves be found through comms traffic? Our ansibles are programmed to encrypt their locations. And Lethe can route your messages in such a way that they are untraceable."

"Fine."

"You will delete your copies of the nav files and create whatever fiction you need to to keep your commander from getting curious." She turned to Barre. "You will show us what you did to make contact with your brother."

"And Jem?" Barre asked.

"His safety is up to you."

"What the hell do you mean by that?" His hands clenched and unclenched.

"I made a promise to him and I don't break my promises. It's not Ithaka that poses the threat. Do you think that if the Commonwealth finds us, they will care that three of their own are here?" Her voice softened. "Do you know why we live in these close quarters when we could spread out across a whole planet?"

Ro shook her head.

"You should do a better job studying your history."

"We don't have time for this, Dr. May. Please." Barre's voice cracked again.

She seemed to become even smaller than she already was. "I'm sorry. You're right. Follow me."

The door opened to her signal. Ro and Barre shared a look and followed the woman into the corridor. Their two guards gave them a startled glance, but fell in behind them.

"Lethe, allow full incoming communications access to Maldonado, Ro. Accept outgoing messages for delivery.

Continue routine monitoring."

Ro nodded. That was fair enough. After all, she had basically threatened the safety of Ithaka, its people, and its future. If their positions had been reversed, Ro wasn't so sure she would have agreed to her own terms.

May had been true to her word. Immediately, Ro's micro pinged with incoming messages. She stared at the display and read Nomi's first. Shit.

Chapter 23

MEDICAL WAS IN the same place it was in every standard-design station build. The door opened and Barre rushed inside. An eerie sense of the familiar clashed with the strangeness. His parents and their team weren't here. But Jem was.

A tall, lanky man in a rumpled jumpsuit crossed the room to intercept him. "You're his brother?"

"Yes. Is he … Is he …" He could barely get the words out. Barre wanted to push past this man and search medical until he found Jem.

There had to be something Barre could do. He thought back to his own neural procedure. It had been weird and painful, but it hadn't harmed him in any way. Barre ran his finger over the tiny scar at the nape of his neck. He could barely feel the slight thickening of the skin that indicated the base station. Inserting that had been the most irritating part of the whole process.

It had been a long time since he thought of the nanoemitters that had taken up residence in his brain. They had become a part of him, and he could hardly remember when he hadn't been able to focus his thoughts and intentions to trigger his micro, or to create the complex music that was equally a part of him.

He took a deep breath. Something of his parents' professional calm washed over him, and damped down his panic. "What's his condition?"

The man frowned at Barre's sudden switch to triage mode. "I'm Dr. Land and I oversaw the implant procedure."

Part of Barre wanted to shake this man for his recklessness. He forced himself to relax his clenched jaw.

"He's currently in a medically induced coma, and his brain function is essentially normal."

"Essentially. What the hell does that mean?" Barre felt his composure crack; at that instant, he envied his mother's ability to suppress all emotion.

"His vitals are stable. The actually procedure was uneventful. We had to choose a few unconventional placements due to his pre-existing damage."

Barre's heart raced. This matter-of-fact report was about his brother.

"The base module was slipped subcutaneously without incident."

He resisted the urge to rub at his scar.

"We monitored throughout and watched the near-field net deploy."

That had been the strangest thing Barre had ever experienced. It was as if a second skin had wound around his brain. Every thought, every sensation created a harsh echo. Sounds were louder, colors more garish, smells turned noxious. The movement of air across his skin had hurt so badly, he was sure he'd have welts.

But it was all an artifact of the amplification field. In time, it had eased, as he learned to habituate to what had become his new normal.

"And then he started seizing, in a rhythmic pattern of excitation and inhibition. Nothing we did could interrupt the pattern. We were concerned about neural cascade failure and sedated him."

"I need to see him. Now." It surprised him how steady his voice was. How much like his mother's tone of command. Of control.

Land nodded. "Follow me. The rest of the team is with him."

There were so many things Barre wanted to ask. Why did he do it? Jem was clearly a high risk patient. His developing brain would have been the least of it. How could he have risked damaging his mind even further? Barre wasn't sure who he wanted those answers from—Jem or Land.

He didn't even glance back to see where Ro was. There was nothing she could do for Jem. Barre set his jaw and followed the doctor into an isolation room.

Jem lay on a telemetry table, his thin body covered by a sheet. Monitors beeped in a cacophony that might have been turned into something musical. Barre shivered, staring at Jem for what felt like an eternity until he saw his brother's chest rise and fall. He didn't even spare a glance for the other doctors crowding the room.

"Damn it, Jem. You should have waited." Waited for him. Waited for another option. Waited until he was older. He straddled the metal stool beside the table and took his brother's hand in his. It was limp. Cool. The room was cold, too. Jem's skin was an ashy gray. Corpse gray. It didn't help to know they had reduced Jem's core temperature to ease the metabolic demands on his brain.

Barre closed his eyes but didn't let go of Jem's hand. "Focus, Barre, Focus," he muttered to himself. He could do this. He didn't know how, but he had to make contact again.

Clearing his mind, Barre let his mind play what he had come to think of as Jem's theme. Full of arpeggios, it reminded him of Jem as a little kid, climbing up and jumping off everything he could reach. Mostly, the music was bright, cheerful—maddeningly cheerful. But that was Jem. The discord, the darkness had come after his injury.

Waves of sound crested and receded, leaving echoes behind. In the stillness between the notes, he listened for his brother's small voice.

Silence.

Come on, Jem. Where are you?

He leaned forward until his head rested on the edge of the telemetry table. How had he done this before? Why wasn't the music enough? Maybe it only worked if Jem was trying to reach him at the same time he was trying to reach Jem.

Stripping out layers of instrumentation, Barre played Jem's theme again, this time as a simple repeating melody. He reached out toward Halcyone. A trill of three notes from the AI answered him. Relief made him tremble. He had been afraid that May would try to retake the ship. He signaled the AI again, and asked Halcyone to pass his musical message through to his brother as if he were just pinging Jem's micro.

It should work.

It had to work.

Moments passed, marked by the irritating dissonance of different monitors. He didn't even know if the med team was still there. They didn't matter. Only Jem mattered. If anything happened to him, it would break something in their mother. Something that was already extremely fragile. His lips twitched into a partial smile. Sympathy for their mother. Jem would think he'd gotten his neurons scrambled.

That would be my brain, not yours.

Jem!

Shit, Barre, you don't have to shout.

I'm here. With you. I mean, I'm talking to you, but I'm sitting next to you. Can you feel me holding your hand?

Jem fell silent for so long, Barre thought he'd disappeared again.

No. But I'm glad you're here.

I won't leave you. I'm going to figure this out. Find a way to get you home.

Look, this isn't your fault.

No. It's —

And it's not Dr. Land's fault either. This was the only chance I had and I took it.

Barre wasn't so forgiving.

Why can't I feel anything, Barre? Am I paralyzed?

They put you into an intentional coma to protect you. To quiet your brain. It was like it was on fire.

Oh. That's a relief. I figured the emitters had done something.

This time it was Barre's time to fall silent.

Barre? What's wrong?

He sighed. *The field triggered seizures.*

Shit. Don't let them take the emitters out.

But, Jem —

If you had to choose losing your music over dying, what would you do?

Barre squeezed Jem's hand, even though he knew his brother couldn't sense it. He didn't need to answer that question. They both knew what he would say.

Tell them to reverse the sedation. I'll either integrate or I won't.

Damn it, Jem. Don't make me do this.

Jem's internal voice got very quiet. *You're the only one who can.*

*

Ro had nearly bumped into Barre as he stopped short just inside of medical. She moved to follow him as they headed across the room, but May blocked her path.

"There's nothing you can contribute here. And we need to talk."

"Fine." Ro frowned as Barre disappeared into a procedure room before she turned to follow May.

The woman led her past the open lab space to a sealed door. It opened at a wave of her hand. "Come in. Sit down."

Ro crossed the room and sat at the edge of the worn chair.

"Compose your messages. Then we'll talk." May sat

opposite her.

This was impossible. How could this be the scientist Ro had idolized and studied for nearly her whole life? She glared at May before pulling out her micro. "You're sure Lethe can obscure the ansible path?"

"Of course."

Ro chewed her lower lip and considered several likely jump destinations close enough to Gal-3 so Halcyone could have conceivably gotten there in a day's travel, but isolated enough that ansible coverage would be thin. It would keep Daedalus guessing, anyway, and buy them some time. Reporting comms issues would delay Mendez even further, though it would also raise suspicions. That couldn't be helped.

She composed a short message for Daedalus and paused. Her private messaging program was pretty good. Daedalus had never discovered it. The question was, how good were May and her AI? And was Ro better? Hacking in to one of May's programs didn't mean much in the universe of things other than that particular hack was a solid one. As far as the messaging program, there was only one way to find out. She quickly replied to Nomi before turning to May, hoping her tiny text message wouldn't attract notice. "Okay, have Lethe route this to Daedalus through the Anistell system."

"Good choice."

Getting May's approval felt wrong. On the one hand, this was her hero. On the other, May's Underworld had allowed her father to nearly start a war and escape Commonwealth justice. There were so many questions she wanted to ask, but she kept her silence.

"It's clear that you're the programming genius." There was both admiration and condescension in May's voice. "I'm puzzled. I've only known Jem a short time, but he doesn't seem the type to take someone else's credit. Yet, he didn't tell me about you."

It annoyed her that May called him Jem. She had no right to claim his friendship. And less right to judge her. But Ro shared the woman's confusion. Why hadn't Jem said anything? Was he trying to protect her? "We're a team. Jem has less experience than me, but he's very, very good."

"Yes, he is. But it's you I'm interested in right now. You and your musical friend." May leaned forward in her chair. Her blue eyes sparkled in the room's low light.

Ro frowned. "You mean Barre."

"Bernard Durbin. There was no indication in his academic record of programming skills."

Ro's face heated. "You work fast."

"We have no choice. I'm responsible for a lot of people's lives here. We needed to know if you were a threat."

She snorted. A threat. Right. "Now what?" Barre wouldn't leave without Jem. And Jem wasn't medically stable. If they had harmed him, Ro didn't know what she would do.

"That's somewhat up to you, Rosalen. Tell me about your hack."

Ro shivered. Only her father called her that. "I'm at a definite disadvantage. Presumably, you now already know just about everything in my records. I was taught you died in the war. Obviously, that's not the whole story."

"Official records rarely tell the whole story. Yours, for example, is fairly thin."

May was playing with her, but Ro could be evasive, too. "You said I needed to study history. Well, I did. But the history I was taught isn't the history you lived. So how about you tell me your side of the story." Ro winced inwardly. It sounded like she was interrogating the great Adiana May. "And then I'll trade you and tell you what I did to get past Lethe's defenses."

"You are definitely something else, Ms. Maldonado. Fine. I'll start. But I warn you, it will be simpler for you to believe what you think you know."

"You've read my files. Have I ever taken the simple route?"

The corner of May's mouth twitched upward. "No." She stood and paced the lab. Her lurching steps created a strange, syncopated rhythm that echoed in the large room. "This planet wasn't always called Ithaka. It was one of dozens of the original mining stations set up in the first years of the Commonwealth. We were close enough so the trip from the hub only took a few jumps, but this was in the early days of quantum travel. There were only a handful of stable wormholes that had been mapped, and jumps were still extremely risky."

The first generations of jump pilots paid the price of getting the quantum calculations wrong. Ro had met an old pilot with end-stage jump sickness once. It still gave her nightmares. She had no idea how the poor bastard survived for so long with a random latency between his sensory signals, his cognitive process, and his motor response. Most of the early victims couldn't bear living permanently out of phase like that.

But the mining companies didn't want to spend the money or deal with the delay of sending colonists through interstitial space in cryosleep. So they burned through pilots and risked passengers. Until May helped create the SIREN code.

"And travel back then was expensive. Nearly all the original colonists were indentured miners or dissidents. And of course, their families; most of them shipped off for a one-way trip."

May seemed comfortable lecturing, which wasn't too surprising. So far, her version wasn't too far off the official accounts of the first diaspora. Except instead of the focus on political dissidents, the official line Ro had learned was that visas were granted to pioneers looking for adventure, fortune, or a different kind of freedom than was available in the Hub. If her father had been of age at the time, Ro imagined he might have been one of the colony applicants.

"My parents came here to work for the mining consortium. My father was an accountant. My mother, a metallurgist. Jobs were hard to find on Earth those days. They figured the hardship bonus would pay off their school debts a lot faster than anything in the Hub could've."

Ro glanced down at her micro, thinking of Nomi. If it weren't for her debts to the Commonwealth and her placement on Daedalus, Ro would never have met her.

"They had it better than most. Their jobs were pretty safe. And paid decently enough that they were able to afford a child. Me. And when I showed aptitude in programming, they paid for access to the virtual schools so I could keep learning."

If Ro's father had done that, Ro would never have had to tinker with Halcyone. She would have been able to qualify for a Hub scholarship. Jem wouldn't have been injured in the ship's wild burn and they would never have been here.

"They should have been able to pay off their debts and leave, but the more I learned, the more I needed to learn, and the more the Commonwealth charged them to provide it. Until they'd been on this inhospitable world for nearly two decades.

"I was given a full scholarship to Uni back in the Hub, and do you know that my parents were charged a premium to send me? A fuel surcharge." She laughed harshly. "You'd think that transportation on and off this rock would have been the cheapest thing around. And it should have been. Except the Commonwealth had a monopoly on aduronium, and practically all the isotope was taken off-planet. My transport added another six months to my parents' debt."

"What happened to them?"

May looked up and blinked at Ro. "They died here when I was working on my doctorate. Never knowing that they had paid their original debt ten times over. But I didn't find that part out until many, many years later. The part about meeting Chaz Dauber at Uni and creating the theoretical models for the SIREN code because we were bored? That's the story you probably already know."

It was easy for Ro to imagine young May and Dauber tinkering and refining what would become the first true AI, because that was the official history. As far as anyone outside Ithaka knew, the two had become victims and emblems of the war that the Commonwealth had gone on to win.

"You'd think that having pretty much invented the AI technology that let jumping become automated and nearly routine would have wiped out my debt to the Commonwealth." May paused. "But you'd be wrong."

How had she become this cynical old woman? "Did your parents die in the war?"

May stopped walking, turned back to Ro, and snorted. "Not hardly. They died because the corporation that ran the mining station never put any money back into the facilities. There was a radiation leak in part of the original residence ring. It killed them and a dozen other families and rendered a large part of the planet unlivable. This compound was built after the first one was condemned."

"I'm sorry."

"I tried to get back for their funeral, but even after the years I taught and did research to cover my debt, I didn't have the credit to pay for the trip. And not long after that, the war started in earnest. A group of several key colonies used the deaths here and elsewhere as a rallying cry for independence. They took over the isotope mining operations and cut off Commonwealth access to fuel. Of course it was mainly a symbolic gesture, since there were other colonies they were able to tap. But symbolic or not, the Commonwealth retaliated."

Ro nodded. That was part of the official history, too. During the war, there had been a famous blockade where Commonwealth forces tried to starve out the colonies. The desperate rebels had risked unstable wormholes to break through. As many died in the attempt as from combat. "I don't understand. If you were from the colony, how could you work for the Commonwealth? How could they trust you?"

May winced. "You have no idea what it was like. To know that the colonists were people just like your parents, your friends. To be part of the Commonwealth and understand that, for all its flaws, it created a stable society that you had been part of for over a decade. That had let you pursue your dreams and change the universe. You can't possibly understand how that can twist your loyalties."

"What made you choose the rebels?"

"I didn't. Until the virus. The one that brought down AI controlled ships. That was me. Well, us. Chaz and I created that virus to support the blockade and attack the rebels."

"Wait. That's backwards. The rebels were responsible for the destruction of ships all over the galaxy." That's what downed Halcyone. Ro creased her forehead. But Halcyone had been a rebel ship. It didn't make sense.

"No. They weren't. Chaz and I—we never thought the virus would be deployed. We thought the threat of it would end the war with the least amount of casualties to both sides, force both sides to the bargaining table."

"Is that what you tell yourself?" As soon as Ro opened her mouth, she regretted it. May looked past her, her eyes clouded.

"Chaz found out the Commonwealth was planning to use our virus to attack the colony on Marast Three. To send a message. The AIs we developed didn't only control ships. They also were deployed to keep the air clear and the water uncontaminated on the settlements.

"It wasn't hard to picture what would happen to all the

civilians on all the colony worlds once the Commonwealth unleashed what we created. It would be what had happened to my parents all over again, but on a much larger scale. In the end, I had no choice. Especially after Chaz died because he dared question his orders. I crippled the virus, but it was still deadly. To both sides."

Ro closed her eyes briefly. What would she have done?

"Now do you understand why I'm here?"

It was so hard to hold onto her anger. "What I don't understand is why you let men like my father infiltrate The Underworld."

"Your father?"

"I thought you had all my records."

May pressed the heels of her hands against her closed eyes. "It's what I told Jem. The Commonwealth redacted much of the information on the lot of you. So I take it you were also involved in the weapons smuggling he told me about."

"Involved?" Ro snorted. "Less involved than victims of. It's a long story. I was given Halcyone as a reward."

"Not to doubt your skills, given what you just pulled off on Ithaka—and we are going to talk about that—but why would the Commonwealth give you a ship?" May lowered her hands from her face and stared at Ro, her head tilted to the side.

Ro shook off her own growing doubts. She deserved that ship. She had brought it back to life. Halcyone was hers. "We uncovered a conspiracy that involved a disgraced diplomat, my father, and their black market contacts, and likely prevented a war. So yes, I earned my ship. And the black market—unless I am mistaken, that means The Underworld. Which means you."

"You are mistaken." May fell silent, her accusing gaze steady.

"So that's it? I'm supposed to trust you because you say so?"

"No. But I have honored my agreements. Your friend received his neural. Your communications have been unlocked. We have only asked for something in return."

"Wow. You're good. You drew us here, practically stole my ship out from under me, performed an illegal and risky operation on a minor, expect us to believe your story without an iota of proof, and be grateful that we're not under arrest?"

"Actually, yes."

Ro couldn't help it. She laughed. At first it was a strangled, mocking sound. And then May joined her, shaking her head and laughing until tears ran down her face.

"But you're wrong about one thing," May said when they had gained control of themselves. "I didn't bring you here."

"I don't believe you."

May shrugged. "I can't dictate what you believe. But think. You're an extremely smart and resourceful young woman. Having you here is a complication we don't need. Your presence puts me and my people in jeopardy. There is simply no good reason why I would have brought your ship to Ithaka, no matter how curious I was."

"Then how the hell did we jump here? And why?"

"Maybe you'd better tell me how you resurrected your AI. And then I'd like to know how you hacked into mine."

Ro looked into May's face, and with trembling hands, set

up several virtual windows. "I think it will be simpler if I just show you." Until this moment, she had never been shy about her own work. As she walked through her process, she kept sneaking glances at the woman who had created the very sandbox in which Ro played. Would she be angry at the modifications Ro had made? She was hoping for something more like 'impressed,' but wasn't counting on it. Especially now, after May had caught them intruding into Lethe's brain.

Ro played several of Barre's musical routines for her first. "I don't know if it would work on all computers, but Halcyone was pretty badly damaged. It had its own version of head trauma." Which brought her thoughts far too close to Jem. Barre was with him. It was going to have to be all right.

"He is a rather remarkable talent, your friend Barre."

Ro nodded. "You should tell him that. He might believe it coming from you."

"Then perhaps I will. Now let's look at your work." May leaned in to one of Ro's displays. "You broke into the SIREN code through the autonomics? Those systems were designed to be siloed."

"Well, they are, but look here." Ro pulled another window over and opened a rough schematic of the ships computer systems for her. Ada May. Damn! She was showing Ada May how to code. The thought nearly made her stumble into the heads-up displays. "There are points of contact. Semi-permeable membranes, really, that let the autonomics receive orders from the AI proper and let the state-data from the autonomics flow into the AI. I just found a way to alter the permeability settings." It made sense to describe it in that kind of anatomical language. As a metaphor, it was pretty apt. And something she'd learned from working with Jem.

"Just?" May lifted her eyebrows. "That's a lot more than 'just,' Ms Maldonado."

Her cheeks flushed with heat at the praise. "It's Ro."

"Ro," May said, smiling.

"So that's how I was able to even get the SIREN source code to reload. But there were complications." Ro had no intention of reliving the out-of-control burns Halcyone had taken, or the time it tried to shut off life support. "I couldn't get the jump drive to work."

"And?"

Ro sighed. No reverse in a wormhole. "Barre found a heavily damaged nav file. It had the words to a poem scattered in it."

"Ithaka," May said in a soft whisper.

"Yes. How did you know?"

"I wrote that program. It looks like you finally figured out at least part of what it does."

"Yes. It worked with the extra linkage in the drive and somehow translated the old maps."

"More transposed than translated. Barre would under-stand. But it was more than that." May nodded. "And that explains how you got here."

"Care to enlighten me?"

May inclined her head. "If you go to the significant trouble to make a place vanish, you can't leave maps around with a convenient arrow labeled 'you are here.' I created a homing routine. After one of our ships made a jump and re-entered interstitial space, the Ithaka program would send out a query, get a ping-back, and re-orient."

"They had to manually run it for every jump? That seems"—Ro paused, looking for a diplomatic way to say it —"less than elegant."

"We weren't looking for elegant. We were trying to survive."

Ro turned away.

"Otherwise, if a ship was captured, the Commonwealth would have found us. There were too many lives at stake to take the risk."

"So Halcyone was simply coming home." Would May take the ship? Ro choked back a bitter laugh. If this were the Commonwealth, she would have a legal claim. Salvage laws were clear. But this wasn't the Commonwealth. And Ro had no standing. It was like being under her father's capricious control all over again. "I won't give her up without a fight," Ro said quietly. It was less defiance and more just a statement of fact.

"I believe you."

"Excuse me?"

"Keeping you here against your will would be nothing but a recipe for disaster. I could isolate you and take away your micro, but I suspect you'd find a way to hack through my defenses with a spoon and a piece of string.

"And if we dumped you somewhere in Commonwealth space? You'd have the motivation and enough stubborn anger to find your way back here just to spite me." May laughed. "Am I wrong?"

"No."

"I thought so. You would have driven Chaz crazy," May said. "I'm sorry. I wish we could have met under different circumstances." She leaned against the chair opposite Ro and sighed. "Charon will think I've gotten soft in my old age, but you're free to leave."

"Wait. What?"

"I'll consider Barre's discovery and the vulnerability you uncovered as payment for your young friend. As soon as he is stable to travel. Take your ship and go."

"I don't understand."

"Go back to Daedalus. But be careful of the questions you ask. You might not like the answers."

"How do you know I won't betray you?"

May smiled. "I don't. But we've managed to survive so far."

Was May manipulating her? What did the woman truly want? She wished Barre were here. Or better yet, Nomi. Her instincts were a lot less cynical than Ro's. "Fine. Take me back to medical."

May nodded.

Ro followed, her mind whirling. What if May was telling the truth?

What if she wasn't?

Chapter 24

Commander Mendez walked into her office. Nomi followed, her mind whirling. Who the hell should she trust here? The lights brightened as Mendez walked over, not to her desk, but to the informal sitting area in the corner. So this wasn't quite so by the regs.

Nomi glanced down at her micro, not so much hoping for a message, but to collect her thoughts.

It's complicated. We're safe.

Her face heated up. Ro. Relief flooded through her. Gutierrez walked in with a tray of coffee and handed her a cup. Nomi's hands trembled as she took it, grateful for the interruption. By the time Mendez turned to her, she had regained her composure. If her face was still flushed, the hot coffee would explain it.

"Thank you, Emma."

Gutierrez nodded and left, but not before meeting Nomi's gaze with her own. It looked like a warning. Nomi took another sip of the hot drink and waited for Mendez to say something, anything that would give her a clue what was going on.

She desperately wanted to answer Ro, and to check for another message. *It's complicated.* When was anything with Ro ever not?

Nomi looked up at Mendez. The commander looked exhausted. Dark circles bruised the skin below both of her eyes.

"We have not been able to find any trace of Halcyone. This is disturbingly familiar."

"I'm sorry?"

"Your friend seems to have a talent for vanishing."

"I'm not sure she would consider it a 'talent,'" Nomi said. "More like an unfortunate accident."

"Fair enough." Mendez smiled briefly. It deepened the fine lines around her eyes. "But losing a ship and its crew after losing the child of prominent crew members has not made my job any easier. If you know something about Ro's whereabouts or plans, now would be a good time to tell me."

"No word from Hephaestus?"

Mendez raised an eyebrow.

Nomi flushed. Shit. Was their involvement not station knowledge? "I thought I heard Targill's name the other day."

"Halcyone is not their mission." Mendez's gaze didn't move from Nomi's face. The set of the commander's jaw made it pretty clear that she wasn't going to reveal anything more.

Nomi's stomach soured. Now what?

Daedalus's slightly nasal, bored voice broke through the silence. "Commander Mendez, message from comms."

"Patch it through."

"Commander, this is Lowell. We've made contact with Halcyone."

Nomi exhaled in a rush. At least she wouldn't have to choose between Ro and Mendez now.

"They're having issues, for a change." Lowell's voice was as dry and as sarcastic as he always was in person. "This time with comms. They sent their message through to the ansible network via a freighter in the Anistell system."

"Send the full text to my secure line."

"Yes, sir, Lowell out."

Mendez turned to Nomi. "Convenient."

"Sir?"

"Convenient that they were able to transmit line-of-sight to another ship."

Nomi knew that wasn't what Mendez meant. No, it was convenient that Ro could only send messages to Daedalus and not receive anything back. The text of her private message scrolled through Nomi's head. *It's complicated.*

It was clear that Mendez didn't believe Halcyone was in the Anistell system, and neither did Nomi.

"If you hear anything more from our search and rescue party, contact me, no matter what shift."

"Yes, sir." Nomi heard the dismissal in Mendez's voice. She set down the half full coffee cup and left, eager to shut herself in her quarters to answer Ro's message. Gutierrez was waiting in the anteroom. Nomi sighed. Now what?

"You will pass your messages to the commander through me."

"Yes, sir." Yes, Ro was definitely right. This was getting complicated. As she walked through the station, she couldn't shake the sense that she was being watched. The corridors were too crowded for her comfort. Now that Nomi had been here a while, everyone on station knew her and in such a small place it was impossible to hide. It took forever to get back to her room. Her micro seemed to get heavier and heavier as she walked.

Finally, she shook off the last of her fellow staffers and retreated to her quarters, relieved to finally be alone. That was a first. Ro was the anti-social one. As Nomi walked toward the sofa, the room lights brightened to her default afternoon settings. A blanket lay folded across the back rest and she ran her fingers across the soft fabric, thinking of Ro curled up beneath it.

Nomi sat and pulled out her micro. The message had vanished. Ro had designed the program that way, but it still made her uneasy to have it gone.

What the hell is going on? Everyone is going crazy here. Hephaestus is out there, looking for you. Looking for Ithaka.

She slid the blanket into her lap and set the micro on top of it. There was no telling how long it would take to get an answer. But she had nowhere to be. She just needed to figure out what to say to Gutierrez. How had Ro gotten her into this mess?

The minutes crawled by. Had Nomi said anything that might incriminate herself if Gutierrez decided to report her to Mendez? She didn't think so, but that didn't mean much.

Her micro buzzed. She jerked upright and it nearly tumbled off her lap. I can't tell you a lot right now. Jem's here. There were problems. Barre's on it. Hold off Mendez and Gutierrez as long as you can. Jem got the neural. It didn't go as planned. I don't know the details. I'm working on getting us home, but it may take a bit.

Nomi curled her fingers around the micro. Poor kid. Jem didn't deserve this. And she had helped him get in contact with The Underworld. Not intentionally, but that didn't make the guilt any easier to bear. I don't think you have a lot of time. Mendez knows you're not in the Anistell system. Where are you?

Ro's response came so fast, Nomi nearly dropped her micro in surprise.

Can't tell you that either. Not now, anyway. I'm sorry. As soon as Jem's stable for travel, I'll be in contact again. Miss you.

It would be easy for Nomi to be angry at being shut out again, but she had a pretty good idea what would happen if the Commonwealth found Ithaka. And as long as Ro, Barre, and Jem were there, Nomi was going to run interference for them.

Nomi stared at Ro's reply until the text slowly faded from her micro. Jem was alive and Ro missed her. No matter what, those were two pieces of good news she was determined to hold on to.

*

Once Barre's presence had disappeared, Jem fought off panic even though he'd been the one to disconnect. If that was even the right word. When he woke up—Jem didn't want to think about the alternative—he would have to try and figure out just how they were able to link. Halcyone had to have something to do with it. That was pretty radical. Maybe he could barter that information for the neural. Dr. May would definitely want to know how to replicate it. And then he could go home.

But for now, his brother's comforting voice and music were gone, and the silence in his head had taken on weight. At least he knew why he couldn't feel his body or open his eyes.

His parents had put plenty of patients into medically induced comas. For lots of reasons. It was a routine procedure which should have comforted him. It was a good thing Barre didn't realize just how scared Jem was, or he never would have agreed to waking him up.

It was impossible to measure time in this floating emptiness. Jem was forced to wait, each moment stretching out endlessly. What was happening in the med bay? What if the doctors were unable to reverse the coma? He thought nothing could be worse than the nausea and the dizziness. He was wrong.

Halcyone? Are you there?

He wasn't sure the AI was actually aware of him, or if the link to Barre was something that his brother had figured out. Either way, there was no answer. Not from Halcyone. Not from Barre.

Then, into his empty world, a bright blue light winked on and off in a regular rhythm. The light was accompanied by a noise that pounded against his ears. And Jem realized he had ears again. His heart raced. The light flashed faster. The sound sped up.

"Jem? Can you hear me?"

His brother's voice boomed against his skull. Each word trailed yellow streamers. The inside of his throat was raw. Jem swallowed what felt like tiny scalpel blades. The pain tasted green.

"He's crashing again!"

"Ready twenty cc's of prantophen."

The voices felt familiar and very strange at the same time. Each one bloomed a different color against his ears. The words were hard to separate from one another.

"No! You've got to give him a chance to sort this out." Those words were yellow. Yellow was familiar. Warm. Like real sunshine through real atmosphere. Yellow was Barre.

Jem struggled to connect his mind to his limbs, but everything in him felt heavy. Purple. He knew that was wrong, but it somehow made sense. Yellow was Barre. Purple meant heavy. Green hurt. Blue was loud.

"If we don't put him under right now, he risks permanent brain damage." Dr. Land's words were laced with red. The color of blood. The tinge of fear.

"Please. It's his only chance." Yellow again. Yellow streaked with red.

He focused on the waves of purple flowing through his arms and legs. Slowly, he lifted one arm. The color drained down the limb and into his torso, leaving the arm light, free.

"We have purposeful activity!" The red paled to light pink, then a pearl white.

A bright light seared his vision. He put his arm down and followed it, blinking furiously at the color trails.

"Pupils responsive. Eye tracking normal."

"We're still getting increased activation across the sensorimotor cortex."

Jem wished they'd all shut up. Between the colors and the pressure against his skin, he was getting a headache. And he'd had enough of those to last a lifetime. "Barre? Tell them to leave me the fuck alone."

His words felt heavy in his mouth, purple against his tongue. It was like eating lilacs. He remembered the intensely sweet smell of what his father had said was his mother's favorite flower. When Jem has been six or seven, they'd traveled to Earth for his mother to speak at some conference. His father had bought her a bouquet of the purple flowers and they made their hotel room smell the way his words did now.

"I know the scans look strange, but I'm going to call this baseline." Dr. Land's voice was steady, as colorless as water and it was a lot easier to listen to. "Jem? Jem, can you hear me?"

"Yes."

"Good. I'm going to repeat some of our sensory testing. The testing we did before deploying the nanoemitters. It will help us understand what is going in your very interesting brain. Okay?"

"Sure, doc. But Barre stays. And get the damned lights out of my face. They're heavy."

"I can do that on both counts."

The bright exam lights faded, taking the intense blue with them. Jem took a deep breath and looked around. He was in a generic medical bay, complete with standard issue transport bed and monitoring system. It was crowded with the entire med team.

"Mariana, I need you to stay. The rest of you, wait in the conference room."

Jem remembered that Mariana was Dr. Chote, the neuropsychologist. At least the ethicist was being kicked out before he could tell the team 'I told you so.'

"Jem? You okay?" Barre's words dripped with red. He looked into his brother's very concerned face. Barre was sitting on a stool at the bedside. He looked terrible. The circles beneath his eyes were dark shadows. They had a lot to talk about, but for now, Jem was just glad he was there.

"I'm not sure." He had never heard colors before. He had never felt sound before. He wasn't even sure how he could explain it. And if he did, would Dr. Land try to remove the neural?

"Your eyes, they're not doing the stutter."

Jem could feel the smile in his brother's voice. No more nystagmus? He would totally trade a world full of impossible colors for the ability to focus again. "Seriously, doc? Is that even possible?"

"I'm afraid that may be the sedation masking your symptoms. But let's get you through the testing, young man, and we'll figure out what's possible."

That sounded suspiciously like a medical brush-off, the kind of 'no' couched in meaningless platitudes. Not something he figured Land would resort to. Barre squeezed his hand. If his brother tried to reassure him now, Jem would rupture an air seal.

He closed his eyes as the doctors moved in and out of the procedure room, gathering their testing equipment. For now, he wanted some time in the silence of his own mind to sort out what had happened. What had changed. Jem had done as much research to prepare himself for this as he could, given the limitations of his vision over the past too-many difficult weeks. No two neural procedures were alike. Training and integration followed very idiosyncratic paths. But there was one common thread: active engagement between the patient's own thoughts and the nanoemitters sped up the process.

But how did he start? He was afraid if he asked Land and Chote, they would counsel him to wait until their testing was finished. And if he waited that long, and the testing wasn't good, they could very well want to remove the emitters.

Which wasn't going to happen.

It totally wasn't going to happen.

Halcyone? Jem tried to ping her with his mental voice as if he were just talking to one of her speakers. *Halcyone?*

The ship didn't acknowledge him. It was hard to keep his frustration and disappointment under control. He tried again. And tried to reach out to Barre, too. But the two of them—the ship and his brother—might as well have been a dozen wormhole jumps away. Jem was locked in his own mind. He tried envisioning what the emitters might be doing, thinking of Dr. Land's pre-op conference and presentation. Was the near-field net stabilizing? Had the silver mesh been able to bridge the damaged connections in his brain? It was weird knowing that something was going on inside him, but being unable to tell what. All the pain and odd sensations had been an artifact of the insertion procedure. Now, with his brain full of artificial neurons, he couldn't feel a thing.

He wished he could look at some of the stored data on his micro. Now that he had some context for what had just been done, the information he'd collected on the integration process would be a lot more relevant. The article was sitting on the top of the virtual pile of research he'd favorited. If he could only read it, it might help him get this thing in his head going.

A window brightened in front of him. The harsh light hit him with physical force and made him wince. Where was the light coming from? His eyes were closed. He blinked. Or thought he did. It was confusing. With deliberate effort, Jem opened his eyes. The display vanished. Instead, there was the procedure room. His brother sat by his bedside and the two doctors talked in hushed tones by the door.

Jem closed his eyes again. The virtual window was a sharp-edged, bright rectangle right in the center of his visual field. Text scrolled across its face. It was his micro. His micro, and it was displaying the case report describing one patient's experience with neural integration. *Holy shit.*

As eager as Jem was to explore more of what he might be able to do now, he also wanted to study the information in case the doctors interrupted him for their testing. He scanned through the article, looking for the patient description that hadn't made a whole lot of sense earlier. It was such a simple joy to just read something again, that Jem wanted to weep.

Could he keep going? Barely daring to second-guess himself, he paged through to the next article in the queue. The display dimmed. Jem squeezed his eyes shut even more tightly, willing the virtual-virtual screen to stabilize.

The page cleared. Jem began to read.

The display browned out again. Then, the words began to waver and warp in his visual field and he wanted to scream.

It was the nystagmus, or its equivalent, all over again.

It wasn't fair.

It wasn't fucking fair.

The window winked out, leaving a cold emptiness behind. He choked back a sob.

"Jem? Are you okay?"

He turned his head away from his brother. "No."

"What's wrong? Jem? Look at me."

The room twirled as his head moved. Hot tears leaked from his eyes. All of this for nothing. He met Barre's worried gaze.

"Oh, Jem. Damn it."

The yellow of Barre's voice bled red. He knew what his brother saw—the saccade of his eyes as they stuttered back and forth, back and forth.

Barre leaned over and rested his forehead on Jem's. "It's okay, kiddo. We'll keep working. You can't ... Don't give up. I'll help you."

Then Dr. Land's voice broke into Jem's misery. "Let's see what's happening, shall we?" He sounded so matter-of-fact, so casual, but Jem could hear the color of his concern.

Chapter 25

THE DOOR TO the small medical bay opened. Barre jerked his head up in time to see Ro charge into the room and stop short, staring at Jem, his small body still shivering against the table. "Is he going to be ... Is he okay?"

"I'm still here," Jem answered. His voice was barely louder than all the telemetry. He seemed so small.

Ro stepped to the opposite side of the bed and took Jem's other hand. The room had gotten crowded again. Dr. Land and Dr. Chote were by the door, leaning down to talk to Dr. May. What was she doing here?

"If you have Jem's results, I think you need to be talking to us," Barre said. He sat upright on the stool and used his best command voice. They needed answers. If the doctors thought they could avoid being straight with Jem, they would soon learn their error. Jem squeezed his hand. He squeezed back.

Dr. Land turned away from the door, nodding at him. "Yes. You are quite correct. Perhaps we should have a private conference." It was clear he meant for Ro to leave.

"We're a team," Barre said. "Jem?"

"Ro stays," his brother said. At least some of the color had returned to Jem's face and as long as he didn't try to focus on anything, the nystagmus was minimal. Maybe it was even a little less than it had been before the procedure, but Barre was afraid to ask Jem about it.

"Fine. I may need Mariana to clarify some points."

"Fine," Barre echoed. No one mentioned Dr. May. The woman half-leaned, half-sat against a low shelf near the door.

Dr. Land stood at the foot of Jem's bed. "Young man, how familiar are you with early neural attempts?"

Barre gave him points for speaking directly to Jem.

"I know the basics."

"Then you probably don't know about PINS."

"Huh?"

"PINS. Post Implant Neural Synesthesia."

Barre knew what synesthesia was. He felt his music as a full kinesthetic experience, complete with color and texture, not just something to process with his ears.

"We don't know why, but in some people, the nanoemitters can trigger a global synesthesia, where the senses map onto one another."

"That's one way of putting it," Jem said.

"There hasn't been a documented case in the literature in years. It was a side effect of some of the early implants."

"What did you do to my brother?"

"Barre, don't," Jem said, wincing, even though Barre hadn't raised his voice.

"Based on what we're seeing in your testing, Mariana and

I don't think it was in the design of the first-gen emitters or in their placement. We reviewed the old studies. Remember —almost all the early research was done on soldiers injured in the war, as a way to enhance control over prosthetics. And if they were injured badly enough to need limb replacement, it's a good chance many of them also had head injuries. We believe PINS is likely a consequence of placing nanoemitters in an injured brain. Like yours."

"Oh," Jem said.

"It is reversible?" Barre asked.

Land and Chote traded a look. "There was only one treatment that worked. We'd have to remove the emitters. And there's a short window of opportunity to get them all."

"No." Jem shut his eyes on what must be sensory overload. "I'm willing to give it a chance. A chance to integrate."

Only Barre heard the hitch in Jem's voice. His fear rang high and sharp through the room.

"But there's no guarantee the synesthesia will fade." Dr. Land frowned. "I'm sorry. This is uncharted territory."

Barre wanted to shake Dr. Land. He had no right to experiment on Jem. The risks were too great.

"Barre," Jem's thin voice interrupted Barre's rising fury. "It's not his fault. It's not your fault. It's not anyone's fault. It just is. I would have found a way to get a neural no matter what. So if you want to blame anybody, blame me."

He hated how resigned his brother sounded.

"There were some unexpected findings." Dr. Chote crowded in around Jem's bed and smiled down at them all. "It looks like what we assumed was seizure activity was just a different kind of integration. Especially across the visual-motor cortex. It looks like the emitters are trying to bridge some of the damage related to Jeremy's nystagmus and vertigo. It may also help his concentration and memory, but I suspect that will take some more testing, and more time."

"But you don't know," Barre said.

"I do," Jem interrupted. "At least now, there's a chance. Even if it's a small chance. So what if things have color and weight or smells and tastes."

"Will the nystagmus go away?" Barre asked.

"I'm sorry, we don't know that either," Dr. Land said.

"But there's a chance, right?"

"I believe so. It may be a case where his young brain is actually an advantage."

"I'd like to keep him in medical to repeat the neuropsych battery—," Dr. Chote said.

"No." Ro interrupted, her voice filling the small room. "Is he medically stable to travel?"

Chote blinked and looked at Dr. Land.

"We have no idea how long it will take for his brain to fully integrate," Dr. Land said.

"Is he stable to travel?" Ro repeated slowly.

"I wouldn't advise it." Land looked over to Dr. May. "Ada?"

"Ro, it's all right." Jem's hoarse voice cut through the tension. Everyone turned to him. Barre had an urge to shield him with his body. "It's all right," Jem repeated. "I made a promise. I'm staying."

Barre jumped up. The stool clattered to the ground behind him. "What? No!" he shouted.

"Ithaka fulfilled its side of the bargain." Jem glanced at

May. "This is mine."

"You can't … This is crazy …" Barre sputtered, shook his head, and started again. Getting angry wasn't going to help. It took several deep breaths before Barre felt like he was in control again. "You can't possibly hold him to any sort of agreement. First, he's a minor. Second, he made a choice essentially under duress. Third, it seems that your part of the bargain didn't work out too well."

Jem closed his eyes briefly. Barre wondered what he was seeing. "This isn't the Commonwealth, Barre, and you can't just carry me away. I knew what I was doing when I came here."

Dr. May nodded at Land and Chote. "I think I should take it from here." The two doctors shared a brief look before leaving. May pushed away from the wall and limped closer. "Your brother is a remarkable young man. And he is correct. He made an adult's choice and we respected that choice."

Jem smirked up at Barre. At least some things never changed.

"But I think you are right, too." May captured Barre's glance with her intense eyes. "As much as working with Jem would be a delight, the risk of him staying—of any of you staying—is too great for all of us."

"So you really are letting us go," Ro said.

"I've been a lot of things in my life, young lady, but a liar is not one of them."

Jem struggled to sit up. The sheet slid down, exposing his bony chest. He looked so frail and so small, but his expression was as resolute as their mother's. "I owe you a debt, Dr. May."

"Yes, you do. And the price of your freedom is your secrecy."

"Why are you trusting us?" Ro asked. Barre wanted an answer to that, too.

"I intercepted your message."

Ro's head jerked up.

"Not the one to your CO." May smiled. "Your other message. That was well done. You are as good as I thought."

"Ro? What is she talking about?" Barre asked.

"I sent a message. To Nomi. How did you find it?"

May smiled, but her eyes had a faraway look. "I figured out something very similar a long time ago. Chaz and I used it to talk when we didn't want anyone else listening." She shook her head as if to toss away old memories. "You could have betrayed Ithaka. You didn't. I'm going to take that as evidence of your character and your word. But I think you'd be wise to add encryption. I have one that might suit, if you're interested."

Ro blushed bright crimson and handed May her micro.

"What about our interface?" Barre asked. "I keep my promises, too."

"Well enough. We need to give your brother a little more time to recover before subjecting him to jumping."

Jem groaned and slid back down onto the table.

"Perhaps you wouldn't mind giving me a tour of Halcyone and showing me what you can do at the same time?"

Halcyone was Ro's ship and this was her call. Barre caught her gaze and raised his eyebrow.

"Fine," she muttered.

"Will you stay with Jem?"

Ro exhaled heavily. "Of course."

Barre held out his arm for Dr. May. "Shall we?"

She smiled and placed her small hand in the crook of his elbow.

All the way back to Halcyone, Barre tried to figure out what was really going on. Finally he just asked. "Why are you doing this?"

Dr. May sighed. "Talk to your brother and to Ro. Between them, they can give you the long version. The short version? We were betrayed by the Commonwealth. Chaz died to protect me. I used what we built to safeguard Ithaka. The private comms program we created became the backbone of a secure communications relay that allowed The Underworld to function and flourish."

"Oh, is that all?"

She laughed and patted his arm.

Barre paused at Halcyone's air lock. "Is she okay? You didn't do anything to her, did you?"

May slipped her hand from his elbow. "No."

"Okay, then. You wanted to see what I figured out?" Barre triggered the command fanfare, but had it play through his micro. The notes filled the small space by the airlock. Then Halcyone repeated it with her subtle variation. Barre added the command for entry and the door cycled open.

"Interesting."

"I can also do it directly from my neural. I just wanted you to hear. Welcome aboard." Barre showed her the whole ship, from the cargo bay where the contraband weapons had been stored, to their quarters, to the bare bones of what had been medical, to engineering, and finally to the bridge. Until they reached the bridge, the only time May reacted was to touch one of Barre's guitars and smile as the sound reverberated through his room.

Despite all the cleaning up he and Ro had done, the bridge still showed the scars of the desperate battle of her last crew to regain control over the virus-ravaged AI. As May limped around the damaged consoles, Barre told her about the snippets of the logs they had recovered. "The ship was on a collision course. The AI wouldn't respond. We think they turned their weapons on her main memory and drives in a last-ditch effort to save themselves. Maybe they figured they could manually land the ship and reconstruct the AI later."

There had been no 'later' for them or for Halcyone. Not until Ro started tinkering forty years after. It was weird. Barre could draw a direct connection between Dr. May, the virus, this ship, Ro, and their landing on Ithaka.

"I wonder if I knew them." May stood, staring at the broken viewscreen. "So many died to protect the secret of Ithaka. Sometimes I wonder if it was worth it."

Barre looked down at the floor, permanently streaked with evidence of weapons fire.

"I did what I believed I had to do. All the years building The Underworld and subverting our way into Commonwealth systems, I always thought it would be the military who found us. Or a smuggler looking to play both sides of the street. I never expected you."

"Me?" Barre shrugged one shoulder. "Ro did all the heavy lifting."

"She is truly brilliant. She and your brother have the talent and the creativity to be better than I was. But you? You were a surprise."

"How about you tell my mother that. Maybe she'd believe it from someone like you."

"What she believes is irrelevant."

Barre lifted his gaze from the floor.

"What do you believe?" May asked gently.

"I'm not sure." She confused him. This was the home of the black market. If Ro and Micah were right, both of their fathers had connections, if not with Ithaka, then through it. Which made May responsible. For the weapons and for Jem's injury. No. That wasn't the full truth. Each of them had made choices that led them here. Including Barre. "If the Commonwealth found you, they would destroy this place and dismantle The Underworld."

"Yes and no."

"No?"

"Sure, the idea of Ithaka is a threat, but what they want, what they have always wanted, is to control The Under-world. And now I'm in a position where I need to protect it, even though it has grown far beyond what it was created to be." She sighed. "Beware the unintended consequence. We needed a system to communicate that took advantage of the existing ansible network, but was untraceable. So I discovered a way to utilize the system's blind spot, much like your friend, Ro. But its very advantages—anonymity, path randomization, and self-healing—made it a conduit for the syndicates and the smugglers."

Barre understood all about unintended consequences. "And even if the Commonwealth knew about it, they couldn't take it out without shutting down the entire ansible system."

May laughed—a short bark of a laugh. "Of course they know about it, young man. The Commonwealth uses The Underworld for its own purposes. And cosmos help me, I created the means for them to do so. Everything we do on Ithaka is an attempt to stay ahead of the Commonwealth."

Maybe Barre had been around Ro too long, but he believed May. It wasn't just paranoia. Paranoia didn't explain the forged diplomatic seals on the weapons that had been in Halcyone's hold. That degree of finesse required the resources of the Commonwealth itself. "You haven't done anyone any favors by bringing us here."

"I know. I'm sorry."

"You helped Jem, and I'm grateful. If I knew how I reached him through our neurals, I'd tell you. But the truth is, I was worried. I couldn't get Halcyone to respond and I did what I always do when I get overwhelmed—I retreated into my music."

May limped over to him and looked up. She wasn't all that much taller than Jem. "I think there's more to it than that. You've created something unique. A musical language to communicate with an artificial intelligence. Your discovery should be all over the literature. In a different life-time, I would research your process and be proud to be a coauthor of the official paper."

Barre turned away from the intensity of her gaze. "None of that matters to me. I just want my brother to be okay." And as he said it, he realized it was true. The papers and the research would validate his skills to his mother, but none of that would change who he was and what he loved.

"So can you show me some of what you've done?"

He placed his micro on one of the consoles and waved Dr. May into the chair. "I can try."

"That's all I have any right to ask," she said.

*

"Are you going to be okay?" Ro asked. She had never seen Jem look so small and frail, even when he was semi-conscious on Halcyone after his injury.

He squeezed her hand and smiled. "I don't have any choice."

"Is there anything you need? Something to drink? Another blanket?"

"No. I'm just glad you're here."

Ro watched his eyes blink more and more slowly until they were closed. Between one breath and the next, he had fallen asleep and his hand relaxed in hers. She hesitated as she pulled out her micro. So May knew about her hack. And because of it, Ro had gotten Nomi even more tangled up in this mess. Now what?

So far, May hadn't given Ro any reason to doubt her word. But she had no idea what to do once they left Ithaka. They had to get Jem home. That was clear. But plotting a course that wouldn't betray Ithaka's location would be the easy part. What would they tell his parents? What would Mendez believe?

There was too much Ro didn't know. Without Nomi's help, everything would fall apart. But if they were discovered, Nomi could be charged with treason. And if May could track their messages, could someone in the Commonwealth?

How had everything gotten so complicated?

Ro swallowed a laugh, not wanting to disturb Jem, and woke the little computer. This would be a lot safer when she could deploy May's encryption to all their micros, but for now, it was the only way she had to communicate with Nomi. The transient nature of the messages should make them difficult to intercept. It was a risk she had to take. One she knew Nomi would accept, too.

Jem's going to be okay. Pretty much. She had to believe that and so did Barre, or it was all for nothing. We're coming home. But need to plan our route. It was so frustrating to communicate this way, not knowing if her messages could be intercepted. There was no way of knowing when Nomi would get them or when she would get a reply. Sometimes the traffic was almost instantaneous. Other times, the tunneled messages got delayed or bumped if the network was choked. Ro had to hope for the best. Will send official traffic as soon as we're able. Maybe best if we let Hephaestus escort us home?

Avoiding the ship would only make it look like they had something to hide. Now they had to figure out what to say about Jem. Ro didn't think it would be possible to lie about contacting Ithaka. But could she use enough information to keep suspicion away from her and Barre while protecting May's location?

All Ro knew was she couldn't do this alone. She stared at the text, feeling how inadequate it was, but not knowing what else she could say. Miss you? See you soon? Be careful? They were all true and all just words. Taking a deep breath, Ro finally added to the message. <u>Be safe.</u> Her hands trembled as she tapped SEND and watched the words vanish.

Chapter 26

"How's he doing?"

Ro had been staring so intently at her silent micro that she nearly fell off the stool when Barre's voice filled the procedure room.

"Asleep," she said, keeping her voice low.

"Awake, now," Jem said.

Barre hastily slid into the seat on the other side of the bed. "Hey."

She looked away as the brothers hugged. "I should get Halcyone ready."

"Ro, wait," Jem said. "We need to talk."

When she turned back to the bed, Barre was holding Jem's hand again. "Maybe we should wait until we're aboard Halcyone," she said. "You do realize that we have no expectation of privacy here."

Jem shrugged. "Dr. May already knows everything there is to know about us. About Halcyone."

"Barre?"

"He's right."

"Fine." Ro glanced down at her micro, but there was still no reply from Nomi. "The clock is ticking. The longer we stay here, the more we put Ithaka in danger of discovery."

"Dr. Land is going to want to do more tests," Jem said.

Ro drew her eyebrows together. If taking Jem home put him at risk, then they couldn't leave with him. But they couldn't show up without him, either. Not unless they wanted to trigger a full-sector search.

"Can Mom and Dad monitor you?" Barre asked.

Jem sighed. "I was hoping we could avoid telling them."

"Do you really think they'll believe you ran away to get a neural and nothing happened? Seriously? And even if they did believe you, once they did a scan, they'd see the implant. We're going to need a good story."

"I'm more worried about Mendez," Ro said. Not only did they need a story, but they needed to scramble their nav logs. And hide the file that contained the Ithaka reference. "How's the ship?"

"Halcyone's fine. They didn't do anything to her and she responds to my neural commands."

"Good." Ro took a deep breath and her shoulders settled.

"May keeps her word," Jem said.

"You trust her?" Ro wanted to. She really did. But it was still hard to reconcile her childhood idol with the woman who was waging a secret war with the Commonwealth through the power of the black market. And May had tried to hijack Halcyone.

"Yeah. I guess I do. There's no sour in her voice."

Ro raised an eyebrow. "Sour?"

"Lies taste sour." Jem shrugged. "I know. It's weird. It's weird to me, too."

"I think we don't have a lot of time. We've already been gone more than a full standard day and been out of contact for almost that long."

Barre leaned in toward his brother. "Are you sure you're up to jumping?"

Jem wrinkled his nose. "It'll suck. But waiting won't make it suck any less. So yeah."

"What are we going to tell your parents?"

Barre and Jem shared a worried look.

"Lucky for both of you, I have a lot of experience with this. The best lies stick as close to the truth as possible. How about—Jem contacted a doctor from the black market. They helped smuggle him off-planet. And then he was taken to an undisclosed location for the procedure and returned to Gal-3 where we found him." She paused. "Wait, we're going to have to change our flight plan so it looks like we jumped from the Anistell system back to Galileo."

"Jem? How were you going to pay for this?" Barre asked.

He looked away as his eyes began to hitch again. "Micah," he mumbled. "His father left him all this money and he didn't want it. He said it should go to where it could do some good. I told him I needed it for an experimental treatment."

"Micah." So that's what Jem meant in his hidden message.

He sat up and stared them both down, holding his head at the awkward angle that minimized the nystagmus. "I didn't lie. It just wasn't the whole truth."

"Maybe you are as good at this as I am," Ro said.

Jem clenched his jaw.

"I'm sorry. I was trying to be funny."

"Look, can we leave Micah's part out? I don't want to get him in trouble."

Ro smirked. "Seriously? He's used to it." She looked at her micro again as text began to scroll across its surface. It was as if Nomi were there beside her, whispering in her ear.

Send your comms traffic asap. Things getting stressful here. Don't know whereabouts of Hephaestus. Mendez said you were not their mission.

She read and reread Nomi's message. They had pretty much run out of time. "Can you walk?"

Jem nodded. "You need to find my clothes."

"What's going on?" Barre asked.

"We basically triggered a supernova on Daedalus when we dropped out of sight. Hephaestus is patrolling, but Nomi doesn't think they're looking for us."

"Shit."

"Can you get Jem aboard and squared away in a jump snug?"

This time both brothers shared the same expressions of disgust. Well, it couldn't be helped. "Lethe, contact Dr. May. Urgent. Have her meet us on Halcyone."

"Acknowledged."

It was weird to hear May's voice from a computer's synthesizer. "I'll see you on board," Ro said.

"We'll be right behind you." Barre rummaged around on the shelves above the telemetry table and found Jem's clothes.

At the door, Ro hesitated. It remained stubbornly shut.

"Lethe, access request, Maldonado, Rosalen, clear route from Medical to Halcyone."

"Approved." The door slid open. Ro sprinted her way back to the ship.

May must have been closer, because she was waiting at the airlock. It took Ro several seconds to catch her breath enough to request entry. At least Barre had fixed that.

"We need to leave before they figure out Ithaka is only a few jumps from Gal-3." It wouldn't matter that it wasn't on the maps if they decided to run a massive search pattern. If the Commonwealth was desperate enough, they'd risk unstable wormholes. Hell, all they would have to do is send drones. Ro couldn't do the math in her head, but there were a finite number of wormholes within a reasonable distance from Gal-3. Each of those had branching paths into more, but there wasn't an infinite number. With enough resources and enough time, Ithaka could be found.

"It's not like this was unexpected. We have other defenses." May placed her hand on Ro's arm. "It's okay."

She flinched, but didn't shake off the older woman's touch. This wasn't her father. She wasn't a threat. In a different set of circumstances, Ro would have begged for a place at this woman's side. There's was so much she could have learned here. "I need your help."

May nodded.

"Follow me." It took all of Ro's willpower to give May access to Halcyone. But it was the only way. With a series of quick gestures, she set up virtual windows above the main engineering console. In one, she opened the garbled "Ithaka" file. In another, the nav logs. The raw data didn't make a lot of sense to Ro, but it would to an astronavigator. Especially one who was looking for a place that didn't want to be found.

The older woman watched Ro and smiled. "I don't think I've ever seen someone as adept with gestural controls."

Ro turned to hide the blush that heated her face.

"So, what would you like me to do?"

There was so much Ro wanted to ask her. If they had the time, she would have loved to go over the SIREN source code line by line, and talk about each subroutine. But that would take months. Maybe longer. "I don't know enough about nav systems to alter our logs. But I'm going to proceed on the assumption that the Commonwealth will impound the files. Is there anything here that will betray you?"

"No. Some of our other defenses in the Ithaka file include a randomizer utility that scrambles the recording of the nav paths. It's why the program needed to be run before every jump. Leave the logs as is. If we make any changes, that will raise more red flags than the nonsensical data."

Ro raised an eyebrow at 'some.' She wished there was time to review more of the program with its creator. "Good."

May gave her a quizzical look. "So you really don't want us to be found."

"I may not trust you, but if you knew my father, you'd know why I don't trust the Commonwealth either." Or anyone. But that wasn't true anymore. Thanks to Jem, Barre, Micah, and Nomi.

"I'm sorry."

"For?"

"That what I built was able to be subverted." She glanced down at her foot. "I've seen too much death and destruction to ever want open war again."

The memory of Micah's ruined feet nearly made Ro gag. "I believe you."

"What else do you need to be able to leave?"

"Some better jump cushioning for Jem. And a nav path that takes us back to Gal-3 by way of the Anistell system."

"Well, you don't, actually. I can program in the most direct jump sequence from here to Gal-3. The Ithaka program will take care of the rest. The logs will spew out a bunch of meaningless data—enough to keep the Commonwealth engineers busy for months."

Ro smirked. It was the kind of hack she would love to have created. It reminded her of her ghost program. "She's all yours." She stepped back and waved May forward. Her breath hitched in her throat as Ada May lifted her hands and took control of Ro's little world.

Watching May use the interface made Ro feel awkward and slow. Even with their slight tremor, the woman's hands moved in smooth, effortless arcs. At first, Ro tried to keep track of every gesture, but she kept getting distracted by splashes of color and light as data swirled through the heads-up display. There was both a beauty and an economy to her work. Even if Ro hadn't known May's identity, she would have understood she was in the presence of a master.

Time slowed as she watched. When Ro looked around, Barre and Jem were beside her. A trundle full of supplies came to a halt behind them.

"I took the liberty of getting you some things," May said, her gaze never leaving her virtual windows.

"Thank you," Ro said.

Barre bent down to empty the cart. In addition to some basic food rations, it held three sets of intact jump cushions. Dense and breathable, they were form-fitting and designed to dampen the temporal vibrations of wormhole travel. They did a far better job than the snugs. Maybe Ro could rig their micros to project a fixed horizon to lock on to, which would make the trip easier still. Though it probably wouldn't work for Jem. Poor kid.

"Wow," Jem whispered, looking up at May's work.

"Pretty much," Ro said. "It's good to see you upright."

Jem smiled thinly. "It's not as easy as it looks."

May stepped back from the virtual screen. "You're all set."

"Dr. May. Thank you," Ro said. There were so many things she wanted to say: Thank you for helping Jem. Thank you for letting them leave. Thank you for not holding Halcyone hostage.

She took an uneven step closer to Ro. "Ada. Call me Ada."

"Ada." Ro wasn't sure what came over her, but she put her arms around Ada May's slight frame. The two of them hugged before Ro disengaged and stumbled away from the uncomfortable and unexpected intimacy.

"Good luck," Ada said.

"You too."

"Young man, I think I'll take this back now." The woman slid Jem's sleeve up. Her fingers slid along the smooth surface of his wrist cuff and it opened with a soft click. She shook Jem's hand. "It was a pleasure. You could do a lot worse than learn from your friend, here. And don't give up hope."

Jem rubbed the bare spot on his arm. "I haven't forgotten

what I owe you."

"And you have a remarkable talent, Barre. I hope our paths cross again someday."

Barre turned from where he had been staring at the file that had started their journey here. "Is this your work?"

Ada nodded. "Chaz started the naming convention. You should have seen all the acronyms he went through before he found SIREN. He loved old mythology. I chose Ithaka to honor him and the journey he didn't live long enough to make."

"Is there a way to safeguard this without losing the data?"

"I thought you had copies on Daedalus," May said.

Ro shrugged. "I lied." The only copies they had were the ones she made to test on Halcyone. Telling the truth was a gamble. If Ada set the file to self-destruct, Halcyone wouldn't be able to translate the old maps that could let them find their way back. But the risk to Ithaka was too great to let it remain.

"I'm sorry. It would be better for all of us if —"

"Wait. I have an idea," Barre said. "What if I bury it behind a musical trigger? No one on Daedalus knows about what I can do. If anyone stumbles across it and tries to access it, it'll just go boom anyway."

The incredible barrage of sound was not something Ro wanted to ever experience again. "Are you sure?"

"Yes, I am." Gone was his hesitation or his self-effacing uncertainty. And as much as it stung Ro to admit it, this was something he could do that she couldn't. "Are we good, Dr. May?"

"Five by five. And it's Ada."

Barre smiled. "All good, Ada."

It startled Ro to hear Nomi's expression coming from Ada May's voice. "So are we ready to go home?"

"Ready as I'll ever be," Jem said.

Barre offered Ada his arm. She patted his hand and declined.

"I know the way. Safe travels," Ada said, before picking her way toward the door in engineering. The trundle wheeled after her. They followed the echo of her uneven steps all the way down the corridor.

"All right, music-boy. Do your thing. Then get Jem secured for the jump sequence."

"Aye-aye, Captain."

"We all know the story, right?" Ro asked.

Barre and Jem both nodded, and despite the differences in their ages and builds, she saw the same determined expressions in their eyes.

"Let's get these rockets firing."

*

Nomi paced her quarters and watched the time, not knowing what to do with herself. Other than her scheduled days off, this was the first late shift she wasn't supposed to work since being assigned to Daedalus. The change would wreck her sleep schedule. But for now, that was the least of her worries. Ro was on her way home. And Jem was with them.

She hoped the poor kid got some relief from the constant

vertigo.

But once they were safe, then what? If Ro had truly found Ithaka, she could claim the finder's fee and would never have to worry about Halcyone again. Hell, with that much credit, she could buy a new ship. And probably leave Daedalus. But for some reason, Ro was working on a plan to divert Hephaestus from Ithaka. Why? She kept going back to Ro's first message. *It's complicated.* No shit.

The visitor chime rang. Nomi stopped in the middle of the room and stared at the door. No one came to her quarters except Ro. And Ro was still somewhere between the silence of interstitial space and the reality-folding of jump space.

The chime sounded again.

"Daedalus, identify."

"Gutierrez, Emmaline."

A chill traveled the length of Nomi's spine. It wasn't like Gutierrez didn't know she was in her quarters. If she didn't answer, that would give the LC more to distrust than she already had. "Fuck," she whispered, channeling Ro, and signaled the door to open.

"Lieutenant Commander, please come in," Nomi said.

As Gutierrez stepped inside, Nomi studied her in an attempt to figure out if this was official station business. The LC was dressed in her military uniform, but that wasn't surprising. Nomi figured the woman probably slept in one. The overhead light glinted on the prosthetic and she forced herself not to look away.

"Would you like to sit?"

"No."

Nomi steadied her hands on the back of the chair and stood facing Gutierrez. "How can I help you, sir?"

"I need to know if Ro has located Ithaka."

"Sir?" She held onto the chair back to keep from stumbling. "As far as I know, that's what Lowell is trying to do."

"Lowell is a fool. I didn't take you for one."

"She's just trying to get Jem home." Her voice faded into a whisper.

Gutierrez folded her arms across her chest. The manufactured one gleamed. "I told you before. I owe a debt. I mean to pay that debt even if it costs the lives of your friends."

Nomi gasped.

"I don't wish it to come to that, but if they unmask Ithaka, the war that follows will make the one I lost my arm and my innocence to seem like a skirmish."

"What do you want from me?" A flash of light caught her eye. Nomi glanced down at the micro, balanced on the edge of the table. *Not now, not now,* she thought wildly and quickly looked away. But it was too late. Gutierrez had followed her gaze and they both saw the message scrolling across the small screen.

Official message inbound. We're at Gal-3 and the headers will match. Hephaestus should have no problem tracking us here. Home soon.

Gutierrez nodded. "What is she planning?"

Nomi closed her eyes briefly, wishing Ro were here with her. "Plan? She doesn't plan." Barre's words replayed in her mind: *Ro jumps first and calculates the course after.*

"She mentioned Hephaestus. What is she trying to do?"

"I think she's hoping to lead them away from Ithaka."

"Your friend is playing a dangerous game."

"And so are you, Lieutenant Commander." Nomi emphasized her title. Gutierrez should be helping the Commonwealth forces, not running her own interrogation sessions.

"Ah, but the Commonwealth isn't officially searching for Ithaka. Officially the 'lost colony' is a spacer's tale. No more, no less than that."

"And the money?"

"There have been crackpots and conspiracy theorists as long as there have been societies." Gutierrez shrugged. "Some of them have money to burn."

"So Ithaka doesn't exist and Hephaestus isn't looking for it."

"Exactly."

"So why did you erase the comms logs?"

"Because Ithaka doesn't exist and Hephaestus isn't looking for it."

"What kind of debt has you orbiting treason?"

Gutierrez stared until Nomi blinked. "I can't tell you that."

They were both on the edge of sedition. How much worse could it get? "Can't or won't?"

"Yes. Both." Gutierrez softened her harsh expression. "I'm sorry. It's complicated."

Hearing Ro's answer come from the LC raised the hair on the back of Nomi's neck.

"So answer me one last question, Nakamura." Gutierrez relaxed her arms and paced an exact trajectory between the door and the galley. "If they make it back to Daedalus, are they smart enough to craft a good story and stick to it?"

"If? What would possibly keep them from getting here from Gal-3?"

She traced the wall with her artificial hand. "Accidents happen. Even in stable wormholes. And their ship is old. Unpredictable."

"You don't believe that."

"It doesn't matter what I believe. Let's say Targill considers them a threat. Or a source of information. Where do you think his loyalties lie?"

Not with Mendez or Daedalus. He answered to bigger fish. "What about yours?" Nomi whispered.

"It's not my loyalties you need to think about. How far will you go to protect what you care about? What are you willing to give up?"

"I don't understand."

Gutierrez stepped closer and dropped her voice. "I think you do. Nothing you've done up to now has risen to the level of treason." She glanced at the micro, nodding when she noticed Ro's message had vanished. "At least nothing documented. But a time is coming where you're going to have to make a choice. Of all of you, who has the most to lose?"

"Why are you doing this?" Nomi's stomach cramped and her mouth flooded with sour saliva. She could lose it all—her position, her future, her family. She swallowed over and over to flush the taste from her mouth.

"Because if you're going to follow the path I've traveled, you need to know what's at stake. You have a chance. Just one chance to walk away and stay out of this."

Nomi looked down at the folded blanket. Her eyes

brimmed with tears. "I can't," she said.

"I'm sorry. Don't say I didn't warn you." Gutierrez left, her steps measured and precise on the hard floor. When the door closed behind her, Nomi clutched the blanket and huddled on the sofa, rocking back and forth.

Chapter 27

"ALL CLEAR. HALCYONE is in parking orbit around Gal-3." Ro's voice sounded a little shaky, and not just because it was passed through the ship's ancient speakers. "Everyone okay?"

The jumps between Ithaka and Gal-3 were easier and harder than Jem expected. Harder because this time he didn't have the benefit of whatever drugs Charon used to knock him out. Easier, because the jump cushions May had provided were a lot better than the worn compartment on Charon's little ship.

"I think I'd rather be a crewsicle next time," Barre said, groaning from the lower bunk.

He wasn't sure cryosleep was the answer either, but Jem was definitely glad they were going to pause here for a while.

"Meet me on the bridge," Ro said.

"Aye-aye, Captain." Jem and Barre said in chorus.

"I hate you both. Ro out."

The small room smelled dingy gray, the color of long-forgotten laundry, a combination of old vomit and sour sweat. "Just like old times."

Barre stumbled over to the sink and wiped his face. "Not quite the way I remember it."

"Help me down?" He didn't trust the vertigo not to betray him as he climbed from the top bunk.

"You got it."

Barre's arms were steady around Jem's shoulders as he made it to the floor. It wasn't home, but being surrounded by Barre's instruments was comforting. He looked up, feeling his brother's concern. Beneath the wild dreads, his face had the pinched worry of their mother's expression.

"It's going to be okay."

Barre pulled him in an uncomfortably tight hug. "You're an idiot," he said. The words were bright yellow, warm against his skin.

"I love you, too, but I can't breathe."

"Sorry. Sorry." Barre backed away and stumbled into one of his small hand drums. The hollow sound filled the room with pale blue.

It was weird and it wasn't. Part of him marveled at the way his senses jumbled together, but the sensations were just there. Like they had always been. Jem couldn't feel any evidence of the nanoemitters buzzing around his brain. The only thing that did bother him was the scar where they had slipped the base station under his right ear. It itched, the sensation a crawling light green.

And then there was the way he and Barre were able to hear each other's thoughts. On a theoretical basis, it made sense. Each neural could directly connect with either a simple processor or an AI. And an AI had the computing power to amplify and relay those commands to another neural. But as far as Jem knew, no one had done it before. And ever since the docs had awakened him from his coma, it hadn't happened again. It was something they definitely needed to talk about. But now wasn't the time. Maybe if his control over the neural got better. Maybe. It was hard to hold on to that hope, but it was all he had. "Okay. Shall we move on to step two of the grand plan?"

"After you."

They walked through Halcyone's quiet corridors, and for a moment, it was like stepping back in time. But the last time he'd been here with Barre, the AI had been trying to kill them, and Jem's head had been leaking blood into his brain. Yeah. Even with the weird color/smell/feel thing going on, this was a lot better. And it could have been the anti-nausea meds on board, but he thought the vertigo wasn't as bad. Or maybe he was just accommodating to it.

Ro was waiting for them on the bridge. Jem caught a whiff of burned plastic. Swirls of red and green danced in his vision for an instant as he glanced at the ruined door. He had already been taken to Hephaestus when Micah had been shot, captured, and then had nearly burned his own feet off to get free from Ro's dad. They had not been able to replace the door that he'd blasted through to save Ro and Barre.

Maybe they should leave it like that. A monument or something. Though it did make it impossible to seal off the bridge.

"Is everybody ready?" Ro asked. Her words also felt yellow, like Barre's. Full of concern, but warmth, too. "I sent a message to Nomi. I have to transmit our official comms traffic to Daedalus. I'm hoping Hephaestus isn't far from here. If they act as our escort, then they can't be looking for Ithaka, right?"

It seemed like a lot to pin their hopes on. "If they think we know something, they're going to keep us under a lot of pressure."

"We haven't done anything illegal. Ithaka doesn't actually exist as far as the Commonwealth is concerned," Ro said. She sounded confident, but Jem felt the red of fear permeating her words.

"But the black market does," Barre said.

"Remember, we didn't contact The Underworld."

"No. I did," Jem said.

"And you're a minor," Ro said. "We just came to find you. And Mendez officially sanctioned our search. Besides, it's all true." She used her fingers to count off each item. "You were drugged. Someone took you to an undisclosed lab. You received the neural in return for payment. You were given money by Micah. And you have no idea what route you took on your trip back to Gal-3."

That was the outline of their story. It was simple. He could even use Dr. Land's name—Barre assured him he didn't exist based on extensive searches. So it was either an assumed name, or he'd been expunged from Commonwealth records by Dr. May. Ada. Jem smiled. He was on a first-name basis with one of the smartest minds the universe had ever produced.

Jem glanced up to find Ro watching him.

"We can't ever tell anyone about her, can we."

"What do you think?"

"But it was real. We got to meet Ada May. That's pretty

seismic."

A slow smile brightened Ro's face. "Yes. Yes it is." She glanced down at her micro before checking in with Jem and Barre. "So we're ready? No questions?"

"Ready," Jem said.

"Five by five," Barre said.

"All right. Here we go." Ro triggered the comms transmitter and sent their message to Daedalus through the ansible network.

Gal-3 was a major hub, at least in this sector of space. Their message should short-hop it to Mendez. After that? Jem wasn't sure what would happen. He dreaded facing his parents, but they, at least, were a known quantity. Though he wondered what colors their words would be.

Mendez and Targill were the bigger problem. They represented the unknown of a Commonwealth that had changed its shape before his eyes. There was a silent war happening that almost no one else knew about, and the ones who did know were dangerous. Who could they trust? How would they know?

Jem looked at his brother and Ro. Even after he'd lied to them, manipulated them, they still came for him. They had his back. And so did Micah and Nomi.

For their sake, and for Ada May's, Jem was going to have to keep trying to get better.

*

They didn't have to wait very long. And when the

response came, it was not from Mendez, but from Targill. Ro wasn't at all surprised.

"Chief Engineer Maldonado, this is the Commonwealth vessel Hephaestus. Given the difficulties you have had with your ship, your CO has requested we place a navigator aboard and assist you in your return."

That was a surprise. Ro made sure there was no live channel to Hephaestus and turned to Jem and Barre. "Anything we need to handle first?" Ro didn't need to worry about the logs—May had taken care of them. Even if their 'helpers' somehow managed the authority to search their micros, the messages Ro sent to Nomi and Nomi's responses were gone. And she'd like to see them try to break May's newly installed encryption.

Both Jem and Barre shook their heads.

"Remember, don't offer any information. Only answer the exact questions they ask." Years of dealing with her volatile father had their advantage. She opened the channel. "Hephaestus, you are cleared to board. Thank you for your offer."

Barre raised an eyebrow.

"It never hurts to be polite," she said. "Jem, lie down. You look like hell. Barre, stay here. I'll greet our visitor. You can monitor over your micro—I'll set mine to live-stream."

"Paranoid much?" Jem asked, but he didn't argue with her as he curled up on the old acceleration foam on the floor of the bridge.

"Actually, yes. You? I trust. Targill and his crew? Not so much."

The flitter was already docked when Ro got to the airlock.

She waited as the pressurization routine finished. The last time she had received a visitor from Hephaestus, it had been her father. At least he was so far out of the picture he might as well be dead. The light above the door shifted from red to green, and Halcyone unlocked it. A tall, trim, uniformed man opened the air lock and stepped through.

Ro let out the breath she had been holding. It definitely wasn't her father.

He held out his hand. "Niles Galen, navigation specialist, Hephaestus."

She shook it on autopilot. "Ro Maldonado. Captain, Halcyone." It was still strange to call herself that, but this was her ship and she wasn't going to let anyone bully her out of it. Especially not anyone wearing a military uniform.

"What seems to be the problem?"

He was typical new-recruit-eager, head freshly shaved, uniform creases sharp. Galen was likely the same age as she and Barre. Which felt odd. Maybe it was odd for him, too, to have someone his peer have her own ship, even one as old and broken as Halcyone. "Other than forty-plus-year-old systems that have a propensity toward crankiness? Not really any problems, per se. There seems to be an issue with the nav logs, but the ship's jump drive is functioning."

Halcyone's placid voice broke in. "Flitter zero three is requesting permission to undock."

"Proceed," Ro said. The flitter headed back to Hephaestus which meant Galen was stuck with them for the duration. She wondered how he felt about that. At least he had no sidearms, which could have meant he was there simply to collect information. Ro thought she preferred the overt threat.

"Follow me. I'll take you to engineering." As they headed down the corridor, Ro wondered if keeping him there was the right choice. It was either engineering or the bridge and she didn't want him there in case Barre needed to access his musical interface. Her paranoia might be getting the best of her, but Ro also didn't want him unsupervised in engineering. That meant dragging two jump snugs in there. So much for the lovely cushioning in her bunk. If there was anything more uncomfortable than a jump snug on a thin pad, it was one crammed into the emergency niches.

The more she considered it, the more she couldn't see any other alternative. When they reached engineering, she triggered the internal comms channel. "Barre? Can you bring us two jump snugs?"

Galen didn't react. Either he was stoic, or had expected the bonus discomfort, given the age of the ship.

"My ship may not be as fancy as Hephaestus, but all the critical subsystems check out."

"With your permission, I'd like to do my own scans." Galen pulled out his micro. It was one of the rugged military ones. According to the specs, the housing could deflect hand-held energy weapons fire. And Ro was certain any of the information on one could be indexed by Commonwealth servers. She had no choice but to give him command line access. Ada May had better be as good as she was supposed to be, or both Halcyone and Ithaka were going to be in the line of plasma fire. Both figuratively, and quite likely, literally.

She nodded and got her micro paired with the ship. It would have been easier simply to pair his to hers, but that felt even more risky than getting him set up directly with Halcyone. There were too many hacks on her device that had come from less-than-reputable places in the eyes of the Commonwealth. "I need your node ident."

He passed his device to her. Either he was overly trusting or supremely arrogant. Either choice made Ro uncomfortable. She set up guest access for him and tossed the micro back. His reflexes were as sharp as she'd expected. "You have access to all of navigation, including all the relevant subsystems. Halcyone will recognize you as a temporary crew member for internal comms. You are cleared for engineering, sanitary facilities, and the commissary. The basic schematic should already be on your micro."

Galen raised an eyebrow before taking a seat by the main nav station. Maybe he was impressed. Maybe just annoyed at her thoroughness.

Barre entered, dragging two jump snugs behind him. Galen didn't even look up from his work. She and Barre both shrugged.

Ro wrote a quick private note. <u>Keep monitoring, okay?</u>

<u>Roger, Captain.</u> He smirked at her and turned to leave.

<u>Jem okay?</u>

Barre shrugged. Ro wished she could offer something more than her concern. It was good to have Jem back. As irritating as he could be, Ro realized how much she'd been worried about him. And not just for the work he could do for her. Nomi would be proud. But for now, Ro needed to channel her inner misanthrope.

As Galen focused on the nav station readouts and his

micro's heads-up displays, Ro crammed the jump snugs into the wall niches. At least they would prevent jump sickness.

"Let me know if you have any questions," she asked, coming up behind him. To his credit, Galen didn't jump or even twitch. Nor did he move to hide any of the displays. Maybe he was simply what he seemed to be.

And maybe Ro could be a concert pianist.

"It looks like the jump drive is working within acceptable parameters."

Ro had to hold herself from making a snide comment.

"I've programmed the jump sequence and done several sims, and all the checksums are valid. You're right about the nav logs, though. That's not something I can troubleshoot from here, but I've taken the liberty to make copies of the files."

Of course he had. Ro forced herself not to react when all she wanted to do was throw the nav engineer and his micro out the air lock. Instead she took a breath and asked, "Are we ready to jump?"

He patted the console. "She should hold together."

"Fine." The sooner they got to Daedalus, the sooner she could get rid of him and figure out if he mined her ship with spy-ware. "This is the captain," she said on the ship-wide channel, imagining the eye-rolling and smirking on the bridge. "Secure for jump sequence. T minus—" She turned to Galen.

"Three minutes?"

Ro nodded. "T minus three minutes."

"Aye, aye, Captain." Barre's voice was almost free of

mockery.

"After you," she said, sweeping her hand in the direction of the jump niches. Ro trusted Halcyone to get them home safely. What they would find there was a different matter.

*

Jem followed Barre back to his quarters and silently swallowed more of the jump-sickness tablets he offered. Only reaching for the next rung when his other hand and both legs were secure, he climbed into the top bunk.

"You okay?" Barre asked.

"I think I'd rather deal with a Commonwealth tribunal than Mom and Dad."

"Pretty much."

"Are you sure we can't tell them I was scammed or stood up or something?" Jem sunk into the dense foam. It fitted and solidified around him. He would be glad when this portion of their trip was done.

"You know they're going to scan you."

Jem sighed. "Yeah. I know. Life would be simpler if you would just lie to me."

"Not the way it works, kiddo."

"Like mother, like son," Jem said.

"Funny."

Halcyone's countdown interrupted Jem's response and he closed his eyes, waiting for the world to turn him inside out again.

Three jumps in quick succession made Jem glad his

brother had remembered the meds. Barre groaned in the bunk below him and Jem smiled. Misery did enjoy company.

Before he had a chance to peel himself out of the form-fitting foam, Halcyone announced they'd arrived in orbit around Daedalus Station. "Is it too late to head back out there?" Jem asked.

Barre half-rolled, half-fell out of his bed and scrambled to his feet. He leaned against the upper bunk. "I won't let you face them alone."

The bright yellow of his words warmed Jem and washed away some of the fear.

"Why don't you clean up. It'll make you feel better."

Jem looked down at his rumpled clothes. They were quite a bit worse for the travel. He had a fresh set in his bag. Changing would also make him feel a little better, but maybe the weary look would make his folks a tiny bit more sympathetic.

They joined Ro on the bridge.

"Where's our guest?" Barre asked.

"In engineering. I wanted to make sure we were all set." Ro looked down at Jem.

"I'm not stupid." A dark orange aura filled his mind and coated his tongue with burnt toast.

"Hey, I didn't say that. I just wanted to give us some privacy if we needed any last minute planning."

Barre took a breath and Jem figured he was about to get in the middle of him and Ro. Which was kind of funny, since that was what Jem had done the last time they were all aboard Halcyone. "No. You're right. I'm sorry." The strange sensations faded along with his anger. "I'm just nervous."

"Yeah. Me, too," Ro said.

None of them mentioned Ithaka. They didn't need to.

"Waiting isn't going to make things easier," Barre said.

"All right, then. Time to go home." Ro opened comms. "Ensign Galen, we are ready for landing. Would you like to double-check our glide path?"

Only Jem could see the irritation glowing around her.

"All set, Captain."

Ro didn't seem to be annoyed when Galen called her that.

"Daedalus? This is Halcyone. Requesting clearance to land."

There was a long pause. Too long. Jem swallowed the sour taste of his own fear. Then a familiar voice filled the bridge.

"Halcyone, you are cleared to land. Welcome home." It was Nomi and the warmth of her words wasn't diminished at all in the transmission.

A rare smile transformed Ro's face. "Initiating approach. Thank you, Daedalus." She cut the connection. "Last chance for questions, comments, or regrets."

"Let's go home," Jem said. He stared down at his feet, willing his dizziness to fade. It wasn't like they had much of a choice.

Halcyone glided down to a textbook landing. Ro patted the captain's console.

Thank you, Jem thought, trying to connect his neural with the AI. He still wasn't sure how he had connected with her earlier.

A single tone reverberated inside his skull, a full, resonant sound. It died away, leaving a comforting warmth behind. Jem smiled. Maybe his brain wasn't a hopeless case after all. "Ready to face the music?" he asked Barre.

His brother swatted him on his arm as they walked out of the bridge and to the airlock.

Galen was waiting for them, standing at parade rest in the corridor. Ro nodded to him. Jem fidgeted as station crew reconnected the umbilical. Barre stood behind him with his hand warm on his shoulder. The old Jem might have shaken him off.

Halcyone released the seals and the air lock opened. Jem groaned when he saw their welcoming committee. Gutierrez looked as if she'd been waiting there ever since Halcyone blasted off looking for him. For all Jem knew, she had. But even her serious expression, rigid stance, and wicked-looking prosthetic didn't make him anywhere near as uncomfortable as the sight of both of his parents waiting behind her. He paused. Barre squeezed his shoulder. It was going to be all right.

It had to be.

Chapter 28

Ro LOOKED AWAY before either of the Doctors Durbin could make eye contact. She may have been the one to bring Jem home, but that didn't mean they would be grateful.

Gutierrez nodded to her. "Chief Engineer Maldonado, the commander requests your presence. Ensign Galen, a flitter from Hephaestus is waiting for you."

Ro glanced up at Gutierrez and then down at her own sloppy clothes. It was too much to hope that the LC would let her wash up and change. Well, Mendez had long experience with her father's appearance. Delay wouldn't make this any easier, anyway.

The Durbins rushed over to Jem, and Ro winced as they brushed past Barre to reach him. So this was going to be a divide and conquer attempt. She should probably be more nervous than she was. But they found Jem and brought him back and Nomi was here, waiting for her. It was more than Ro had counted on.

Ro followed Gutierrez through the busy station. Checking her micro for local time, she realized it was first shift. That didn't make sense—Nomi had been in comms. She felt a little off balance and the crowded corridors didn't help.

Members of the crew called out to her, or nodded and smiled. Ro wanted to retreat back into Halcyone. At least until she had a chance to change and grab a shower. But that ship had already jumped. Gutierrez guided her into Mendez's office without a single word. Ro had tried to capture the LC's gaze, but Gutierrez had just stared straight ahead. What had Nomi told her? Whose side was the LC on?

Ro's earlier confidence vanished. There was a lot more at stake here than Halcyone.

Mendez stood behind her desk, with her back toward the door. Ro swallowed hard. That was a power position. One her father used to use all too often. One that said he hadn't considered Ro enough of a threat to face her. Ro glanced behind her as Gutierrez left the room and the office door sealed.

The last time Ro had been here, she was offered coffee and a job.

Mendez turned. The woman's uniform was as impeccable as ever and only made Ro feel even messier. "Chief Engineer, good to have you back." The commander looked as weary as Ro felt—which was interesting. "Please sit."

Ro took the waiting seat in front of the large desk. Mendez waited several seconds before taking her seat. Was that another power ploy? Or was the commander as distracted as she appeared?

"While I will be expecting a full written report, supported by your ship's logs, this is our chance to speak informally."

Informally. That was an interesting choice of words, given the way Mendez had set up their meeting. Well, the logs were a mess and wouldn't add much of anything to Ro's report, other than that Halcyone was still a work in progress. That suited Ro's purposes on a number of levels, not the least of which was that no one else should want a broken ship.

"Yes, sir." Ro made an attempt to straighten out her bearing. "As you know, we followed Jem Durbin's path to Galileo 3, but there was no record of him on the station or at their med facility. Nor did he answer any messages. We knew he was looking for medical help outside of normal channels, so we analyzed the likely destinations he might have taken from Gal-3. We thought it was worth looking into the clinic at the fringe of the Anistell system." She looked up. Mendez was watching her with a predatory concentration. "We began to have some difficulties with the comms at that point and could only broadcast ship to ship."

"Yes, I am well aware of that. Continue."

"When we were able to reconnect to the ansible network, we received an anonymous message that Jem was recovering from his neural implantation procedure and that he would be returned to Galileo 3. The message self-destructed before we were able to copy the headers or send a reply. And while we knew there was a chance we were being manipulated, we didn't have any better options, so we returned to Gal-3 to wait."

"I see."

"Jem contacted us from there and rejoined the ship. Then we reported in. The rest you know."

"It sounds fairly straightforward." Ro could hear the skepticism in Mendez's voice.

Mendez steepled her fingers and stared across her desk, letting the silence build. That was also something Ro's father used to do. She knew how to deal with that. If Mendez figured the waiting would push Ro to keep talking until she slipped and revealed something, well, the commander was wrong. Ro only hoped Barre and Jem could follow her advice.

Finally Mendez broke the room's quiet. "It appears that Halcyone either does not have a beacon, or the one she has is not functioning."

"Sir?"

"For your safety, and for the safety of your crew, we will install one. Without charge, of course."

Mendez studied her as if waiting for some reaction. Ro focused on her breath and on keeping her expression neutral. "I believe the ship's manufacture pre-dated the common use of beacons. It will require careful integration with the old ansible system."

"I'm sure we can find help for you in comms."

At the thought of Nomi, Ro's cheeks warmed. But it wasn't as if Mendez didn't already know about their relationship and trying to hide her reaction would only make the commander suspicious. Maybe it would even work in her favor.

"You are, of course aware, that the young Mr. Durbin received his neural through a black-market supplier."

There was no gain in denying it. "So it seems, Commander."

"And you had no personal interaction with his contacts?"

"The only communication we received was the anonymous message."

"Did Jem mention anything about Ithaka?"

Ro was surprised that Mendez asked about it so directly. She must be under a great deal of pressure from higher ups. "The lost colony? I wish. I could use the credit to overhaul Halcyone."

Mendez leaned forward. "If you remember any other details, even something you might consider irrelevant, contact me at any time."

"Yes, sir."

Mendez must have signaled for Gutierrez because the door opened and the LC entered. Ro stood and left. Gutierrez followed right behind her. She escorted Ro across the anteroom and out of command.

"It seems Nakamura has placed her trust in you," Gutierrez said, as Ro stepped into the corridor.

Stopping short, Ro turned to face the LC, her face heating up again. She kept her silence. Her relationship was none of Gutierrez's business.

"I knew your father. I hope Konomi won't regret her choice."

Ro squared her shoulders. "I am not my father," she said and stomped into the crowded corridor, seeing only his face with its casual sneer and the weapon that sat so comfortably in his hand. It seemed like a lifetime ago on Halcyone's bridge. Her father threatening Barre. Threatening her.

She wasn't him. Gutierrez had to know that. Of course the LC knew that. Ro stopped short and mumbled an apology to the security officer she nearly tripped up.

What was Gutierrez playing at?

She needed to talk to Nomi.

*

They walked to their family quarters in a tense silence. At least Barre was beside him. Jem knew his mother wasn't happy. The glances she gave Barre nearly smoldered. Some of Jem's perceptions were products of his scrambled brain, but he was learning to trust the sensory oddities he experienced.

His father's shoulders were tight, his eyes narrowed. Before Jem would have pegged him as furious, but his whole body shouted fear. Jem wanted to shake the two of them. To tell them that he was here, that everything had worked out. But that wasn't exactly true, either.

Everything had changed.

He paused, trembling at the doorway. Could he go back to being the old Jem? The Jem who lived and breathed for the kind of hacks that would make Ro's work look sloppy and amateur? Everything seemed trivial next to the truth of the war and the reason for the hack that had created Ithaka.

"No one is in trouble here," his father said.

Even without the short-circuiting of his senses, Jem would have seen the lie. Of course they were in trouble. It's just that his parents didn't know it yet.

Barre lightly brushed his hand across Jem's back. They crossed the threshold together and stood side by side, facing the small living room area where so many family conversations had gone wrong before. Jem stopped to take it all in, as if he'd been away for years instead of days. In some ways, it had been a lifetime.

"Please, sit," his father said.

His mother was already sitting on the edge of a sofa, one knee bouncing up and down rapidly. She probably wasn't even aware of the nervous tic. His father sat with her and placed his hand on her leg to stop its angry motion.

He and Barre took the opposite sofa. His brother was like a wall next to him. Neither of them spoke. This was their parents' show.

"We want to run a full medical diagnostic," his mother said. She stared straight ahead as if she couldn't risk meeting Jem's eyes.

"Of course, Mom," Jem said.

Her dark cheeks flushed a dusky red. "And until we're convinced you are medically stable, you are confined to quarters."

Jem jerked his head up and stared at his mom, not caring if it triggered a new round of vertigo. "You can't be serious."

"Or if that's not to your liking, you can stay in medical."

Shit. She was serious. Jem looked up at his dad, but he sat rigid and stone-faced. No help there.

"I'm fine. I swear."

"You have no idea what kind of risks you have exposed yourself to, Jeremy." His father's voice trembled. Or maybe it was just how he heard it now. "You need to tell us everything you can about the procedure."

"Who did this to you, Jeremy?" His mother leaned forward, her gaze locked on a point midway between them.

"We need to know. So we can find them and prevent them from ever harming another child again."

It was the most emotion he had ever seen her display. Again, he wasn't sure if what he experienced was because of the synesthesia. He'd have to check with Barre later. If he could carve out any private time with him. Jem opened his mouth and closed it again. He couldn't answer her questions. He couldn't defend Dr. Land and Dr. Chote and the rest of the team without betraying them.

He didn't need to turn to his brother to feel his concern. Barre was practically vibrating with it. Stick close to the truth, Ro had said. Okay. There was no public record of Land, so that was a safe place to start. "They used pseudonyms. Dr. Land. Dr. Sea. Dr. Sky. And they never took off their face masks. No one forced me. I was the one who insisted. They tried to talk me out of it." Other than the made up names, it was all the truth. "Mom. Dad. I had no other options. And I have no regrets."

His mother drew breath to speak. To argue with him. Jem knew what she was going to say. Hadn't they already been through it all? He interrupted her before she said a single word.

"You told me I needed to be patient. That things would improve. But I saw the way all your specialist colleagues looked at me. And I read all their notes. The official ones. Not the sanitized and overly hopeful versions they gave me. Not only was I not getting better, I was getting worse."

His mother winced and looked away. Damn it, she knew. Of course she knew.

"Where did they take you, son?" His father took over the

interrogation, good cop to his mom's usual bad cop.

"I don't know. I was sedated during transport." Which also was true.

"What can you tell us, Bernard?" his father asked.

Jem wanted to answer for him, to shield his brother from their parents and their unreasonable anger. It seemed they were always angry at Barre.

Barre looked straight ahead. "We got an anonymous message telling us that Jem would be waiting on Gal-3. That he was recovering. Then we got a message from him. The rest you know."

"I doubt that," his mother said. She ground her jaw so hard, Jem could believe that sparks would fly out the next time she opened her mouth.

Barre opened his arms. "I'm sorry, Mom. There's nothing else I can tell you. We picked him up. I managed not to shake him apart for running away. We came home."

Home. He knew Barre didn't think of Daedalus as home, much less this sterile apartment. No. Home to him was now Halcyone. It was hard not to be jealous of that.

Their father scowled. "How did you get off Daedalus? Where did you get the money to pay for the procedure?"

In a way, he understood his parents. They were just looking for someone to blame. Jem sighed. He knew he couldn't keep Micah's role out of this. He hoped his friend wouldn't get in too much trouble. "Look. He didn't know. I lied to him, too. Just like I lied to everyone. It was my only chance and I took it. I'm not sorry I got my neural, but I am sorry how I had to do it."

"Who. Who helped you?" his mother demanded.

"Micah. I told him I needed to see a specialist. That I couldn't tell you about it because I wasn't sure they could help me and I didn't want you to be disappointed again. That's all Micah knew. He offered me the money I needed."

His mother sprang up from the sofa and paced the room.

"It isn't his fault. He was trying to help out a friend. And I owe him an apology." Micah wasn't the only one Jem had used. Nomi, Ro, and Barre. He'd lied to and used them all. Jem glanced back at Barre, whose presence was a steady warmth beside him.

Barre nodded. Then his voice was in Jem's head, a comforting bright yellow glow. *You got this, kiddo.*

Jem held his breath and tried to reply, but the easy connection he'd had before slipped away.

His mother must have seen his momentary lapse of attention. She stood beside him and pulled out her micro to scan his head.

"I'm fine." He pushed her hand away. "I'm just tired. I need a shower, a change of clothes, and some food. Then we can all go to medical together, like one big happy family." Fear made Jem snippier than he meant to be, but it was enough to distract her. She frowned at him before walking away, her arms tightly folded across her chest.

"Are we done here?" Barre asked. "I have work to do on Halcyone."

"If you have nothing relevant to add, then yes," his mother said.

Barre looked away, but not before Jem saw the hurt in his eyes.

"I'm not being quarantined, am I?" Jem asked.

"No. Of course not," his father said. "We just want to manage as many environmental variables as we can while we conduct the needed tests."

"Good. Barre, see you later?"

Barre stared briefly at each parent before answering. "A supernova couldn't keep me away."

Jem stood with Barre and the two brothers hugged. There was so much Jem wanted to say, but it would have to wait until later.

Stay strong.

Jem blinked back tears as Barre left. The room felt as cold and as empty as space. The way his parents were: cold, empty, and unforgiving.

*

Watching his parents interrogate Jem made Barre understand how much of their need to control came out of fear. And it had little to do with him or his brother. It was an uncomfortable thought. Uncomfortable, too, was the sympathy that came with it.

He made it back to Halcyone to find a pair of technicians waiting at the air lock. One was a short, balding man, the other a taller woman. Ro was not with them.

"Orders from Mendez. We have a brand new beacon for you," the man said.

Shit. He needed to talk to Ro, but he couldn't risk open communication now that they were back on Daedalus. Everything they said was liable to be scrutinized. Barre suddenly appreciated the level of paranoia Ro had to operate under every day just to survive her father.

Maybe he could delay the inevitable. "Hey, Chief Engineer Maldonado's not here right now. Can you reschedule this for later?"

"We just need access. It's all routine," the woman said. Their work trundle bumped into the closed airlock and the technician canted her head. "You can open her up, right?"

"Yeah. Sure." Damn. Barre requested access through his neural; the ship complied. The musical confirmation she sent him sounded upbeat, happy. Ro would tell him he was projecting. "Engineering's this way."

How was he going to keep them from crippling the ship? The beacons were used for map updates and communicating navigation hazards, but he was sure the Commonwealth could turn them into trackers. Or at least a vehicle to add spyware to the AI. He was channeling his inner Ro, but he couldn't help it. If they even suspected Halcyone had made contact with Ithaka, they would monitor them so closely they wouldn't be able to sneeze without someone knowing.

Damn it, Ro should be the one here.

But she wasn't. For all Barre knew, she was still in Mendez's office. Or worse yet, under arrest. "Anything I can do to help, just let me know. Halcyone's an old ship and she can be a little quirky."

"These things are plug and play," the woman said. Barre probably should have known her name, but he spent so much of his time on Daedalus feeling sorry for himself he'd never learned it. In the few months Nomi had been here, she probably knew more of the station staff than Barre did.

"I'll stay out of your way." He took one of the seats at the periphery of the room. It was a good vantage point. He could see what the techs were doing, but they couldn't really watch him. "How long will this take?" Maybe Ro would show up and have some brilliant and wonky hack ready to deploy.

"Why? Taking this bird anywhere?" Both techs laughed.

They set up the trundle as a workbench beside the main nav station. Barre winced as they pried open the access port at the base of the console. It was like having his own skin torn.

"Man, you weren't kidding about this heap." The shorter tech poked his head up from where he had been studying the wiring. "You sure it flies?"

"Oh, she flies, all right." Ro would be burning mad if she were here. But maybe it was better that she wasn't. She couldn't prevent this. And if she protested, it would only heighten Mendez's suspicions.

They were going to hurt the ship. The techs probably had no idea they weren't just doing routine maintenance, but the beacon would make it impossible for Halcyone to use the old maps without detection. It would obliterate their only path to Ithaka. Worse, still, her nav array wasn't standard. If they spent too much time poking around and found the extra linkage, would they be able to put it all together the way Ro had?

Barre wasn't the engineer Ro was. Even if he studied what the techs did, there was no way he could undo it.

"You're lucky you didn't blow up when the interstitial engines came on line," the first tech said.

The other tech laughed. "Or jump into never-never land,"

she said.

The two of them dug into the wiring with an enthusiasm that made Barre queasy. Halcyone sent a musical question through his mind. It was what he had come to know as the 'are you okay' melody.

How was he going to respond? A simple 'no' wouldn't tell Halcyone what to do. Ro wasn't here to write a program. All Barre could do was craft simple routines, based on code snippets someone else wrote. But if he didn't do something, the ship would be crippled again, this time by Commonwealth design. Halcyone repeated her question, louder and more insistently this time.

Barre stared past the intrusive technicians and took a deep breath. He wrote a brief melody he hoped would convey danger and caution. The AI played it back, using a tone that added a question. How could he explain this to the ship? It was impossible.

The old anger and frustration built inside him. What good was his musical talent now? For a minute, he entertained blasting the techs with a wall of sound. All he'd have to do was trigger the Ithaka program without running it through the nav transposer. But as tempting as it was to chase them off the ship like that, it wasn't a viable solution.

He tugged at his dreads. Jem would probably know what to do, but as usual, the wrong Durbin brother was here.

But maybe Jem could help him. Ever since his brother was woken from the induced coma, he didn't seem to be able to answer Barre mind-to-mind anymore, but it was worth a shot. A torrent of swearing from the techs made Barre smile. At least they were having as much difficulty with Halcyone as he and Ro had had. Maybe it would buy him some more time.

He played the music he associated with Jem. When he knew Halcyone was listening he tried to explain the problem, hoping Jem would be on the other end of the mental line and have some solution. They needed to find a way to wall off what the technicians were doing from Halcyone's main systems. Keep the beacon from integrating across nav and comms without disabling it outright.

He paused, waiting for some sign that his brother heard him.

Then, note by note, thought by thought, he started all over again.

Barre worked to keep his breathing under control, but he knew time was not his friend. If the techs finished the installation before he came up with something, they were sunk. Mendez would definitely not buy another convenient systems failure should something break on the beacon.

Come on, I need a little help here.

Please wait. Program compiling.

Barre nearly fell out of his chair. The techs were still busy cursing over Halcyone's ancient wiring and didn't notice.

Halcyone? He sent out a musical query.

The melody came back to him as an answer. Then the verbal message repeated in the AI's flat tone, but the voice sounded in his head, just as the music did. *Please wait. Program compiling.*

What the hell was happening?

Program ready.

What program? What had the AI done?

Halcyone's voice repeated the status, this time with what seemed like annoyance. *Program ready.*

"Oh," Barre whispered. He closed his eyes and reached out to the computer. *Run program.*

A bright note rang in his mind. Barre could have sworn it sounded pleased. *Navigation and communications subsystems isolated. Program complete.*

"I don't fucking believe it."

"You talking to us?" the male tech asked.

"Nope. Sorry." Barre fiddled with his micro so he'd look like he was busy with something in case they glanced his way. Wow. This was crazy. As far as Barre knew, no one had ever communicated with an AI like this. He smiled and opened his mind to the ship again.

Well done, Halcyone.

She didn't answer. She didn't need to. A gentle ringing note echoed in his head.

"Okay. We're done here." The female tech started gathering their tools and organizing them back on the trundle. "It's a nonstandard installation, but it was the only way to marry the old with the new. You should be all set."

"Great. Thanks." Barre stood.

"We can find our way out." The other tech sealed the access hatch and stood, arching his back. "I'm getting too old for this."

After they left, Barre walked over to the station they had cannibalized and he stroked his hand across its smooth surface. "You clever thing, you. Wait until I tell Ro." And Jem. Barre smiled. For now, for once, this was something he could own. Maybe Ada May was right. He was much more than just a musician.

Though that was okay, too. After all, his music had started all of this.

Chapter 29

Nᴏᴍɪ ᴋᴇᴘᴛ ɢʟᴀɴᴄɪɴɢ at her micro, counting the minutes until shift change. Even on first shift, there wasn't nearly enough work to distract her from knowing Ro was home. Ro was home. Nomi smiled. She hadn't been able to keep the hitch from her voice as she'd passed along Halcyone's official landing clearance. It had only been a few days since the ship had gone off after Jem, but it seemed like far longer. At least this time Ro had been Halcyone's captain instead of accidental cargo.

Which didn't make the worry any easier. The small engineer had made a complicated mess out of Nomi's once organized life.

Her micro finally signaled shift change. Nomi wanted to run from comms, but she switched her station to auto, slipped off her headset, and slowly pushed back from the console. When she looked up, Cam Lowell was standing over her. The other crew members were handing off their stations to the relief, giving their reports in low voices that didn't carry across the soundproofed room.

Lowell leaned down. "I heard a rumor that your friend has some intel about Ithaka."

Cold washed through her. How could he know that? Were he and Gutierrez playing some kind of game?

"Suckers have been searching for the lost colony for decades, but I have some pieces of the puzzle. I think Ro has a few, too. I'll cut you in on the prize money if you can convince her to work with me." Lowell nearly shook with his eagerness. Sweat shone across his forehead and his grin was all teeth.

"All I know is she's home, safe, and so is Jem. But I'm sure we'll talk as soon as she's done being debriefed by Mendez." And Nomi still needed to understand what Ro meant by 'it's complicated.' They had led Hephaestus away from their search. Why? Once Jem was safe, what reason could she possibly have for protecting The Underworld and Ithaka?

Lowell nodded. "She's someone with discretion. Tell her I sometimes worked with her father. On special projects."

Nomi kept her face blank. As if that would be the deciding factor for Ro's trust. Actually, it would, only not in the way Lowell expected. "I'll be sure to let her know." She released the chair lock and rotated toward him, forcing him to step back or be trapped between her seat and the next row of consoles. "Excuse me," she said in her most polite voice. He moved aside. As she left, she felt his gaze like a plasma burn between her shoulder blades.

Outside comms, she leaned against the corridor wall, her heart pounding. She pulled out her micro. At least now that they were both on station, the messages would fly between their micros. <u>Ro? Are you okay? Are you free?</u> Nomi meant it in more ways than one.

<u>Where are you?</u>

<u>Just leaving comms. Meet me in my quarters?</u>

<u>Fine.</u>

The messaging app was so unsatisfying. Just words, without any of the clues that went with more sophisticated communication methods. But soon they would be face to face and none of that would matter. It was all Nomi could do not to race from comms to the residence ring, but as eager as she was to see Ro, she didn't want to attract any more notice from station staff than she already had. If she counted Mendez, Gutierrez, and Lowell, there were three more people than she was comfortable with who knew Ro had some connection to Ithaka.

Ro was waiting for her inside, pacing the length of the small galley area.

"Hey," Nomi said.

"Hey." Ro took a hesitant step forward.

Nomi closed the distance between them and opened her arms to hug her. It always surprised Nomi how much shorter Ro was than she, given her ferociously big presence. Ro's head rested on Nomi's shoulder.

"Everything is fucked. I don't know who to trust. Who knows what."

Nomi breathed in the scent of Ro's hair and sighed. "I don't know either. I thought Gutier—"

"Don't say it. Don't say anything. Not here."

"Ro, this is crazy," Nomi whispered. "What happened?"

She lifted her head from Nomi's shoulder and smiled. "I'm not sure you'd believe me if I told you."

"Told me what?"

"I would just about kill for a hot shower," Ro said, raising her voice to its normal conversational level.

"Huh? Of course." Ro had kept a change of clothes there since Halcyone was grounded the last time.

Ro towed her across the apartment to the small head, opened the door, and drew her inside. There was barely room for one person in the cramped space. She was hyper-aware of Ro's scent—a spicy note still bright after several days on Halcyone in the same clothes. Ro set her hands on Nomi's shoulders and pushed her to sit on the closed toilet. Then she leaned over fiddled with her micro. "Okay, that's better."

"It's going to be difficult to shower in our clothes. And without towels." Though she wouldn't mind trying to negotiate the one-person stall with Ro someday, Nomi didn't think that's what she was suggesting. Ro's pale face turned crimson.

"Are you sure you want to know?" Ro asked.

Nomi didn't know whether to laugh at the two of them crammed in the head or yell at Ro for trying to shut her out again. But the grim look on Ro's face kept her silent. She nodded.

"We found Ithaka. You already know that."

"That information is worth a whole lot of money, Ro. You and Halcyone could be set."

"It's not ... I can't ..." Ro tugged her fingers through her hair. "It's bigger than that. Bigger than any of us."

"What do you mean?"

"The Commonwealth. The war. So many lies."

Nomi thought of Gutierrez and her shiny prosthetic arm. She had fought and nearly died in that war. On the Commonwealth side. But even so, she was protecting Ithaka. Or at least that's what she'd led Nomi to believe.

"I'm afraid, Nomi."

"Afraid to tell me? Afraid to trust me?" A quiet anger built inside her, and a deep disappointment, too.

"No," Ro cried. She caught Nomi's hand and interlaced their fingers. "I'm afraid you'll get hurt. Afraid for what might happen to your family."

Even though the room was warm, a chill ran through her. That was basically what Gutierrez had said. "I'm a big girl. And besides, look at us. I'm already in deep."

Ro looked at her with a strange sort of pleading in her eyes before taking a deep breath and relaxing her shoulders. "We were taught that it was the rebels who released the AI killer virus. That it was the rebels who were responsible for murdering Dauber and May, for the destruction of ships and the deaths of their crews. That the Commonwealth battled back and won the war."

Nomi nodded.

"Well, that's the holovid version of events. Complete with symphonic soundtrack. The convenient heroic tale of the Commonwealth of Planets." Ro paused and gripped Nomi's hand even tighter. "Yes, we found Ithaka. Yes, it's where The Underworld began. But it's more than that. Much more." The red returned to her cheeks and her eyes blazed an intense green in the bright overhead light. "It's all backwards. It wasn't the rebels. They didn't make the virus. They didn't kill Dauber and May."

"Ro, of course that's what they told you. Why are you suddenly convinced their version is the truth?"

"You're not going to believe it." Ro grinned and shook her head. "Because she isn't dead."

"Who? Who isn't dead?"

"Ada May."

"Excuse me?" Nomi's voice squeaked. Dr. Adiana May. The brilliant young computer engineer who along with Dr. Charles Dauber pretty much created the AI revolution. The May Institute at Nomi's Uni was named for her.

"Ada May. She's very much alive, despite the Commonwealth's attempts to make it otherwise."

"Oh." Dread coiled deep in Nomi's stomach. If she hadn't trusted Ro so completely, if Gutierrez hadn't tried to warn her away, she might have tried to laugh off her friend's paranoia. But this—this was more than 'complicated.' If the Commonwealth discovered what they knew, more than their lives would be in danger. Nomi looked up at Ro. Her normally dour face was alight with wonder.

"Yeah." Ro smiled. "I know."

"Do you have any idea ...?" Nomi sputtered to a stop. "We are so spaced."

"It's going to be all right."

"So that's it? Everything we thought we knew is wrong, and we just go on like nothing's different?"

Ro relaxed her hold on Nomi's fingers and stroked across her knuckles. "Of course not. This changes everything. We have a job now—to protect Ithaka."

"What about your father?"

"What about him?"

"Ro. Think. He had connections to the black market. That means Ithaka. And May."

"I told you, it's complicated. There's work to do. For Halcyone, me, Jem, and Barre. Are you in?"

Water dripped from the spigot over the sink. She should put in a work order for that. Nomi closed her eyes. She didn't know whether she wanted to laugh or cry. The gentle plink could have been rain back home, singing on the roof of her grandfather's porch. What would happen to her family if the Commonwealth figured out her part in this? Would helping Ithaka be an act of war? She was still part of the larger military structure, at least until she could pay off her debts.

The irony nearly choked her. The money for finding Ithaka could have freed her from the Commonwealth.

Gutierrez had tried to warn her. *If you're going to follow the path I've traveled, you need to know what's at stake. You have a chance. Just one chance to walk away and stay out of this.*

She opened her eyes and took a deep breath. "Yes."

Chapter 30

"So now what?" Nomi asked, blinking back tears.

Relief flooded through Ro. She wasn't sure what she would have done if Nomi had chosen to stay out of this. The only thing Ro had to lose was Nomi. But Nomi had a life. A family. Ro put her hands on the counter to steady them. "Can I take a shower for real?"

They both laughed, a high, nervous sound. Ro opened the head's door, backing out so Nomi could fit through.

Nomi rummaged through a cabinet. "Here," she said. In her hands were a folded towel and a change of Ro's clothes.

"Thank you."

"It's nothing."

"No, it's not." Ro reached for her hand, brought it to her lips, and kissed it. "I'm not an easy person. I ask a lot of the people around me." She thought of May, alone and bitter. "If you're willing to stick around, I promise to try and be better."

"That's all I can ask," Nomi said, softly.

Ro knew she deserved far more. "Will you be here when I get out of the shower?"

"Um, Ro, this is my room. Where else would I be?"

"I don't know. Wait. Shouldn't you be sleeping?"

"I'm on first shift now. Gutierrez's orders."

"Hmmm." They would definitely need to compare notes on the LC. "I need to get back to Halcyone. To talk to Barre. And after that? I don't know." There was so much to process. But she wasn't alone. She had Nomi and Jem and Barre. And probably Micah, too, but she didn't want to drag him into this. Not when he had just gotten a chance to start a new life.

There were still a lot of questions. Gutierrez was a puzzle. Was it possible that they had an ally deep inside the Commonwealth itself?

Nomi put her hands on Ro's shoulder. "Go. Shower. I'll grab us all some food and meet you on Halcyone."

Ro smiled. "Hey. I owe you one."

"At least."

After a shower, Ro felt a lot more ready to deal with their new reality. Or at least head back to the ship and figure out what Mendez had done with the beacon. It would take all of Ro's skills to disentangle it from her ship.

Nomi had already left by the time Ro emerged from the head to get dressed, but her scent still filled the room. Ro breathed it in deeply before heading back into the stark corridors of Daedalus Station.

The whole way back to Halcyone, Ro worried about the ship. If the Commonwealth wanted to, it could claim the battered freighter and nullify the agreement that had made Halcyone hers. But if that happened, the Commonwealth would essentially be admitting what it suspected. The official line was still that Ithaka didn't exist. Even though Mendez had asked her about it.

There wasn't enough Maldonado paranoia in the galaxy to handle all of this.

As Halcyone's air lock swung open for her, Ro exhaled her relief.

"Welcome aboard, Captain Maldonado."

The AI's voice seemed smoother. Barre's handiwork. Ro grinned. "Halcyone, locate Durbin, Barre."

"Engineering."

"When Ensign Nakamura arrives, tell her to meet us in engineering."

"Yes, Captain."

That was interesting. Barre must be tinkering with Halcyone's vocabulary and syntax modules. When she got to engineering, he was sitting at the main nav console, his feet propped up, and grinning like an idiot.

"Ahoy, Cap!"

Things must have gone a lot better with his parents than she had anticipated. "How's Jem?"

A brief frown shadowed his face. "He'll be better once our parents finish scanning him from head to toe. You don't have to tell me how things went with Mendez. She sent a squad to install a beacon."

He was smiling again. Actually, it was more like a smirk. What was going on? Ro ran a security sweep and a privacy hack before confronting Barre. "What are you so happy about? Those things are as hard to hack as the Commonwealth banking network."

"You don't have to."

Ro knelt down to open the access panel at Barre's feet. "Have to what?"

"Hack into the beacon."

"I don't know about you, but I don't appreciate having a spy on board, even if it's just some components and wire."

Barre crouched beside her and took the panel out of her hands. "It's all set. I took care of it." There was that smile again.

"Oh. Did you do that mind-fuse thing with Jem again?" That was pretty seismic. She was going to have to figure out how Barre did it. Maybe it was worth the risk and the expense to get a neural after all.

"Not exactly."

She waited, but Barre just stood there looking smug.

"You're not going to tell me, are you?"

"Take a look for yourself. The beacon is there. It's pinging the system all green. It's just not integrated with anything."

"Okay." Ro set up her micro and interfaced with Halcyone. A couple of quick gestures and she was looking at something as sophisticated as she'd ever seen in the way of hacks. "You did this?"

"You could say that."

"Wow." The beacon was nestled in the nav hardware, but where it should have been activated within the AI code infrastructure, it was isolated in its own virtual machine. "That's—"

"Amazing? Clever? Elegant?"

It was all of the above, but Ro wasn't going to give Barre the satisfaction. Besides, he didn't have the skills to create it.

"Interesting." She waited for him to tell her more, but he just waited, looking extraordinarily satisfied with himself.

"Fine," Ro said, collapsing the windows. "How did you do it?"

He tapped his forehead. "I can talk to her. And not just with music. I can talk to her and she talks back. She wrote the hack. Not me. I just told her what we needed."

Ro's mouth fell open as she stared at the tall musician. If she hadn't been there when Barre 'talked' to Jem, she would have believed he was on drugs. Ones a lot more powerful than the bittergreen he used to use. "Wow." That was all she could say. A computer that could directly communicate with a mind. Wow. Scientists had been theorizing about that for more than a decade, but as far as Ro knew, no one had demonstrated it was actually possible.

"Um, Barre? I think you just got elevated to secret weapon status."

"What am I? The helpful sidekick?" Nomi walked in carrying a heavy sack. She set the food bundle down on the nearest console and ran over to hug Barre. "How's Jem?"

"I don't know, really. But he's safe and I'm going to help him."

"Thank the cosmos," Nomi said. "So what's the plan? I brought dinner ..." She glanced down at the time display on her micro. "No, that would be lunch. I brought lunch for all of us."

Nomi wasn't anyone's sidekick. If anything, she was Ro's center. And if that was so, it made Ro some kind of satellite that was always just about to break orbit. She opened the bag. "Oh, joy, meal bars."

"Isn't there some kind of old expression about beggars and choosers?" Nomi asked.

"But we're not," a quiet voice said from the doorway.

It was Jem.

"Not what?" Ro asked.

"Beggars."

"How did you escape prison—I mean, medical?" Barre asked.

Jem shrugged. "They ran every scan they could think of. Twice. As angry as they are, even they couldn't find a reason to keep me. I mean, it's not like my nystagmus and the headaches are new or anything."

"Are they any better?" Nomi asked.

"Yeah. I think so. A little." Jem puffed his cheeks out. "Look, Nomi, I'm sorry. I owe you ..." He glanced around the room. "I owe you all apologies. I shouldn't have lied. I should have trusted you. I'm sorry."

Ro passed him a food bar. She knew all about that particular painful lesson. "What do you mean about us not being beggars?"

He unwrapped the bar and nibbled on its edge before making a face. "Micah's money. He gave it to me. And I'm giving it to all of us."

"How much money did he give you, exactly?" Ro asked, narrowing her eyes.

"It's a lot. There are a lot of zeros attached."

"Oh." She could get Halcyone fixed. Really fixed without her having to work as the station's engineer. And Nomi could pay her debt to the Commonwealth. Would Micah be okay with that? Did they have to ask him? Ro sighed. Yes.

They did. She did. If she wanted to use his funds, it was the right thing to do. Her lips twitched into a brief smile as she imagined his sarcastic response.

"We should give it back," Barre said. "And we need to let him know what's going on."

"He won't take it," Jem said. "Besides, he wanted it to go to where it could do some good. Undo all the shit his father had caused."

Ro slipped Nomi's hand in hers. "What would you do if you didn't have to work off your obligation?"

Nomi's eyes widened.

"And we could help our friend with that money." Even with safeguards in place, Ro didn't want to say Ada's name. They all understood how fragile Ithaka's safety was.

"We can't leave Daedalus," Barre said. "Not without raising suspicions we can't afford to raise."

"But, Barre—"

"Think about it, Ro. If we leave, if Nomi pays out, if the ship gets a major overhaul, what will Mendez think? Where will they believe the money came from? And if we leave Daedalus? Sure, it's a big universe, and we've managed to sideline their beacon, but do you think the Commonwealth won't send our description to every ship in the fleet to search for us?"

"Fuck."

"So we stay right where we are, and we fix Halcyone a little at a time. And we keep our ears and eyes open. Our friends did just fine before we blundered along. I think they'll be okay a little while longer."

She nodded, watching Jem hoist himself onto a console

and swing his legs back and forth. "Well, I guess that means I'm stuck with you hanging around the ship wanting to help fix things."

"I'll do what I can, Ro. But I'm still a work in progress."

It was good to see the kid at least willing to try. "All right, then. Barre's right. We stay. We watch. We wait." At least it would give Ro a chance to figure out what Gutierrez wanted and whether Lowell was a threat. "We—" Her micro buzzed. A plain text without any identifiers scrolled across its screen.

Ro blinked.

She stared at the message again, opened her mouth, and closed it.

"What's wrong?" Nomi asked, her hand warm on Ro's arm.

"Son of a bitch." Her heart raced. This changed everything.

"What?" Barre demanded.

"Look. Are you seeing what I'm seeing?" she asked, turning the micro so the rest of them could read its message.

Barre whistled low and long.

"Is that what I think it is?" Jem asked.

Three lines of glowing text were written across her micro: her father's name, Alain Maldonado, followed by a set of coordinates, and the words 'take care.'

A parting gift from Ada May.

Ro met each of their eyes in turn.

Barre and Jem stared back at her, open mouthed, nearly identical expressions of disbelief on their faces.

"What do we do now?" Nomi's cheeks were flushed.

"We have to tell Micah," Barre said, recovering first.

Ro nodded and set down her micro. It would have been better for all of them if Alain Maldonado had died in Halcyone's escape pod, but she knew she'd never be that lucky. Now that they had proof he was alive, they had no choice.

Finding her father could very well make things unpleasant for herself and maybe even for Ithaka, but the consequences of leaving him free to pursue his dangerous self-interest would be far, far worse. The Commonwealth and The Underworld were dangers Ro could understand. Her father was like an unstable wormhole: he would turn their lives inside out. Even Micah's.

She took a deep breath and answered Nomi's question. "We plan."

* * *

Acknowledgments

When I started on the journey that would turn into DERELICT and this second volume of the adventures of Halcyone's crew, ITHAKA RISING, I had no idea where it would take me. Like Ro, Barre, Jem, Micah, and Nomi, I, too, have been changed.

To know that my words have reached and moved thousands of readers is a gift beyond price. Thank you for taking this jump through the wormhole with me.

I owe a debt of gratitude to Chris Howard, writer, artist, and all around talented human for the cover. Working with Karen Conlin for the second time has convinced me I'm a one-editor gal. Keep trying to teach me the proper use of the subjunctive, Karen. I may get it one day.

I had a super team of beta readers, starting with my husband, Neil, who never lets me get away with anything just because he's family. Thank you to readers Cathy Pelham, Sally Smith, Richard Durham, DJ Buckles, and Lisa DiDio for their excellent suggestions and incisive comments despite my tight deadline. The book is better because of you.

To the readers who have taken these characters into your lives, my eternal gratitude. I look forward to future travels with them and with you.

~LJ, June 2015

About the Author

LJ Cohen is the writing persona of Lisa Janice Cohen, poet, novelist, blogger, local food enthusiast, Doctor Who fan, and relentless optimist. Lisa lives just outside of Boston with her family, two dogs (only one of which actually ever listens to her) and the occasional international student. When not doing battle with a stubborn Jack Russell Terrier mix, Lisa can be found working on the next novel, which often looks a lot like daydreaming.

Connect with LJ online:

Homepage: www.ljcohen.net/
Blog: www.ljcbluemuse.blogspot.com/
Newsletter: www.ljcohen.net/contact.html
Facebook: www.facebook.com/ljcohen
Twitter: @lisajanicecohen
Tumblr: www.ljcohen.tumblr.com
Google+: www.google.com/+LisaCohen
email LJ: lisa@ljcohen.net

Want to read more?

Sign up for Blue Musings, an occasional email newsletter complete with free, original, short fiction offered in a variety of drm-free formats. (www.ljcohen.net/contact.html)

Other titles by LJ Cohen:

Halcyone Space
Derelict (book 1)

Changeling's Choice
The Between (book 1)
Time and Tithe (book 2)

Future Tense

Stranger Worlds than These (Short Stories, ebook only)

Pen-Ultimate: A Speculative Fiction Anthology (co-edited by LJ Cohen)

Made in the USA
Lexington, KY
03 February 2017